BOUNCER

Thank you. . .

. . . for the inspiration & friendship	. . . for the much needed assistance	. . . for your early, positive feedback
Rob Higham	Katie Standefer	Annette Barker
Barrett Dodds	Grey Gunderson	Jenny Poon
James Kein		

. . . for the constant push, criticism, emails, texts, phone calls, attitude, mancations, and incessant haranguing

Tim Peterson

. . . for your love and confidence throughout

Angela ◻ Ellie ◻ Brenner ◻ Xander ◻ Cienna ◻ Mom ◻ Dad ◻ Tim

BOUNCER

KIPLING PETERSON

iUniverse, Inc.
Bloomington

Bouncer

iUniverse books may be ordered through booksellers or by contacting:

iUniverse
1663 Liberty Drive
Bloomington, IN 47403
www.iuniverse.com
1-800-Authors (1-800-288-4677)

ISBN: 978-0-5954-9139-1 (sc)
ISBN: 978-0-5954-9143-8 (hc)
ISBN: 978-0-5956-0981-9 (ebk)

Printed in the United States of America

iUniverse rev. date: 10/14/2011

☼⌁ 1 ⌁☼

It was close to one in the morning and the night had lumbered on without a fight or any major displays of drunken idiocy. The only excitement had been a spastic dancer falling off the stage and a couple of underage kids trying to sneak into the club. Still, an uneasy feeling lurched at Georgell Butler. The night was too serene, too quiet, the type of night when chaos inevitably burst.

As a bouncer for the better part of his adult life, Georgell had worked in many nightclubs, bars, and at hundreds of concerts. He was a professional; no longer guided by a lust for violence or the ever present need to play on the advances of women. Money wasn't the catalyst either; though good, Georgell felt an unseen magnetism to the club world. It was a need ingrained in his very being; a natural inclination to protect. He was a bouncer. He had always been a bouncer.

The dance floor seemed an ocean of waves as bodies moved with the hypnotic percussion and churning lyrics that blared from the speakers. Georgell glanced up at the high-vaulted ceiling as a burst of fog erupted from blowers and descended on the cheering crowd. A smile creased his face as the familiar scent touched his nostrils and reminded him of a recent birthday party. The fog smelled exactly like silly string. The haze dissipated and the laser show commenced its flashy dance of color and pattern on the walls and crowd. An interruption of darkness would blanket the floor every few minutes and then creep away in the flash of strobe lights that hung from the rafters. For a moment the crowd would be caught in a stop-motion frenzy as the lights blinked on and off to the thumping melody.

Georgell shook his head at the peculiar sight. Exiting the dance floor down a rear staircase, he passed two patrons locked in an oblivious kiss and emerged on the main level of the club. He marveled at the amount of people that continually visited the aging nightspot and credited the vision of the owners for imaginative events and an ever changing decor. In a calculated routine, his eyes darted around the crowded central bar, surrounding tables and couches, and to the shadowed corners of the room. His head turned slightly as he passed numerous windows and glanced outside. With a controlled swagger, but light on his feet, Georgell nodded cordially at people he recognized but kept moving. Nearing the end of the room he made eye contact with a cocktail waitress and with a slight nod, suggested she move out of the narrow hall. She returned a knowing smile and shuffled by with a group of infatuated males following close behind.

The dimly lit hallway smelled of sweat, perfume, and alcohol. The old brick walls were peppered with posters and shards of tape from past signage. Big banners hung from the rafters advertising beer specials and upcoming events. Beams, pipes, and ducting were painted a dull black to disguise their obtrusive appearance but were otherwise left visible. On either end of the hall were mirrors that gave the space an illusion of vastness. Opposite the entry to the main bar, down the hall, and passed a vivacious blonde pedaling beer from a fully stocked ice cart, was a wide staircase that led back up to the dance floor.

Georgell made eye contact with several clubbers as he headed toward the staircase. A tall lanky kid dodged Georgell's gaze while briskly walking down the crowded corridor and slipping out of sight. It was amusing how ignorant some people were, Georgell thought as he keyed his microphone and said, "Kool-Aid, tall blonde kid coming your way. Check him."

"What for," Kool-Aid quickly responded.

"He's dealing. Pull his stash, and toss him!"

"Copy that."

Georgell liked giving action to Kool-Aid because his face would swell up and turn red when he was angry. It was amusing to watch the horrified expressions of onlookers as this 6'1", 400-pound mass of a man threatened lives. Funnier still were the brave clubbers that tried to fight him. Kool-Aid would stand motionless as they punched him square in the face and then, with surprising speed, wrap them up in his fleshy arms and squeeze until they fainted or apologized.

"Flushed the weed and tossed the kid. No problems."

"Copy that," Georgell said as he leaned on the exterior wall of the stairway. He peered in the mirror for a reflective view of the crowd descending the steps and then slowly began the climb back up to the dance floor. Any other night Georgell would have been at the entry watching as backup, but he knew that Sampson, the grim-looking long-haired doorman, had heard the radio chatter and would provide ample assistance if needed. Georgell wanted to keep moving. The prognostic itch of trouble was tight in his chest and he had to stay mobile and aware.

A group of muscle heads, each with a smile or nod of cordiality, lumbered passed Georgell on the stairway. The overbearing scent of Drakkar and Elsha trailed behind them like an unseen tail. They were bouncers from a local strip club and traveled in a ravenous pack looking for girls or a brawl. They were trouble. Permanently kicked out of most clubs and bars, they would come to Club Momentum because they knew a fifty dollar tip at the door would get them passed the entry line and into the club. Georgell tolerated their antics and ultimately allowed their entrance because they spent a lot of money. More importantly, Georgell's crew had soundly suppressed their fits of rage many times. Sure they had muscle but no street smarts, and escorting them from the club was always exhilarating for the staff.

About ten yards behind the muscle heads, hidden in the descending crowd, followed Bug. Bug was an inconspicuous 5'8" and a slight 140 pounds. He was the best set of eyes Georgell had. If the muscle heads started harassing anyone Bug would radio their location and the keywords, "Roid-Roid." It would only take seconds for Georgell's designated squad of bouncers to respond.

Georgell gave Bug a slight smile and continued up the last few steps toward the main dance floor. As he passed through the crowd, Georgell nodded at familiar faces and voiced empty greetings while thinking how ridiculous they all were. Night after night, hopping from one club to another and for what? They would spend their money, maybe get lucky and go home with someone, and then do it all again the next night. What was the point? *Insanity*, he thought. Mindless hordes drugging up on alcohol and whatever pocket candy they carried, hunting for likewise shallow beings of the opposite or same sex to share the waning hours. Georgell always thought a goldmine would be the reality show that captured the stunned and confused mornings as clubbers woke to whomever they slept with from the previous night. Which would it be; horror, confusion, happiness, what? *The Morning After, tune in Wednesday at seven when Harry wakes up in a tub, missing a tooth, and lying next to an overweight librarian with one eye. A goldmine,* Georgell thought.

A known Ecstasy dealer caught Georgell's eye and pointed at an attractive girl sitting oblivious on his lap. "Pleasure, man, not business!" he said with a smile. Georgell nodded as he topped the stairs and headed for the entryway. He knew the guy was lying. The girl was tripping on something and Georgell was certain it didn't come from a competitor. Bug would be watching "Mr. Pleasure" after the muscle heads.

The itch pressed uneasily at Georgell as he entered the dance floor, vigilant. Dealers and muscle heads weren't the priority tonight. The unpredictability of alcohol-induced-judgment and the degrees of danger rising with every sale and every swallow kept Georgell on his toes. The unexpected surge of anger, the spontaneous eruption of stupidity, and the sudden lapse of thought were a constant in the club world. Sight was everything. Eyes had to be everywhere and constantly moving. *Expect the unexpected or get caught sleeping,* he thought. Adrenaline was the bouncer stimulant. Georgell thrived on its pending rush, as did most of his staff.

Georgell had no history of martial arts training nor did he have a background filled with competitive wrestling or boxing. He was a street fighter. His experience didn't come from childhood beatings or struggles in a rough neighborhood. He simply had an innate fight savvy that molded his personality and made him who he was. He knew how to brawl and could absorb pain without thought. Ultimately, Georgell's tolerance for stupidity and arrogance gave him the cool required for such a volatile environment and he rarely lost control of a situation.

At 6'1" and 213-pounds, Georgell wasn't a mass of muscle or unusually large. He was big enough to be imposing and strong enough to handle most people without injury to himself or others. A daunting appearance was important for a bouncer and Georgell felt his shaved head and five-inch braided goatee exuded that menacing edge. Besides, the goatee allowed Georgell and his wife, Emma, a moment to talk when she patiently rebraided the thing.

Georgell was most proud of his eyes. Not that they were exceptionally colored or significantly set but Georgell used them as a necessary weapon. New bouncers would always hear his lecture: *Never let them see fear. Keep your eyes locked on theirs. Show how serious you are with a stare. Beat them with your eyes and you'll win the fight without throwing a punch.* Georgell drilled this directive into his staff and performed it flawlessly with his cold blue eyes and intimidating stare.

"Keep sharp guys," Georgell said as he passed a team of bouncers.

"What's up Doc?"

"Just stay alert. I've got an itch tonight," Georgell said without acknowledging the questioner. The itch always excited the bouncers because the itch meant trouble. Georgell's itch was dead on and rarely mistaken. There was going to be action.

Doc, Georgell thought. A college degree and the once admitted goal of being an English professor had earned him the label. He didn't mind though; it could have been worse. Every bouncer had a club name. Rarely one they chose. Names were usually commensurate with appearance or style: Tiny, Mammoth, Gremlin, etc. but every time Georgell heard "Doc" he wanted to smile. *Boy would I break the stereotype for English professors.*

Georgell surveyed the masses as he passed a chrome pillar, making his way to the balcony steps. Nothing had changed since he left the dance floor minutes earlier. He climbed the steps, deftly moving between throngs of people. Once on the balcony, Georgell found an empty spot on the rail and leaned over to scan the vacillating crowd below. The music thumped a popular tune and repetitively hammered away at the night. Cigarette smoke, a non-distinct generic brand, crept into his nostrils and ate away at his concentrated scanning. *I need another Excedrin*, he thought.

"Pink, can you grab me a Coke please," he asked a glittering cocktail server as she passed.

"Sure Doc, gonna be here?"

"Yeah, for a bit." He smiled and turned his gaze back to the surging crowd. Coca Cola and Excedrin were the two addictions Georgell gladly admitted to. He was never much of an alcohol drinker. The impairment was just too ridiculous to bother with. As a teenager he would go to parties and purposely not drink just to enrage other partygoers and get in fights. As he aged it just seemed pointless to imbibe in that which caused so much trouble. *Without alcohol, immaturity would be the only thing keeping bouncers employed*, he thought with amusement. Alcohol just never fit into Georgell's world, and now with a family of five it just seemed wasteful. Of course Emma constantly harangued him about the Coke drinking, but it had become somewhat of a family joke. One of the kids would bring him a can, he would pop the tab, hold it up and declare, "This . . ." and then in unison everyone would chime in, " . . . is the last Coke I will ever drink!" They loved it.

Georgell swept the floor with his eyes. Bouncers were in position at every station and in clear view of another. Every bouncer had a partner. Eye contact had to be kept and backup immediate. Chopper, a name somehow morphed from the mass of silver capping on his teeth, watched the dance floor from the west rail. This was a dangerous station because the 4-foot rail was the separation point between the dance floor and the service bar. Chopper's back was exposed to the impatient throng trying to get booze. It didn't seem to bother him though. He had a large black 6'6" frame, massive arms, tightly braided corn rows, and a ridiculously huge golden pirate hoop that dangled from his right ear. He wore the ornament as a distraction. "Man," he would say, "kids always trying to pull it out, gives me an open shot!"

Georgell agreed with the theory—the goatee he wore was also a drunk-magnet and provided him with easy access for restraining holds when distracted brawlers focused on it; but Georgell always thought Chopper's hoop was overkill.

Tequila, a short, stocky, ex-pro boxer from L.A. covered the North wall. He leaned against a balcony riser and looked at ease with one eye on the crowd and the other on Chopper. Georgell recalled how nonchalant Tequila was when he had first moved to the area. How peaceful and quiet he had expected Salt Lake City to be. He recalled the first major fights they had been involved in together and how quickly Tequila had realized that this quiet city nestled in the Rocky Mountains of Utah was no different than L.A. It had just as many ignorant people willing to fight over the most ridiculous circumstances. Despite his ability to fight, Tequila rarely had the opportunity to throw a punch. He was fast and quick to dodge attacks but Chopper would usually have an assailant lifted from the ground and begging for mercy before Tequila could reciprocate.

On the stage to the east was Troll, a quiet monster of a man. Conversation, in fact a whole sentence would be quite a show for Troll. He was 6'5", a young 22, and just not attractive due to an abundance of pock marks and scarring. Troll was green for a Bouncer but a quick learner. His stoic gaze and frightening appearance seldom gave him occasion for violence but his best friend and partner filled that void by causing more than enough for both of them. Taz, stationed on the South wall next to the balcony stairs, had a mass of curly red hair and a temper to go with it. Many times Georgell had to pull him from fights before he injured bystanders in his whirl of rage. Troll and Taz were inseparable and a fantastic team.

Across the dance floor and up on the opposite balcony leaned Bear, staring, watching. He was a roaming bouncer, free to wander the club, and Georgell's partner. Bear was 5'6" with a short well-groomed beard, shaved head, and a seasoned veteran gaze. He had a solid base of muscle and powerful strength. In fights Bear would go straight after the biggest guy, leap on his back and lock his massive arms around the target's neck. Rarely was Bear knocked free before the victim would drop unconscious. Georgell trusted Bear implicitly and appreciated his no fear attitude. He, like Georgell, had years of experience and knew what to look for and how to react.

As if on cue, Georgell heard Bear's deep raspy voice through the earpiece, "Everything okay?"

Georgell gave a reluctant thumbs-up and shrugged.

"Door! Door! Door!" A loud bellow screamed through the earpiece. Immediate action took place on the dance floor as all the bouncers bolted from their stations toward the exits. Something was going on at the entrance. Georgell pushed through the crowd as people, seeing the bouncer exodus, curiously began to follow. "Security!" Georgell screamed as he shoved a guy to the side. Sampson would only use the emergency call in an extreme situation and being the furthest away from the call, Georgell was very concerned and desperate to push through.

Georgell raced down the stairs, passed the beer cart, rounded the corner into the main bar and immediately noticed a horde of people crowding the entry. *What's going on*, he wondered.

"Do not exit!" The frantic voice of Tequila screamed over the radio, "I repeat, do not exit! Stay in! Stay in!"

Bear hurled people to the side as he scrambled toward the entry. Georgell, seconds behind, followed in his wake. Both ignored Tequila's plea. The distinct sound of a shotgun blast thundered from the street and a wave of hysterical screams followed. A throng of frightened clubbers ran through the entry and heaved Georgell back against the membership desk. Another sickening boom pierced the frenzied scene. He was close. His team was out there. He needed to help. Georgell pressed his body against the wall and desperately made his way toward the echo of death. Another blast sounded as Georgell rammed through the door. A warm salty spray of red flecked his face and a young brunette fell at his feet, eyes wide open. The nightmare unraveled before him.

Georgell could see and react to volatile situations because he had the ability to mentally focus and determine what was needed. As chaos forced others to panic, Georgell's mind would sharpen, his heart rate would slow and his senses heighten. He would lock out all peripheries and instantly zero in on the problem and react.

At the bottom of the entry steps was a man screaming incoherently and wielding a smoking shotgun. His searing maniacal eyes were familiar to Georgell. The convulsing of his shirtless muscular body and the veins which bulged from his neck and temples masked the person within, but Georgell knew the eyes. The raging face only framed the murderous change in the man's lost gaze. The black smoking shotgun jumped in his hands with a flash of light and a hollow echo. Another body dropped.

Who is he? Where are Bear and Troll? Georgell silently questioned. Kool-Aid lay motionless at the shooter's feet, two or three people pinned below his massive weight. To Georgell's right lay Sampson, blood steaming from his splayed chest and a cold lifeless stare glaring into the clear night sky. Amidst the bodies, dead and barely living, an acrid scent of urine, sulfur, blood and fear gently lifted through the settling smoke. A distant girl was vomiting in the street.

Georgell noticed Chopper, also on the right, alive and holding his broad blood-stained shoulder as he crouched behind a brick column. Matted among the bodies on the steps lay Tequila and Taz face down. The stain of death painted the scene and Georgell knew his friends were clinging for life, if they weren't already gone.

Though only a flash of time had elapsed, Georgell felt as though he had been surveying the scene for hours. There was only one option and, without hesitation, Georgell accepted his fate and moved. He took one step from the front door and leapt headlong toward the enraged assailant. He sailed over the stairs, bodies, and screaming chaos. He felt nothing of the shot that penetrated his skin and tore at his neck as he pounded squarely into the madman. The shotgun bounced free from the murderer's grip and slid into the street. Georgell was numb to the crushing weight of body after body piling, pinning both him and the assailant to the hard concrete ground.

Sirens wailed in the background, screams echoed in the crowd, and inside the hypnotic rhythm of music continued to thump. He could see his children home in bed snuggled with their favorite stuffed animals, his wife unknowingly reading a novel on the living room sofa. *Would she be mad? Curious*, he thought as his mind wandered, *why a Thursday*.

☼⌇ **2** ⌇☼

Mmmm, looks appetizing, Georgell sarcastically thought as he slid the aging cafeteria salad aside and wondered when Emma would arrive. A mindless reality program was playing on the television across from his bed and he thought about changing the channel but didn't. He wasn't watching anyway. Georgell tenderly fingered the bandage on his neck to ease the itching and drifted away in thought. Weeks had passed but his mind was only recently reengaging with time and reality so he tried to recall things but still struggled with his memory. The stifling hospital room became a prison in his increased mental awareness and it felt as if he were wilting away like his uneaten salad or the many vases of dying "Get Well" flowers on the nearby table. *Why don't they throw them away?*

The bed groaned as Georgell shifted his weight. Happily, he recalled that the lung machine was no longer attached to his chest with its obtrusive tube jammed between his ribs. His left lung had collapsed and the machine was used to inflate and repair the damage but it was nice to have it gone. Georgell pulled up his gown and stared again at the massive circular bruise just below his chest where the tube had been. The darkness of the bruise was lessening but it was still an ample reminder of the assailant's shotgun. The blunt barrel of the weapon had cracked a rib and caused the collapsed lung.

The itching returned and Georgell gently pressed again on the heavy bandages that covered his neck. Most of the shotgun pellets had shredded his shoulder but a few had penetrated his neck and ruptured his carotid artery. Everyone talked about how lucky he was, how he should have bled to death. He owed his life to those men that had piled on top of him and the murderer. The weight of their bodies had pressed his ruptured neck onto the skull of the shooter and reduced the hemorrhaging. The prompt arrival of the EMT unit and the close proximity to the hospital made the eighteen minutes from injury to operating table a life saver. He was lucky, it was a miracle.

Georgell didn't feel lucky. Seven people died in the Club Momentum shooting; five were victims of shotgun wounds, an unfortunate girl trampled by the frightened crowd was the sixth, and the last was the crazed shooter. Georgell had played a part in the last death by slamming the shooter to the sidewalk with enough force to lodge a broken beer bottle into his skull. Ironically the same crushing weight of men that had saved Georgell's life had ended the perpetrators by pressing the splintered bottle deep into his brain. Three of the dead were Georgell's friends, bouncers: Sampson, Taz, and Tequila. Georgell reeled at his inability to attend their respective funerals.

The physical pain of recovery was manageable but Georgell could not free his mind from the nightmarish images that constantly plagued his hours of solitude. The same dream played over and over; echoing shotgun blasts, the stench of death and smoke, screams from all around, blood everywhere, and the dull thumping of music in the background like a dark theme. Everything burned in his thoughts just as it had happened, except for the addition of a ghostly figure that seemed to hover above the murderer. The being was old, almost fragile, with a thick red cloak that enshrouded his skeletal form. His gaze was magnetic, powerful, and yet hollow of soul. His face gaunt and his eyes black, empty, void of pupils. At first Georgell assumed the man was a manifestation of death conjured up by his shocked mind; but the dream kept returning and the haunting image more lucid as the nights progressed. The devilish figure was clearly connected to the murderer like a visible puppeteer. The man would point and the killer would shoot—point again and another victim would fall—but the demonic puppeteer always kept his eyes locked on Georgell; staring, laughing, and mocking him. Day after day and night after night the dream infected his thoughts like a parasite of life and always ended with the cold stare, pointing finger, and cackling laugh of the hovering menace.

The itch beneath his bandages subsided but the whining of the reality show contestants pressed on. Georgell wondered where Emma was.

The door to his room clicked shut and Georgell opened his eyes still hearing the nightmarish laughter deep in his clouded thoughts. A new program was on the television, a cooking show, but Emma was there, in his room, standing with her back to him, still holding the knob of the door. *How long has she been here,* he wondered. *How long have I been asleep? When did I fall asleep?* The salad was no longer on his bedside table and some of the wilted flowers were gone as well, replaced with fresh bouquets. *What time is it? What day is it?* The days had somehow run together and Georgell felt anger begin to rise with his loss of time.

Emma didn't turn to greet him and Georgell wondered what she was thinking; standing there motionless and clutching the door like a life vest. Her long black hair rested on her blouse with specks of fluttering light trapped in its length. She kept it long for Georgell. He loved the touch of it, the warmth of it on his body. He loved the smell of it and the accentuating flow of it down her shoulders and back. Georgell marveled at her shape and found her as beautiful as ever. Even after three children she maintained an attractive figure that never failed to arouse him.

"Tell me," Georgell said in a low raspy voice.

Emma's hand dropped from the doorknob and she slowly turned as if she knew he had been watching. She lifted her brown eyes to meet his. A pained smile brightened her features and blossomed below her high cheek bones, "What?"

"I know you've told me but it's still a shadow in my mind. Tell me again, please."

Emma moved to a blue-cushioned chair by the bed. The chair wasn't there before, *or had it been,* Georgell wondered, confused again by the lapse of time. She silently sat and for a moment just held Georgell's gaze, "Franklin tried to get in the club earlier but Sampson turned him away . . ."

"Franklin?" Georgell said. He knew the name, Emma had told him but he couldn't be certain and wanted to hear everything again.

"Sorry," Emma stammered. "Um . . . yes, Franklin, Paul Franklin, he was apparently a bouncer that you wouldn't hire at Momentum. He was the shooter."

Georgell pictured the face from news reports on the television and nodded.

"He was wearing a security shirt . . ." Emma continued as she placed her hand on his, " . . . and Sampson told him to change or he couldn't enter. Kool-Aid came out a few minutes later to check on Sampson and walk the line."

Georgell swiveled his hand over Emma's and squeezed, urging her on. He closed his eyes and tried to recreate the event in his mind.

"As Kool-Aid reached the bottom of the steps a car stopped in front of the club and Franklin jumped out with a shotgun and started screaming something about bouncers. That's when Sampson made the emergency call. Franklin shot him for that, I don't know maybe he was going to kill him anyway but to do it so quickly, I don't know . . . I guess that's when Kool-Aid jumped on some girls in line and tried to shield them. Nobody knows why Franklin didn't kill Kool-Aid too, but he didn't; instead he clubbed him in the back of the head and knocked him unconscious then pointed the gun at the doors, like he expected more security? Anyway . . . when Taz and Tequila came out . . ."

Emma's voice faltered and she pulled Georgell's hand to her chest. He felt her steady heart, her warmth, her life.

" . . . They had no chance, Georgell."

"Go on."

Taking a deep breath, she continued, "Chopper came out next and tripped over Taz and Tequila. As he fell another blast grazed his shoulder. Then Franklin shot Tequila again because he heard him radio the second warning not to exit . . ."

With the narrative pause came a visual change in Emma's demeanor; an expression that Georgell had become familiar with over the last few visits. Georgell knew she was holding back, not wanting to cause him more pain, but he had grown tired of the doting wife routine and her forced restraint was wearing on his nerves. He wanted to hear her true feelings. "What is wrong? You've had something to say for some time now and I need you to open up."

"Why didn't you listen?" she quickly growled. "Why didn't you stay in the club?"

Georgell was surprised by the quick reply and stammered for an answer but found none. Emma patiently watched and said nothing. "Please Emma," he finally said hoping for some time to formulate a sufficient explanation.

After a long silence, her voice now a whisper, Emma relented. "You came out as he fired at a guy trying to get in. I don't know . . . they say he was wearing a black tee-shirt that looked like a security uniform so Franklin shot him in the back. Then an off-duty cop made a move and Franklin shot him in the face from like three feet away. That's when you leapt from the stairs. Those that saw it say you slammed open the door, ran and jumped from the edge of the stairs without even looking . . . as if you knew what to do before you even got there."

Emma dropped her head to the mattress and began to cry. "Why didn't you listen? You could've died."

"Emma I'm here," Georgell said softly. "I'm sorry." He tried to offer comfort by stroking her head but knew she would only continue when she was ready.

Several minutes passed and finally the sobbing dissipated and she lifted her head from the dampened blanket. She smiled more genuine then any smile Georgell had seen in quite some time; as if by revealing her pent up frustration she had relieved a great weight from her life. Her eyes were swollen from tears and her mascara was streaked but her expression had softened and she willingly continued, "Troll never made it out of the back stairwell. Everyone was watching from the window bay and he couldn't get through. Bear didn't make it out either. He grabbed a girl that was being trampled in the entry and pulled her to the side as you ran through the doors. He and Chopper were the first to pile on your back. The police arrived a couple minutes after that."

"I was up getting Gina a drink when the phone rang. Pink called and told me you were being rushed to the ER. She told me a guy was shooting."

Georgell could not recall Emma ever telling him this part of the tale and listened intently. He could feel her spearmint breath and could almost touch her words as they slipped from her tongue. He was there and could imagine his own sense of pause had the roles been reversed. His heart sank and his mind wavered with her beleaguered recollection.

"I didn't know what to do. I sat down for I don't know how long and just, just, couldn't think. I was so mad at you, so angry! Gina finally came in and snapped me out of my stupor but I was lost, totally lost, I couldn't focus!"

Georgell mourned with her, understood her pain, hated himself for being the cause of it and tried to express that understanding with a smile. She understood. They embraced and let the dreary coldness of the hospital and its angular-suppressive room, slip away from the moment.

☼~ **3** ~☼

After his release from the hospital, Georgell immersed himself in the media blitz still buzzing around the Club Momentum shooting. He read the papers, and barked at Emma when she tried to clean up a stack of clippings he had strewn about the dining room table. He watched every broadcast and searched the web for information that he might have missed or hadn't heard. Sleep was avoided. Fatigue and a short fuse were better than dreaming.

The barrage of information began to fill gaps that Georgell deemed necessary to his recovery. He learned that a fully loaded 9mm was tucked in Franklin's pants. Reporters surmised that as many as a dozen more people could have been killed. The car he had driven to the club was stolen from a known steroid dealer. The dealer was found dead a few weeks later in a locker at an abandoned boxing clubhouse. The shotgun was believed stolen as well and the owner, though unidentified, assumed dead. Club Momentum reopened after a few weeks but plummeting sales and a lingering stigma forced its permanent closure after two months.

As for Paul Franklin; Georgell definitely knew the guy. He had applied to be a bouncer three times but was never hired. His pointed features, extended jaw, abnormal size, and inability to remain still were all indicators of steroid use. Georgell simply refused to hire anyone that used steroids and Franklin was more obvious than most. Steroid rage was real, and after seeing its affects on friends, Georgell made it a no exceptions rule. With fondness, Georgell recalled Franklin getting aggressive in the office and could still picture Bear rushing in and dropping a wicked choke on him after the third failed interview. He remembered the exact time they tossed his unconscious body into the cab; and had since calculated exactly 37 days, 7 hours, and 17 minutes from that moment to the first shot that took Sampson's life. *Was that the reason for the shooting? The motive? Kill the bouncers because I can't be one?* Georgell was completely dumbfounded by the idea.

Everyone hailed Georgell a hero and hounded him for interviews. Even national media, which usually shied away from Salt Lake stories, offered him big paychecks for any comment. He refused them all. It seemed that anyone remotely connected to the affair had done an interview with a paper or tabloid and the opinions Georgell heard and read—from close friends to the dullest of clubbers—began to wear on his nerves; but to his astonishment and relief, Bear had refused interviews as well. Georgell wondered why and often thought of calling Bear but never followed through. After one particularly ingratiating television interview, Georgell jumped to his feet and screamed, "Hero? Hero? I'm no hero! People are dead! My friends are dead!"

The outburst startled Gina who had been reading on the floor. Emma slammed her pen on the kitchen table and with a furious expression, stood up, walked to the television, turned it off, and directed Gina to her room. "Your stitches are loose," she said as she stormed out pointing at Georgell's neck.

A warm stream of blood flowed from Georgell's wound and soaked thickly into his shirt. Rage grew heavier and anger pulsed as he stood in the darkness alone. He ignored his wide-eyed daughter and cared nothing for the fear he had caused her. The pain of his neck and the flowing, dripping blood, along with Emma's display of frustration, merely fueled the fire that stoked within his overwrought shell of contempt. He screamed a blood-curdling echo of defiance and kicked the television from its stand. It popped and sparked as it slammed against the wall and fell in pieces to the marbled carpet.

After his outburst, Georgell ignored the papers, disconnected his phone and turned off the cable. No more reminders, no more theories, and no more condolences. He wasn't a hero and didn't need the added aggravation. The required hours of physical therapy became his only outside activity and though he felt a return of strength and ability, his mental recovery continued to darken. Moments of laughter and a glimmer of happiness was found in the distraction of DVD rentals but movies always ended and reality returned with its shroud of self pity and guilt. Like an addict seeking a constant high to escape the demons, Georgell kept a steady flow of distraction rolling on the downstairs television; but the ticks would always return and often a DVD menu would repeat for hours while Georgell stared blindly at the screen.

Sleep still avoided and never lasted more than a few hours when it did happen. The taunting stare and demonic laughter from the hovering figure in his nightmare was never far from his thoughts and kept him awake despite the assistance of sleeping pills that Emma forced him to take.

Georgell could see that his children didn't understand regardless off Emma's efforts to assure them that everything would be okay. He tried to offer a smile or hug but often missed the opportunity or simply let it slip by. On many occasions the kids would bring him a can of Coke pleading with him not to drink it, hoping he would pop the can and play the game but Georgell wouldn't break. He would accept the drink and send them on their way with a sullen "thank you" or a nod of his head.

Emma began sleeping more in Gina's room. She told Georgell it was only temporary, *until he was feeling better*, but Georgell knew his cold demeanor was beginning to take its toll on her as well. He didn't argue or complain just accepted the change and ignored it as he had every other aspect of his daily life. He simply went through the motions; adorned a paper smile for family and friends, marched mindless through the routine of physical therapy, and buried his thoughts in the distraction of movies. Silently, he hoped to dissipate into the furniture unnoticed.

Waking one night in a cold sweat, Georgell found he was alone in the bed. Emma wasn't there to reassure him. The ever-joyful scent of Gina's bubble gum shampooed hair was absent. Neither of the boys was snuggled up against him for security. Even the annoying Chihuahua was gone. He missed them all tremendously and longed for them. After searching the house he finally came to Gina's small room and slumped against the doorway. They were here, all of them, cuddled in a mass of security on Gina's twin mattress. Georgell slumped deeper into the doorway, guilt weighing monstrously on his mind. Here was his sweet family massed together on a tiny bed away from him, away from the king-sized bed that would hold them all. His hands gripped his scalp and he pulled his fingers down his haggard face as the foreign sensation of tears rapt him.

☼⁓ **4** ⁓☼

Georgell returned home from his last physical therapy session, tossed his gym bag to the kitchen floor, grabbed a bagel and a Coke from the fridge then wandered over to his dark corner of the living room. The curtain was open and Georgell reached over to close it, to block out the light, but stopped, mesmerized by the scene outside. Wolfy was running down the sidewalk wearing no shirt and a pair of tattered shorts that barely clung to his body. His face, chest, and hands were a messy red from a melted cherry Popsicle that he still brandished like a weapon. He was growling and chasing neighborhood kids that ran in mock alarm. Gideon and Gina were a happy part of the fleeing bunch and pressed Wolfy to continue the chase while desperately holding on to their own dripping sticks. A smile found its way to Georgell's face. He remembered the many times he had picked up his little Wolfman and joined in the chase. He stood up. *Why not*, he thought as a positive beam of light found purchase on the dark torment of his mind.

Georgell turned toward the door and slowed to a halt as he heard banging coming from the laundry room downstairs. It was Emma. She was upset, really upset. It sounded like she was tearing the laundry room apart. Georgell stepped back and slumped into his chair triggered back into his melancholy state. The phone began to ring and his fuse grew short as Emma shrieked something. The phone rang again; she wasn't answering it, just yelling. He wouldn't answer it either. It wasn't his idea to reconnect the thing. She screamed again. The phone rang again. Another hammering sound, a laundry bucket tossed against a wall no doubt. *I don't care*, he thought. The ringing stopped.

An angry march rumbled up the stairs. Georgell new Emma was coming and quickly took a swig of his Coke in preparation of the assault.

He had no idea what her rampage was about, really didn't care, but stood to meet her as she rounded the corner of the kitchen.

"I can't take it anymore!" She said and tossed a crumpled piece of paper at him. "Are you done?" She raged. "Going to give up and leave me here alone? Seriously . . . what are you thinking?"

Georgell was stunned. He leaned over and picked up the paper trying to avoid her burning stare. Unsure of her reference or what was on the sheet, he slowly pulled open the folds and immediately recognized his own penmanship.

"Sooo . . . sounds pretty grim to me?" Emma said, "All this time I've been staying away, trying to give you space to recover, keeping quiet, trying to empathize while our family falls apart. People keep telling me to leave—telling me you might be suicidal. No, I tell them, not Georgell . . . was I wrong? Look at me!"

Georgell stared blankly at the scribbled poem, remembered it was in his jeans from a few days ago and realized Emma must have found it in the laundry. He read the poem again, ignoring her.

> My cage of sanity has rusted
> My barrier of future eroded
> Sin beckons,
> Enshrouds me with its warm enticements
> Not instantaneous
> > Immediate
> > > Spontaneous
> The parasite of wickedness
> Has leeched on my soul for years
>
> My blood has dried
> My bones decayed
> My soul is ash
> My life filleted
> > I am not me!
> Me is gone!
>
> I am outside, beyond, beside myself
> That is not me
> Me is gone!

I am no longer balancing life on the edge
I am hovering landless over the abyss!
I cannot float
My parachute of faith has been misplaced.

Eyes are closed
Sound is gone
Floating stops

May chaos break my fall

"Well?" Emma said.

"I'm not suicidal Emma." Georgell said meeting her stare. "I'm in a dark place. Why are you making this into something it isn't?"

"Excuse me, a dark place; this house, our marriage, your life—a dark place?" Emma stepped forward and snatched the paper from Georgell's grasp. "Weeks go by without so much as a 'good morning' then I find this and how am I supposed to react? Frame it? I need to know where you are because I can't take this anymore!"

Georgell jammed a finger to his temple and with cold eyes replied, "In here Emma. The dark place is in here."

"Yeah, we can all see that but where does it leave us? My patience is gone and your dark place has become our dark place. I—don't—like it!"

Emma's eyes stripped Georgell of reason and he felt an eruption of anger press forth. He wanted to explain the poem. The mental place he was in when he wrote it but the explanation was out of reach as her eyes and anger exposed his raw emotions. He clenched his teeth and suppressed an outburst as a vision manifest itself in his mind. The picture of Emma and the kids snuggled on the small bed in a sanctuary of contact and slumber, away from him, laid bare the dark place they were living in, the darkness he had created for them. He had no response.

Obviously frustrated by the lack of explanation, Emma shook her head in disgust and stormed back into the kitchen. Georgell heard her grumble, "Whatever" as she passed through the kitchen and headed back down to the laundry room. The door slammed and he knew it was now his play. He thought back over the last few weeks and realized they really hadn't said much or at least he hadn't. There were moments of casual interaction where Emma had tried to involve Georgell in the details of life but he had consistently ignored her. He hung his head, frustrated but still not in a place where he was ready to open up.

The banging in the laundry room returned. Georgell stood motionless, engrossed in his thoughts, staring at nothing. The phone began to ring again. He closed his eyes and shut out the intrusive meddlesome ring.

"Georgell, it's for you!"

"I don't want . . ." he started to say but found his voice silenced by a scream.

"I don't care what you want! It's for you—get it!"

Georgell broke his stupor and forced his body into the kitchen where he registered the putrid stench of Spaghetti-O's still lingering from lunch. Another thundering boom shook the house as the laundry room door slammed again. He shook his head, rolled his eyes, and inhaled deeply as he pulled the receiver to his ear and said, "Yeah."

"Mr. Butler?"

"Yeah, is this a reporter?" Georgell growled.

"No. This is Peter Pratt. Ben, um . . . Troll's father."

Georgell didn't respond.

"Uh, anyway I thought you should know that Ben is gone. He took his own life last night."

Georgell heard a gasp and immediately knew Emma was eavesdropping. A long pause waned in silence and finally Mr. Pratt spoke up again, "Could you please pass on the news? It's nobody's fault. He just . . . I don't know, the doctors think that he blamed the death of Taz on himself. Those two . . ." he laughed a hollow chuckle " . . . they were inseparable."

"I know sir, I'm sorry!" Georgell said staring down at the floor.

"Anyway could you tell the others? You're the only one I have a number for."

"Yes sir, I will. Thank you for calling and if there's anything we can do."

"No nothing," he interrupted. "We've got everything taken care of. Goodbye."

Georgell hung up the phone in a daze. A flicker of sun caught his eye and he slowly focused his sight on the open curtain in the dark corner of the living room. He turned as he heard a ruckus echo from the backyard and through the kitchen window saw Gideon climbing up the side of the garage toward the roof, a friend close beside him. He stepped to the window, peered out at the sun, at the world his children were enjoying. A calming sense of peace blossomed in his thoughts. The grim news was relieving in a way; like a stab of reality that opened his mind for a moment.

Emma hesitantly approached from the stairs and Georgell turned to face her. She glared at him but the anger seemed distant now, replaced by a genuine concern. Georgell smiled weakly but reassuringly and saw Emma soften, her face change, she tentatively smiled back.

"I'm sorry," Georgell said.

Emma's eyes widened, surprised by the pronouncement, and she lowered herself into a nearby kitchen chair. The familiar creak of aged wood echoed like lightning in Georgell's mind and he wondered why he hadn't heard the sound for so long. He knelt in front of her, clasped her hands and peered into her eyes. She looked away. *Why*, he thought. He kissed her hand. She closed her eyes. "What," he tentatively asked.

She shook her head.

"Emma," he whispered. She opened her eyes and met his gaze.

"I'm sorry!" he said again then pressed forward and kissed her softly. A flash of excitement charged his mind and he gently touched her face, pulled her closer, and kissed her more passionately. He slid his hands gently down her neck and over her shoulders then pulled her into a tight embrace. It had been months since they had kissed or even touched and Georgell mourned the loss. He felt a rush of emotion convulse from Emma. He said nothing, just held her and let her cry.

☼~ **5** ~☼

"No, Georgell! I can't believe you're even thinking about it!" Emma yelled. "Seriously, I can understand your need to overcome some sense of loss or whatever but do you honestly expect me and the children to sit around and wait for another night like the last one? Another eight months of hell? Or maybe you aren't so lucky next time and it's your funeral we attend. Come on Georgell, do we play any part in your life? Do we get a vote?"

Georgell thought of the past week. The house was filled with laughter again; there was wrestling, silly dance contests and the warmth of sunlight and fresh baked cookies. The curtains were open and the light was free to roam in the shadows where Georgell once cowered. He was riding high on the good moments and cherished the rediscovery of Emma during their quiet nights alone. Things were getting better and despite the tiny arguments and inevitable lapses of sadness, Georgell was looking forward to the future instead of dwelling on the past.

Today was different, this was a big argument, they had just returned from Troll's funeral and Emma had overheard a discussion he and Chopper were having about bouncing. He knew the subject would come up eventually but didn't want to ruin the happiness they were enjoying. Then, without warning, Chopper dropped the grenade in his lap and Georgell unknowingly pulled the pin.

The kitchen chair wailed its familiar creak as Georgell repositioned. Emma paced across the dining room floor, furious. Her sleek black dress shuddered with each new step and Georgell found himself mesmerized by her movement. Emma seldom had reason to adorn herself in such a way. She was radiant. Watching her pace reminded him that high heels always hurt her feet and yet there she was ranting back and forth in the heels without the slightest hint of pain. Her feet had to be blistering.

Georgell felt the nagging urge to hermit back into his depressive shell but fought to keep it locked away. It was a daily battle, one that he was learning to win but still, the demons of guilt were ever-present in Georgell's mind. On the particularly bad moments, when the darkness seemed too overwhelming to avoid, Georgell had found that a good five-minute assault on the body bag in the garage helped him focus. But now, Emma pacing furiously, the body bag was not an option.

They had been arguing for close to an hour, neither willing to listen or compromise. Georgell slipped his points of discussion deftly into the argument but knew they had no bearing on the outcome. As long as Emma fumed there would be no real discussion. Georgell wanted to say with finality that he was going to bounce no matter what she argued, but he knew such a proclamation would not go over well. Besides, their marriage had always relied on combined thought, discussion, and problem-solving. He longed for an end to the battle, but just couldn't settle on a decisive plan—so instead, he found distraction in Emma's fireball beauty. The tables were usually turned, Georgell fuming and Emma calmly trying to defuse the situation, but this time Emma had the upper hand on anger and Georgell submitted to her rage, listened and waited.

A smile crept onto Georgell's face as he recalled the park hopping a few days ago. In order to keep his mind occupied and entertain the kids, Emma had forced him into visiting fifteen parks in five hours. Gideon posted swing-jump records while Gina made friends and Wolfy wreaked havoc on whomever or whatever he could. *Sweet Day*, Georgell thought.

"Georgell! Are you listening? Do you even care what I have to say?"

Georgell erased the tiny smile from his face and nodded. Emma shook her head in disgust then renewed her ranting lecture.

The funeral was interesting, Georgell thought while trying to maintain a sense of attention to Emma's lecture. The battle of police trying to keep reporters at a distance seemed more of a focus than the actual proceedings. It was apparent that Troll's suicide rekindled interest in the Club Momentum shooting and everyone wanted another sound byte.

Emma's lecture was now focused on some of the funeral attendees and Georgell tried to focus on the relevance but quickly lost interest again. He reflected on the conspicuous absence of Bear and realized that he had become so wrapped up in his own depression and misery that he had selfishly ignored not only his wife and kids but also those individuals that really meant something to him. He immediately decided to track his friend down and try to help.

" . . . And Chopper—I can't believe he even brought bouncing up with you? What is going through his head? Come on . . ."

The pause forced Georgell to utter a response but his attempt at inclusion was ignored as Emma blazed on oblivious to his effort. He thought again of Bear and marveled at Chopper's explanation of his absence. Bear had been locked up over the weekend. Two counts of assault and another for destruction of property. Apparently he had seriously injured a couple of muscle heads in a club brawl. One he slammed headfirst into a neon sign for groping a waitress and the other he tossed out a window for interfering. Although Georgell found the story oddly amusing, he still couldn't accept the idea of Bear being so raw as to throw someone out a window. It seemed too outrageous.

"What was it he said?" Emma asked, hands on her hips?

Georgell tried to focus.

Emma snapped. "Chopper! What did Chopper say about that concert?"

Georgell recalled the shiver of cold sweat that danced up his neck when he realized Emma had overheard Chopper discussing a job with him. "Uh, he said there was a heavy metal concert coming up that he could get me in on."

"Right, a heavy metal concert no less—it couldn't be Hanna Montana or a film festival—straight to metal, insane!"

"Emma, I can't keep apologizing for my depression. I know you had to deal with a lot and I know I was a major burden, but please—try to understand."

Emma spewed her reply as she left the room. "Understand?! Understand?! What am I supposed to understand? Why can't you overcome this adolescent need for violence and try being a father." Down the hall she raged and Georgell leaned over in his chair to watch as she left. *She is hot in that dress,* he thought. The bedroom door slammed.

"That went well," Georgell said to Gina's shivering little Chihuahua. "Is there any hope, Kitty?" he asked. She looked at him with her huge watery eyes and then trotted out of the room in what appeared to be an indignant huff. It was quite obvious that Kitty was on Emma's side.

Georgell stared at a rip in the kitchen linoleum; tried to remember its origin. He rubbed his eyes and stretched his fingers hard over the skin of his neck. He could hear the distant sound of the sink in the master bath, drawers slamming, a shoe hitting the closet wall, then another. *There go the high heels*, he mused. A spider dangled in the corner of the kitchen and seemed curious, like it wanted to know the outcome as much as Kitty.

Georgell banged his head on the table a few times hoping to pound some sense into his thoughts. He understood Emma's concern but wanted her to see it from his point of view. Just to listen. He would give her some time to cool down then take her for a ride in the mountains. Or maybe they would hike up Ensign Peak where they could sit, look over the valley and get some perspective on things. There had to be a solution; he was certain they could figure something out. They were a team. If they couldn't come up with an amicable decision, maybe they could at least figure out some sort of tolerable compromise.

Georgell stretched his legs and looked for the spider. It was gone, disgusted no doubt. A barely audible jingle caught Georgell's ear and he listened intently. It was an ice cream truck coming down the street and immediately Georgell knew the solution, or at least a plan of action. He ran down the stairs and burst into the dark family room where the kids were watching a movie. Wolfy was sleeping soundly in the rocking chair while the other two were snuggled under a blanket and captivated by the animation on the TV screen. Georgell snatched a pair of shorts and a dirty tank top from the floor then picked up Wolfy and changed him out of his grass-stained funeral pants and perspiration-soaked shirt. He then told Gideon and Gina to turn off the movie and change into play clothes. After some complaining and the promise of ice cream, they finally did as they were asked.

"Where we going, Dad?" Gideon said, scratching his blonde, almost white, hair.

"Cold Stone and then to the park."

"What park—can Muppet come," Gina said, her big blue eyes pleading?

"Castle Park," he said. An exuberant yes chimed in from Gideon's room and Georgell added, " . . . and no, Gina, Kitty needs to stay here." Muppet was the real name for the Chihuahua, but Georgell insisted on calling her Kitty while everyone else addressed her properly.

"Dad! She's not a cat."

"Are you sure?" Georgell teased. "She uses a kitty litter box and wears a small kitty collar. And she always comes when I call 'Kitty Kitty.' I think she is a cat."

"Dad, stop." Gina smiled and hit Georgell in the shoulder.

Gideon came out of his room wearing homemade jean shorts, different colored socks pulled up to his knees, red rain boots, and tucking a plastic sword into his belt. "I'm ready, Dad," he said matter-of-factly.

"Going to war son?" Georgell said with a grin. "Better get Wolfy's sword or he'll take yours."

"Yeah," Gideon said and ran back into his room.

Wolfy grumbled a refusal to wake and Georgell began to tickle and tease him. "I don't want it," the tired child argued.

"Ice cream—Castle Park," Georgell taunted over and over as he nibbled on Wolfy's chubby belly.

Wolfy's eyes blinked open as Gideon returned to the room and handed him a gold-handled sword. Georgell motioned for the boys to get up the stairs and chuckled a bit when he noticed the shape of a plastic dagger outlined in Gideon's sock as he bolted out the door.

Georgell loaded the kids into their beat up Chevy Blazer, then returned to the house and knocked on his bedroom door. "Emma, let's go to the park and talk."

The door swung open and Emma stepped out wearing jeans, sandals and a breezy loose-fitting blouse with a sunflower print. Her hair was pulled back into a tight braid and she had on her favorite pink tinted sunglasses with little rectangular lenses. "Okay," she said, walking passed Georgell. A fine misty aroma of lilacs followed her down the hall and Georgell knew she was preparing for battle. *My favorite perfume, tight jeans, those sexy glasses, and where did she get that blouse,* he wondered. *Distract me with beauty and desire. That's her plan,* he thought and then smiling, said, "She's good."

Quickly Georgell stripped out of his funeral garb and threw on a tee-shirt and jeans. He grabbed his favorite ball cap off the shelf and jammed some cash into his pocket. Then a thought grabbed him and he bolted down the stairs and into his cramped little office. Opening his filing cabinet, Georgell found his poetry cache and thumbed vigorously through the contents. Finally he found what he was looking for, yanked it from the file, and folded the copy neatly into his back pocket. *It might help,* he thought.

☼ ~ **6** ~ ☼

The ice cream was gone; the boys were happily playing on the castle structure, swords in hand, and shouting "Death to the dragons!" while Gina was busy talking with a group of girls by the baby swings. Emma hadn't said much and Georgell too waited for the right moment. They were sitting beneath a towering oak, listening to the kids and the soothing trickle of a nearby stream, when Emma finally spoke, "Okay, tell me why. I'm not sure I will agree or even understand but I'm willing to listen."

"I'm not sure how," Georgell said. "It's hard to explain." He shook his drink; the sound of rustling ice distracting him for a moment as he thought. "Remember a few years ago when we went through this same argument after I injured my knee? I quit bouncing and managed that copy center downtown, remember?"

Emma nodded.

"Do you remember how depressed I was?"

"Yes I do," she said. "And I agreed to let you return to bouncing, and I'm glad that I did because you were a better person—look I understand there is some weird male drive that has you sucked into that seedy underworld but I thought for sure you would have no problem leaving now."

"Why?" Georgell took a long sip from his Coke trying desperately to maintain a calm demeanor.

"You nearly died, Georgell. What do you mean, why? You have a family. This dangerous lifestyle just doesn't fit anymore." Emma stared out at the kids as if to remind him of their existence. She waved and smiled at Gina who caught her stare. "I honestly—never for a second in all these past months—*never* did I think you would return to bouncing. I hoped you would break through your depression and you did. I hoped you would love me again and you have. I hoped you would wake up one day and remember the kids you'd been neglecting, and that you did as well. But never did I think bouncing would be a factor in my life or our life again. I'm sorry that I got so upset and screamed at you but you've got to see why I was shocked. Don't you?"

"I think I understand," Georgell said as he batted away a fly. "And I didn't mean for the idea to be sprung on you like it has, but that's how it happened, and here we are. Listen I know that you have a hard time accepting the idea, but somewhere in my soul I truly believe this is a calling. I know you think I am merely acting out some form of testosterone-driven lust for violence. But Emma, I am not doing this because I love the atmosphere or like the attention of horny little girls. I am happy with this relationship! I am happy with our marriage! I love you! I love the kids and I don't want anything to destroy what we have created."

Georgell jammed his straw like an ice pick into his drink for a bit as Emma stared at the playground. "But I cannot go against who I am. I know that I nearly lost you back there. I was so caught up in self-pity and anger that both of us suffered tremendously. I know the kids were affected as well. I don't want to put you through that again and I certainly don't want to put myself through it again. But what else is there? Do you want me to come home every day bitter about work, depressed at life, and grumpy all the time?"

"Let me put it into perspective. I know that you love being a mother and all the school meetings, plays and homework fulfill that need in you. Our kids depend on you; you're always there for them and me. The house is always clean, clothes are always folded and put away, meals prepared, and you practically bake for the entire neighborhood. And somehow, in the middle of all that, you manage the bills and keep yourself looking fantastic. But if you had to work again, where would all this end up?"

"We would do alright." Emma turned to look at Georgell, her features softening a bit as she swept hair back over her shoulder.

"No, that's not the point, I know we would be okay, we've done it before. What I mean is how would you feel? Would you be happy? You love being a mother and you love doing all those meticulous little things that keep us all happy. You always wanted this life and now that you've got it why do you want to give it up? I'll be grumpy again and you'll be worn out because you'll try to maintain a job and continue doing all the mother stuff. Remember our fights, our arguments? I know you're happy and I don't want you to do anything else. It was always your calling to be a mother. I know it and you can't deny it."

Georgell stopped for a moment. The edge in his voice was too harsh and he didn't want to come across as angry. He took a deep breath. "Emma, you take care of everything. I am grateful and lucky to have you. I can't complain because there is nothing for me to complain about. I am amazed that you married me and more amazed that you have stayed with me, especially after these last few months. So somewhere there is a feeling in you for me that rivals mine for you. I have to believe that."

Emma held his gaze and softly nodded.

"I don't understand and I won't try to understand. I'm nothing special—well, maybe I'm a great lover . . ." Georgell paused, watching a little smile creep onto Emma's face, pleased by her subtle reaction. He reached over and picked up her hand. "Give me the benefit of the doubt. I believe, strongly believe, that I am a bouncer not just as an occupation but also as a person. Like you being a mother, bouncing is part of me. It's what I have to do to fill the void in my soul. Besides—the money is good enough that you don't have to work. That in itself has got to count for something, right?"

A fat round pinecone flew over their heads, bounced off the tree, and hit Georgell in the shoulder before coming to a rest on the blanket. Gideon offered a carefree apology as he approached and then, in a barely audible mumble, asked if they could hold his grenade for a minute. He then hustled back to the castle.

Georgell sat in silence watching Emma as she watched the children. She still held his hand and Georgell knew she was mulling over the conversation. He hoped for a positive outcome but as of yet there was no indication of her thought. She just sat, motionless, watching the children and thinking.

"Mom, Dad, watch," Gideon bellowed from the swing set. He was swinging high and, after confirming full attention, he jumped from the swing landing a good distance away. "That's a record," he triumphantly screamed and then yelped as Wolfy whacked him in the back with his sword while bolting for the safety of the castle.

Near a picnic table, Gina and a friend were busy securing flowers they'd picked to every available hole or rip in their clothing, and humming Once Upon a Dream. The sun was beginning to dip behind the mountains and a radiant haze outlined everything in the park.

Georgell reached into his back pocket and pulled out a frayed piece of paper, "I want you to read something. I wrote this when I was working those three jobs after Wolfy was born. I was real depressed after loading trailers all day and was driving to the copy center when this poem came to me. I had forgotten about it until this afternoon. I think it will give you an idea of what I was feeling during that phase in my life." Georgell unfolded the frayed paper and said, "Here, just read it."

Emma held the poem for a few seconds and then handed it back to Georgell, "You read it."

Georgell figured she would say that. She had always preferred listening to his poetry rather than reading it. He too preferred this because he could emphasize words that demanded attention and recite the poem as he had meant it to sound. It was much more meaningful this way, he thought, happy to oblige her.

The sun was nearly gone, just a shimmering of light skirted across the graying sky as Georgell began to read,

> I've accepted the role of mindless minion
> Droning on through senseless dominion
> Thoughtless, needless, hopeless, trudging on
> I'm Being
>
> Mechanical motion, day in and out—speeding by
> Moving me closer to the grave where I'll lie
> Pointless to wonder, think, or explain
> My half full glass floods the unplugged drain
> Suicide, Depression, phantoms for the feeble
> Tranquil in acceptance for the phantom free people
> Wishes wasted, dreams skewed, faith unfounded
> Just Being
>
> Outlets aplenty for happy seeking souls
> Liquor, drugs, chiseled lists of happy goals
> No outlet for me, I'm fantasy free. I live. That's life.
> I'm Being
>
> My world, my stage, happily I bow and wave
> My production perfect with underworld raves

Eyes, smiles, handshakes and thank yous
Grind the stone, chew the fat—pay the pending dues
Posture on, blissful on, pretension maintain
Follow the sheep of humanity—ignoring the obvious game
All kneeling, not seeing, accept the common insane!
Just Being

One of the living but living with the dead
Prescription free sedation—iceless water I tread
Zombiotic momentum extreme
Just Being

Two positive steps forward then slide a mile down
Forget the glittering diamond and follow the cackling clown
Freedom from light comes in bitter shade
Snapping with the thunder of a guillotine's blade
Comply with scheduled eternity or burn in failures flame
Escape not the paradigm enshrouding your name
Just Be

Hear the rod, see the rod, wander serene in the fog
Drift through the motions on a motion free cog
Sirens hear, pleasures see, desperately trying to mangle the free
Just Be,
Tranquil in the Bog

Georgell's voice trailed off as he finished the poem. He quietly folded the tattered page and returned it to his back pocket. Off in the distance an ice cream truck whistled its enticing tune, a reminder of where this evening began. He was troubled by Emma's silence and began to open his mouth but found himself muted by her sudden voice.

"I can't handle another phone call," she said with a strong whisper.

Georgell felt her piercing eyes and knew she was serious.

"How can I deal with the anxiety and stress of waiting for another phone call?"

Georgell said nothing. He couldn't answer.

"I don't know how to accept it. I am willing to relent but you've got to help me find a solution to my anxiety. I am a mother, and yes, that makes me happy because it always has been my desire. But you forget that I am also a wife and I cannot be who I am without you. I don't want to do this alone. We created this together and I guarantee your poem is a perfect mantra for single mothers. How can you promise me that I won't become one—that you won't be hurt again? I honestly don't want to receive another phone call like that, I just . . ."

"I can't. How can I promise you I won't get hurt? I really don't believe a situation like that could arise again but I can't say I won't react the same way that I did. Fights are going to happen. People are going to get injured. Will I get hurt again? Probably, will it be serious—I don't know. It's part of the job. The uncertainty is what keeps a bouncer on his toes. I'm good at my job and I can promise that I will never take unnecessary risks but I can't promise an end to the phone calls."

Georgell could see that he wasn't helping the situation and then a thought occurred to him, "Why don't you work with me? Whatever club I work for I'm sure will give you a job too. Mom could watch the kids. It will get you out of the house and if something happens you'll be there and won't get a phone call. You'll get to know the staff and maybe even find some new friends. Even if it's just a few nights—what do you think?" Georgell sat up engaging Emma with his excitement and hoped she would agree.

"I don't know," she said. "I think it could ease some of my worries and might even help my self-esteem but I still struggle with the idea. Are you sure you are ready to go back? It's great that you've made such a strong recovery but what about your mental state? Don't you think there are some issues inside that you haven't completely overcome?"

Georgell still battled depression and the dream still haunted his thoughts but he felt like he was gaining control. He could feel the darkness creeping up and believed he could keep it suppressed with distractions. He knew Emma was right but refused counseling and wouldn't discover any problems with fear or apprehension unless he put himself back out there. "I think I'm okay. Physically I feel great. But honestly I can't say I'm a hundred percent until I go back and see."

"You're not a hundred percent why? If you won't seek therapy can you at least open up to me?"

Georgell paused. "There's a dream that I can't shake," he said. "It's crazy but I can't get it out of my mind."

Emma looked intently and Georgell knew he would have to divulge everything. "It's the night of the murders," he said, "and I'm standing at the top of the stairs watching the entire thing without reacting. But in my dream there's a man that hovers over Franklin and points at every victim that he kills, directing him. The eerie thing is that while this old man points out each victim he stares at me and finally points at me, as I stand there doing nothing. I can't get his eyes out of my mind. Not to mention the fact that he is laughing at me like a demonic hyena . . . I know it's crazy but honestly I think about it all the time. I just can't shake the pointing finger, the eyes, and that laugh echoes in my head twenty-four seven. Even the smells of that night . . ."

The description hung in the air momentarily, Georgell was about to add more when Emma clearly spoke. "No I don't think it's crazy, I think it's normal. You went through a traumatic experience. Most people would never recover without clinical help or some kind of medication and yet here you are, less than a year later, ready to dive right back into the same pit you barely escaped from."

"I don't know how to interpret your dream and I don't know how to erase it from your thoughts either but maybe you're right. Maybe the best thing for you to do is to confront the nightmare, go back to bouncing and overcome the demons. I don't know?"

Minutes ticked away without a word and finally Emma broke the silence again, "When is the concert?"

"Two weeks, on a Saturday."

"Okay, if you promise me that you won't agree to work at any clubs—that means no searching for jobs, no phone calls, nothing, until you have worked the concert—then I will agree. I want to see how you handle the concert before you agree to do anything else. I know you aren't weak-minded and that you feel invincible but please give me this. Until you get your feet wet I just don't think it is smart to jump back in full-time. I think you underestimate the strain that you've been through and I'm scared that this dream might have a more serious affect on your psyche than either of us can understand or foresee. Let's make sure your head is clear."

Darkness was falling and the mosquitoes began to swarm a little heavier. Wolfy was chasing Gina and Gideon around some trees and the streetlights were buzzing to life. Georgell was happy with Emma's stipulations and smiled. "I think I can deal with that. What about you? Do you want to go back to work?"

"You're breaking my rules already!" Emma smacked Georgell in the thigh. "I don't want you thinking about the future until we get through the concert. If you feel good and handle yourself well at the concert then we can discuss the future but for now let's just take it one step at a time, okay? And yes, I will go back but only if you agree to be honest with me about the concert. Don't make me send spies. I want your assurance that if you are clouded by stress or anything out of the ordinary that you will tell me. Do you promise?"

Georgell scooted closer and squeezed her hands. "Yes, Emma. I promise that if I feel uneasy or overwhelmed that I will tell you and we will look into other possibilities. And I promise that I won't inquire about any available bouncing positions, or even mention this discussion, until I have successfully worked the concert. Now do I need to sign something or are we okay?"

Emma gave him a stern look but seemed happy with his response. Georgell stretched out his legs and then rested his head on Emma's lap. "You know, I think you should get a degree in Psychology. I would enjoy having you probe my mind on a regular basis."

"Yeah," Emma said, twisting her eyes and brow, "your poetry is another topic of interest. Can you write me something cheerful as a sign of recovery?"

"I'm better at showing my cheerfulness," he said with a nudge.

She smiled wickedly back and they kissed.

☼~ 7 ~☼

The night of the concert came and Georgell felt the unease of starting something new. The queasiness had lurched at him all day, growing increasingly tight as the day wore on and despite his regimented routine of preparation, he couldn't shake the nerves. After shaving his head and relaxing in a hot shower, Georgell peered at himself in the mirror. "I'm not going to let you trip me up," he said. The stare-down continued and Georgell rolled his neck from side to side and clenched his jaw. The scars on his neck and shoulder were still red from the shower, a visual reminder of what he was willingly walking back into; the possibility of more. He shook his head, took a deep breath and threw a flurry of shadow punches. "I've got this," he said.

Georgell slid on black loose fitting jeans, bulky gray socks and heavy steel toe boots that had recently been resoled. He unfolded a thick extra large black tee-shirt, the word "SECURITY" emblazoned on the back, pulled it over his head and chest, and tucked it into his jeans. Then he tightly rolled the short sleeves of the tee-shirt, not because he had massive biceps but because he had been rolling his tee-shirt sleeves since he was fourteen and it just felt odd not to.

A gold bucket was snatched from a nearby shelf. Inside, Georgell grabbed Mint Chapstick and a packet of Juicy Fruit gum and slipped them into his left front pocket. In his right pocket he dropped an old aspirin vial that he had stocked with Excedrin, a small ID wallet with a pocket clip, and a black space pen. The last item in the gold bucket was a mini black flashlight that he clipped to the backside of his belt.

Emma tightly braided Georgell's goatee as the children slurped their chicken noodle soup and munched on biscuits. "Dad can I braid your goat next time?" Gina asked.

"Sure, honey," Georgell said with a smile. He loved the nickname she had given his beard. Emma attached a rubber band to the end of the braid and smiled. Georgell kissed her, thanked her, and then said, "I love you."

"I love you toooo," Emma mockingly mouthed to keep the moment light.

Georgell winked and then looked sharply at the kids, growling. "Where's my loves?" Gideon and Gina jumped up from the table and ran over to Georgell both embracing him tightly. Wolfy ignored him and kept eating a biscuit.

"Wolfy, I'm going to bite your ear," Georgell said as he stood up still holding the other two and took slow steps toward the table growling.

Gideon yelled, "Run Wolfy, run!"

Gina added a yelp of her own but Wolfy ignored them. Finally, as Georgell leaned in for the bite, Wolfy looked up and with a mouth full of biscuit slurred, "I'm on yours team Dad."

After a few minutes of laughter Georgell gave everyone goodnight kisses, stepped towards the door and said, "You guys better help Mom clean up dinner or else." Gina's eyes widened with concern but the boys just groaned. Georgell stepped out of the house and shut the door.

Chopper met Georgell at the back entrance of the arena with a huge grin on his face. "Hey man ready for some fun?"

Georgell returned the smile, shook Chopper's massive hand, and asked, "Where am I?"

"Tony is running security and wants you to roam if you feel up to it."

"It's like riding a bike right?" Georgell replied as he admired Chopper's new gold earring.

"Yeah man, but it hurts more when you crash." Chopper laughed deeply. "I've got right stage."

"Who's my partner?"

"Some old cat like us. His name is Moose. Don't know much about him but I know he's old school. Over there, man." He pointed at a big guy standing next to the stage attaching a microphone to his shirt. He had a shaved head and a heavy brown beard. He looked to be in his late thirties and, though he appeared to be strong as an ox, he wasn't bulging with muscle as he might have been as a younger man. His stomach pressed tightly against his faded security shirt, his belt bulged a bit from the weight and his pants had a large hole in the knee. Georgell noticed a hefty tattoo on his left bicep with vivid coloring but could not make out its design. As they moved closer, Chopper rambling on about somebody he had thrown out of a club recently, Georgell noticed the deep inset eyes and heavy character lines that chiseled Moose's face. *I bet this guy has some stories,* he thought.

It was always interesting to meet bouncers, especially experienced ones. A lot could be gathered in mere seconds from their appearance and attitude. Moose's unkempt look and scraggly beard had clearly indicated that the man was not bouncing to pick up girls. Georgell also thought it would be a stretch if Moose were doing it for the adrenaline rush or the thrill of violence. His maturity made that option seem absurd. Besides, a thick silver band with a curious Celtic design adorned his ring finger. Moose was a married man. It was possible that he worked as a bouncer part time for extra cash but Chopper had said he had been doing this for years. Georgell wasn't sure what to think but was certain his motives would be obvious when they spoke.

"Hey man, this is Doc. He's your partner tonight." Chopper slapped Moose on the back and wandered off to find Georgell a radio.

Moose nodded at Georgell and extended his hand. The gesture caused his tattered shirtsleeve to rise up and expose the entirety of his unique tattoo. Georgell was surprised to see a scene from The Nightmare Before Christmas; the boney figure of Jack Skellington in his trademark black suit leaning over to kiss the wide-eyed Sally with her sewn-together limbs and patchwork dress. The characters were framed within a giant yellow moon and holding hands on top of an unraveling hill. Georgell smiled, saying, "Tim Burton," as he shook Moose's heavily callused hand.

Moose's rugged brow furrowed. "Huh?"

"The tattoo, Nightmare Before Christmas . . ."

"Oh—right. My kids picked the design."

"Yeah, how many do you have?"

"Five," he replied with a slight sneer. "They spice up my life."

"Sure do." Georgell agreed. "I've got three."

"Really . . ." Moose interrupted, "you still with their mother?"

"Sure—twelve years," Georgell answered a bit perplexed by the question. "Why?"

Georgell and Moose stared at each other for a moment, both a bit confused by the direction of their dialogue, unsure how to proceed.

"Sorry," Moose finally interjected. "I just haven't met many bouncers with more than one kid and rarely any that stay married. Most guys quit bouncing once they have kids or get divorced and then bounce more cause they're angry or horny or both. I've been married nine years and I'm still bouncing and happy at home too." Then abruptly, he said, "You look familiar. We work together before?"

"No, I think I'd remember you. I used to work at Club Momentum."

Moose nodded as if registering the face with a cache of information somewhere in his brain and then said, "That's it, Butler right?"

"Yeah, Georgell Butler."

"Why Doc?"

"Because I have a degree in English."

"And you're still bouncing?"

"Better money," Georgell lied with a smirk. He didn't discuss his real reasoning because it just didn't add up with most bouncers. Emma would remain his only confidant in that regard.

Moose was a few inches taller than Georgell and had to be at least 350 pounds. Georgell was impressed. Moose wasn't cocky, not a jerk, not a tough guy, he was genuine. There didn't seem to be any front or hidden agenda with this guy except for something Georgell noticed in his eyes. His gaze had something peculiar about it that Georgell couldn't pinpoint. *Oh well,* he thought, *I'll figure it out.* Georgell knew Moose was smarter than what his appearance displayed but felt secure that he wasn't a threat. Still, he couldn't help wishing Bear were his partner. Georgell knew what to expect from Bear and how he would react—but most important, he trusted Bear. Moose was unknown and untested.

"Hey man here's your radio, channel twelve." Chopper said as he tossed a radio to Georgell and began attaching his own. Moose continued to look at Georgell as if seeing something or looking for something but Georgell pretended not to notice.

After testing their radios Chopper walked off to his station and Moose resumed their discussion as if there had been no interruption. "No, not the degree, I mean after getting shot and all—why are you coming back to this?"

Georgell thought for a moment, unable to shake Moose's stare. He finally replied, "Hard to explain. Can we leave it at that?"

Moose shrugged and nodded his gruff head. "Sure, for now."

"Moose, Doc, come to the ramp," Tony said over the radio.

☼~ **8** ~☼

The crowd began flooding into the arena. It was a huge building on the state fairgrounds that was typically used for demolition derbies and rodeos but tonight the bleachers were gone and the arena was an empty shell. On the far end was an ornate design of what appeared to be steel beams strewn about in a haphazard mess. The beams were in fact an elaborate stage design that embodied the industrial trademark of the performing band. Two 10-foot jackhammers were suspended from the rafters on either side of a Plexiglas platform that seemed to hover above the mangle of steel. Emblazoned above the stage in a ragged, chiller type metallic script, was the name of the band, Todeswunsch-Jungfrauen.

Georgell was informed that the band played loud thrashing music with a deep hammering base and that a couple of chainsaws were actually used as instruments. He was also informed that flamethrowers were part of the show and that the fire department was aware and present.

A low bass hypnotically beat through the sound system and Georgell noticed the tempo and volume slowly increasing as the start of the concert drew near. After a time Georgell realized that the lights were slowly dimming as well. He wondered if the crowd was aware of the steady change. Were they so caught up in the growing excitement that their immediate surroundings had no relevance? He had to admit the subtle changes were genius. As the beat became faster and the volume louder he felt his own heart quicken with anticipation. The dimming lights began to shadow the massing crowd and Georgell felt uneasy and anxious. *The crowd is going to explode*, he thought. *They're being primed and don't even know it.*

An hour passed and the guttural beat was deafening. The lights were completely out and visibility was minimal at best. Georgell's nerves were screaming and he had no idea where Moose or any of the other security personnel were. He wanted to radio for location updates but wasn't in charge. Tony was the lead and Georgell had to accept his authority and find a way to calm down. Tony was smart, he had to be aware of the circumstances and so Georgell begrudgingly decided to maintain his position and wait for instructions.

The maddening beat drummed on. Georgell's thoughts began to darken. The lack of sight and frenzied roar from the crowd, wore away his patience. His heart was pounding. Sweat dripped from his forehead and his entire body was tense with anticipation and concern. *Maybe Emma was right. I'm not ready for this. I'm totally overreacting and stressing over nothing.* Georgell felt an urge to act; he had to let Tony know he wasn't ready. He had to get out. *What if someone gets hurt because I hesitate? I'm not ready.* Georgell felt dizzy as the crowd began to cheer

"Brace yourselves, it's about to get crazy. Roamers head to the front." The ring of Tony's voice echoed somewhere in the back of Georgell's mind but in his whirr of stress the command went unanswered. He couldn't move, and could not defuse his panic. His knees buckled beneath him and everything went black. Georgell collapsed against the wall and slumped to the ground. No one noticed. No one cared. All eyes and attention were directed to the dark stage. The rapid beat overcame the screaming crowd and then suddenly stopped. A frenzy of cheers erupted followed by a simultaneous blast of lights, drums, guitars, smoke and a rush of the crowd as the band appeared amidst the fire and glitz of the stage.

In the subconscious darkness of Georgell's mind the explosion reverberated and echoed like the blasts of a shotgun. Visions of the nightmare danced in his memory, laughter echoed, and again the shotgun blast sounded. Georgell opened his eyes as the smell of cigarettes, leather and sulfur slapped his senses back to the moment. The darkness was gone, the panic was gone, his heart had steadied and he felt a stabilizing calm. He rose from the floor and looked over the scene with complete focus and undeterred sight.

"Doc, right stage!" Moose blurted in the earpiece.

"Copy that," Georgell responded as he headed toward the industrial mass. Nobody saw him falter. The darkness covered his moment of weakness, the nerves were gone, now he could work. He was a bouncer: focused, alert, and ready for the unexpected, ready to act.

As he made his way forward, Georgell continued to sweep the scene with his eyes, assessing everything in his path and planning every step to the stage. The crowd was lost in the hammering screams and thrashing rhythm of the show; pushing against each other, pressing, pounding and bruising themselves without notice. The music and excitement buoyed them into a frenzied need to get closer; they were oblivious to anything else.

In his hurried approach Georgell noticed odd figures, not dancing or pushing, but standing above the crowd, looking into it. He did not stop to look at the visions because they did not seem real, almost fantastic, hovering like apparitions or ghosts but the spectacle was enough to give him a shudder of concern. The similarity of these images was immediately associated with the cloaked man in his nightmare. *All in my mind*, he thought and pressed on trying to shake the imagery.

Georgell broke through the surging fans to the right of the stage and saw Moose and another bouncer dragging some men toward an exit. Two girls scratched at Moose's helper in an attempt to free his bloody captor while Moose had an unconscious figure tucked under one arm and tried to subdue the enraged girls with the other. To the right of Moose, Georgell saw someone pull a baton from his coat and snap it to its full, 3-foot extension. He couldn't understand how the weapon made it into the concert but immediately bolted into action as the angry aggressor moved toward Moose. The attacker swung the baton toward Moose's head but to his surprise found it blocked by Georgell's forearm. In a quick motion Georgell slid his arm down the baton and gripped it tight with his hand. He then pulled the stunned assailant toward him. Yanked off balance, the attacker fell forward and with a solid crack connected face first with Georgell's lifted knee. Georgell let the man fall to the ground and then slammed his boot to the man's back. He then spun around to confront any other attackers. No one else seemed interested so Georgell directed his attention to the pestering girls. Chopper had joined the melee and in a single scoop lifted both girls away from the preoccupied bouncer and carried them to the exit. The situation had been diffused.

After escorting his victim to the exit Georgell asked Moose if he was okay and found a wicked smile adorning his face. "Of course, let's get back in there!" he answered. Concert police had cuffed the five fuming fans to a rail and a medic was attempting to clean their wounds. The bouncer who was assaulted by the girls had some bloody scratches on his neck and arm but refused first aid, following Moose and Georgell back into the arena.

Georgell respected the refusal of treatment and understood the wicked smile that Moose carried on his face. A similar smile press its way onto his lips, *Once more under the breach dear friends.* This was real and he felt completely alive. The door slammed shut behind them as they returned to the arena. Chopper and the other bouncer stepped passed some barricades and leapt back onto the stage. Moose looked at Georgell and nodded toward the hyper crowd in the center of the arena. A few frenzied kids were getting out of hand and it was time to pull them. Georgell nodded back and they waded into the screaming crowd.

Georgell focused on the thrashing group while keeping his sight also on Moose wading into the crowd on his left. The kids were provoking docile fans and would certainly be pummeled if they weren't pulled soon. Georgell slipped confidently through the crowd and yanked one of the boys off his feet in a hard lock. The kid was a featherweight, maybe 100 pounds, and didn't put up much of a fight. With his free hand Georgell pointed menacingly at one of the other hyperactive boys and yelled, "Come with me!"

Moose had likewise gathered up two others and the entire group made their way to the side. What had appeared to be four wound-up boys ended up being a group of nine; but no one argued and after a firm warning they agreed to settle down.

Georgell watched as the group made their way to the back of the arena and felt certain their troublemaking was done. Still, he thought it funny that they were so willing to follow when he and Moose were the only ones opposing them. Old enough to be bold but not arrogant enough to test limits. Given another year or two and they would have fought without question. *Still would have lost though,* Georgell chuckled.

Throughout the evening Georgell kept an eye on Moose, coming to admire his skill at spotting problems before they occurred. His abilities were as honed as Georgell's and they made a great roaming team. Even the first fight might have been avoided if Georgell had not fainted—but he was nonetheless glad he had arrived in time to help.

As Georgell ducked in and out of the crowd with Moose, breaking up minor scuffles and helping out exhausted fans, he continued to glimpse dreamlike beings floating above the mass. The figures seemed to hover over the people—watching but never acting. With growing frustration, Georgell tried to maintain sight of one but the visions always seemed to dissipate. He would catch a glimpse and than try to decipher what exactly he was seeing when the image would fade. Inevitably he would be called to a situation or spot a problem himself and never fully magnify what he was witnessing. Was it the concert lights causing the visions? Was it part of the show? *Is it all in my mind*, he thought.

After a little more than two hours, the concert coming to a close, Georgell was pleased with himself. He was confident and felt that—aside from the bewildering figures—he had acted with great skill, and never felt as focused as he had been tonight. He couldn't wait to let Emma know that everything was okay.

As the band left the stage and darkness fell over the arena the crowd began to chant, "More—More—More!" Georgell closed his eyes, anticipating another blinding light as the band returned for an encore.

The blinding light came, the barrage of sound, the elated screams, more smoke and the shrieking melody of another song slashed into the darkness with a shower of flame. Georgell opened his eyes with forceful intent and looked into the crowd for any last minute chaos. He felt a surge of adrenaline pump into his veins as before him, not ten feet away, stood a young man in the crowd, maybe eighteen years old with what appeared to be a man hovering over him. The boy screamed and yelled like the rest of the fans around him and seemed oblivious to the intruder.

Georgell stared in disbelief. This was no light show. No projected image. This apparition was there and real as the floor Georgell stood on. A dark black almost liquid three-piece suit adorned the figure and his legs seemed to fade at the ankle into the shoulders of the oblivious young man. Shards of light bled off the shimmering blue shirt hidden beneath his black tie, vest, and suit coat. His hair was a dark brown pulled tightly into a fisted bun. A slick mustache spread across his aged face, his dark eyes scanning the crowd without defined pupils. The ghastly figure radiated evil.

Ripples of cold quivered through Georgell's body. He was completely dumbfounded. Then, as he watched in disbelief, the figure turned his gaze, bearing down upon Georgell with his lifeless stare. Georgell had never felt such cold fear. His body froze, and his mind seemed blocked from any thought. The being reached into his jacket, gaze still locked on Georgell, and pulled out a shimmering dagger with a six-inch blade. The dagger had a double edge that danced in the concert lighting, hypnotizing Georgell with its glowing menace. The figure raised the dagger and with a vicious scowl, pointed it directly at him.

The young man stopped jumping, pulled his eyes from the stage, and turned to look at Georgell with a calculating stare as if directed by the being above him. Sweat streamed down the boy's face and drenched his shirt. He began to make his way toward Georgell through the crowd, intent on reaching him. Georgell stared as he approached, unable to act or move, he felt utterly helpless and the stark realization that his life may be over, sprang to his mind.

Cackling laughter resonated in the abandoned corridors of Georgell's mind, dulling the concert screams into a frenzied background hum. He recognized the pounding cackle and through his paralysis, mentally acknowledged the similarities of the two events.

"Close your eyes!" Moose bellowed through the earpiece. "Now!"

Georgell recalled Tequila's warning at Club Momentum and how upset Emma had been at his refusal to adhere to the direction. This time he didn't think twice about the command; wasn't even sure if it were directed at him but immediately closed his eyes anyway.

A numbing sensation came over him. Georgell felt an odd rush of warmth surge through his eyes and down his face, extending through his arms and burning out through his fingertips. Hearing a nearby grunt from Moose, Georgell slowly opened his eyes. Moose held the unconscious body of the sweat-drenched kid in his arms. The apparition was nowhere in sight. "Come on," he yelled as he scrambled toward the nearest exit.

"He saw you, Doc! We have to get him out of here before he wakes up. Hold the door." Moose blasted through an exit. Georgell followed and watched as Moose tossed the kid against a brick wall and ran back into the arena. "Shut the door," he said then hit Georgell on the back with a sharp slap. "I knew you had the sight!"

"What?"

"You don't know?" Moose asked, a bit surprised then laughed. "Wow!" He hit Georgell hard on the chest and said, "Don't worry about it now. Shake it off and keep focused. Just don't stare at anymore guardians."

"Guardians? Shake it off?" Georgell was completely lost.

Moose slapped him in the face, smiled, and then ran toward the entry, calling back, "Wake up! After the concert, Doc! After the concert!"

The sting on his face snapped Georgell to attention. He watched as Moose pushed through the crowd. Could he be losing touch or was this actually happening? The thoughts whirled in his mind, begging resolution, but logic could not explain what he had seen or felt.

Moose was trying to snap him back to the moment, Georgell understood this now. He had to finish the night. He had to concentrate on the crowd, do his job, and above all—not stare at any more guardians. *Whatever that meant,* he thought. Touching his stinging cheek, he resigned himself to the task at hand and would wait for answers after the concert.

A fight broke out near the entry and Georgell bolted into action as Tony's call sounded in his ear. "Roamers to the door!"

☼～ **9** ～☼

After three encores and an hour of corralling fans from the arena, Georgell nursed a Coke in the entry and waited with the others for their payout. He pretended interest in an exaggerated tale Chopper was spinning to a rapt group of eager young bouncers but quietly wondered where Moose had gone.

"Good job guys!" Tony bellowed as he wandered in from a final check of the arena. "No big problems tonight. Come get paid."

Georgell watched as the other bouncers lined up and cashed out, then wandered over. Tony smiled as Georgell approached and said, "You seemed pretty sharp out there. Feel like your old self?"

Georgell nodded and nonchalantly asked if Moose was still around.

"He left early, something about dealing with a problem. I didn't ask." He handed Georgell four twenty-dollar bills and with a hopeful grin asked, "Can I call you for the next one?"

Georgell held up the cash and with a tone of disgust answered, "Not for this."

"Sorry man, I couldn't pay the old rate. I didn't know where your head would be so I brought in a couple extra guys. I got you next time though."

"Yeah, I'll be around just call." Georgell shook Tony's hand and headed toward the exit. A cool breeze swam across his face as the door locked behind him. He was upset that Moose had left but more curious as to why. Crossing the east parking lot, Georgell could make out someone sitting on the hood of his car and realized, as he strolled closer, that the loiterer was Moose.

"Let's get something to eat," Moose said as he slid from the hood and stood by the passenger side of the Blazer.

Despite not knowing what Moose was up to or how he knew what car was his, Georgell decided to play along. He said nothing as he unlocked the doors, got in behind the wheel, and started up the vehicle.

Moose scrambled giddily into the passenger side and pulled the door shut. "There's a 24-hour Mexican place on Fifth South. You're buying."

Georgell knew the restaurant and nodded as they drove from the fairgrounds parking lot onto Tenth West. The dull neon of a 7-Eleven lit up the cab of the Blazer as they stopped at the North Temple streetlight. "Why didn't you tell me you were going to leave early?"

Moose ignored Georgell's question. "I can't tell you how excited I am that you can see those buggers," he said. "I've bounced in clubs all over the place but never found anyone else with the sight. I had a feeling about you though. The way you stared at me was different, I had a feeling . . ."

"Wait, I asked you a question," Georgell interjected as he rolled through the streetlight and turned left onto North Temple. "Why did you make me sit in there so long? What was so urgent that you had to take off early?" And then, remembering the reason for their meeting, he sputtered, "And what the—what—what—what are those things?"

"Listen," Moose said as he adjusted the seat to its full extension. "I left early to send that boy of yours home in a cab. Besides, I never told you to wait inside. It's your own fault for waiting so long. About those things, well, I don't know everything but I can give you some heads up. Maybe together we can make some sense of it all."

"How long have you been able to see them?" Georgell queried.

"Going on three years . . ."

"How . . ."

Moose raised his hand in a halting motion and said, "Wait. Just let me get some history out of the way before you assault me with questions."

They were stopped at another light and though irritated, Georgell said, "Fine."

"What chicken strips!" a haggard vagrant said to a fire hydrant as he pushed a shopping cart down the deserted sidewalk. The light turned green, the Blazer rolled forward, the vagrant spewed a chorus of profanity at a distant cat, and Moose began to tell his story.

Georgell listened as they drove on the overpass, a train rumbling on the tracks beneath them. He was at a loss for the purpose of the lengthy narrative but listened despite his annoyance.

Moose had started bouncing at the age of nineteen after a back injury forced him out of a football scholarship. Bitter about life and with no friends or family to help him, Moose turned to bouncing and found a welcome outlet for his frustration. Eventually he met his wife Naomi and her ever-positive attitude gave him purpose again.

Moose talked about loving life again. How Naomi had turned his world inside out and though he lost contact with his family—they disapproved of Naomi because she was black—he didn't care. After their marriage, he quit bouncing and went back to college but after their first child the financial strain was too much and he reluctantly returned to the nightclubs. Each subsequent birth, Moose would try a new career: plumbing, painting, electrician's apprentice, but as the bills piled up he would always return to bouncing. He never stayed in a career long enough to earn the position or elevated income large enough to provide for his family.

Once it was apparent that he could only sustain his family as a bouncer, Moose settled into the career fulltime. He moved the family to Atlanta and found a gig at a raucous club where the tips were plentiful and the paycheck regular. After a few years he was well known as a bouncer and his family was doing well.

The traffic was minimal on Fourth West, sidewalks and parking lots void of people as they drove. Moose continued his background narrative and Georgell listened; surprised to hear Moose talk about Atlanta and captivated by the lifeline. They passed Pioneer Park; the homeless seemed content in their little groups on park benches or huddled under pine trees—a few still wandering about.

Moose admitted that his pride wouldn't allow him the discernment of status and that he roughed up anyone that stepped over the line, no matter who they were, who they knew, or what they controlled. Because of his pride, he crossed the wrong guys one night and was jumped after work. He took a real beating and was hospitalized. After his recovery an unhealthy obsession with revenge took over his life. He lost his ability to trust other bouncers and became paranoid and reckless.

Georgell marveled at the many parallels he shared with Moose. The similarities were eerie but oddly comforting as well.

"I bet I was one of the highest-paid bouncers in Atlanta," Moose said. "I knew what to expect and could stop most problems before they happened. My biggest hitch then and now is—well, I'm trigger happy. I start throwing punches way too fast. I don't control my temper too well." He paused for a bit, lost in moments that he couldn't change. "I've done some things, hurt some people . . ."

Georgell could see Moose drifting. "We've all done some things and hurt some people," he said. "It's part of the job. Makes you better, right! I wish I could take back a lot of nights. One in particular, but it's gone, now I can only chalk it up as experience." He paused. "But how does this lead to the—what did you call them—guardians?"

Moose shuffled in his seat as if shaking a memory from his mind. Then, with a tightly rolled magazine he had taken from the glove box, he pointed at an approaching street. "Take a left."

Georgell turned the wheel and followed the direction though he already knew exactly where they were headed; Albertos, Emma's favorite place for nachos and horchata.

"Yeah, that's it Doc, that night changed you. It made you a better bouncer. More focused. You have the sight because of that shooting; because of your injuries. After I was jumped I was better too. Always watching and waiting. I began to see the guardians hovering over people and it really twisted my mind. I started hammering down booze to erase the images. I thought I was going crazy. Whiskey eased my pain, but made things worse as well. My skills dropped, my home life went to the dogs, and I felt worthless." He thoughtlessly pointed left again. "I didn't care though—I couldn't see the guardians anymore and for me, it was worth it."

"I nearly blew it man," Moose said as he tossed the magazine onto the dashboard with an angry grunt. "One night Naomi woke me up—I was out cold in my car, I had crashed through the fence in our front yard and completely trashed a bike and some toys. She was screaming at me. I still only remember pieces of that night?" He stared out the window trying to remember, "There was blood all over. My forehead was split open pretty good, my knuckles were bloody, my clothes ripped—I have no idea what happened. There was a big dent in the hood of the car too—like I hit somebody."

The Blazer was parked and idling in front of Albertos. Moose was on a roll and Georgell didn't want to turn off the engine for fear that it would halt the flow of information. He kept his hands on the wheel and stared out the window, into the restaurant, watched the workers, and listened to Moose.

"I may have killed someone that night? I'll never know—we left town the next day. It's hard to explain it all."

That was the wake up call and exact moment that changed Moose. His solitude and distrust of life had been fractured and he made the immediate decision to confide in Naomi. He told her everything. "Because of her, I'm sober! She's my world dude."

Moose stared out the window, not seeing the restaurant, not realizing they had stopped moving and were parked—he was in the moment, lost in the past. He carried on about his struggle with alcoholism and how focused he had become as a bouncer.

"One night I was working the door and was really pumped up. Busted three kids with fake ID's, tossed a couple of junkies too, I was feeling great. Then it happened, I saw a girl standing in line with some friends and a guardian hovering above her, plain as day. The dude didn't fade in and out like I'd seen them before. I remember just staring, like you did tonight only I was lucky, mine wasn't a threat. I remember he had a white goatee and white hair. He seemed old, but ripped; you could really see his muscle definition through the tee-shirt he was wearing. It was bizarre, you know what I mean! Anyway the girl was with a group of college kids and I'm guessing she'd probably never been in a club before. She was joking with her friends but didn't look too excited . . ."

"A tee-shirt?" Georgell interrupted not quite sure he had heard Moose correctly.

"Dude, there's no uniform. I've seen them in skirts, chains, old Shakespeare clothes, all kinds of stuff and they ain't always men either. I've encountered some real frightening chicks too. Anyway this guy was different. In fact I haven't seen one like him since that day. He was a good guardian."

"How'd you know?"

"You can feel the difference. In your heart, mind, everywhere, you just know."

"There's no other distinguishing mark?"

"Don't need one, like I said, you feel it."

"But . . ."

Moose raised his hand again and held off the question, "Let me continue before I get lost." He then described how the guardian's features and body language changed as the girl slowly made her way closer to the door. "It was like he was psyching himself up for a fight or something," he said. Steps away, the guardian was suddenly holding a two-handed sword that appeared from nowhere. Moose described the shivers he felt as the man pointed the massive weapon at the club entrance, poised for an attack. With visible excitement, Moose then described how the guardian had seen him staring and returned the gaze with a silent plea. He expressed his unease at the awkward moment and how he felt compelled to help the being.

"So I decided not to let her in. I told her she had a fake ID. Her friends were irate but the girl seemed almost relieved. She told her friends to have fun and walked away without a debate. As she left, the guardian turned to me and bowed. It was awesome! I felt like I really did something meaningful."

"Naomi figures I'm working for the Man upstairs. I'm not sure about that but no matter how tough it has gotten, she hasn't let me quit. She's the one that came up with the name 'guardian' and every morning over breakfast I have to summarize my night, every detail. She writes everything in a journal along with descriptions of the ones that have recognized me."

"Wait, wait, wait," Georgell blurted, "What do you mean recognized you?"

"Oh, sorry, yeah I'll get to that."

They had been sitting in the parking lot of the restaurant for close to an hour and after an audible grumble from his stomach, Moose said, "Basically the sight has made my life hell but it has strengthened my marriage and made me hungry. Let's eat!"

Georgell turned off the car with a glance at the gas gauge as Moose blasted open the door. The chilled air pricked Georgell's skin as he too exited the vehicle. The scent of grilled meat and potatoes hovered in the early hour mist. The distraction increased as the spitting sound of the grill sang while Moose held open the outer door of the eatery.

"Have you ever seen them outside the club?" Georgell asked trying to ignore the tantalizing sounds and smells that begged his attention.

"Nope, only when I'm working; venue doesn't matter though—concerts, clubs, bars, they show up at all of them."

They ordered but before getting comfortable, Georgell decided to call Emma. She was glad he called and the conversation was brief as he assured her all was well and that he would explain things in the morning.

Georgell made his way to the corner booth where Moose was already comfortably lounging, his drink half gone, and was just about to slide onto the cushion when their order number was called. "While you're up," Moose said with a grin.

Georgell collected the tray of food; two heaping platters of Spanish rice, refried beans and steaming carne asada. As he reached the booth, and before he could sit or even set the tray on the table, Moose grabbed one platter and started shoveling forks of meat into his mouth. The big man smiled as Georgell settled in and finally took a bite. After a few mouthful's, Georgell realized he wasn't all that hungry and decided to concentrate on his beverage while he waited for Moose to finish.

"Recognized, when I say 'recognized' it means the guardians can see you, and recognize the fact that you can see them." Moose began after a gulp of Coke. "I figured out that by staring at a guardian long enough it would see me, like the good one had, but the bad ones don't like it."

"Is that why you told me to close my eyes?" Georgell asked.

"Yeah," Moose answered. "But it was too late; he was already locked in. You're lucky I was there to help you out, Doc! I was alone the first time a dark guardian recognized me."

With dramatic emphasis Moose then described his fateful encounter with a chubby little, loud mouth, Indian kid and his Indian chief of a guardian. A good deal of time was spent describing the guardian's headdress until Georgell pushed the narration on by motioning with his hands and a pointed whisper, "Don't care about the headdress."

Moose didn't know what to do about the guardian but could feel its evil as prominently as he had felt warmth from the good guardian, and wanted the thing out of the club. Eventually the kid began arguing with a group of college students and Moose made a move to boot him from the club. Not knowing the consequences, he admitted staring too long at the guardian. The result of this action was a menacing assault from the guardian with a bone dagger that Moose had previously not seen. When he approached the boy he caught the thrust of the guardian's weapon and dodged just enough that the blade pierced his shoulder and not his neck.

This was a stunning revelation and Georgell struggled with its realism but, as if expecting his lack of belief, Moose decided to offer proof of the event by rolling up his sleeve and pointing at his tattoo. The scar was cleverly disguised in the vast yellow moon that shone behind Jack and Sally; but under close scrutiny the disfigurement was obvious. The skin was too smooth, cauterized in a near perfect circle, roughly the size of a quarter, and inset slightly deeper than the normal bulge of his skin. Moose proudly displayed more scars by ripping a bigger hole in his jeans where two similar circles marred his upper thigh. Then he leaned forward, yanked up his shirt, and displayed a series of four circular scars lining his lower back.

He went on to explain that when a guardian's weapon pierced the skin it felt like an intense muscle cramp and that the tissue immediately scarred over with the circular markings in accordance with how severe the puncture had been. He also clarified that despite the menacing appearance there was no lasting affect, other than normal bruising for a few weeks and permanent numbness around the scarring. He also made the assumption that the guardians targeted the heart as the only place where damage could really be inflicted; but had no way of knowing for sure. "I'm not willing to test that theory quite yet," he said.

Georgell touched the scar on Moose's back and marveled at its perfect symmetry. Each circle connected in a smooth transition from one point to the other. He ran his finger the length of the blemish from the outer ridge of the top scar down to the fourth in a smooth line. He then sat back in his seat and pushed his food aside. "How do you fight back?"

"Two choices; turn and run or knock out the speck."

"Speck?"

"Yeah, specimen, speck, like the Indian kid; he's the speck of the Indian Chief guardian. Naomi and I just figured they were like human specimens, y'know. Anyway, when Chief Hatchet stabbed me," Moose tapped his tattoo, emphasizing the scar, "one of the guys his speck was razzing knocked him out and the guardian vanished. After that I figured I could just take out the speck and eliminate the guardian. I was right, but it ain't as easy as it sounds. The long scar on my back came after I crept up on a speck standing in a hallway. I thought I caught him off guard but the guardian recognized me earlier in the night and somehow knew I was coming. That's when I realized they don't need physical sight. Once you've been recognized they know where you are. Anyway, like I was saying, I thought I had the jump on the dude but the guardian was jabbing down with his sword as I turned the corner and lunged. I cracked the speck's head against a wall and knocked him out but not before I got those nice ringlets on my back."

Moose went on to explain how he received the scars on his thigh in a second encounter with the ghostly Indian Chief. He believed that guardian's had an ability to control specks and emphasized this conclusion by using the second attack as an example. He said that the speck snuck up from behind and cracked him with a chair followed by a tomahawk slash from the guardian. He successfully rolled away and the kid was subdued by other bouncers but the surprise confrontation prompted Moose and Naomi to move. They had been nomads ever since. Whenever Moose was recognized by more than a couple guardians they would relocate.

Georgell listened without interruption. His own troublesome dream fit perfectly with Moose's conclusion that the guardians had an unseen control. It made absolute sense. He thought back to his own encounter with mounting gratitude for Moose and his intervention.

Moose snapped his fingers. "Still with me Doc?"

Georgell nodded, perturbed by his lack of attention and Moose continued, "That's why I left early tonight. I guessed your new friend would be waiting outside and I was right. His guardian didn't know I could see and I cracked the boy, tossed him in a taxi, and told the cabby to take him home."

Georgell stared at Moose and marveled at his nonchalance and jovial attitude. He didn't understand and a sense of contempt quickly overtook the gratitude he had previously felt. "So what are we supposed to do?"

"I don't know. I figure the only way to eliminate the guardians is to kill their specks but there's no way I'm going to prison for murdering some stupid punk. Nobody's going to believe we can see demons floating above bad guys."

"Okay, so what do you do—and why?" Georgell leaned back in the booth and folded his arms. He couldn't understand the motive and was growing irritated by Moose's lack of genuine concern.

The weighty question silenced Moose and he leaned forward with a hard stare. His fidgeting stopped and he plainly stated, "I can't just quit."

"Naomi and I agree that I need to do this; that I am protecting those that aren't aware. In the back of my mind I always see the girl I turned away and the gratitude on the guardian's face. That drives me man!" Moose hit the wall in an attempt to cement his conviction. He continued sternly, "I may not act serious enough for you but humor is my only outlet. Don't get my lighthearted attitude wrong. I'm scared! I'm scared for my kids and for the future. But there's no way I can ignore my ability and stay home."

Measuring his next statement, Moose paused for a moment and then continued, "I work clubs and concerts and look for guardians. When I see them I toss their speck. Something always happens if I don't. A guy was stabbed, a girl raped, and both times it was from a speck that I didn't pull.

So I hurt them; knock them out, whatever it takes to legitimately pull them from a crowd without raising suspicion or questions. I do it to prevent harm. But I never let their guardian's recognize me. Not anymore."

Georgell and Moose stared at each other with evaluating eyes. Then, barely audible, Georgell said, "Then what? Is that it? Keep moving when it gets too hot—help where you can but never take a stand?" Georgell couldn't believe Moose's only drive was conscience. There had to be more. He was holding something back.

"Take a stand?" Moose forced a laugh. "How do you take a stand without killing specks? I can't take a stand if I'm sitting in a cell. In fact my guess is that most inmates have their own little guardian and not the good kind. How long do you think I would last in there? I can only do what I think is best for me and my family, and that don't include jail time."

Moose was growing angry and Georgell could see he wasn't kidding about the short fuse. "How can this be good for your family?"

"Quit then!" Moose hit the table with both fists and leaned back hard against the bench, exasperated. "That's why I'm alone. I know there have been others like us, but guardians have probably killed most in their first few days of seeing. I was lucky. You were lucky. Walk away if you want but don't ever forget that kid from the concert because his guardian knows your face and I guarantee he's hunting you."

Georgell held his gaze and thought of the situation. He measured the reality of what was happening and could not logically piece it together. Frustration bloomed into anger. Fear twisted into rage. His vision clouded and he felt a loss of reason sweep over his thoughts. "No! There has to be more to this," he shouted.

Moose didn't say a word. A nearby janitor, startled by the outburst, dropped his broom and stared at Georgell, unsure if he should run, hide, or continue working. Moose motioned for Georgell to settle down and he obliged, giving the frightened man a calming nod. The janitor picked up his broom and resumed cleaning in a different part of the restaurant.

Moose, with a devilish grin, calmly said, "I'm hoping together we can figure this out. I'm not much of a thinker. I let Naomi do that for me. I'm a worker, a blue-collar roughhouse worker. I know how to bounce and I have a gift. You have the gift too and you, my friend, are definitely a thinker. Maybe together we can unravel some of this mess."

Georgell said nothing.

"Like I said, Naomi and I have taken this gift and done with it what we felt was the best for us. Is there more? I don't know, probably, but I need someone else to help make those discoveries. What do you say?"

Georgell nodded but didn't look at Moose. He then stood and softly said, "I need to go."

"I'll walk," Moose said. He handed Georgell a napkin with his number scrawled in a hasty script across the face. "Give me a call."

Home in bed, Georgell dozed off and found himself once again on the steps of Club Momentum. Taz, Tequila, and Sampson dead at his feet, Franklin blasting his shotgun under the specific direction of his dark guardian; the cackling laughter mixed with the blasts booming in a thunderous, sickening, echo. This time it was different though. The guardian never pointed at Georgell. The shooting continued randomly into the crowd and street. Georgell watched in horror as death raged in front of him. People died with screams and pleas of hopeless despair. The guardian smiled as he orchestrated the bloody massacre without hindrance. Georgell felt his muscles tense while trying without success to act. He wanted to help but stood motionless—watching the horrific scene.

Emma's voice sounded from his left. He turned to find her standing on the steps amidst the chaos, Wolfy in her arms. Gina and Gideon were clinging to her legs, fear magnified in their expanded eyes. Georgell felt the gaze of evil and turned to see the skeletal finger of Franklin's guardian extended and pointing at his family. Shots punctured the already pounding atmosphere and the scene froze with a silent scream.

Emma, the kids, everything stood still. Georgell felt warm tears searing his cheeks and then a touch. Again the touch and Georgell opened his eyes. "Dad, can I get in bed with you?" Gideon asked, holding tight to his blue frog.

"Yeah," Georgell said, barely able to mutter a whisper. He wiped away the tears from his eyes. Reached out and pulled Gideon close, hugged him tightly and rearranged the covers snuggly over his little body.

Could a man know this, know such things existed and do nothing? He thought. The world was more dangerous now. He could literally see the threat. It was a real reason to fight and protect. A door had been opened reaffirming his need to be a bouncer. He had found the resolve but felt nauseated and overwhelmed by the uncertain implication of his decision.

☼~ **10** ~☼

Georgell woke to a tickling attack from his boys. He tenderly subdued the onslaught with a barrage of his own tickles and the boys begged for mercy. Emma entered the room and apologized for the ambush, freely admitting that she had been the mastermind. Georgell deftly pulled her on the bed and enlisted the boys in another assault while holding her down. They happily obliged. Muppet began yipping her disapproval as Emma squirmed and wailed. Seconds later, Gina raced in to investigate the commotion and she to fell victim to the tickling melee. After thoroughly destroying the bed and amidst another fit of laughter, Georgell smelled something burning and looked at Emma.

"Yeah, I uh, made you an omelet." She punched him hard in the stomach with a smile and leapt off the bed. "I'm anxious to hear about last night," she said as she bolted from the room, Gina and Muppet chasing behind.

Georgell directed the boys to crack open the windows and the crisp scent of morning rain swam into the room as they did. As smoke began to filter into the room, Georgell smiled. The boys ran out to assist their mother and Georgell lay back down with a contented sigh. The burnt egg was still the overpowering aroma in the room but the rain added a welcome freshness and the breeze pushed back the creeping smoke. A steady drizzle tapped on the glass and Georgell lay happily listening. He felt an amazing sense of peace despite the terrifying dream. His greatest obstacle would be Emma's acceptance but he was determined to get her blessing and return to bouncing. After a few moments calculating his approach, he finally slid out of the bed, pulled on some blue sweats from the floor, and headed for the kitchen. The smoke alarm began to blare.

After ridding the house of smoke and taking out the garbage, Georgell detailed the concert to Emma while she made a batch of french toast. He told her about the raucous band and the juvenile crowd. He detailed the unsteadiness he battled early in the evening without disclosing his fainting spell and described the altercations he had been part of without any mention of the guardian. He wanted her to know of his readiness before he divulged any new concerns.

When breakfast was over, Georgell helped Gina with the dishes while continuing his narrative. Emma sat attentively at the kitchen table sipping chai tea. As Georgell dried the last dish he looked into Emma's eyes and knew she wasn't fooled. She was waiting for the rest. "So what do you think?" he laid the towel on the table and sat across from her.

"Sounds like it went pretty well, but there's more—what else happened?"

Georgell pondered Emma's ability to read him so clearly and finally broke into the grim reality. He admitted the overpowering stress that had enveloped him. He reluctantly told her about fainting and appreciated the concern she displayed in her eyes. Then with a bit of excitement, he ventured into a discussion of his nightmares and the real presence of guardians. He talked about Moose and how he and Naomi were dealing with the sight. He told her about the scars and everything he could recall from the meeting at Albertos. He spoke fast, unable to stop the flood of emotions and events that blazed in his mind and crumbled from his lips.

Emma listened intently, the concern obvious on her face. She began to nibble on a piece of toast that Wolfy hadn't finished and Georgell thought he might be losing her. He spoke more passionately, hoping she would accept the truth and help. She didn't have to believe everything, just enough to allow him the freedom to work. Her blessing was all he needed and he hoped his blatant truth would elicit that response.

"This is not easy to listen to," Emma said. "I'm having a hard time understanding where this is coming from."

"I'm telling you everything Emma. Ask me any question, I'm an open book. I need you to understand because I can barely believe it myself. I need you to be a part of this—to help me make sense of it."

Hours went by, rain continued to fall in spurts, and Georgell did not move from his chair. He answered every question as honestly as he could. He knew Emma was grilling him in an effort to extricate inconsistencies but the truth didn't leave room for cracks. He remained rational and spoke in an upbeat and positive manner no matter how ridiculous or pointless the questions seemed.

Finally, after hours of discussion, the conversation reached an end. "I can't say I believe all this but I won't close my mind to the possibility. You have obviously been deeply moved by whatever it was you saw and despite the craziness, I have a hard time believing you'd make it up. So for now I'm going to ignore the insanity of it all; but you have to answer one more question." Emma stopped for a moment, clearly not finished, and with a searing intensity said, "Are you ready to bounce again, full-time?"

Georgell felt the severity of the moment. Emma had not believed his story but was ultimately willing to listen without shutting him down. He knew it was absurd and wasn't sure himself if it were true but could not falter in his belief. He had succeeded in being completely honest and was now convinced it had been the right choice. Returning her stoic gaze, he said, "Yes."

Emma contemplated the answer for a few moments, keeping her eyes locked on his, then simply said, "Okay."

☼~ 11 ~☼

With Emma's blessing, Georgell made a few inquiries and found a new club nearing the end of construction. The club was scheduled to open in a month and the staffing process had just begun. Head of security was an open position and after a stellar phone conversation, Georgell was asked to come down for an interview the following evening. He was confident that the job was his and decided to contact Moose about the news hoping that he too would get hired at the club. Moose heartily agreed to join him.

Emma gave Georgell a genuine kiss upon hearing the news. She expressed encouragement but Georgell could tell she was secretly rooting for the other guy. *She's crazy*, he thought, *there's no way anyone in this town is more qualified than me. The job is mine whether she likes it or not.* He smiled, smacked her on the butt as she walked off with the laundry basket, and said, "The job is mine honey, you know it is!"

"Of course it is dear," she said while heading down the steps.

Georgell drew in a deep breath of air, the scent of Emma's cherry blossom shampoo still tantalizing his senses. The phone rang and Georgell caged his rapidly growing desire and snatched the phone from its cradle.

A few hours later, Chopper called and gruffly chastised Georgell for not inviting him along as well. Georgell was pleased at the interest and sarcastically apologized for the oversight with an open invitation to join in.

"Man you know I was going whether you invited me or not so quit trippin! What about Bear?"

Georgell hadn't thought of Bear and immediately felt compelled to get him involved as well. His confidence and excitement level rose exponentially. "I'm on my way to talk to him now."

"Good luck. I mean it man, good luck. Not about bringing him on but controlling the dude once we're in. Did I say good luck?"

"Let's not get prematurely employed. We may not get the job so don't get too excited."

"I thought you were getting better. Guess not. Man you must be crazy to think the job ain't a done deal. You probably already have the schedule made, huh!"

"Where are you going?" Emma asked from the living room.

"Call you later," Georgell hung up the phone and walked into the living room. "I'm going to see Bear. I won't be long."

Emma snatched up a folded sweatshirt from a pile of clean clothes on the floor and threw it at Georgell. "Good luck," she said with a grin.

Georgell pulled on the sweatshirt and as he bounded out the door, said, "How about a movie tonight?" He didn't wait for a reply but was certain Emma would have a babysitter arranged and a list of movies in hand when he returned.

Bear's apartment complex was weathered and beaten but oddly glowing in the pelting rain. Georgell immediately noticed the absent brown Range Rover from Bear's parking stall and guessed that he was not at home. Unperturbed, he decided to run up and check the apartment anyway. If nothing else he could leave a message on Bear's fridge as he had many times before.

Georgell bolted from his car, ran across the slick grass, and hurdled up the stairs three at a time. With the chill of the rain biting at him, he briskly jogged down the exterior walkway to apartment number seven. He was in a great mood, despite the weather, and was excited to tell Bear about the club. At the door, Georgell pounded loudly and screamed, "FBI! Open up!" A curious neighbor looked out a window and, seeing Georgell's ragged goatee and unkempt apparel, said something in an exasperated Russian dialect and slammed the window shut.

Georgell chuckled at the curious intrusion then returned his attention to the door. It had been a long time since their last discussion so his plan was simple; act as if nothing had happened. He knew that if Bear were touched with the same depression he had suffered, talk of the past would go nowhere. They would discuss it someday but now wasn't the time. Again he pounded. "Candy-gram—flowers." Still no response. He tried the knob and found the door unlocked. A blast of cold air from the humming AC unit welcomed him as he entered the dark apartment.

"Hello, anyone alive in here?" Georgell flipped on the light switch and looked around. There was no answer and he repeated the query. Oddly, nothing seemed out of place. The collection of medieval weapons still adorned the walls like hunting trophies. Royal red paint loomed sedately in the background. The black leather couch and claw foot armchair sat snugly against the wall as usual. Bear wasn't a real social person and rarely entertained, so finding the apartment in such a familiar state wasn't surprising; however, the oppressive cold streaming from the AC unit seemed to intensify an unseen chill. There was a change, a feeling that tugged at Georgell, but nothing tangible. The apartment had an altered sense of self. It was eerily cold beyond the frigid hum of the air conditioning. Something wasn't right.

Georgell wandered into the kitchen and found a similar lack of activity. Everything was in order and familiar. Not even a spoon littered the sink. The dishwasher was empty and the cupboards neatly stacked with plates, glasses and other small wares, while an adjacent shelf held canned goods and boxes of pasta noodles. The refrigerator had recently been replenished as well; fresh vegetables bloomed from the shelves. The bottom rack had two parallel rows of Guinness beer, a half-gallon of whole milk and a near depleted half-gallon of chocolate milk. And, with a smile, Georgell found a six-pack of Coke hidden in the back. It had been nearly a year since he had visited the apartment but one can was still missing, a can that Georgell had drunk.

Don't mind if I do, Georgell thought as he reached in and pulled another free from the six-pack. He popped the tab and took a long drag. The ice-cold burn felt good as it rolled down his parched throat. "Ahhh!" Georgell exhaled as he lifted the can from his lips and continued his search.

A dull glow caught Georgell's attention as it crept from beneath the bedroom door. He took another swig of the Coke and headed for the entry, more curious than concerned. Inside he found two faux candles flickering on either side of Bear's bed. The queen-sized bed was covered with a comforter made from the skin of an Alaskan Kodiak brown bear and Georgell oddly recalled the day Bear had bought the trophy and how excited he had been. Above the bed a tapestry loosely hung from a long ornate wooden staff. Two pointed dragon talons protruded from the wall and held the staff parallel to the ground, the tapestry draped between them.

The tapestry was new and Georgell was completely mesmerized by its dancing colors and curious workmanship. It was definitely old and the intricate design was saturated in some cryptic meaning beyond Georgell's ability to grasp. Still he stared in rapt curiosity. The border of the piece appeared to be carvings and sculptures but the symbols were unrecognizable due to the vines that snaked around them in a covering blanket of vibrant forest green. A sea of blood-red waves swam across the interior of the tapestry and crashed against the vine covered borders on all four sides. The central piece appeared to be some sort of runic symbol engraved in jade and floating on the sea of blood like a raft of preserved knowledge. The symbol was so real it seamed to leap from the tapestry.

"Bear?" A woman's voice called from the entry.

Dropping his gaze from the tapestry, Georgell stepped back out of the bedroom and looked to the front door where a short, well-endowed, young woman stood in the entry. A mass of thick red hair sat in a jumble on her head with pencils jutting out at skewed angles. She wore baggy cargo pants with knick-knacks stuffed in every pocket and a black jacket that shimmered from the rain. The unzipped jacket hung loosely from her shoulders, framing a pale white tee-shirt with large green Celtic symbols stretching across the snuggly fit surface. Georgell guessed she was in her early twenties and silently hoped she and Bear were an item.

"Sorry, Bear isn't here. Can I help you with something?" Georgell asked.

"Oh, I'm sorry. I didn't mean to barge in; I saw the door open and thought . . ." She paused for a minute and then with an accusing glare asked, "Who are you? I've never seen you before!"

Georgell raised his hands as if to calm her and with a laugh said, "Maybe I should be the one apologizing. I'm an old friend."

"How do I know that?" She said with a growl. "You could be snooping around and looking for a quick snatch. Maybe you've been scouting out the place. Maybe . . ."

Georgell took a step forward, nodding as he did so, and said, "Yeah—and maybe Scotty beamed me in from the Enterprise?"

A look of sheer contempt blazed in the girl's emerald green eyes as he approached and Georgell thought she might tear his throat out for the sarcasm. "Sorry!" he stammered, as the girl pulled a pencil from her hair and held it like a dagger. "I'm a friend, I swear it! Look I haven't taken anything but a Coke from the fridge."

Her lips were opening for another barrage when a grunting voice from behind the door interrupted, "There better be a dollar on the counter for that Coke! No, make that five dollars. It's pretty old and probably worth something." Bear came into view and laid his thick hand on the woman's folded arms. "Alys McFadden, this is Doc" he said, looking at Georgell. He then crossed the room, and with a slightly noticeable smirk, reached out his hand.

They clasped hands in a powerful shake and stepped into a quick respectful embrace with a mutual pat on the back. Retreating, Bear said, "I'm not joking about the five dollars."

"I left ten in the fridge," Georgell said without hesitation. Both broke into a hearty laugh and another embrace.

Alys, confused and still standing in the doorway, cleared her throat and said, "Should I come back later?"

"Sorry Alys. Come in and shut the door." Seeing the wicked look in Georgell's eyes, Bear then swiftly followed with an introduction. "Alys lives in five. She's studying Ancient Runes and Symbolism at the U and uses my place as a private study hall away from her obnoxious roommates."

Georgell noticed the backpack strapped to her shoulder as she shut the door and slid the carryall onto the couch. He also caught a slight shake of Bear's head and sadly understood they were only friends.

Alys approached and shook Georgell's outstretched hand. She sheepishly apologized for her inquisition and Georgell waved her off. He then asked, "Irish or . . ."

"Yes, my grandfather came over on a boat," she replied.

Georgell acted stunned for a moment and then sarcastically said, "Did you just say your grandfather came out of a box? Like a cereal box?"

Alys laughed and with surprising familiarity, punched Georgell in the arm. "No! I said he came over on a boat. His name wasn't Lucky!"

"So what does the tee-shirt mean?" Georgell asked while rubbing his arm.

Alys grinned, as did Bear, and then replied, "It basically says quit staring at my breasts."

After a few minutes of laughter and small talk, Alys excused herself and Georgell said, "Maybe next time you can explain to me the significance of the tapestry in Bear's bedroom."

Alys looked at Bear questioningly then at Georgell. It was obvious she had no clue what he was talking about. "Yeah sure," she left the apartment and the door clicked shut behind her.

Bear turned his gaze back to Georgell for a moment then walked over to the AC unit and switched it off. "It's cold in here," he muttered to himself and turning back to Georgell, said, "I'd rather we stayed out of my bedroom, if you don't mind."

Georgell crushed his Coke can, nodded at Bear, and tossed it perfectly into the garbage as Bear held open the lid. "Come on, Harvey; please tell me she isn't just a friend," Georgell said, using Bear's given name with a motherly tone.

"She's barely eighteen!" He shot back, "And don't call me Harvey."

"I thought she was a grad student."

"Nope, a senior. She did start early though. She's smart! Graduated High School at sixteen and has a full ride scholarship. She hasn't been accepted to grad school yet but she'll get in."

Georgell could see that Bear liked the girl and was puzzled by his hesitation to act.

"So, what are you, twenty-seven? What's the problem? Need some pointers? She is legal you know! It's obvious you like the girl," Georgell rang into Bear with a barrage of questions, silently pleased for the distraction that Alys had provided. The stress and concern he felt for their first encounter since Club Momentum had quickly been dispelled.

Bear ignored the remarks and pointed a stout finger squarely at Georgell, "Why are you here?"

The distraction gone, Georgell let the question hang for a moment and wandered over to the refrigerator. He reached inside, grabbing a Guinness and another Coke, shut the door with his elbow and tossed the Guinness to Bear. "There's a new club opening up, Euphoria, heard of it?"

Bear opened his can as Georgell opened his. Both gulped down a couple of swigs and Bear nodded.

"They don't have security yet. What do you think?"

Bear took another heavy swig of his beer and said, "Have you done any work?"

Georgell wandered over to the couch and sat. Bear followed and slid into the leather armchair. "Yeah, I worked the concert last night. It was tough at first but I'm fine. Chopper is in, and Moose—do you know Moose?"

Ignoring the question Bear said, "Things are different, I'm different, I can't control my anger anymore. Rage comes over me, I keep hurting people and I can't help it. I don't think you want me on your staff."

Georgell knew that Bear had just opened the door for a conversation but wasn't sure where to go with it. "Look, I'm not going into this thing with blinders on. Things are definitely different. I don't expect either of us to perform the same as before but as long as you're on the other end . . ." Georgell tapped his ear to indicate a radio and continued " . . . I know I've got back up I can count on. That night did some damage and I don't expect to ever escape the nightmares but I'm not willing to bow out quite yet. So if I have to wrestle you off a few idiots to save their lives, you know I won't hesitate." Georgell wasn't sure if his pep talk was working but he knew that Bear was listening. "Besides someone has to keep you out of jail otherwise Alys may lose interest."

A flying can of Guinness tagged Georgell in the side of the head and spewed beer on his head and chest. Bear smiled at his accuracy and admired the dripping mess on Georgell's face. With a grin, Georgell lifted his Coke and toasted Bear, "Here's to you, then, beer-chucking-guy, and all the rage that comes with you. Club Euphoria, watch out!"

☼⁓ 12 ⁓☼

Club Euphoria was a long rectangular structure with its length extending south over a sloping hillside in the Avenues. The club entrance was street level on the high north end of the block. The south end of the building had two black fire escapes reaching down from emergency exits on the upper level and bordered a row of dark bay windows. On the roof of the building sat a giant blue, green, and pink neon sign that hummed "Club Euphoria" to the Salt Lake valley below.

Passed the doorman and through the main entry, a double wide flight of stairs extended up and to the right. Solid black walls lined the stairway with inset television monitors behind thick Plexiglas. The screens soundlessly displayed music videos and sporting events to waiting guests. At the top of the stairs a length of velvet rope hung between stanchions that led up to a granite-topped entry desk.

Georgell stood by the entry desk and watched the astonishment of patrons as they took in the décor. The foyer was a vision of fire that opened up from the mouth of the stairs. The walls were thick sheets of glass that danced with pseudo flames and radiated a warm heat. The ceiling had thousands of multi-layered lights that constantly flickered to life and slowly dimmed like floating ash. To complete the combustible atmosphere, smooth charcoal cobblestone-like tiles covered the floor.

Georgell pulled his attention away from the gawking guests and entered a dark tunnel across from the entry. Above the opening a red laser inscription fluttered, "Swerve of Love." The tunnel was covered from floor to ceiling in a rounded arc with the familiar cobblestone tiles and was dimly lit with throbbing strobe lights. Plush black couches lined both walls with small tables set between them. A few couples were already taking advantage of the romantic setting with heavy kissing and whispered conversation. The tunnel swerved to the left and then back to the right and finally opened up to the dance floor with the thumping beat of music.

Lounge areas with blue tables, white chairs, and black couches swept out on curved angles atop sparkling blue carpet. The carpeted areas tiered up on three one-step levels separated by stainless steel handrails, openings every few feet. Directly to the left and right of the tunnel, and located on the top tier of each lounge, sat fully stocked bars with granite tops and a crew of three bartenders working each.

To the left was the donkey bar. A stainless steel, six-inch frame, bordered the three station bar with blue silhouettes of donkeys glowing behind a plexiglass cover. To the right was the elephant bar, also with three stations bordered by a stainless steel frame but the silhouettes on this bar were of elephants and they shimmered with a dull red glow behind the plexiglass cover.

Georgell crossed the dance floor and chuckled at the design. The surface was covered with a checkered pattern of 6x6 black and mirror-like tiles that extended the entire length of the floor. Guys were constantly looking down at the reflective surfaces but with the lighting variations and constant movement, Georgell knew they would see nothing.

The sound booth hung from the ceiling, DJ's bobbing their heads as they controlled the lighting and music. A burst of smoke blasted into the audience and the lights dimmed. Blue lasers spun within the rippling cloud of smoke and the dancers screamed with an electrified pleasure. A pounding rhythm accompanied the light show and a new song thundered from the strategically placed speakers that bordered the dance floor.

On the darkened ceiling and hidden within the lighting was a catwalk that extended from the DJ booth to the center of the mirrored back wall where a door was barely visible. Another catwalk followed the length of the mirrored wall with ladders extending down to dance cages at the midway and end points. The four cages hung eight feet above the crowd with a dancer gyrating provocatively in each.

Georgell was heading down to the sports bar but as he neared the back wall an overzealous clubber jumped onto one of the dance cages and dangled with one hand while grabbing the dancer's leg with the other. Georgell yanked the startled gymnast to the ground and the kid quickly apologized as Georgell shook his head. The cage dancer retied the strap of her high heel boot, straightened her dark leather mini and resumed her clawing and swooning with a thankful nod to Georgell.

On the mirrored back wall, and situated behind each pair of suspended cages, were corridors that led to the lower level. The corridors were covered from floor to ceiling with black cobblestones like the tunnel and a misty red light flickered from faux torches ensconced every few yards apart. The corridors sloped and turned in behind the mirrored wall where they met and framed a landing beneath three massive bay windows. Each window was framed like giant medieval paintings and displayed an awesome view of the Salt Lake valley below. A wide stairway descended down from the window landing and into the sports bar on the level beneath the dance floor.

The expansive sports bar had pool tables, electronic dartboards, a dozen big-screen TV's, foosball and air hockey tables, pinball machines, and a myriad of sports memorabilia adorning the ceiling and walls. Scattered throughout the area were tables, chairs, and barstools and across the entire back wall a service bar hummed with activity as six bartenders filled drink and food orders. Above the lengthy bar, neon signs buzzed with various product logos from beer to whiskey.

Georgell walked through the buzzing area and smiled at faces he recognized. He thought of the weeks that led up to this grand opening and was pleased with the outcome. He had been hired as head of security and after some negotiation was given a very respectable salary. He was also given free reign over security and full control of staffing. The one drawback was the budget limitations. The staffing allowance was based on revenue projections that seemed tremendously low. The budget hampered his ability to hire sufficient crew, but what he lacked in staff he decided to make up for in experience. He hired a smaller crew at a higher wage and hoped the budget would increase over time.

Georgell decided to run a crew of three roaming teams, one doorman and one watcher; totally eliminating position bouncers for the time being. He was concerned about his lack of staff in relation to the size of the club but his pleading had no affect on the owner's decision. He would have to depend on the combined experience of his crew until extra staffing could be justified. For this reason Georgell required every club employee to carry or have access to a radio. This was the one stipulation that the owners finally allowed, given the lack of security staff. Georgell had taken the time to train bartenders, cocktail waitresses, coat check employees, and the club manager on the proper etiquette and procedure for radio use.

Each section of the building had simplified radio codes to alert security of possible trouble. Every employee was required to know the codes and understand when and how they were to be used along with what to expect as a response. These codes quickly became part of employee speech and were used in normal banter as well as flash response.

For immediate action a code had to be repeated three times in succession. This flash alert would call every roaming team to the designated area, and as every team was currently considered roamers, this meant everyone. When additional staff was eventually hired the flash response would be modified.

Georgell saw an approaching cocktail waitress and pulled a spare laminated card from his back pocket and placed it on her tray.

BASEMENT	=	Sports Bar
CAGE 1, 2, 3, or 4	=	Dancer cages from left to right from the tunnel
DANCE	=	Main dance floor
DJ	=	DJ booth and catwalks
DONKEY	=	Left bar from tunnel
DOOR	=	Main entrance
ELEPHANT	=	Right bar from tunnel
ENTRY	=	Foyer and coat check area
EXIT	=	Outside exits from the foyer and basement
LANDING	=	Bay windows on the sports bar landing
OFFICE	=	Main office area
SLOPE	=	Corridors from dance floor to bay windows
TUNNEL	=	Swerving tunnel from foyer to dance floor

"Learn the codes Magpie," he said.

"Yeah—yeah, donkey, monkey, door, DJ, blah, blah," she said as she passed.

Georgell smiled at her mockery and silently knew, despite the cards and training; most would panic and forget protocol anyway.

Moose was lounging on a nearby stool with his back leaning against the wall. He could see most of the sports bar from that vantage point but seemed more interested in the WWE wrestling match on a nearby TV. Georgell had assigned Moose as his partner, roaming team one, primarily so they could keep an eye on each other and watch for guardians as well. They had even created a radio code to inform each other of guardian sightings. 'Eyes on me' signified a visible guardian. After the verbal alert, basic hand gestures would indicate location and approach.

Bear and Chopper made up team two. They would concentrate on the sports bar but make constant sweeps of the stairs and corridors. Chopper's added responsibility was keeping Bear under control which meant he had to be quick to react and quicker to inform Georgell of any situation.

For the last team, Georgell hired a muscular six foot tall brunette with mesmerizing silver-gray eyes who worked days as a correctional facility officer. She was inexperienced but her size and police training made her an easy choice; besides having a female bouncer to check restrooms and deal with out-of-control women was a huge asset. She immediately insisted on using her real name but Georgell would not allow it. Instead, he tagged her with the name "Nemesis" after the Greek Goddess of Vengeance.

Georgell hired a seasoned bouncer named Pineapple to partner with Nemesis. He had recently returned to the area and had worked with Georgell in the past. Pineapple was not a name directly affiliated with his Samoan heritage but more because of his talent for crushing the hard fruit with his forehead. Pineapple was 6'5" with a thick black Afro and was an imposing mass of muscle. A menacing tribal tattoo adorned the entire left side of his face, clawed at his neck and extended down his left arm to his wrist.

Pineapple and Nemesis would stay vigilant on the dance floor and make frequent checks of the foyer and restrooms. They would also respond to all alerts involving women.

Bug, after some prodding by Georgell, Bear, and Chopper, agreed to work again as a watcher though he hadn't worked in a club or even entered one since the shooting at Momentum. Bug would continue his role of following whomever Georgell felt would be a problem. His girlfriend would also get paid when she came to the club on the weekends as his date and cover.

The final addition to Georgell's Club Euphoria crew was the doorman, a square-jawed Russian warmly named Red. He was in his forties but his massive torso and 6'6" frame did not reflect his age. Only his face, rugged with lines of a hard fought life, gave any indication of his years. In Georgell's estimation, Red's twenty years as a Russian soldier coupled with his fearless persona, daunting features, and booming voice, made him one of the top doormen in the city, if not the world. His heavy accented dialect and reverberating tone would carry over any ruckus and demand immediate attention. Red also had a great eye for catching fake ID's and scaring off underage kids. Georgell was immensely pleased when he had successfully sniped Red from a competing club by offering steady hours and a higher wage.

Georgell looked at a nearby clock and was surprised to see that the first hour had already passed. He made his way back up to the dance floor, through the tunnel, and down to the exit doors. There was a healthy line extending to the right of the front doors and down the sidewalk. Red was directing the line with the aid of Chopper who waited for Bear to arrive. Georgell had previously excused Bear from being on time because of a prior commitment and wasn't too concerned about problems in the first few hours anyway. People would be too enamored with the whole layout of the club to get involved in petty arguments or stupidity. The problems would come as the alcohol worked its magic.

Nodding at Chopper and Red, Georgell re-entered the club and made his way to the dance floor. He then headed left up to the donkey bar where Emma worked with a couple of other bartenders. She wore the name "Cherub" on her red silk blouse; a name Georgell had tagged her with years ago. She didn't notice him watching and continued taking orders and pouring drinks. It was obvious how she made such good tips; she attentively listened to customer orders then repeated the request back with a magnetic smile and cheery demeanor. She was radiant. Her hair had been braided and spun in a fashionable twist on her head with little glittering butterfly clips that held it in place. All day Emma had been stressed about her age, appearance, and bartending knowledge but now, in the middle of the rush, she seemed totally at ease and more than capable.

Georgell was pleased that she had agreed to bartend again and even happier that she didn't feel obligated to work but was doing it for fun. She had been skeptical but warmed to the idea relatively quickly when Georgell guaranteed the part time shifts that worked best for their family.

"Doc, come to the office please," the club manager called over the radio.

"Copy," Georgell responded and began walking toward the mirrored wall in the back. He passed Moose, who was munching on some fries from the sports bar grill, and told him to stay put.

On the wall beneath dancer cage one Georgell located a black door, unlocked it with his key, and wandered back to the office as the door automatically closed behind him. The office was in back, with a visibly open door and a dim light glowing within. Georgell entered and saw Terrance with a perplexed look on his face. "What's up?"

Terrance Bond was not a big guy but had a wiry athletic build from years of professional soccer. He had short brown hair and wore a loose, long-sleeved shirt to cover the tattoos that adorned his forearms. He wanted to look professional and didn't think the flaming soccer balls would convey that message.

"What can you tell me about these guys?" Terrance asked as he pointed to a security camera. On the screen a group of well-dressed men were talking with Red at the entrance. "I've heard they are involved in drugs and prostitution and who knows what else. Should we let them in?"

Georgell chuckled and said, "The Greeks? They're harmless. And trust me; whatever business they're in won't be a factor here. These guys have a lot of money and come to blow off steam, meet women, and have fun. They won't be a problem. In fact having them around eliminates trouble."

"How's that?"

"Like I said, I know the guys and they respect me. Bear and I have helped them a few times and they have returned the favor. They're all cousins or in-laws or something because they stick together and do whatever it takes to help each other out, maybe it's a Greek thing, I don't know, but they are good guys and friends of mine. Our problem isn't the Greeks it's anyone trying to keep them from having fun. In fact . . ." Georgell watched the screen and not seeing who he was looking for continued, " . . . Huh, it doesn't look like Cosmo is with them. Anyway he's the big man and definitely someone you'll want to get to know. Just don't piss him off or you might get whacked."

Georgell looked at Terrance seriously, and after a rewarding look of concern, winked. "Just kidding—they're harmless and excellent clientele. Don't worry about it—hey why are you hiding in here?"

Terrance shook his head. "Resting—it's going to be a long night, after a long day, and a long morning, and a long two months getting to this point. So if you don't mind, I would like to return to my siesta. Oh and sorry about the Greek thing. You know the crowd and if there is a problem you'll let me know, right?"

Georgell nodded and shuffled out. As he left he turned out the light, whispering, "Goodnight Sir."

"What the . . ." Terrence growled from the office.

☼~ **13** ~☼

Georgell entered the dance floor still smiling at his prank when the radio chirped in his ear, "Um—Doc, eyes on me." The words came like a riptide yanking Georgell from his complacency. He turned to where Moose had been and saw him still there, grimly pointing to the tunnel.

It had been three weeks since the concert and the work of setting up the club, hiring staff, and just the normal function of life had buried guardians in Georgell's thoughts and disillusioned him from the reality. Now it was happening, it was real; Moose was directing Georgell to the nightmare he had so earnestly forgotten.

The mechanical wave of the crowd hummed and flowed in a slow motion bounce as Georgell turned his sight toward the tunnel. His eyes focused through the flickering lights and darkness and finally rested on a hulking figure, possibly seven feet tall, standing above the crowd. It was a guardian. His features were hard to decipher from the distance but his massive barrel chest, glimmering shirtless in the dancing lights, gave off the illusion of a moving wall. It was also easy to make out some sort of spiked helmet on the head of the beast; a head that seemed to rest on enormous shoulders without the extension of a neck. The guardian's human counterpart was lost in the crowd below but steadily moving through the throng of dancers. The monstrous guardian edged forward as well, swaying his gorilla arms back and forth as they progressed.

Georgell quickly looked away, hoping not to draw the attention of the beast. Then, with more discretion, looked again and noticed Chopper walking in the crowd ahead of the hulking apparition. He followed Choppers progression to the right slope and with a horrifying revelation watched as Bear emerged from the crowd carrying the hovering beast above him.

"We're not in Kansas anymore!" Moose said as he reached Georgell's side. "That is the biggest guardian I've ever seen," then realizing that Bear was the speck, added, "Really?"

Both stood dumfounded and watched Bear disappear in the red glow of the right slope.

"Chopper you in position?" Georgell asked a moment later, finally breaking from his stupor.

"Copy," Chopper carelessly replied.

"Bear—you copy?"

"Copy, in position," Bear responded.

Georgell radioed each bouncer to cover his query and after positive returns from all he looked at Moose and said, "He's coherent."

Moose nodded and said nothing.

"Any suggestions," Georgell asked hopefully.

"We've got to take him out."

"Not an option," Georgell responded. "Look, Bear is still our friend and he seems to be in control, right? So we keep an eye on him and try to figure out what to do. In the meantime—don't look at that monster!"

"Yeah," Moose heartily agreed with a nod to cement his compliance. Then he smiled and with a grunt said, "Dude, I think it's Goliath! Like the real Goliath!"

Georgell smiled but couldn't muster a laugh. After a moment he told Moose to check on Red, and radioed Bug. Moose nodded and headed to the front, saying, "I'm checking his forehead later."

"Who's forehead?" Bug asked as he slipped in beside Georgell.

Georgell ignored the query as he unlocked the back door and stepped into the quiet office hallway. He ushered Bug in and allowed the door to slide shut behind them. "I've got a target but it's a tough one," Georgell said, with hesitation. "I need you to shadow Bear. He has some issues since Momentum and I need you to watch him. Don't get too close, and find a target that you can watch to cover any inquiries. I can't explain it all right now but I need you to do this. Got it?"

Bug looked perplexed but agreed. With a nod, he turned and opened the door to leave when Georgell grabbed him by the shoulder and said, "If something happens—I mean any sort of aggressive behavior—engage the radio three times without a word and I'll find you."

Bug nodded again and headed back to the dance floor. Georgell wanted to follow, to get things going, but watched the door shut without moving.

His knees felt weak and his thoughts were bouncing around in his head without focus. He rubbed his face furiously, flexed his muscles, pumped his fists and bounced on his toes. *Got to get it together*, he thought, grabbing the doorknob. With a deep breath, he yanked the door open and rushed through the dance floor crowd with no objective other than movement. A ripple formed in the crowd to his left as he noticed Pineapple and Nemesis pushing toward him as well.

Georgell stopped in the strobe lit tunnel. When Nemesis and Pineapple arrived he motioned for them to follow. They pressed through the tunnel and foyer, down the exit stairs, and rammed through the double crash bar doors. Moose, who was strolling up the sidewalk from checking the parking lot, was startled by the frantic exit and nearly tackled the rushing trio.

"Whoa, what's up?" Moose said recovering from the shock.

"Did a tall guy in a brown coat just come out here?" Georgell questioned while looking right and left.

Moose shook his head and Georgell snapped into command mode, "Moose go check the line. Pineapple you and Nemesis go back and sweep the restrooms then return to the dance floor. Blonde curly hair, brown jacket, tall, maybe six feet, oh, and white converse, find him—he's dealing!"

The staff headed to their assigned tasks with no further questions. Georgell smiled as he briskly walked toward Red searching for the fictitious perpetrator. His heart was pumping, and he knew the cobwebs of boredom had been shaken from his crew as well. This was a trick he had learned years ago to stimulate the staff on a dull evening. No one ever caught on to the effectual ploy, not even Bear, and it had always worked wonders on the overall vigilance of his bouncers.

The night pressed on with no serious concern and, to Georgell's delight, no other guardians appeared. At one point Georgell congratulated Pineapple and Nemesis for finding a man who was an uncanny match to his fictitious dealer and regretfully allowed them to toss the guy. He took solace in the fact that the man had no companions and spent very little at the bar but still felt a fleeting pang of guilt.

For most of the evening Georgell's thoughts were spent contemplating what affect the guardian was having on Bear. He was convinced that the beast had to be infecting Bear with some kind of negative rage but nothing happened, it was quiet. Bear had done nothing out of character and on the few occasions when Moose and Georgell ventured down to the sports bar, they made the visit quick; didn't so much as talk to Bear—let alone steal a glance at the forceful mass above him.

At closing, Georgell assisted the crew in shuffling people from the club. Bear came up from the right slope pressing a group of girls and an overly flirtatious guy toward the exit and Georgell, with a deep breath, decided it was time to interact. Without a glance up at the guardian, Georgell slid in beside Bear and nudged him with an elbow. "I'm shocked! You didn't throw anybody out a window. What's your problem?"

Bear said nothing and kept pushing forward without so much of a nod.

"You alright," Georgell asked.

"Fine," Bear sharply answered, continually stepping forward with an unseen focus.

"Can you check the basement." Georgell said, gently tugging Bear's shoulder to stop him. He could feel the cold stare of the hulking guardian above him. Chills cascaded down his back but he refused to look up.

Bear turned with a jolt and snapped at Georgell, "What?"

"Sweep the basement," Georgell said, locking eyes with Bear. Defiance and anger flamed in Bear's gaze. The crowd continued forward but Georgell and Bear were motionless.

"It's clear," Bear growled.

"Check it again," Georgell huffed back. "Please."

Bear, maintaining his gaze, brushed passed Georgell with an aggressive nudge and headed back to the basement. Chopper looked startled at Georgell's non-reaction but Georgell ignored him and resumed the push of straggling conversationalists. He had successfully distracted Bear from whatever it was he had been intent on doing and ultimately reduced the chance of a harmful outburst. The night was nearly over.

Finally, the customers were gone and the doors locked. On a normal evening a wrap-up discussion would ensue but, given the eerie presence of Goliath, Georgell decided to skip the meeting. Instead he invited everyone to Albertos where they could talk, eat, and most important, not have guardians to worry about.

Once dismissed, Bear slipped out the door without saying a word to anyone. Georgell saw him leave and was surprised that the guardian was no longer in view. Excusing himself from a discussion Emma and Moose were having, he raced down the stairs, and out the entrance doors. He spotted Bear nearing the corner and shouted, "Hey, you coming to eat!"

Bear stopped and turned, "You want me to?"

"Why wouldn't I?"

Bear stood for a moment saying nothing; his eyes focused on the sidewalk, "I'm sorry about what happened in there . . ." Georgell made no response and Bear continued, "Like I told you at the apartment—I don't think I should be bouncing any more. I don't know what's wrong with me—with my head—I'm scared I might hurt someone." Bear looked up with a stern gaze and seemed to quiver. "Did you know I was about to thump a guy?"

Georgell shook his head, "When?"

"Right at the end there," he pointed at the building. "When you sent me back to the basement—the guy didn't even do anything. I just wanted to hurt him—I'm telling you Georgell, my mind isn't right. You distracted me but I nearly assaulted you instead. I was fighting myself . . ." he said jamming fingers into his forehead " . . . trying to keep cool, but I still tried to provoke you—I wanted any excuse to fight."

"Come eat with us," Georgell said without reproach. "This whole thing stems from Club Momentum and I want to help you deal with it, okay."

"What do you mean?"

"Just come eat, we'll discuss it there, alright?"

Bear stared at Georgell for a moment but as Emma, Moose, and Terrance walked out of the club, he nodded, and with barely a whisper said, "Alright." He then turned the corner and headed for the back lot.

Terrance locked the entry doors and smiled as Georgell approached. "I'm not a bouncer but I can kick real good, does that grant me the privilege of eating with you guys?"

Georgell heard the question but ignored him as Moose shot a questioning glare. Georgell nodded at Moose as Emma replied to Terrance. "What are you talking about? I can take both these guys and I can't even spell kick; of course you can come." She took Terrance by the arm and walked off with a smirk. "Who needs them?"

When Terrance was out of earshot Moose pulled close to Georgell. "Any idea why Goliath left?"

"Yeah," Georgell said. "He's going to eat with us—we'll talk about it there; but please keep in mind that he has no idea what's going on. It's important that we talk with him in a way that won't scare him off. We've got to keep him on our side. Maybe if he can give us some insight as to what goes through his head we can work out a solution. We've got to try."

Moose said nothing and Georgell assumed this was not a point they were in agreement on. Still, he refused to leave Bear in the dark. He had to be included and Moose would simply have to agree. They followed Terrance and Emma across the street to the east parking lot in silence. Georgell ignored his wife's arm in arm stroll with the boss. He was not a jealous man. Upon reaching the car he threw Emma the keys and said, "You drive, I've got a lot on my mind."

"Shotgun," Moose blurted with excitement and jumped in the front seat.

Georgell smiled and crawled into the back.

☼～ **14** ～☼

It was crowded around the corner booth, but no one seemed to mind. Georgell, Emma and Terrance squeezed into the middle while Chopper and Moose sat on the edges. Terrance devoured a breakfast burrito and nibbled on the nacho platter that Emma and Georgell shared. Moose and Chopper ate heaping combination platters and guzzled their drinks with barbaric veracity then pointed and laughed at each other while their mouths were still packed with food.

Emma grabbed the nacho platter and pulled it close as Chopper and Moose both turned her direction and smiled. "Back off you heathens," she said with a grin.

Georgell forced a smile, trying to enjoy the moment with his friends but his mind was wholly preoccupied with his concern for Bear. What was he doing, when would he arrive, and how, he wondered, would he broach the subject with Terrance and Chopper still around.

"Come on man, Doc don't care. Give us a taste," Chopper said, reaching for a chip.

With a heavy nod toward Chopper, Moose said, "Give him a taste. I want the platter."

Georgell shook his head as Emma gave him a side glance; she then threw up her arms in surrender. The two men lunged at the remaining morsels, Moose growling like a beast protecting its kill. Terrance tried to retrieve one last nacho and nearly lost a finger. Emma laughed at the mock frenzy.

Georgell began to wonder if Bear would show. His reaction seemed positive and yet maybe he misread him. He wasn't the same person anymore and maybe his expressions no longer held the same meaning they once had. *No*, Georgell thought. *I know Bear and guardian or not, he wouldn't say he was coming and then bail.*

After a failed attempt to shove Chopper aside, Terrance politely asked the big man to move. Chopper huffed and slid from the booth. Terrance stood next to Chopper, then facing the other three, said, "Don't stay out too late, kids, we all need to work tomorrow." He then threw a few bucks on the table. "That's for whichever one of you fine folks cares to clean up my mess, I'm out!" Chopper followed Terrance to the front.

"How do you like that timing," Georgell said to Moose and Emma as he pointed at the parking lot where Bear was exiting his vehicle.

"Yeah," Moose said with a hint of relief. "I was wondering how you were going to deal with that. What about Chopper?"

Georgell watched Bear stop and talk with Terrance in the parking lot and then turned his gaze to the counter, where Chopper seemed to be ordering more food. "Let's not worry about Chopper. I think we should discuss everything in the open, guardians and all. Let's just see how he takes it."

Moose nodded.

Emma leaned back and gave Georgell a hard stare. She seemed stunned but said nothing. Georgell realized there had been no discussion of the guardians since the morning after the concert and figured she had simply glazed over his explanation as mad rambling. "It's real Emma, and more than that, Bear has a guardian, a big guardian. Moose and I need to tell him. We need to help him."

Emma continued to stare in disbelief. Georgell reached out and squeezed her hand. There wasn't anger in her stare or a sudden burst of verbal disregard so Georgell felt a smidge of relief. Still, he felt stupid for not keeping the guardian topic alive, and though he too hoped the visions weren't real he could understood her reaction.

Georgell maintained an unspoken gaze with Emma for a moment then looked at Chopper as he slid back into the booth with another order of nachos. "Sweeeet," Moose said as Chopper slid the food between them with a nod.

Bear set his tray on the cleared corner of the table, grabbed a chair from an open setting, smiled at Emma, and sat down. He left his burrito in the wrapper and ignored his drink. "So what's my problem, Doc?"

Stunned by the sarcastic query, Chopper looked at Georgell while shoving another loaded chip in his mouth. Georgell simply said, "I need a little more information before I can jump into my prognosis. Can you answer a few questions first, with the truth?"

Bear sipped his water and peeled back the wrapper from his food, stalling.

"Should we leave?" Emma asked, pointing at Moose and Chopper. Neither protested her query and all looked to Georgell for an answer.

Georgell was not ready. Still not sure how to handle the delicate situation and taken aback by the sudden willingness for Moose, his partner in this craziness, to leave him alone. "No!" he said with a glare at Moose. "Moose has valuable insight and I need him to stay."

Georgell then looked softly at Emma and said, "I would like you to stay. Your perspective is unique and critical, despite what you may believe."

"Man, ain't nobody kicking me out of this—whatever it is?" Chopper said.

"I want you all to stay, if Bear agrees?" Georgell slid his eyes from Emma and back to Bear.

Bear dropped his burrito to the tray and looked angrily at Moose then back to Georgell. "I have no problem with Chopper or Emma staying but I really don't know Moose and frankly I'm not sure why you trust him so much."

Moose grinned. Chopper finished chewing the mass of chips in his mouth, washed it down with a drink, and then slid the nacho platter aside.

"He needs to stay, Bear. I think when we are done you might have a better understanding of the situation and be more willing to cut Moose a little slack."

"I'm not hostile. I just want to know what's going on."

"Fine. Can you trust my judgment on this?" Georgell asked. "What about the honesty? I don't care how insane or ridiculous you might think an answer may be—I've got to hear the truth. Can you do that?"

Bear shrugged and picked up his steaming burrito.

"That's not good enough, Bear! Look, this is serious stuff and I—we—can help but I need you to talk openly, without hesitation." Georgell leaned into the table and with a dead-on stare asked again, "Can you do that?"

Moose's grin widened, Emma shuffled her position a little, and Chopper, unaware of what was about to take place, just sat attentively. Bear withdrew from taking another bite of his burrito and instead, wrapped it up and placed it back on the tray. He then looked at Emma. She shuffled a bit more but nodded her head. Bear then turned his eyes to Chopper who, feeling the gravity of the situation, raised his eyebrows a bit, shrugged his shoulders and said, "C'mon man, don't put this on me. I don't know what's going on but if Doc says he can help, let the man try. Either way you know who I am and where I'm going to be every night."

Bear nodded, and ignoring Georgell, turned his gaze to Moose.

"Listen," Moose said without hesitation or concern. "Three weeks ago I sat in this same booth with Georgell and helped him deal with a similar problem. I'm no witch doctor but I know what's going on and to be honest with you, I'd rather see you quit." Bear's face hardened and Georgell thought there may be an issue as Moose continued. "But . . . for some reason Georgell thinks we can help you and hey, I'm as curious, no—more curious than you to find out what that plan may be."

Georgell felt a jab in his side—a hint from Emma to intervene but oddly enough, Bear seemed to soften.

"Alright," Bear said with a nod at Moose. "I appreciate your candor." He then looked again at Georgell and raised his hands in a now-what gesture. A minute passed and the tension thickened as the second hand raced around the face of the overhead clock.

Chopper broke the silence, "Man this is crazy! What is it with you two? Either start talking or I'm going home. Zardoz is playing on the Sci-Fi channel."

"What I've seen and felt isn't easy to describe. Are you sure you want to hear it?" Bear leaned back in his chair. Georgell and Moose nodded. Emma seemed to sink in the booth and Chopper was as eager as ever. "Do you really think you can help?"

Georgell simply replied, "Let us try."

"Alright, I'll be as honest as I can, but if I don't feel good about a question I won't answer. I'm only saying that because I'm not sure where you're going with these questions and I don't want them getting too personal."

"Fair enough," Georgell said.

Bear took a sip of his drink and rotated his head around to release some stress. Georgell, still holding Emma's hand, squeezed it reassuringly. "Can you describe what you're feeling at the club? You told me that you want to hurt certain people and that you mentally fight with yourself not to lose control."

"Yeah, that's right."

"Does the feeling come over you all at once or is it a gradual build?"

Bear unwrapped his burrito and tried to explain, "It's like a wall that I walk into. Seriously, I walk into the club and from the first steps I'm overcome with anger and hatred. I look for anything, any reason to make a move, even with other bouncers."

"Like at Stone's," Chopper interjected. Seeing Moose's confusion, he added, "It's a bar we were working at across town. Bear picked me up for work one night and we were having a good ol' time but man, when we got to work . . . he didn't say one word—ignored me all night. Is that what you mean?"

Bear's face contorted a bit. "Yeah, something like that. I get so wrapped up in reasons to be angry that I have to focus on staying calm. It frustrates me to talk and trying to smile is just plain out of the question. I concentrate on staying cool. Violence seems to be a catalyst though; when a fight breaks out my body takes over and I just react—like that incident with the muscle heads. I completely lost control and wanted to do as much damage as I could. I didn't care about the consequences."

"Yeah man, like that. That's what I was telling you at the funeral. He gets hateful," Chopper said, looking at Georgell and pointing at Bear.

"Has this rage ever jumped out of control without a fight?" Georgell asked.

"A few times . . ." Bear looked down at his tray, " . . . I'll be walking down a hallway or something and then, almost like I'm watching from the outside, I'll attack someone who hasn't done a thing." He raised his head and addressed Chopper, "Remember that kid I pummeled in the hall at Stone's?"

"Which one," Chopper said with a huff.

"The one I said was spitting."

Chopper nodded and Bear continued, "That kid didn't do a thing! In fact I don't think he was in the club for more than ten minutes. He was looking for his sister or something and I took his head off. The spitting thing was the only excuse I could come up with. When I got home that night I was sick to my stomach for what I had done." Bear shook his head in disgust.

Georgell looked at Moose who raised his eyebrows and slurped another gulp of his Coke. Then Emma stepped in with a question, "How long was it before you started bouncing again? After Momentum, I mean?"

"I don't know, a couple of weeks maybe. Why?"

"Yeah that's right," Chopper said. "We both started at Stone's the weekend of that wet tee-shirt contest, remember?"

Bear nodded and Emma jumped right in with another question, "Was the rage in you then?"

"Nah man, he was cool. We were cracking jokes all night," Chopper answered for Bear.

"That's right," Bear agreed. "I remember feeling a little hesitant, being my first night back and all, but I never felt aggressive or the rage I do now. Even when a brawl broke out I felt normal and we handled it without any problem."

"Yeah man, that's right. Like old times." Chopper said with exhilaration.

Moose, having been relatively silent, nudged Georgell on the shoulder and asked Bear, "Do you remember seeing anything that night, anything that didn't seem right?"

"Anything you couldn't explain or thought was an illusion or hallucination?" Georgell added. He felt Emma tense up and knew they were heading into a line of questioning she wasn't comfortable with.

Though Bear didn't immediately answer, the look on his face betrayed him. Georgell didn't want Bear to rationalize his recollection and quickly tried to hook an easier response. "People, Bear. Did you see people hovering in the crowd? Did you see ghosts or apparitions or something standing over a person that you couldn't explain?"

Bear looked up at Georgell with grateful surprise and nodded. Moose's face brightened with relief and Georgell squeezed Emma's hand. He wanted to scream, *there it is!* But thought better of the response and instead nodded and said, "Okay." Chopper looked wide-eyed at Bear, completely at a loss, and then at the other two bouncers and finally at Emma.

"I saw something like that. I'm not sure what it was. But the next weekend I worked a private party at the Lounge and that's when I really saw something, or at least I think I did." He began to waver a bit and Georgell reassured him with a nod.

"This guy paid me to just hang out on the couch. He wanted me around but didn't want it to be obvious, y'know. I had a few beers and some food when I noticed the guy sitting next to me had this other dude standing above him."

"At first I thought he was just standing behind the couch but I kept looking and realized he was floating. I remember thinking I must have had a cookie laced with acid or something because the whole idea was a trip. Not much else happened though; I feel asleep and woke up after everyone had left."

"Since that night I haven't seen anything weird, that's when the other stuff began though; the constant rage, the anger, the sudden bursts of aggression. I can't believe I'm just now making the connection." Bear looked down at his fists, entranced by them.

"I knew it Georgell, I knew it," Moose exclaimed. "He got the sight just like you, from Momentum. That was the trauma."

"Okay but he doesn't have it now," Georgell replied. "And if he does he isn't using it like us."

"I know! But he did have it. Something must have happened."

"What could have happened?"

"Maybe he was stabbed, or knocked out, I don't know . . ."

Emma squeezed Georgell's hand and he looked at her. "You have a confused audience," she said sliding her eyes toward Chopper and Bear.

Georgell interrupted another hypothesis from Moose with a heavy elbow and apologized to the others. Moose grunted his disapproval and said, "Sorry guys, I got excited and forgot you were here."

Forgot you were here, Georgell pondered as if Moose's words were a key to something. "Bear, do you remember anything else from that night? Have you forgotten anything? Did the guardian look at you?"

"Guardian?" Bear asked confused.

"Sorry, I mean the guy standing over the other guy at the party, the ghost, did he look at you?"

"I don't know? Like I said, I don't remember anything else from the party. The guy that hired me said I fell asleep, nothing else happened. Not that I can remember anyway," Bear said, his words trailing off. "Why?"

Georgell slumped back in his seat and tried to figure out what he was missing. He could feel the answer dangling in front of him but couldn't unlock the solution.

Chopper leaned in to Emma and quietly said, "Are we seriously talking about ghosts? I thought I was the sci-fi geek here?"

Emma squeezed Georgell's hand again.

"Chopper, I know this sounds crazy, and trust me it will only get crazier, but try to listen and have an open mind."

Chopper offered a golden toothy grin, as if to reassure Georgell that nothing would seem too outrageous and with a quiver of his head, a bulging of his eyes, his shoulders shrugged up, and a quick motion of his hands he mutely said, bring it!

Reassured by Chopper's magnetic smile, Georgell just decided to talk and hoped he could flush out the missing link in the details. "I—well Moose and I—have a gift. We can see what we call guardians; they hover over people and protect them. Actually there are good guardians that protect and bad guardians that force people to do bad things, like shooting up a club. It seems that surviving some traumatic experience makes you more aware of your surroundings and more apt to see the guardians. Anyway, they also attack if they're seen. Moose has . . ." Georgell stopped abruptly and, having discovered the missing link, nearly leapt over the table and said, "Bear take off your shirt!"

"Wait a minute," Emma broke in. "What's going on?"

"Bear, please," Georgell said ignoring Emma.

Bear looked quizzically at Georgell and put up a finger to quiet another reaction from Emma. He then said, "Tell me why."

"Don't shush me" Emma said.

"Sorry Em," Bear said, still looking at Georgell. "I didn't mean it that way I—I—I just need to know . . ."

"Yeah man, tell us why," Chopper added with his trademark huff.

Georgell returned Bear's look. "You know why, don't you? You have a scar. A scar you have no recollection of getting. It's smooth, round and numb to the touch."

Moose unexpectedly stood, yanked off his shirt, and turned around, exposing his back. Surprised by the action but equally pleased at Moose's willingness, Georgell pointed to the ringlets on Moose's lower back and said, "It looks something like that, doesn't it?"

Bear stared at the scar on Moose's back, then looked at Georgell, and again back at the scar. Finally in a steady fluid motion he rose, slid the chair back, and stripped off his shirt

Chopper began to laugh, "You guys are playing with me aren't you? C'mon, what's up man?" His laughter started up again when he noticed the three smooth ringlets in a triangle pattern directly over Bear's heart.

A couple of well dressed Hispanic patrons, seeing the large men staring at each other with their shirts off, snatched their order from the counter and quickly exited the restaurant. The timid janitor, recognizing Moose and Georgell from their previous encounter, hastily grabbed a mop and headed for the restrooms.

Jorge, the friendly manager, hustled over to the group and quickly stood between the shirtless men like a bug between dueling fly swatters. "Please, no trouble, please, guys please sit down, I will bring more nachos, okay."

"Its fine Jorge, we don't need anymore nachos."

"What?" Chopper and Moose said in unison with a glare at Georgell.

Emma stacked the scattered plates on the used trays and handed them to Jorge, then with her calming smile and soothing voice said, "Nachos would be great. The boys are just showing of their scars. Everything is okay."

Jorge took the tray and said, "Yes, good—no charge." Emma thanked him and as swiftly as he arrived, Jorge shuffled back to the counter.

"Okay, start over about these guardians," Bear said pulling his shirt back on and sliding into his chair.

Chopper lowered his head and tapped it a few times on the table. His eyes were focused when he raised it again, and more to himself than anyone else, he said, "Man, does anyone else here the Twilight Zone?"

Over the next hour Georgell and Moose explained all they could about guardians. Bear listened intently with very few questions. Chopper couldn't stop grinning, as if all his other-worldly beliefs were somehow being realized in the unveiling of these guardians. Emma listened as well, but not with the same enthusiasm as the others, she was looking for holes.

Bear shook his head, "So I'm being haunted by a dark guardian that is hovering over me and trying to control my actions because I was stabbed by some other dark guardian who recognized me because I stared at him and now I'm a speck to this thing that you guys can only see when I'm in a club. Is that about right?"

Moose and Georgell nodded then Georgell began to laugh when he realized how ridiculous it sounded. Bear joined in and Moose looked at them curiously.

"What," Georgell said, "if I were listening I would think you and I were completely out of our minds!"

Chopper began chuckling uncontrollably as well while Emma just stared in cautious awe and nodded in agreement with Georgell. Moose still didn't get the joke and returned to the problem at hand, "I was wrong about them trying to kill us. They're trying to turn us, not kill us—like to the dark side or something."

Chopper hit the table and said, "There it is man! I knew it! Star Wars had to come into this eventually."

"So what do we do?" Bear questioned after regaining some control. "If I continue working is this thing going to rot my mind and follow me home at night? Am I going to wake up someday with the urge to commit mass homicide in a mall? What's the plan?!"

Georgell's immediate strategy was to discover how Bear was involved. Now that the primary objective was complete there was no set plan of action and he immediately felt the gloom of uncertainty. He believed there had to be a way to eliminate guardians; now, with Bear under guard, he was more determined to find that solution. But how would they do it without putting Bear, or others at risk. "We have to eliminate the guardian," he said.

"Right," Bear sarcastically agreed. "And do I live in the process?"

"Come on Bear, we have to think this through. I'm not trying to get you killed but if you stop bouncing how will we discover its weaknesses? We're all in this, as a team, to help; but you have to be involved and willing to take a chance. I'm not even sure what kind of chance I'm asking you to take. Could you possibly die, yes? But remember Moose and I can see that thing too and we have just as much at stake. I want it to work out."

"No offense, Doc, but the whole thing seems pretty asinine. I'd have left already if I didn't have this scar over my heart." Bear pounded his chest then pointed at Chopper. "He thinks this is some kind of low budget movie. And again, no offense, but your own wife doesn't believe it. Do you Em?"

Emma didn't look up, but acknowledged the accusation with a solemn shake of her head. "So tell me again how *we* are going to find a solution without *me* ending up on a cold slab in the morgue."

Georgell didn't have the answer. He knew Bear was right but could do nothing more to persuade them of the truth. *I'm done*, he thought, *I have to give it time.* A wry smirk slowly appeared on his face. He tugged the rubber band from his goatee and unraveled the braid. He knew Bear wouldn't walk away no matter how life-threatening the problem was, despite his skepticism and sarcastic tone, he would be there, ready to work—ready to defeat this thing. He shouldered Moose to let him out of the booth. Pulling Emma up behind him as he stood, Georgell looked down at Bear and said, "I'm going home to think." He then slugged Chopper and asked, "You going to quit?"

"Man—not now," Chopper decisively responded.

"Moose?"

Moose looked at Bear and said, "I've got a slingshot I want to try on that monster. I ain't quitting!"

"Emma?"

Emma leaned over and kissed Bear on the cheek. She then whispered in his ear, "A few hallucinations aren't going to scare me off even if they are infectious. Let's work this out."

Georgell then said, "Who's to say it doesn't follow you home already? You're different, Bear, and I want to help find that person you used to be. The guardian has to be eliminated for that to happen! Tomorrow, nine, I hope to see you at the club. Or stay home, work it out alone, either way I'm tired . . . goodnight."

Chopper's deep laughter followed the couple to the door and out of the restaurant.

☼～ **15** ～☼

It was close to nine and already a hundred-plus guests were crowding the sports bar and trickling onto the dance floor in anticipation of the DJ. A line had been slowly gathering in the front of the club as people talked excitedly about the previous night and how posh the setup was. A desk attendant called over to Georgell, "Doc, phone, I think it's Bear."

Georgell walked over to the desk and felt a looming disappointment as he reached for the phone. "Bear?"

"Yeah, listen, I'm not sure about all this. Can we talk for a bit before I commit to this?"

"Where are you?" Georgell asked excitedly.

"Back lot."

"Be right there." Georgell hung up the receiver and engaged his radio, "Moose, I'm heading to the back lot. Hold down the fort."

"Copy," Moose replied.

Georgell saw Bear leaning out of his car and staring at the full moon. It was ironic that on a night when the future was so unknown, with such dark implications and uncertainty, a full moon haunted the sky. "Not a good sign is it," Georgell said as he opened the door and sat down on the passenger seat. "Difference is we always looked for the crazies on nights like tonight and now we are the crazies." Georgell's attempt to lighten the mood had little effect on Bear's gloom.

"What's the plan," Bear asked matter-of-factly.

"I wish I had a simple solution, but I don't. Right now the only thing we know for sure is that the speck has to be unconscious to eliminate a guardian. You being the speck makes that proposition a little more difficult, but we'll do whatever it takes. In the mean time we'll keep you in the sports bar with Chopper. He's going to keep a close eye on you and try to keep situations to a minimum. Moose and I will make regular sweeps in your area but we won't be hanging out. Spending too much time in the same area with that thing is difficult." Georgell was planning to keep Bug on him as well but wanted to keep one ace up his sleeve.

"Listen, Bear, I'm glad you're willing to put yourself through this. Try to keep us informed as much as possible and fight the aggression and rage. We're going to work this out. There is a solution and we will find it."

Bear attempted a smile. "Tell Chopper if it gets crazy he can't expose his back to me. If I wrap a choke on him it's over."

"He knows."

"Another thing. I've thought it over and I don't think it's a good idea for me to have a radio. If a call comes over the wire I'll be pumped with adrenaline and less able to control my rage."

Georgell let the idea stew for a moment and then agreed, "Alright, but you need to have one to avoid questions. Keep the power off."

Bear agreed, pulling the keys from the ignition.

"All in place," Moose buzzed in Georgell's earpiece.

"Copy that," Georgell responded. He then opened the door and stepped out of the car as Bear did the same. During their stroll from the back lot to the entrance, Georgell slyly removed the batteries from his radio and held the empty shell in his hands. He wanted to remove any temptation Bear might have to listen in on the chatter. Chopper greeted them at the door, whistling the Twilight Zone theme, but abruptly stopped when Georgell threw him a cold stare.

Passing guests on the stairs Georgell felt uneasy, and wondered if the behemoth had appeared yet. As they walked by the desk he grabbed a radio and deftly switched it with his own. When he handed the inoperable radio to Bear he ventured a quick glance overhead and felt an uneasy jolt of nerves as the guardian hovered in place, looking about. Georgell forced his eyes away, trying to concentrate his sight and mind elsewhere, but was heavy with concern.

"It's here isn't it?" Bear asked. Georgell wasn't sure if the beast would understand a reply, so he ignored the question.

"Right, I seriously want to hit you for not answering me so I know it's there." Bear attached the radio to his belt and walked through the tunnel. Chopper followed and winked at Georgell as he passed.

"Be careful," Georgell admonished. Chopper's massive hand flipped a thumbs-up as he and Bear turned the corner out of sight.

As Georgell wandered through the club over the next few hours he continually thought of the guardian over Bear. At times he would began to rationalize what was happening and have to do a quick sweep of the sports bar to reground his thoughts in reality. His stomach always reminded him of the truth as it tightened every time he saw the thing.

There was also a lingering regret for not spending more time with Emma during the day. She was gone most of the afternoon and Georgell had spent the day hauling trash to the city dump. They had barely seen each other. He knew she was upset, that she needed some attention, but didn't know what else to say and chose to ignore his own need. Now he missed her, regretted his choice and wished she were working.

It was quiet, despite the blaring music, hundreds of conversations, dancing, laughing, singing, and yells of friends across the way. The level of noise, when so loud, became static noise, wind, nothing. Georgell could hear a pin drop. He decided to perform a radio check to breakup the monotony. He called every bouncer by name and each responded in turn. When he radioed Bear a fuzzy acknowledgment came under the disguised voice of Chopper. Earlier in the evening Georgell had mentioned to Chopper that Bear's radio was not functioning and that he should not react to any call unless he was mentioned by name. Chopper wasn't happy about the order but understood the need to keep Bear out of trouble and agreed. He also agreed to cover for Bear on any radio check. This was the second successful test.

Georgell tossed his empty plastic cup of Coke into a garbage can and reached in his pocket for some gum. Realizing he was out, he made his way to the office where he had another pack hidden in a jacket pocket. He pulled the jacket from a hook and found an envelope next to his gum. Georgell slipped the gum in his pocket, opened the envelope, and pulled out a letter from Emma. He immediately felt excited and apprehensive at the same time.

Georgell sat in the chair behind Terrance's desk and began reading:

> Georgell,
>
>   I am sorry we didn't get a chance to talk today. I wasn't avoiding you. I just needed to think on this whole guardian thing. I'm not sure there is anything more you can tell me so I decided to talk with Naomi. Honestly, I was a little upset with her that the subject has never come up. We've seen

each other nearly every day for a month and she has never said a thing? Anyway, I wanted her perspective . . . a female's perspective, or maybe more so, that of a wife and mother. I just have a hard time understanding all this. It's simply not believable? I can see how real it is to you and Moose, even Bear seems willing to accept it after the whole shirt thing—I admit those scars are bizarre—and Chopper will latch onto anything "sci-fi," I think he believed before Bear did?

Anyway, Naomi and I took the kids to the park and just talked. Nothing new just the normal yada-yada but I finally asked her if she really believed all the guardian nonsense and her whole demeanor changed. Seriously it was not the reaction I expected? She clammed up so I pressed her; I think if she didn't see my sincerity it would have gone different. Anyway I explained my concerns and how I trusted her and needed her perspective. It was obvious that she believed in the stuff but said nothing so I changed my question to, "Why do you believe this?"

She looked me in the eye, took my hands in hers, and said,

"BECAUSE IT IS TRUE!"

I can't describe the feeling that shot threw me, it was insane, and I had no doubt that she was serious! I began to tremble, like something was being freed in my mind, a truth I had locked away or something. Anyway, she apologized for not talking about it earlier. She said she didn't want to lose me as a friend. She said she didn't have friends, her kids didn't have friends, Moose especially didn't have a friend, and it was a luxury she didn't want to lose. She said you were an answer to her prayers and that the kids and I were a bonus. She is such a spiritual person! Anyway she thanked me for accepting them and making them feel loved. Of course at this point I was bawling like a baby and felt like an idiot, but it was nice to hear. Anyway, she was scared that if I heard about the guardians she would lose my friendship so she selfishly avoided the subject.

I guess I can understand. After the shooting it seemed everyone wanted to be a part of my pity party and it made me crazy. The kids and I became pet projects for people and I was tired of the fake attention. I honestly feel like my relationships with family and close friends have dissipated. No one wanted us to stay with you. They all thought it was a destructive relationship and begged me to leave. I couldn't, I knew you still loved us; I had to believe that. Anyway I lost some close friends and confidants during this recovery process.

The last month has been awesome though because I too feel like a prayer has been answered, minus the whole guardian thing of course. Naomi, Moose, and the kids have accepted us; and changed us. It's like I can be me around her. I can drop the tough wife and mother act and be me, that teenager who likes to gossip and laugh and enjoy life, Naomi has helped me realize that again. I think you know what I mean, you've seen it. I think you've felt it as well. Moose makes you laugh. <u>I LOVE YOUR LAUGH!!</u>

Anyway, I'm not as strong as you and I am definitely lacking the faith that Naomi seems to have. I don't think I can fully accept the guardians yet. I still need time. It's too surreal and simply doesn't mesh with what I have always believed? I'm trying to work it out but I just can't seem to get passed my personal chunk of reality. How do I open my mind to alternative realities when this one takes so much of my energy? Naomi said to give it time. She said I have a front row seat when I work at the club and that she envies the time I get to spend with you guys. Anyway, if it is true—than I am sure she is right and that it will come. Just, please don't push me, let me find it; let me absorb it in my own time.

WOW! I can't believe I've written so much. I started this because I wanted you to read a note Naomi gave me . . . funny huh? Anyway, she had a note in her purse, beyond weird I know!! And she gave it to me today. She wrote it a couple of days ago . . . Anyway, it's awesome! She wrote the note because she had an impression that I would need a boost soon. Again, is this woman for real with her spiritual feelings or what? I didn't enclose the note from her because I think I basically told you everything anyway but if you want just ask and I will let you read it, K.

I LOVE YOU! BE GOOD! Wake me when you get home

wink-wink . . .
~Your Cherub

Georgell was relieved. He felt a weight somewhat lifted form his thoughts and immediately wanted to call Emma, he reached for the phone but heard someone coming down the hall. He quickly slipped the letter back in the envelope and returned it to the jacket pocket. He then laid his head on the table and pretended to snore as Terrance walked in.

"Whatever," Terrance said. "Get out of my office!"

Georgell laughed and obliged. As he headed toward the dance floor entrance he engaged his radio, and said, "Moose meet me at the door."

"On my way, Doc."

☼~ 16 ~☼

The perimeter walk was refreshing. Moose and Georgell had walked through the back parking lot and were headed back toward the front in a steady stroll up the steep sidewalk. "Naomi talked with Emma today," Georgell said.

"Yeah."

"Thank her for me. I think she made a difference." Georgell sucked in a couple of deep breaths of crisp air.

"Yeah."

"I think . . ." Georgell stopped midsentence as he noticed a guardian half a second before Moose grabbed his arm. They slowed their steps and silently studied the situation. The guardian hovered over a middle-aged man a few patrons from the entrance. The speck stood with a group of guys, all of whom seemed well built and athletic. *Maybe a visiting baseball team or something*, he thought. The guardian was a young guy, maybe twenty, and seemed to dance with excitement as his speck neared the entrance. The figure held no real menacing features other than a wicked smile and flaming red hair but the glimmering swords in each of his hands made for an eerie change. *There's always something*, Georgell thought while making a mental note of the oddities. He then engaged his radio, "Red, this is Doc, do not respond."

Red took some identification from the next guy in line, looked at it, then at the guest, and again at the ID. Handing back the card he nodded approval to the patron but also made a sly acknowledgment to Georgell.

Georgell was excited. This was the first guardian he would have the opportunity to purge and Moose was right there with him. Taking out the speck would be no problem, but the ensuing fight—if the other men decided they weren't happy—could get ugly. He engaged his radio to call

Pineapple and Nemesis to the front but changed his mind as a couple of black Suburban's pulled up. Georgell smiled as well-dressed Greeks began to exit from the vehicles.

"White shirt—Next group—No entry! I repeat no entry!" Georgell cryptically spoke into his radio. Again Red responded with a nod as he allowed a couple of girls to enter. No entry meant Red would do whatever it took to keep a patron from the club and Georgell knew he would do it.

Cosmo, the boisterous leader of the Greeks, stepped from the suburban with his arms outstretched. He was a slightly pudgy man with broad shoulders, a full head of dark hair, and an infectious smile. He stood nearly six feet tall and wore clear glasses with a bluish tint. His hands were adorned with different colored rings and two thick gold chain bracelets danced on his right wrist. A tie was visibly missing from his tailored suit and his blue silk shirt was unbuttoned enough to expose a mass of black hair on his chest.

"What's up Doc," Cosmo bellowed as he embraced Georgell. The other Greeks laughed hearing Cosmo's rendition of Bugs Bunny but Georgell didn't waste time with pleasantries.

"Coz, these guys at the door are about to be a problem. Can you hang back for a sec and help out."

"Absolutely!" Cosmo smiled and quickly relayed the situation to his boys. Moose and Georgell headed to the entry.

The ignorant speck was first in the group to reach Red and nonchalantly displayed his identification. Red shook his head and bore down on the guy with a bitter glare. "Tonight I don't like baseball, you guys go," he said sweeping his gaze over the group daringly.

"What? You can't . . ." the man began to protest but his words were cut short as his body went limp and he fell unconscious to the ground. Red had surprised him with a powerful head butt then faced the others as he tossed his clipboard to the ground.

Moose and Georgell had just reached the line and hastily went to work as the other team members lunged for Red. Georgell slashed his boot against the back leg of his closest target. The leg buckled and Georgell pulled the man back by his shoulders and sidestepped him as he fell. He knew the Greeks would pounce on him before he could get back up and so he lunged for the next target.

Moose hurled himself head first into a couple of guys that were clawing toward Red and the threesome fell scrambling to the ground. Moose had one man pinned beneath him and grabbing his lengthy hair, slammed the man's head to the walk. Unable to avoid an attack from another, Moose dropped his head and braced himself as a full on kick blasted him in the forehead. Georgell saw the brutal kick and three well-dressed Greeks pummel the kicker as he recoiled.

The first man to reach Red connected with a short jab that Red absorbed by stepping into the swing. Red returned a crushing blast to the man's midsection followed by an uppercut that snapped the guy's head back and propelled him against the entry doors. The second assaulter managed to leap on Red's back and lock an arm bar around his neck but the choke was short lived as Georgell delivered a kidney punch to the choker. Georgell then wrapped his own choke on the man and yanked him from Red's back. The man threw his arms in the air and squealed, "Okay."

Georgell loosened his hold but did not release the man. He told him to relax and then backed up against the wall and surveyed the scene. The fight was already over.

Cosmo and a couple of Greeks stood over a bloodied but coherent blonde guy who sat on the walk with his hands up. Moose had left the unconscious body of the guy he had tackled and was pressing toward a couple of others who were backing away submissively. Against the club wall, the man that kicked Moose lay curled up and screaming as another throng of Greeks yelled at him to shut up. Red, shaking off the arm bar, stepped toward the slumped body of his uppercut victim and pulled him by the feet away from the door. The last member of the team was the unconscious speck, his guardian no longer visible.

Georgell smiled and thought, *that went fairly well*. Then, loosening his choke, said, "Can I let you go without any trouble?" The man agreed—anger thick in his voice. Georgell released his grip but kept his hands ready for any quick reaction.

The man slowly stepped out of the lock and turned to address Georgell but said nothing. Georgell's hand held his microphone and without engaging the radio he calmly requested police back up while eyeing the fuming man. He then broke eye contact for a moment as he noticed the speck beginning to stir. In a calm voice he said, "Cops are on the way.

I suggest you gather up your friends and leave. Otherwise you may be tomorrow's front page."

A few cabs pulled up with exiting customers and Red whistled for them to hold. Still fuming, the man knew he had no other option and waved his teammates over to help load the injured players into the vehicles. Moose—unsatisfied with their speed—picked up the speck by his shirt and pants and tossed him hard into the back seat. "Hurry up!" he grumbled.

As the taxis drove away and the Greeks vigorously hugged one anther, Red wiped some blood from his eyebrow, picked up his clipboard and yelled, "Next!" The stunned crowd was a bit slow to react but eventually overcame their shock and stepped forward. Conversations erupted throughout the line as groups relived the brawl with excitement and disbelief.

Georgell slapped Cosmo on the back and said, "Thanks Coz. First round is on me."

Cosmo shook his head slightly and said, "Now where was I?" Then, knowing he had an audience, he bellowed, "What's up Doc!" and gave Georgell a crushing embrace. Everyone laughed. Cosmo then said, "I will not allow you to buy me anything. I should pay you for this excitement, are you kidding?"

"Right! Get in the club, and be good," Georgell said, motioning to the door.

Cosmo stepped toward the door and with a glance at one of the others said, "Take care of our Russian brother." He then swung open the doors and entered the club. Red turned and accepted the handshake from the designated Greek and then watched as the remainder of the guys entered the club. Red refocused his attention on the bustling line.

Georgell knew the friendly handshake included cash, probably a hundred-dollar bill, and was pleased to see Red appreciated. Working the door was not an easy job—it took a great deal of patience and attitude—but given time it was definitely the most rewarding. On a busy night Red could easily go home with a thousand dollars, and Georgell firmly believed, as a solo doorman, Red earned every cent. Experience, skill, and the willingness to befriend the crowd always paid off in tips.

Red is good, Georgell thought as he reached into his back pocket, pulled out a folded bill that Cosmo had deftly deposited during their embrace, and transferred it to his front pocket.

Moose had a trickle of blood oozing from his forehead and the start of a nice bruise but his cheerful demeanor and gaping smile showed no concern. Georgell motioned him into the club, slapped Red approvingly on the back, and then with a wink said, "I'll try to call off the cops." Moose and Red both knew his declaration was a ruse. The boys they had beaten were professional athletes and that meant they would duck the media exposure. Right or wrong, they would be fined or reprimanded if the incident made the news. It was a perfect setup with no serious injury or resulting ramification.

"Exit!" Pineapple radioed as Moose and Georgell began to enter the club. They looked at each other and bolted back down the walk and around the corner to the exit doors. The doors blasted open and a couple of guys came stumbling through. Pineapple rolled out behind them, tripping on the last few steps.

Nemesis hopped over the sprawled Pineapple and slammed the nearest guy to the pavement screaming, "Don't move." She then dropped her knee into his back and pressed her hand to his neck. The other guy bounced off a parked car and turned to help his buddy when Moose stepped in front of him, sending him back against the car with a thud.

Pineapple jumped to his feet, turning to face a couple more guys who were exiting the club behind them. Both immediately threw up their hands. "Just leaving," one said.

Georgell nudged the side of Nemesis' prey with his foot and asked, "Any more trouble or are you leaving too?" The muffled reply sounded like an agreement to leave so Georgell tapped Nemesis on the shoulder. She reluctantly released him and stood up. The man rolled on to his back and looked up at Nemesis. Georgell lightly kicked him and barked, "Apologize to the lady!"

"Sorry, sorry, I apple-gize," the man said. He stood, swayed unsteadily on his feet, and glared at Nemesis. He grumbled something as his friends grabbed him by the arms and walked away. The man pinned against the car slid passed Moose and sheepishly asked, "Are we eighty-sixed or can we come back?"

Pineapple gave a slight nod and Georgell, while pointing at the departing trio, replied, "You can come back if you keep that idiot under control."

The man agreed and trotted down the street after his friends.

Moose howled at the moon and screamed, "I love this job!"

Georgell looked at Pineapple and with mock concern asked, "You alright?"

"Yeah I just missed a step."

"I've got to say; watching you roly-poly out the doors was quite funny. But Nemesis having to hurdle over you, wow, I won't forget it," Georgell said as Moose howled again.

Pineapple smiled and brushed himself off.

Nemesis, unsure of procedure, was bouncing on her toes, adrenaline clearly still surging in her veins.

"I'm impressed," Georgell said. "You handled that last bit well. How was the first part?"

"The guy grabbed my butt! I asked him to leave and he grabbed my butt," she said. "He'd been harassing a bunch of girls and we warned him twice," she said defensively.

Georgell kept a straight face as she hurriedly retold the incident but he wanted to burst into laughter. She must have thought he was angry but in fact he was very pleased with her performance. "Alright, alright, calm down. So did you hit him?"

"No . . . I kneed him in the balls," she hesitantly replied.

"Okay well that wasn't the best choice but it all ended good right? So shake it off."

Nemesis looked up somewhat surprised and asked, "That's it? No incident report?"

Georgell smiled and said, "I hired you because I trust your judgment. Besides, if you were out of line Pineapple would tell me. But right now we have only two bouncers inside and the night is far from over." He then spread out his arms and in a corralling motion shuffled the bouncers back in through the exit.

When everyone had settled back into their respective roles, Georgell and Moose were cornered by Chopper as he noticed them descending the stairs. "What's going on up there man?" Then, noticing Moose's bruised and bloodied forehead, he added, "You already busted up? C'mon man its dead town here. I'm losing my mind staring up there." He motioned above Bear's head but didn't point and neither man looked.

"It was a guardian," Moose said. "Outside—he was with a whole group of guys—but we handled it."

Chopper sighed with jealousy.

"How's he doing?" Georgell said with a nod toward Bear.

"I can't see nothing but I can tell he's concentrating. He slapped a guy earlier but I got him out before it got worse. He's been pacing a lot and he told me to quit staring—yelled at me actually. There's nothing up there man. How do you see it?"

"Maybe you shouldn't stare so much," Moose said. "I think the guardian is beginning to notice."

"What?" Georgell asked and then noticed the guardian in the mirror looking their direction. A shivering chill ran up his spine as, for a moment, Georgell thought the beast were looking at him but relief discovered it was Chopper that held the evil gaze of the menace. "Yeah, maybe you should quit staring, probably making it harder for Bear."

"Man, you're probably right. Every time I try to get close he walks away—been keeping opposite me for most the night."

Moose walked back up the stairs and Georgell followed. Chopper looked at them with a bewildered stare and Georgell said, "Sorry, its tough hanging around that thing. Keep us informed. Sixty minutes man, just hold it together."

"Copy that," Chopper responded in the earpiece.

Forty-five minutes later, Georgell was discussing the night's incidents with Terrance when three distinct beeps echoed in his earpiece. He knew this was the distress signal from Bug but had to ignore the beeps because Terrance heard them as well. After a minute, he calmly excused himself with the ruse of doing rounds and swiftly headed to the sports bar. Moose was a step behind.

Bug met them on the stairs above the bar and explained the situation. He told them about the growing distance between Chopper and Bear and how they weren't communicating or even paying attention to the guests. He also explained that he had felt a sense of urgency to let Georgell know but wasn't sure if there was any significant concern. Georgell told him he was right to call and continued down the steps as Moose passed to his right.

Chopper and Bear stood on opposite corners of the bar. Chopper stared blankly above Bear and Georgell knew immediately the problem. Goliath had removed his spiked helmet and continuously slashed it in the air with a stabbing motion at Chopper. Bear was gripping the handrail like an anchor and with focused concentration, stared at a buzzing neon sign.

"The guardian thinks Chopper can see him. It's trying to force Bear to attack," Georgell said not even checking to see if Moose was nearby. A grunt reassured Georgell of Moose's presence and he continued, "Bear's resisting it."

The beast thrashed and pulled, pointed and mutedly screamed, but Bear held tight to the rail and didn't budge.

"This isn't fun anymore," Moose grumbled.

"Chopper, eyes on me," Georgell radioed while trying to formulate a plan.

Chopper broke from his stupor and successfully located Georgell. With a jerk of his head, Georgell motioned for Chopper to come over and in a serious voice said to Moose, "You may have to intercept a charge, get ready."

Chopper began to walk toward them. Bear didn't move despite his lunging guardian but Moose took a protective step closer anyway.

"Watch out!" came the screaming voice of Bug, and in a sudden whirl of motion, everybody reacted.

Chopper pointed at something behind Georgell and broke into a run. Bear released the rail, spun with a menacing growl toward Chopper, and bolted after him. Moose took another step forward and with the sudden rush from Bear, he too broke into a run, skirting the edge of the bar.

In quick response to the warning, Georgell crouched and felt an intense pain sear into his right shoulder as he spun to his left and took a step back. A knife slashed across Georgell's shirt as a familiar young man with crazed eyes and a wiry frame recoiled and lunged again. At the same instant, a guardian, from above the wild eyed boy, thrust a jagged dagger down at Georgell as he circled back toward the stairs. Another searing flash of pain stung Georgell as he twisted to avoid the guardian's dagger but allowed the speck's blade to slice his upper abdomen.

A ferocious yell came from Chopper as he leapt onto the entry. Raising both arms above his head, Chopper made a fisted sledgehammer that he thrust down on the speck's shoulder. A sickening crack echoed from the snapping bones. The knife dropped and the kid fell to the ground. Chopper, unable to stop his momentum, trampled over the fallen kid and bowled into Georgell.

Georgell fell beneath Chopper's crushing weight and was momentarily pinned on the steps beneath him. The speck wailed in agony but was not unconscious. Georgell recognized the lifeless stare of the guardian now standing above him. It was the guardian from the concert. His suit, the hair pulled back in a bun, and the six-inch double-sided blade were unmistakable. It was the same guy, the guardian that recognized him. Georgell was helpless to the rushing thrust of the guardian's blade.

A sprig of hope shot into Georgell as Chopper turned to his right and raised his arm in an attempt to block the guardian's assault. The blade penetrated completely through Chopper's forearm but protected Georgell from the thrust. The guardian swiftly pulled the dagger free and lunged with greater intensity toward Georgell's chest, his wicked glare fixed on Chopper.

Chopper rolled off Georgell, grabbing his wounded arm.

Georgell kicked his left leg hard at the kid's exposed head and felt his foot connect. The guardian and dagger vanished, inches from Georgell's heart, as the speck's body went limp.

Moose made a hard right turn to intercept Bear and knocked a couple of startled girls to the ground. The girls shrieked but Moose didn't seem to notice as he lowered his shoulder and blindsided Bear. A table shattered as their combined weight thundered onto its surface. Chairs flew in every direction as they continued to slide across the floor and finally came to rest against a pool table.

Bear had somehow twisted during the intense fall and lay facing Moose with his body jammed against the table. In a quick defensive response, he thrust his thumb at Moose's eye but gouged the upper socket instead. Blinded, Moose reached over the edge of the pool table, found a billiard ball, and slammed it hard into the side of Bear's head. Bear slumped unconscious to the ground.

Georgell looked on in horror as he watched the crushing blow of the billiard ball against Bear's temple. He leapt to his feet, screaming orders as he ran into the bar following the shattered wake of Moose's assault. "Bug, get an ambulance. Chopper, get that kid out of the club! Don't let him wake up!"

Guests were backing away from the scene. Some ran out of the sports bar as quickly as they could, others were too shocked to move, and a few angrily protested the melee. The disheveled girls gathered themselves up from the floor and one screamed when she saw the blood surrounding Moose and Bear.

"Pineapple, Basement! Clear it out," Georgell blared into the radio as he reached the disheveled impact zone.

"Is he okay?" the screaming girl managed to ask as her friend yanked her toward the exit.

"Get out of here!" Georgell barked.

Moose lay with his head buried in Bear's chest. "We've got to get him out of here," Georgell said resting his hand on Moose's shoulder. Moose didn't respond. Georgell grabbed him by the shirt pulled, and yelled, "Moose, we've got to get him out of here! The guardian!"

Finally Moose rolled off Bear and on to his back. His face was a gory mess, a steady stream of blood pouring from the right eye socket. Moose spit blood from his mouth and quietly asked, "Did I kill him?"

Georgell ripped off the dangling bottom half of his tattered shirt and thrust it at Moose then pressed his hand to Bear's neck and felt a strong pulsing beat. "He'll be fine. Hold that on your eye." He then leaned over and hefted Bear's limp body onto his shoulder, lumbered to the emergency exit and pushed through the door. A shrieking alarm wailed but Georgell ignored it and moved as fast as he could to the back lot. His legs were heavy and his breathing laborious as he turned from the sloping sidewalk and into the lot.

A couple of guys leaning against a wall and sharing a cigarette ran over to help Georgell as he staggered around the corner. They pulled Bear from Georgell's back and asked for direction. Georgell pointed at the Range Rover as he shuffled over and opened the door. The men placed Bear's unconscious body on the front seat. "You alright?" one of the men asked, looking at the blood oozing from Georgell's midsection.

"Yeah, thanks for the help," Georgell responded. He fumbled in Bear's pockets, pulled out the car keys and stuffed them into his own pocket. Then he engaged the door locks and slammed the door shut. Seeing his helpers walking reluctantly back to the wall, he thanked them again, sucked in some heavy gulps of oxygen, and sped back toward the club entrance. As Georgell ran up the sidewalk, a group of girls gasped and moved to the side, no doubt disturbed by his frantic bloody appearance.

Red stood on the street looking around—the emergency exit door still blaring its alarm. Georgell quickly directed him to go in and help clear out the basement. He then stepped back in the sports bar, pulled the door tight until he heard the lock engage, then slid his key into the alarm port. The shrieking siren ceased.

Moose was still sitting near the pool table with the blood soaked shirt pressed against his eye. Georgell leaned down and asked how bad it was and in a whisper, Moose informed him that he could see out of his left eye but wasn't sure how bad the damage was to his right. "I'm sorry, I'm so sorry—I didn't know what else to do. I'm sorry . . ."

Georgell touched his shoulder and said, "You did what was necessary. Bear would've done the same to you." Georgell wasn't sure if that was the reassurance Moose wanted to hear but he knew the stakes. More than anything, Georgell was enraged by his own attack, furious that he had been blindsided so easily. Bug's warning ultimately saved him from the dark guardian fate that Bear suffered, but tonight's lesson was a tough one to swallow. Then a sudden realization came over him, "Chopper can see!" he blurted out.

"What?"

"Chopper can see the guardians. He saved my life!"

Moose lowered the bloody tee-shirt and focused on Georgell with his good eye, "What?"

"Come on," Georgell said and pulled Moose to his feet. As they slowly walked through the club searching for stragglers, Georgell voiced the details of Chopper's intervention. "The guardian stabbed him. I saw the dagger cut right through his arm!"

Terrance came around the corner as Moose and Georgell entered the foyer. "What the . . ."

"We're fine," Georgell said and then asked "Is the ambulance here?"

Terrance nodded and pointed to the front. "Three, oh and six cruisers. This doesn't look good, y'know!"

"Maybe now I can get the staff I need," Georgell said as he and Moose headed down the steps.

Outside, police were directing traffic and shuffling patrons away from the front of the club. Red, Pineapple and Nemesis talked with an officer as another guided two hand-cuffed men into a cruiser. Georgell wondered what had happened but could not inquire as a couple of EMT's quickly approached and asked if they needed help.

"He got a thumb in his eye," Georgell said to one of the men while nodding at Moose. "I was slashed across the midsection but don't think it's too serious."

Georgell and Moose followed the EMT's to their ambulances. Deciding his shift was over, Georgell engaged his mike, and said, "Pineapple, finish up and help Terrance lock down. Moose, Bear, and I are done for the night." He then pulled the wire from his ear without hearing a response and saw Moose do the same. Bug sidled up to them from the shadows and took the burdensome radios while asking if Bear were alright.

"Yeah," Georgell lied and watched a sigh of relief spill across Bug's face. Then with a gesture of sincerity he said, "Hey, thanks for the warning. You saved me tonight."

Bug nodded and with the placating knowledge that all was well, said, "If this is going to be a standard night I'd like to tender my resignation."

Georgell heard Moose laugh and wanted to do the same but—unable to erase Bear from his thoughts—he just nodded. Moose followed his laughter with a shrieking howl at the moon as he entered the ambulance. Georgell shook his head.

"Wait," Georgell said and waving Bug back over said to the EMT, "Will you excuse us for a minute." The EMT nodded and stepped into the ambulance to retrieve some equipment.

"Seriously Chris, thank you, but you're not done."

Bug looked at Georgell and listened.

"The incident with Moose and Bear never happened. We've got to make sure the whole night gets pinned on that punk, alright," Georgell said pointing at the departing ambulance.

Bug nodded.

"Tell Chopper and Moose before the cops question them. Let me know the story when you've got it."

The EMT returned and beckoned Georgell into the ambulance but Georgell held him back with an outstretched hand until Bug nodded again. Georgell then stepped into the ambulance, secure in the knowledge that Bug would cover the bases.

☼~ 17 ~☼

"Hey Butler, you dying in there?"

Georgell didn't bother opening his eyes or responding. He recognized the burly street voice of Sergeant Bernard Jackson and was pleased to hear it. His wounds had been cleaned and the attending EMT was stitching up the three-inch slash on his mid-section when the cop intruded, and despite the night's trouble Georgell was relieved.

"Looks like Moose is going to be wearing a patch for a few days. Punk missed his eye though, lucky. Hey how did that skinny punk do so much damage? Three strapping boys like you roughed up by a weasel like him? Something don't add up . . ." Jackson looked down at his notepad and after a moment asked, "You with me, Doc?"

Sergeant Jackson had been working the nightshift for over twenty years and knew the club scene in and out. He was a large balding black man with an ear for liars. Jackson knew how to wean the truth from the wildest tale and had become familiar with all the club regulars, owners, and especially the bouncers. Jackson liked Georgell because of his honesty and refusal to allow drugs and prostitution in the club. Georgell in turn respected Jackson for his loyalty to bouncers and dislike of drunks. This mutual admiration grew into a respectable friendship in which both could trust the judgment and action of the other.

"Yeah Barney, I'm listening," Georgell grunted.

"So clear this up. Chopper and Moose are confused. The kid slashed you. Chopper broke the kid's shoulder. Moose picked the boy up and was gouged in the eye. Is that right or did it happen like this; kid slashed you, Chopper broke his shoulder, Moose tripped on the way to help and gouged his eye on a broken chair. Oh and where was Bear during all this?"

Georgell listened to the different stories but had no idea which version Bug had passed on. He wasn't concerned though and, ignoring the query for Bear, answered, "What do you think? Did you notice the huge goose on Moose's head? His memory is a bit fuzzy; give him some time to gather his thoughts."

"Gather his thoughts, right . . ." Jackson said with understanding. "Right," he said again, "and how is your memory of the incident."

"I'm a bit banged up as well, give me a minute," Georgell said as he flashed an okay sign with his left hand. In the distance Georgell recognized the smooth monotone voice of Bug in a conversation and yelled for him to come over. The conversation ended and Bug jogged over to the ambulance and cleared his throat.

"Ah," Georgell sighed with his eyes still closed. "Bug, I mean Chris, has Moose straightened out his story?"

"What do you mean?" Bug asked.

Georgell laughed a bit, noting Bug's concern for the looming officer and said, "Sergeant Jackson, meet Chris Roland, he's our memory for tonight."

Jackson looked at Chris with a serious glare and licked the end of his pencil. "Son, you have something to tell me," he said in a gruff voice.

"Be nice," Georgell shot from the bed, laughing.

Jackson chuckled and then in a friendly voice said, "Spit it out kid. I've got a report to make and Doc needs his memory refreshed."

Bug hesitated, still uncertain of the situation, but after another stern look from the officer, spilled out the details. Jackson listened and scribbled notes on his pad. Then, seeing Georgell sit up in the ambulance, he thanked Bug for his cooperation and waved him off. Jackson helped Georgell out of the ambulance and accompanied him over to the other unit to check on Moose.

"Seriously, what happened? I've got the official report but what's the real deal?"

Georgell wished he could divulge the entire insanity of the guardians but knew this was neither the time nor place for such a discussion and instead gave Jackson as much of the truth as he could, "Bear and Moose had a little confrontation but they worked it out and I think everything will be okay."

"A little confrontation? How's that?" Jackson asked a bit surprised.

"It's a long story, Barney, but they worked it out. I just didn't want any heat to come down on them for the damage in the club. Guys like that fight and things get broken, know-what-I-mean?" Jackson nodded as Georgell continued, "I know this all sounds peculiar but I need you to trust me tonight and let it go. I'll explain it all when we have a little more time."

"Where is Bear?" Jackson questioned.

"He's waiting in his car. He got a nasty knock on the head, though, and I need to go check on him." Georgell stopped, thanked Jackson with a handshake, and then turned to address Moose who had come up beside them.

Concern obvious on his bandaged face, Moose asked, "I know you said he's okay and all but I feel sick and I need to see for myself. Where is he?"

Georgell mused at how, only moments earlier, Moose had been howling unconcerned at the moon and now he was a concerned friend again. *Maybe the bandaging triggered his compassion nerve*, he thought.

"Goodnight Georgell," Jackson interrupted.

Georgell acknowledged Jackson with a nod and knew the conversation was far from over. As Jackson headed toward his cruiser, Georgell moved toward the back lot and motioned for Moose to follow.

"Georgell," a voice beckoned from the street.

Georgell and Moose turned toward the voice and saw Alys jogging across the street with a frantic look in her eye.

"Georgell," she said again. "Bear called me a few minutes ago. He sounds hurt. Where is he?"

A wave of relief came over Georgell as the impact of the words hit him. Bear was okay. He called Alys. "He's in the back," Georgell responded.

Alys bolted passed them. Georgell pulled the car keys from his pocket and yelled, "Wait! Here's the keys!" He tossed them in a low arc as she halted. Alys made no attempt to catch the spiraling keys but swiftly scooped them up from the sidewalk as they skidded to a stop near her foot.

"Don't go anywhere! I'm right behind you."

"Kay," Alys answered. She sprinted down the walk and turned the corner.

Georgell pondered this for a moment and wondered if the platonic relationship of student and study-hall proctor had ended. He then reached out and grabbed Moose with a halting tug. "Hold up. Leave them alone for a minute," he said.

Moose turned, confused and hurt but willing to wait.

The ambulances and cruisers dispersed and the milling crowd waned. Pineapple exited the club with Nemesis, Terrance, Red, and Chopper following behind. Terrance locked the club and approached the bouncers as they all began chatting.

"Check this out!" Chopper said to Moose holding up his arm as a trophy.

Georgell nudged Moose who immediately understood the concern and stepped toward Chopper waving down his arm. "Zip it," he said as they walked a few steps closer to Georgell.

"Yeah, sorry man, I forgot." Then, ignoring his reprimand, Chopper raised his arm again and with animated joy exclaimed, "Check it out!"

A complete series of cauterized ringlets circled his upper forearm. Chopper twisted his arm to emphasize the orbital scar and touched it again with wonder. "Don't even hurt man! I saw the blade go completely through. Man I felt it go through! But now, nothing! It's like I've always had this thing."

Moose smiled and admired the scarring, "Yeah that is something—it's pretty cool!"

"Yeah," Chopper said. "Now I need one on this arm."

"Nah," Moose answered. "Looks better just on the one. It's a statement."

Chopper's eyebrows raised as if Moose had let him in on a grand new idea then he grinned and slowly nodded in agreement.

Georgell raised his hands in mock surrender and walked toward Terrance. "Sorry, dude. I don't know what to tell you? Tweekers get a little crazy and when you ad a weapon to the mix, well, let's just say property is the least of our concern."

"Yeah-yeah," Terrance said. "And . . ."

"And, well, from a financial perspective, the damage in there could have paid for at least three more bouncers."

"Could've used the help," Pineapple agreed.

"Put one at door and I can come for help," Red resolutely spoke as he placed his monstrous hand on Terrance's shoulder.

"Okay, alright! I'll talk with the owners tomorrow. We're definitely meeting our budget requirements. I'm sure we can get a green light for more staff. Just don't crush me!" Terrance said with a chuckle.

Moose returned to Georgell's side as Chopper headed down the street mumbling something about church. "He's pretty excited," Moose said with a gesture toward Chopper.

"That's a good thing, right?" Georgell asked.

Moose lit up and looked quite ridiculous with the bandage on his head and his giant childish grin, "With that guy? Absolutely!"

Georgell and Moose headed to the back lot and found Bear sitting on a curb at the far end of the lot, his eyes closed. Alys sat next to him, stroking his arm with one hand, talking soothingly, and, with her free hand she dabbed a damp cloth at Bear's throbbing wound. As they neared, Georgell could see a massive bruise just above Bear's left ear and knew that his head had to be pounding. He was pleased that Bear wasn't in worse condition and even more pleased that his guardian wasn't visible and waiting for round two.

Alys jumped to her feet when she saw them. "You could have killed him!"

As Moose was about to respond, Bear reached up and roughly pulled Alys back to the curb. Alys turned to Bear with a startled look and found his eyes open and softly begging her to forgive his action. "Sorry, I didn't mean to pull so hard," he said. "Moose did what was necessary. I'm not dead, just throbbing a bit." He then looked up at Moose and with visible concern said, "Your eye?"

Moose shook his head, ignoring his own injury. "Sorry, it was the quickest way."

Bear nodded.

"Wait," Georgell interjected, pointing at his bandaged midsection. "I'm the one with the permanent beauty mark. What about my condolences?"

Bear closed his eyes again and flashed his middle finger at Georgell. Moose and Georgell began to laugh and Bear just shook his head.

"Why is this a joke?" Alys said, still fuming.

Georgell wasn't sure how to take her verbal abuse but found relief as Bear came to the rescue. "Alys don't," he said and pulled her tightly to his side. "You don't understand. Everything's fine. We weren't fighting each other over something simple. I'll explain later." He looked up with appreciation at Moose. "We're friends. He was helping. I'll explain at home."

Moose nodded at Bear. With a telling smile he said, "Friends."

Georgell helped Bear to his feet and guided him to his car.

Alys kept quiet, focused only on Bear as they slowly approached the vehicle. She was obviously fighting back her temper and trying to keep cool.

"You're not driving, are you?" Georgell asked.

"No, Alys will drive. We'll get her car tomorrow. I may stop by your house though, you going to be home?"

"Yeah, I'll be home," Georgell answered.

☼~ **18** ~☼

Georgell could hear Emma talking in the basement when he walked in the house and assumed she was on the phone with Naomi. He picked up the phone in the kitchen and said, "Hi Naomi." The women laughed. "Hey I'm going to bed. Love you."

"Love you too," Naomi mocked.

Georgell smiled and hung up the receiver.

The bedroom door creaked open and Emma entered. She shuffled off her shirt and sweatpants and slipped into bed. "What happened to Moose's eye?"

Georgell squinted at the dull red alarm clock: 4:23 AM. He lay on his side, his back to Emma, and he pretended not to hear the question. She touched the jagged shotgun scarring on his shoulder and felt his knotted muscles. She snuggled closer and began to massage his neck. The tension slowly eased as she worked her hands expertly down his back and up again to his neck.

Georgell loved the sensation of her soft hands. He loved the smooth touch of her legs comfortably hugging his. Her warmth soothed him and excited him at the same time. Her hands magically worked his sore muscles, relieving the stress he had accumulated throughout the evening. He welcomed the peace and silently yearned for the moment to never end.

Georgell's repose came to a sudden, abrupt, halt as Emma quit massaging and bolted upright with a gasp. She reached over Georgell and fumbled to turn on the light.

"What?" Georgell said shutting his eyes against the sudden brightness.

He rolled over to find Emma sitting upright and staring at him. She was pale and looked almost fearful, hands now covered her gaping mouth.

"What?" Georgell asked again.

Emma dropped her hands slightly and said, "Your shoulder." Her hands jumped back to her mouth and with a muffled amazement she repeated her words, "Your shoulder!" She then extended one arm and pointing, said, "There's a scar."

Georgell sat up and reached over his right shoulder searching for the cause of Emma's concern. He felt the smooth circles and immediately recalled the searing pain he had felt when Bug had first warned him of the attack. In the ensuing action of the night Georgell had forgotten the pain and had never thought to check. He expected a bruise or maybe a pulled muscle but never guardian scarring.

"It's true. This insanity is true," Emma whispered, closing her eyes.

Ignoring his desire to find a mirror, Georgell reached out to Emma. Her head was shaking in disbelief as she allowed him to pull her close and then reached around and touched his new scarring.

Emma leaned back and peered into Georgell's eyes. "This is really happening to us, isn't it?"

"Yes it is," he responded. "I'm sorry." Georgell didn't know what else to say.

A smile brightened Emma's lips and she said, "I'm relieved you're not insane, but I never thought, I never . . ."

"I know," Georgell said as Emma's words trailed off. He leaned over and kissed her. He was beyond exhaustion but felt Emma deserved his full report. Over the next forty minutes he told her about the guardian battle and about Chopper's scar and his new ability to see. He told her about Bear and Moose and even about the odd appearance and reaction of Alys. He also removed the bandage from his stomach and displayed the stitching on his physical wound.

Emma was surprisingly quiet and listened attentively without interruption. As Georgell's account came to an end she reached over and turned out the light, then leaned in and gently kissed him. Her lips were soft and enticing. A wave of excitement mummified Georgell's exhaustion and the early hour no longer mattered.

Georgell lay in bed; beads of sweat rolled off his chest and soaked the bandage on his abdomen. The light went out in the bathroom and Emma slid back under the covers. She draped her leg over his, snuggled close and rested her head on his chest. "Uh-oh," she said. "I think we irritated your stitches."

Georgell looked down at his midsection and noticed blood splotches forming on his bandage. He pressed his fingers into Emma's thick hair, massaged her head, and said, "Worth every second." She smiled, closed her eyes and snuggled close. Georgell listened to her steady breathing as she dozed off and danced his fingers like butterflies across her leg. Her beauty mesmerized him. Then, with a jaw-breaking yawn, he collapsed into a deep welcome slumber.

☼~ **19** ~☼

Georgell, Emma, and the kids were huddled together on the sectional couch in the family room when the doorbell rang. "Intruder alert!" A voice bellowed from the entry. Muppet scrambled from her nest on Gina's lap and leapt from the couch. She yipped all the way up the stairs and slid across the linoleum floor of the kitchen to the living room.

Georgell recognized Moose's heavy voice and decided to stay put. A stampede of feet tromped on the upstairs floor as kids barged through the entrance with excitement. "Down here," Georgell yelled.

Wolfy and Gideon heard the foot-riot on the living room floor and raced up the stairs. Chitty Chitty Bang Bang played out its last scene on the television and—as the credits began to roll—Gina too clambered up the stairs. *Perfect timing*, Georgell thought. It was close to noon, close to lunchtime.

Emma's eyes opened amidst the commotion and she smiled, pleased with the length of her nap. She wore a pair of wrinkled pajama shorts and one of Georgell's oversized security shirts. Her hair was pulled back in a haphazard braid but she hadn't bothered with anything else. Georgell had yet to make an effort either; he sat in a pair of old sweats and an undershirt. The boys were still in pajamas but Gina had gotten up early and dressed immaculately as usual.

"Was that Moose?" Emma asked.

"Yeah," Georgell responded and playfully shoved her off the couch. She fell with a yelp and retaliated by tossing a nearby shoe at Georgell's head.

The shafts of sunlight from the window in the door at the top of the stairs disappeared as Moose eclipsed their beaming paths and trotted down the steps. "It's a beautiful day," he said as he entered the family room. "We brought steaks and hot dogs for lunch."

"Great," Emma said as she stood and straightened her disheveled clothing. She then walked behind Moose and, before heading up the stairs, shoved him as hard as she could towards Georgell.

Moose, whose one good eye had not yet adjusted to the darkness, stumbled and fell onto Georgell. An elbow crushed Georgell's midsection and an audible gasp shot from his lips as he felt the pull of stitches. "Get off!" He wheezed.

Moose rolled off the couch and lying on the floor said, "We didn't bring any Coke—we're out. Please tell me you have some?"

"Yeah," Georgell said then referring to Emma added, "Ask Cato where it is."

Moose laughed and lumbered up the steps. As he reached the top he laughed again while heartily repeating, "Ask Cato."

Georgell laughed as well, not because the Pink Panther reference was particularly funny but because Moose kept repeating the phrase. It was also difficult to ignore Moose's unique style of dress without a snicker. He wore tattered cut-off parachute pants that dangled unevenly below his knees, faded flip-flops from the movie Old School, and a blue and yellow striped rugby jersey that complimented the thick white eye patch he sported on his bruised face. *A man after my own heart,* Georgell thought.

It was a gorgeous autumn day. The sun blazed high in the sky and a few scattered clouds offered an occasional break from the heat. The boys chased each other through the house and around the yard with sticks, and anything else they could use as swords, while Gina and Flora, Moose and Naomi's oldest, headed off on a bike ride. Georgell and Moose lounged in flowery lawn chairs with giant jugs of iced Coke, eyeing the sizzling grill with anticipation. Georgell still wore the old sweat pants but had donned the security shirt Emma had been wearing earlier.

"Hey, I think I owe you some tip money from last night," Georgell said. He and Moose had decided to pool their tips and with all the craziness hadn't settled up yet.

"I doubt it," Moose said. "The Greeks set me up pretty good. I probably owe you money."

"Two-eighty."

"Three-forty," Moose said with an air of superiority. He fished some cash out of his pocket and held it out to Georgell.

"Nice," Georgell said.

"Indeed," Emma agreed as she suddenly appeared, snatched the money from Moose, and slipped it into the pocket of her brown capris. Georgell wondered where she had come from and tried to mentally decipher when it was she had managed to take a shower. Her hair was up and she had on a loose yellow blouse that Georgell found tantalizing. He twisted his neck watching her as she scooted back into the kitchen. The screen door banged behind her and Georgell could hear her talking with Naomi in the kitchen.

"Where did she come from?" Moose asked.

"No idea," Georgell said picking up his drink.

A brown Range Rover pulled up behind Moose's banged-up station wagon, and Bear jumped out in time to tackle an unaware Gideon. Seeing the assault, Wolfy ran to Gideon's aid but quickly fell prey to Bear's tickling as well. Alys stepped out of the car and stood over the melee, patiently waiting for Bear to escape.

"Run," Moose half-heartedly warned Bear as he saw his three boys running over to help. Bear looked up and tried to surrender but was unable to stop the onslaught. He lay on the ground and tried to defend himself as the pack of boys attacked him like a swarm of land piranha. Alys stepped back to give the battle some room.

"Stop," Georgell said with no conviction. "Get off, leave him alone, stop, stop, stop . . ." his voice trailed off as he took a long sip of his Coke.

Moose laughed and followed suit, "Enough boys, he surrenders, watch his head." He laughed again.

Bear finally escaped, grabbed Alys by the hand and jogged over to the guys. "Thanks for the help, what happened to the band of brothers?"

"You started it," Georgell chuckled.

Emma and Naomi stepped from the house laughing about some unknown discovery when Emma noticed the gruesome bruising that extended from Bear's ear to his forehead. "Bear!" she said. "That is a lot worse than Georgell described. Are you okay?"

Bear shook off Emma's concern with a wave and said, "It looks worse than it feels." He then nodded at Naomi and said, "I'm fine. No worries." Alys gave him a discrete nudge and he added, "Ladies this is my personal nurse Alys. Alys, this is Emma and Naomi." He then tickled the baby in Naomi's arm and said, " . . . I can't remember your name."

"Marla," Naomi said.

"That's right, little Marla."

Alys seemed uneasy, no doubt from the previous evening's outburst, but she managed a cordial greeting then looked at Moose and hesitantly said, "Sorry I yelled at you last night. You didn't deserve it."

Moose, not expecting such an act, tried to offer a magnanimous bow but couldn't quite accomplish the deed as one of his boys cannon-balled onto his lap.

"Girl, do not apologize to that man!" Naomi said while waving at Moose. "He needs to be yelled at twenty-four seven or his stupid genes surface."

Georgell pointed at Moose and snickered like a little kid. Naomi smacked him in the back of the head and Moose returned the snicker.

To put Alys more at ease, Georgell said, "So Bear, I take it you and the Leprechaun have become . . ." He purposefully left the end hanging and waited for some clarification.

"Alys," Bear said emphatically, "and I have become closer than we were . . . thanks to a little prodding from you."

"What?" Alys asked, shooting Bear a quick glance.

"Yeah, Georgell kind of gave me a shove." Bear said lifting Alys' hand and giving it a sheepish kiss. "I was concerned that our age difference would be an issue but after his urging I decided to take a chance."

Alys smiled at Georgell and said, "I never knew? I guess that will make up for the Leprechaun remark." She then looked over at Emma and said, "I'm sorry we just dropped in. I hope it's not an inconvenience."

"Not at all," Emma replied. "Hungry?"

Bear nodded and Moose jumped up to get more steaks.

"Actually," Emma added. "We were about to make a run to the store for Coke and other necessities—want to go?"

"You'll have to leave Bear here with the other Neanderthals though," Naomi said as she handed Marla to Moose. Moose shoved a boy from his lap and took the baby.

"Thank you," Naomi said and batted her eyes at Moose.

"We're taking your car, Bear," Emma said, winking at Alys.

"There's some money in the ashtray, Alys," Bear said.

As the ladies walked over to the Range Rover, Naomi locked arms with Alys and Emma and said, "It's been so long since I had some good girlfriends."

Emma bumped Naomi with her hip and Naomi laughed as she forwarded the bump to Alys who threw her head back and smiled at Bear.

"You dog!" Georgell exclaimed as the vehicle turned the corner. "How long have you been seeing her?"

Bear grinned and explained that they had been dating since Alys busted Georgell for intruding. He added that the last few weeks had been especially hot and that things were getting serious. He then apologized for not admitting to the relationship earlier. "I wanted to make sure it wasn't just me, y'know?"

Georgell nodded but Moose said, "Well—I hope you don't have any secrets because Naomi is going to use that sista charm of hers and I guarantee she'll know everything about everything by the time they return. As for not being sure—I'm still not sure why that woman has stuck it out with a redneck like me, but I'm not complaining."

Georgell nodded again.

"Anything left in the garage?"

"Yeah, I think so," Georgell said, raising his jug of Coke. "Help yourself."

Bear disappeared into the garage and came out holding an ice cold can of Guinness that Georgell kept for him in the garage refrigerator. Moose chuckled and said, "You've got something for everyone, don't you."

"Yes, I have to bribe people to visit." Then, hearing a deep thumping beat, Georgell laughed and pointed down the street. A long black Cadillac rolled towards them with the trunk propped open, "Speaking of visitors."

The Cadillac rolled to a stop and the tinted driver's side window buzzed down. "I found some street rats," Chopper said over Sugar Hill Gang's, Apache. Gina and Flora jumped from the back seat holding popsicles.

"Want one?" Bear said to Chopper as he held up his beer and backpedaled toward the garage. Chopper didn't respond but Bear grabbed him one anyway and when the big man lumbered out of his car, Bear tossed the Guinness at him.

"Don't mind if I do," Chopper said as he caught the beverage. He then lifted up his left arm and showcased his scar to Bear. "Check this out man."

Bear looked intently as Chopper opened the can and took a swig. "Wow," he said. "Last night?"

"Yeah man, last night. The dude was going to stab Doc in the heart and I took the hit. Blade went right through my arm, man."

Georgell pulled the bicycles from the trunk and closed the lid as Bear continued to admire Chopper's scar. He then pulled a phone from his pocket and informed Emma they would need more supplies.

When the food had been devoured and the clean up completed the adults sat outside talking. The kids had all retired to the basement where they watched Pinocchio and ate brownies smothered in ice cream. In a moment of quiet, Georgell decided it would be a good time for a serious discussion and asked, "As I understand it everyone here is aware of the guardians, is that correct?"

Everyone nodded but looked quizzically at Alys. Bear put his arm around her and said, "We didn't sleep much last night. I told her everything I could remember."

"Good," Georgell replied. "Next question and this is a big one, does everyone believe?"

Chopper raised his left arm, emphasizing his trophy scar, and said, "Are you serious man?"

Moose nodded as did Naomi, gripping her husband's hand.

Bear raised his can of Guinness in emphatic agreement and Alys also nodded but with cautious hesitation.

Emma was standing by the grill and shot Naomi a thankful glance and then addressed the group as she tossed some errant sandals toward the house, "I've been skeptical. You all know that I didn't want to accept this but I've come to realize the fantasy is somehow real. No matter how bizarre it all sounds, I can't fight the reality anymore. I too believe." As she spoke she deftly maneuvered through the group and sat down on the grass in front of Georgell. "Especially after finding Georgell's guardian scar."

Georgell squeezed her shoulders and Naomi gave her a big smile.

"When did you get hit?" Chopper asked.

Georgell explained the circumstance then stood and showed the scar by pulling his shirt up around his head. Seeing a startled reaction from Alys, Georgell let the tee-shirt drop back into place and sat back down. He then said, "Alys I know this is all fresh for you but if there are any questions or concerns we want to help." Everyone agreed and Georgell continued, "We, as a group, need to make some decisions. I don't know what brought you all here today but I'm glad it happened. We can't keep going about this blindly. We need some combined thinking. We need to brainstorm."

"I don't think it's a good idea for me to work anymore," Bear flatly stated.

"I agree," said Moose. "Look at us." He touched the patch on his injured eye. "Chop, I know you're excited about that scar of yours but last night could have been much worse."

Chopper nodded. "I know man. Do you think I slept much last night? This whole thing has me praying more than ever and thinking a lot more about the man upstairs. Man, I even volunteered to take my aunt to church tonight."

"We're all taking this serious," Georgell added. "And I agree. Last night was a wake up call and we don't need anymore unnecessary injuries. But do you agree to come back if we can discover an answer?"

"Of course! But I'm not the same. There is definitely an influence that prods at me and I want that feeling gone! I . . ." Bear said, then looking at Alys continued, " . . . I mean, we, want to do all we can to help. Just let us know what needs to be done."

Alys agreed with a nod.

"Okay, good. So any theories?" Georgell asked.

Naomi nudged Moose, and seeing he was not going to speak, cleared her throat and said, "Glen and I," Chopper let out a huff at the mention of Moose's real name but after a cold glare from Naomi he quieted. "As I was saying, Glen and I think that the speck from last night should be used." The group did not respond and she added, "Like an experiment."

Skeptical, Georgell said, "But his guardian recognizes both Chopper and I. How do we get to him?"

Moose answered, "It doesn't recognize me." He leaned forward in his chair. "Why not tie him down? Trap him, y'know, so he can't move. Maybe we can learn something?"

"Didn't Barney take him?" Bear asked.

"Yeah," Georgell answered, contemplating the idea. "He could get us an address. It wouldn't be hard to find him. But that still puts us in a situation. I mean it's a good idea but we can't keep the kid locked up as we try to figure things out." He paused for a second and seeing Moose and Naomi a bit perturbed he added, "I think it's a solid idea but not one that should be acted on quite yet."

"What about good ones?" Emma asked. "Has anyone besides Moose seen a good guardian?" No one answered. "Listen—it's quite obvious that these things thrive in clubs but they have to be other places too. And if there's bad shouldn't there be good?"

"Opposition," Alys jumped in. "Yes there must be opposition! Good–bad, hot–cold, day–night, there's always opposition."

"Okay so maybe we should try to discover some good ones," Georgell said. "They won't be hanging out at the club but maybe churches or something."

"I'm going later. I'll let you know," Chopper piped in.

"Good," Georgell said, rubbing Emma's shoulder in response to her clever idea. "Maybe by observing some good guardians we can find a way to free Bear and do things better."

Naomi hit Moose on the chest and said, "All this time I've been going to church while you sleep at home. Why didn't we think of that? You're coming next week."

Moose winced and gave Emma a spiteful eye. "Thanks a lot."

Naomi hit him again.

The door opened and Gina came out with the phone, "It's for you, Dad."

"Has anyone been to Club Sanctuary?" Georgell asked with his hand over the receiver.

"Yeah," Alys answered. "Why?"

"Bug's on the phone. He's thinking about going there tonight but doesn't know anything about it," Georgell said.

"It's a Goth club, 18 and older. A lot of Vampire wannabes and black make up. They play a lot of Ministry, Sisters of Mercy, Nine Inch Nails and other heavy stuff. My friends and I used to hang out there a lot. I haven't been for awhile but its okay."

"Snake works the back door," Bear interjected. "Knock three times and give him a twenty." Georgell passed the info to Bug and told him to have a good time.

Naomi pushed herself up from Moose's lap as a cry came from the house. She rubbed her back as she opened the door and headed in.

"That tapestry above Bear's bed . . ." Alys said to Georgell " . . . you asked what it meant."

Georgell nodded and Alys began to explain the meaning. Seeing the blank stares of the others, Georgell raised his hand in a stopping motion and said, "Maybe we should tell the others what we're talking about."

"Right, sorry," Alys haltingly apologized as Naomi wandered back outside with the baby in her arms.

"Bear tell us where you got that thing and describe it for everyone," Georgell said.

Bear agreed and said, "I took a few weeks off after the shooting and found this little Celtic village up on the Washington coast. It was a typical tourist stop but I found this awesome antique store with weapons and kilts and all kinds of stuff. Anyway I found the tapestry in a back room there. I saw it and had to have it. It ate up a good chunk of my savings but I couldn't walk away from the thing."

"A Celtic village?" Moose asked and then looked at Naomi pleadingly.

"Yeah," Bear responded. "You'd like it."

"I want to hear more about the rug." Chopper flashed his teeth.

"I'll let Alys describe it. It's her specialty and right in line with her thesis," Bear stated, nudging his beaming girlfriend.

"Right," she said, and described the tapestry in broad terms.

Georgell listened and tried to remember the piece but wished it were present as a visual aid. He then said, "Okay, so give us the meaning."

Alys took a deep breath and with her hands drew circles in the air. "There's a double ring in the center of the tapestry which signifies power and divinity but it contrasts with the five pointed spikes in the foreground which is a rudimentary peace rune. Wait," she said and pulled a black Sharpie from her pocket. She then grabbed a napkin from the ground and roughly drew the symbol, stood, quickly displayed her model, and passed it around.

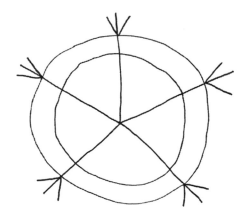

When the sketch made it to Georgell, he remembered seeing the symbol floating on the sea of blood and tried to decipher what it could mean. Alys continued, "I believe that these two symbols in their combined usage mean peace through power. That's my basic assumption anyway." Alys then tried to clarify her statement. "Okay, so there is a sea of blood behind the peace-through-power symbol. The sea represents the result of war and death. The ornate depiction of green vines climbing sculpted wood on the borders has two meanings . . ."

"I'm sorry," Naomi said. "Can you slow down? I'm a visual person and I'm trying to keep up but there is a lot here."

"Not to be rude but is this even relevant to the guardian issue," Emma asked.

"Possibly," Georgell said. "It's not like we have anything else to go on."

"It's relevant," Bear said.

Emma accepted Bear's remark and said to Alys, "Sorry, go on."

"It's okay Emma," Alys said. "But I agree with Bear, it might have some relevance." She then smiled at Naomi and said, "And please feel free to interrupt me anytime, I tend to get wrapped up in my explanations and lose my audience. So back to the border, it has two meanings: the wood signifies the ingenuity of man while the vines portray life and growth. Basically, peace and growth come from force and power." With animated body language she forged on, "People die, blood is shed, but the future is secure as long as righteous humanity acknowledges the need for force through divine sanction."

Georgell grinned as she finished and looked into a number of blank stares. Undaunted she said, "Let's start from the outside and go in. So—humanity grows and prospers as seen by the wood and vines on the border. With this growth comes inevitable war brought on by jealousy, greed, and all the other human frailties. Now—when wars erupt, growth stops, and knowledge only expands in terms of making war a more efficient beast of destruction; this path leads to a sea of blood and the utter end of life."

"Amen," Chopper said. "I can understand that!"

Alys grinned and continued, "So the lesson comes from the symbol. There will always be unrighteous men who seek only for themselves and act on primal urges. These men cannot be ignored or their propensity for war will cause the cycle of death. But if they are dealt with swiftly and with righteous direction, then growth will continue. This cycle is evident in any history book. Maintain peace through power but only with just cause and divine right. That's it." Alys ended her tutorial and Bear grabbed her belt from behind and yanked. She flew back onto his lap and scowled at his brutish behavior.

"Peace through power," Georgell said as he looked at the sketch in his hand. He nodded his head. Moose grunted his approval as well and snatched the napkin.

"Don't forget the divine sanction part," Alys reminded.

"I think we've been given that," Georgell replied.

"Another amen from this guy," Chopper said. "We can see the unrighteous!"

"Or at least the ones that strongly oppose the righteous," Georgell added.

Bear interjected with concern, "Wait a minute. Sure it's a gift, and quite possibly a divine one, but let's not get crazy. I've got a dark guardian and I don't particularly believe I'm all that evil. There has to be more. If there's a way to save me from this beast without violence, I'm all for it."

"You're right, Bear. It's not as cut and dry as I was saying. I do believe this is a divine gift but I also believe we should do what we can to preserve those that are trapped like you. There's a lot for us to learn," Alys said.

"Have you ever found any literature to support this?" Georgell asked Naomi.

Naomi shook her head and replied, "No. I've looked through numerous libraries and done searches on the internet but never found any information on human interaction like we're dealing with; but that's coming from a mother with limited time and resources to do a proper search. Alys is much more capable in that regard. What about that store though?" She then asked with a hopeful chirp.

"I was too caught up with the tapestry to notice anything else, sorry."

"What time is it?" Chopper asked.

"Just after five," Emma replied as she picked up Wolfy who had wandered out.

Chopper tossed his latest can of Guinness toward the trash and missed, "Man I better get; I got some religious recon to do." He stood and stretched his massive arms. "My aunt is expecting me around five-thirty for services so I better get home and change or man she'll hound me for weeks."

"Better find some mouthwash too," Bear reminded Chopper as he watched him pick up his errant shot and dropped it into the garbage. "How many of those did you drink anyway?"

"Man I could down about five more and still handle!"

"Whatever!" Bear laughed.

Chopper ignored the mocking laughter and pointing at Bear, said, "Man, you know I'm coming over tomorrow to take a good look at that rug." He then made his rounds kissing the ladies and hugging the men. He hesitated at Alys but she initiated the motion and kissed him as Naomi had. As he reached Emma, the last in his procession, he snatched Wolfy from her arms and trotted toward his Cadillac. Wolfy whooped with excitement as Chopper said, "You're coming with me, man!"

Georgell watched their hasty escape, calling after, "Make sure he pees before bedtime."

Chopper lifted Wolfy high above him and with an apologetic tone sadly said, "Sorry boy, I'm not good with bedtimes." He gently placed Wolfy on the ground and with a soft smack on the rump, sent him back toward the house. Wolfy turned back and kicked Chopper in the shin for getting his hopes up; he then swiftly ran across the street and jumped back into Emma's arms for safety. Chopper growled at Wolfy but smiled as he slid into his car, engaged the engine, and waved. Apache blared from his speakers as he drove off and everyone could hear his deep voice echoing the chorus, "Jump on it! Jump on it!"

"Should we think about dinner?" Emma asked turning to Naomi.

"Aren't there hot dogs left?" Moose asked.

Emma nodded, and Moose stood to relight the grill.

"How about steaks?" Georgell asked receiving a broad smile from Moose.

"You are crazy! You can't eat that much red meat in one day," Naomi argued.

Ignoring his wife, Moose looked at Bear with eyebrows raised; Bear shook his head and said, "Not for us, Alys has some work to finish. We'd better get going as well." He then stood, gauged the distance to the garbage, tossed, and expertly landed his empty can in the garbage.

☼~ **20** ~☼

A screech of tires echoed from the street followed by two loud blasts from a horn. Georgell was helping Emma clean up the mess in the kitchen and figured Moose and Naomi had forgotten something. Another honk blared from outside and Georgell curiously stepped to the living room. He pulled back the curtains and saw Chopper running toward the front door. The Cadillac was still running and partially parked on the lawn with the driver's door flung open.

Chopper blasted through the front door. "Man, you gotta come to church!"

"What," Emma said stepping in from the kitchen as Muppet slid across the kitchen floor, yipping wildly.

"I don't have time to explain—you were right!" Chopper said, pointing wildly at Emma. "I saw good guardians! There's another service at eight—you gotta come—for real!"

Georgell was stunned by the sudden intrusion and was trying to process Chopper's funeral garb when Emma bolted down the hall and into the bedroom. "C'mon man!" Chopper pleaded with Georgell. "You gotta see this."

From the bedroom, Emma yelled, "Where are your nice shoes?" Georgell let go of the curtain, tried to shake the cobwebs from his head and stared at Chopper as he headed to the bedroom.

"Put these on," Emma said tossing clothes at him as he entered the room.

As Georgell hastily pulled on the slacks and white shirt he realized she was not making an effort to change. "Aren't you coming?"

"What am I going to do with the kids," she said throwing a dark paisley tie at him.

Right, he thought buttoning up the shirt.

"Come on!" Chopper barked from the living room.

The tie loose around his neck and shoes in hand, Georgell followed Chopper to the car and yelped when he stepped on jagged rocks in the street.

"Sorry, I didn't call but I left my phone at home," Chopper said as they rocketed down the quiet street.

Georgell winced, realizing he too did not have a phone. "So what did you see?"

"Man," Chopper began, "I went to church with my aunt Rosa . . . You remember her?"

"Yeah, Chop. I remember her," Georgell said as he recalled all the stories Chopper had shared over the years. Rosa Means had been a middle school teacher for most of her life and though she was unable to have children of her own, she played an integral role in the raising of Chopper and his sisters. When Chopper's father received a promotion from the railroad and relocated the family to Seattle; Chopper was allowed to stay with Rosa and finish his senior year in High School. Georgell knew Chopper and Rosa were extremely close and remembered how Chopper had almost moved back into Rosa's house after his uncle died. "Where is she?"

"I took her home. Man, listen, I saw two good guardians. They were protecting an old man, Samuel Walker. I think they were his daughters because Rosa mentioned they had died at college in a car accident. They were something though . . ."

"Could she see them?" Georgell asked confused.

"No, man, I asked about the guy 'cause he was with a bunch of kids, oh and he's nearly blind. She said his daughters died like twenty years ago, they were twins, and instead of getting angry and remorseful the dude became more faithful and started a home for troubled teens. I guess his wife died a few years ago and he's been going blind ever since—sure didn't act blind though."

Chopper stepped hard on the gas and the Cadillac raced through a light as it turned red. Looking in his rearview mirror, Chopper said, "Rosa said he has a gift and somehow turns the hearts of troubled teens back to the Lord."

Chopper started to laugh and Georgell, having cinched up his tie, smacked him on the arm. "What?"

"It's just funny, man, if Rosa could see what I saw she would understand how his gift works. The man looked like he was sleeping through the whole meeting. His head was bowed, eyes closed, or maybe he was praying; anyway his daughters were both there, hovering above the old man. One watched the kids on his left and the other watched the ones on the right." Chopper said, pointing with his hands as if visualizing the scene.

"Every time one of the kids would start acting up the girls would somehow tell the man and he would lean over and squeeze the kid's knee or shoulder or something, and that was it, the kid would shape right up."

"They were nice looking too," Chopper continued "both had on white gowns, they were young and fit—and had thick gold armbands. Man, I thought they were glowing, kinda looked like it anyway."

Georgell listened, excited by the story and glad Chopper had come and got him.

"The preacher was giving a sermon on showing gratitude for the talents and gifts the Lord has given us; thought that was funny too."

Georgell grinned, happy to see his friend so animated.

"After the sermon, we all stood to sing a hymn and the old dude had a voice that I could almost feel, man," Chopper said dragging out the thought, "It was deep and strong—and he sang without a book—he probably knows all the hymns by heart. The kids were all singing too; even the guardians seemed to be involved? It sounded good; I closed my eyes and let the feeling soak in, then, man, then . . . well, I opened my eyes and the girls, the guardians they were staring at me and smiling. They bowed at me—it was awesome! That's why I came to get you, man, I can't describe it and I hope there are some at this next sermon."

"I hope so too," Georgell said.

They were late so Chopper pulled in front of the old brick chapel and let Georgell out while he went to find parking. Georgell walked to the entrance and stopped with his hand clasped on the door handle. Inside he heard the congregation singing a reverent hymn. His stomach fluttered and he paused for a moment. He wanted to clear his mind, to focus and remember his gift; he wanted to see the good side. After a few deep breaths, and an opportune lull in the hymn, Georgell pulled open the door and entered.

The warm glow of the interior lights cast a halo over the congregation. The organ hummed its melodious hymn lifting the spirits of the gathered souls. Georgell was amazed at the startling difference between this place and the club. He felt a warm sensation as he looked over the standing congregation as they lifted their united voice to God. These people came to this place willingly, not to drown their sorrows in booze and mortal addictions but to bask in faith and pray for a better future. They came to strengthen their spirits in a combined celebration of spiritual hope.

There was an empty pew near the back and Georgell moved over to the row and sat as the hymn ended. A queasy feeling danced like butterflies in his stomach. It was the same feeling he thrived on as a bouncer going to work in the darkness of nightclubs only now he embraced the nervous anticipation in a place of worship.

Slowly looking through the vast audience, Georgell's heart leapt as he spotted a guardian. The man hovered above the crowd with his arms folded. He wore no shirt and his defined torso seemed to glow in the soft lighting of the chapel. The guardian was middle-aged with close-cropped hair and a stubbly beard. He wore grubby jeans secured by a heavy belt with an odd black buckle in front.

Georgell stood and let Chopper slide into the pew passed him. Chopper was breathing heavy from his run and hadn't noticed the guardian so Georgell nudged him and pointed at the intently focused man. Georgell followed the guardian's gaze to the front of the chapel where, sitting in a wheelchair with a microphone in his hand, a well-dressed young man was speaking to the audience. He spoke of overcoming trials in life and working toward personal perfection. He talked about his accident, a result of drug abuse and alcoholism. Tears welled up in the speaker's eyes as he described the heavenly intervention that saved his life. How he believed an angel had pulled him from the burning car and carried him away from the accident moments before the car exploded.

Georgell listened and had no doubt that the young man was telling the truth. Above him a bearded guardian stood with his right hand touching the young man's head. The guardian wore a white suit and tie and his demeanor was soft and comforting to look upon; but more than that the sight of the man seemed to radiate power and strength. Georgell elbowed Chopper and looked over to see a gaping, golden smile and eyes wide as pancakes, as he too absorbed the scene.

As the boy concluded his testimony, the bearded guardian raised his eyes to the back of the chapel, lifted his hand from the young man's head, and pointed at Georgell and Chopper. The grubby guardian turned his hardened gaze to the men as well.

Chopper touched is heart and respectfully nodded. Georgell, witnessing the action and wondering where he had learned the salutation, did the same. Both guardians smiled and returned the gesture. Georgell was exhilarated by their display. He felt connected to a power that he could not describe and yet felt its potency coursing through his veins. *Chopper was right*, he thought and couldn't wait to tell Emma and the others.

Near the end of the service, Georgell leaned over to Chopper and whispered, "There's a ten o'clock Presbyterian service in the avenues. Want to go?"

Chopper turned and glared at Georgell sarcastically. *That's a yes*, Georgell mused. They were both addicted to the recognition of good guardians and couldn't wait to find more.

After a quick dash to the avenues, Chopper and Georgell ran up the street after parking the car. An elderly gentleman held open the door and welcomed them as they entered the chapel hall. Georgell returned the greeting and smiled as he noticed the clock on the foyer: 9:57. They entered the chapel and found seats a few rows from the back. As they sat, Georgell did a quick survey and found it interesting that although the congregation was half the size it seemed similar to the one they had recently left. *Switch the buildings and preachers and the people are the same*, he thought. The same familiar sensation permeated from this group as it did from the other—a people united in divine praise.

An organ was playing near the front as people trickled in from the back and side entrances to fill the few remaining seats. Georgell immediately noticed a short pudgy guardian with bottle cap glasses and thick bearlike hands hovering next to the side entrance. A pleasant looking usher played host to the guardian while directing people to vacant seats.

Georgell continued his survey and found another guardian at the back entrance above the elderly gentleman that had welcomed them to the service. *How did I miss him*, he thought then figured his haste must have clouded the vision. The guardian had long gray hair and a thick gray beard, both seemed curiously wet. The man wore heavy rubber boots and a long yellow fisherman's slicker.

During the opening hymn, Georgell scanned the remaining audience and found no other guardians; he did however notice a degree of reverence in the congregation and quickly surmised it was due to the lack of children attending the late service. The quiet was peaceful and Georgell thought for a moment about how comforting it was that appearance was no indication of soul. The grubby guardian from the previous church lifted his spirits in the same manner as the two in this chapel. All were good and Georgell knew this to be true without question, despite their different features, dress, or heritage. The only obvious exception was the bearded guardian in the white suit from the previous service. He radiated a power that Georgell had physically felt and watching how he comforted his speck and directed the other guardian, Georgell assumed the man had a higher calling or rank but had no idea how such things worked.

A few minutes into the service Georgell noticed a boy seated on the right of Chopper holding a folded piece of paper in his hand. Chopper accepted the note and while unfolding it looked at the boy then to his right where the boy's mother sat attentively listening to the sermon. Georgell leaned into Chopper and noticed the attractive script written in dark red crayon as Chopper flattened out the paper:

James,

Do you remember me? We went to school together. I know it has been 18 years but I was hoping you might recognize me. This is my 5-year old, Daniel, my pride and joy! Anyway, maybe we can talk after the service?

Chandra Wilkins

Georgell felt like a teenager sneaking a peak at something intimate and looked away as Chopper no doubt reread the note. Chandra had on a burgundy skirt and a form fitting white blouse, her smooth dark legs extended to her shoeless feet. A pair of brown suede shoes lay on the ground next to her black purse. Daniel sat quietly between Chopper and Chandra and colored in a Batman coloring book while his mom held a variety of crayons in her open palm.

For a time Georgell lost focus, finding captivation in Daniel's concentrated coloring. The scene reminded him of his own children, watching them color and draw in their nice Sunday clothes, playing hangman with Gina when he should be listening to the speaker. He hadn't been to church in a long time and thought it would be nice to start attending again, as a family.

Minutes passed and finally—when the congregation began to lift its collective voice in a rousing hymn—Georgell recalled the purpose of his attendance and looked again for the guardians. Both specs were now at the side entrance singing and watching the chorister while the guardians methodically scanned the crowd.

Suddenly Georgell felt a shift in the air as a sudden sensation of cold swept over him like a blast of winter from an open window. There was a new presence in the chapel and Georgell knew it was bad. Both guardians turned to the back entrance and their expressions proved what he had guessed. Slowly Georgell turned to the rear and saw a massive figure hovering above a teenage girl. The guardian was a disheveled mess of dark matted hair, grease, and dirt. He carried a heavy ax in his powerful grip and his blackened eyes darted about the room as he became more and more enraged by his surroundings. The girl had a visible scowl on her face but walked dutifully toward a bench where her parents sat motioning to her.

Georgell couldn't believe the physical chill the grim lumberjack exuded as he walked up the aisle toward his bench. He saw Chopper reflexively reach around Chandra and Daniel in a protective manner that earned a flash of surprise from Chandra. Georgell ribbed Chopper in an attempt to pull his gaze from the guardian and the big man nearly jumped out of his shoes. Regaining his composure, Chopper shot Georgell an angry look. Georgell shook his head and motioned with his hands to take it easy as the speck and guardian passed. The girl continued up the aisle and finally shuffled into a middle row where she reluctantly found a seat between her parents.

The guardian, now stationary above the girl and positioning himself in a fighter's stance, turned and directed a menacing glance at Chopper and then back at his ethereal enemies. Georgell groaned in disgust as he realized Chopper had stared too long then looked away to find the ushers. Both men were looking at the girl and reverently walking to the rear of the chapel. Georgell wondered if they could see the intruder or if they were being guided by silent prompts from their guardians. They walked with their arms folded and never turned their gaze from the girl. The guardians pulled swords from unseen sheaths and began to spin and parry the weapons as they eyed there gnashing foe and prepared for battle.

Georgell leaned into Chopper and whispered, "Get out of here. You've been recognized!" Chopper shook his head and Georgell ribbed him again.

Chopper turned to Georgell and with a serious gaze mouthed, "No!"

Georgell looked at the time: 10:50. *What can I do*, he thought. *I can't take her out. Not here!* His mind raced and he could think of no other alternative but departure. He peered again at the dark guardian and his menacing smirk. The guardian gripped his ax with both hands and made a slicing motion directed at Chopper. Georgell also noticed the gaze of the teenage girl; her bloodshot eyes, framed in black, were glaring at Chopper as well. *This is not going to be pretty*, he thought, and a little too loudly said, "Let's get out of here!"

Chopper glared at him as did Chandra and a few other people that sat nearby. Georgell ignored the looks and, grabbing Chopper's arm; readied himself to leave with one last glance at the ushers. The guardians stopped their flexing and wrenched their eyes from their enemy to look reassuringly at Georgell, as if they had known of his presence the entire evening. The longshoreman above the elderly man motioned with a steadying hand for Georgell to stay then gave a slight bow. The pudgy guardian gave a reassuring nod and then he too gave a slight bow. Georgell felt sweat bead on his forehead as he tried to steady himself. Chopper nodded at the guardians and despite the sinking feeling that gathered in his gut, Georgell released his grip on Chopper's arm and nodded to the guardian's as well. They would stay but he had no idea what role they would play and silently cursed Chopper for allowing the dark guardian to recognize him.

"Are you okay?" a pleasant voice asked and Georgell opened his eyes to see Chandra addressing Chopper.

Chopper mustered a wild-eyed nod that seemed to unnerve Chandra and she pulled Daniel up to her lap. Georgell looked around and marveled at the surreal scene; here in a church, a place of righteous gathering and worship, a battle would soon commence. Unseen beings would clash sword to ax and presumably fight to the death. But amidst the danger a beautiful woman, unaware of the coming fray, worried about the well-being of someone she barely knew.

"I'm fine," Chopper managed to say.

Really, Georgell thought.

The service ended and the crowd began to rise from their seats. Georgell didn't move. His eyes were locked on the guardian-haunted girl as she continued to glare at Chopper. Her parents were speaking to her but she heard nothing. Her guardian flexed his filthy chest and bore his teeth in a monstrous growl. Chopper stood and Georgell wanted to pull him back down to the bench but an unseen force prompted him to do nothing.

"James, you okay? You look angry," Chandra said looking at Chopper with genuine concern. Chopper completely ignored her query. "What are you looking at?" she asked, trying to follow his gaze.

"Um," Georgell stood and stammered to say something reassuring about his friend but Chandra ignored him, lifted Daniel to her hip, and angrily pushed her way out of the pew.

Chopper didn't notice and Georgell felt bad but returned his gaze to the girl. Somehow she had wrenched away from her mother's reach and shoved her way aggressively toward Chopper as her guardian raised the axe above his head. Chopper took a step toward the rushing girl and Georgell grabbed him by the belt and wrenched him back to the pew.

The guardian's axe hurtled toward Chopper, but two swords suddenly blocked its descent and pushed it back toward its owner.

The grizzly guardian fell back and landed hard on the unaware crowd below him. He rolled and stood again. He was no longer above his speck but hunched in a defensive stance over the exiting crowd, waiting for an attack. The good guardians had left their specks as well and circled the menace. The longshoreman lunged at the beastly man but his sword ricocheted violently as the axe repelled its force. Taking advantage of the defensive exertion, the pudgy guardian stepped close to the lumberjack, and in a fluid motion, thrust his sword deep into the unprotected abdomen of his foe. The axe fell from the dark guardian's grip and vanished as a look of surprise shot from his gritty eyes. The longshoreman's slicker billowed with a wave of yellow as he recovered his footing and spun around to cleanly sever the mangy lumberjack's head. The menace vanished.

The adolescent girl, freed from her dark captor, stumbled and landed with a thud in Chopper's surprised arms. He quickly stood and helped her regain her feet. Her eyes were no longer glazed over with hatred but seemed to have an apologetic but dazed glow.

"Sorry," she said trying to compose herself as she looked at Chopper.

"No problem," he said.

"Missy, are you alright?" the girl's mother said with concern as she frantically reached for her.

"I'm fine mom. I just tripped." The girl looked at Chopper with a rewarding grin that seemed laced with confusion. Chopper nodded as her mother softened her gaze and thanked him for his kindness.

Lady, you have no idea, Georgell thought as Missy and her thankful parents exited the chapel. "Wow!" Georgell said slapping Chopper on the back. He then looked up at the guardians who had rejoined their specks, and despite the hectic event, he curiously wondered where their swords were hidden. They bowed, first at Chopper then at Georgell, as their mortal hosts shook hands and thanked departing members for their attendance.

After reliving the event with Coke's and donuts from a nearby convenience store, Chopper dropped Georgell off at home. "She was definitely interested. Too bad you were acting completely stoned out of your mind."

"Man, I know—she was hot!" he shook his head disgustedly. "And I remember her from high school, man. She was on the track team. Tall, skinny, big glasses, what . . ."

"That was then my friend," Georgell said exiting the vehicle.

"Man, I know, I know!"

"Later, I've got to tell Emma what happened,"

"I know, I know," Chopper continued saying as he drove away.

☼~ **21** ~☼

"Georgell, its Sergeant Jackson."

"Barney? What time is it?"

"Almost three—I'm sending a car to pick you up."

Georgell sat up in the bed, startling Emma. "Why?"

"Listen, I can't explain now I just need your help."

"Okay, I'll be out front," Georgell said and hung up the phone.

Emma sat up as Georgell rolled out of bed and slipped into some sweats. "Barney's sending a car to pick me up. He needs my help with something—didn't say what."

Georgell went into the bathroom and turned on the faucet. "Is everything okay?" Georgell heard Emma say over the sound of running water.

Georgell splashed water on his face and head then pulled water through his goatee, straightening the kinks. "I don't know," he answered, toweling off. "I'll call as soon as I can." He walked from the bathroom and over to his dresser where he found a tattered tee-shirt and a black sweatshirt with the faded word STAFF barely visible on the back. He pulled both on and stretched his arms to the ceiling then down to the ground. Blue and red lights flashed through the curtains and Georgell grabbed some socks and running shoes. There was a knock at the front door. Georgell rolled his eyes as Muppet began yipping from Gina's room. "I'll call," he said again, and kissed Emma reassuringly. As he left the bedroom he snatched Emma's cell phone off the dresser and slipped it into his sweats.

The officer knew nothing of the situation, only the address where they would rendezvous with Jackson. *This is the second time tonight that I'm putting shoes on in a car*, Georgell mused as he donned his socks and shoes and tried to make sense of the situation. He felt completely blind

141

and uncertain about what Jackson was involving him in. *Why me?* He wondered.

The cruiser pulled up to a barrage of flashing lights. Georgell felt uneasy as he stared up at the old church turned nightclub. Jackson strolled over to him and said, "You familiar with this club?"

"Sanctuary," Georgell said.

"That's right," Jackson agreed and put his hand on Georgell's shoulder. "Listen, I know this is awkward but I need your help identifying a body."

Georgell was stunned by the words. *A body*, he thought. *Identify a body?* Jackson started walking toward a group of EMTs but Georgell was immobile. A few seconds passed and Jackson turned, realizing Georgell had not followed. "Please Georgell, just a quick look and I'll get you home."

Georgell felt the cold of the night grip him as he stepped toward Jackson and followed him to the grisly scene. They walked down an alley where a body lay covered in a white sheet. Georgell felt faint but his resolve kept him steady. Blood pooled in various cracks where the body lay and seeped in dark stains through the cover. Georgell stared down as Jackson exposed the face. It felt as though he were peering through the wrong end of a telescope; but still he tried to focus on the bludgeoned victim miles below.

The phone call during the barbecue, Alys' description of the club; the whole conversation exploded into his mind as Georgell recognized the lifeless stare of Bug. He turned and walked away. Jackson followed.

"Chris Roland," Georgell stammered.

"I thought that was the kid," Jackson said. "There's no identification on the body but I knew I recognized him from last night. Sorry I had to bring you down here for this."

Georgell waved off the apology and felt his mind racing for answers. "Any ideas?" He fought back a surge of nausea and placed a steadying hand on a nearby wall.

"Not yet. We've questioned the staff and clubbers that were still hanging around but no one seems to know."

"Where's his girlfriend?" Georgell wondered out loud as his thoughts began to settle.

"Can you describe her?" Jackson asked.

Georgell nodded and Jackson guided him over to a squad car where a short man dangled an unlit cigarette from his mouth. The man's suit jacket seemed two shades lighter then his slacks and though fit, the man was probably many years younger then his weathered face portrayed. "Fitzy, this is Georgell Butler."

"Detective Fitzhumme," the man said in a gravelly voice and thrust out a hand at Georgell.

Georgell shook the man's thick hand and after a brief introduction, explained his association with Bug and their phone conversation from earlier in the evening. He then described Bug's girlfriend and said he was certain they would have been together. The detective summarized Georgell's statement, thanked him for his help and then motioned for Jackson to get him away from the scene.

Thirty minutes ticked away as Georgell waited for Jackson by the cruiser. His head was swimming with questions and possibilities. *This isn't just a mugging,* he thought. *It's too brutal, like a statement or revenge. But what could he have been involved in?* Georgell wondered. He raked his face with his fingers and tried to focus his thoughts when he remembered the cell phone in his pocket and called Emma. She answered the phone on the first ring and listened dumbfounded to the bad news. Georgell began to spit out possible scenarios and motives but nothing seemed plausible. Bug's girlfriend was a good kid; she didn't even like going to clubs. She was a student at the university and seemed a bit prudish to Georgell and the others. She just didn't fit the profile of this nightmare.

"No, it couldn't be Sarah. She's on vacation with her family, remember."

"Oh yeah," Georgell said and felt a pang of guilt for implicating her to the detective. "So who did he come with?"

"Maybe he met someone new. I'm not sure they were exclusive," Emma offered. "Hey didn't you say Bug warned you the other night? About the assault—revenge is a powerful motive."

Georgell thought it over for a moment and decided it was a very good possibility if the kid wasn't locked up. "I'll call you later Em. I think you may have something," Georgell said. But before he could disconnect, Emma's voice caught him.

"Are you okay?" she asked.

Georgell tried to sound upbeat. "It's tough. I'm trying hard to ignore my guilt for bringing Chris back into this—I practically begged him to come back. If this turns out to be premeditated it's going to be hard to swallow."

"Just keep it all in perspective," Emma counseled. "And remember our perspective has broadened immensely. Learn what you can. Let's give Bear a future."

Georgell knew she was right and wondered how she was handling the news so evenly. He felt a need to mourn Bug's death, a need to dwell on the moment but knew moving forward was the right decision. Still, it was difficult. "I love you," Georgell softly said into the receiver.

"I love you too," Emma replied, disconnecting.

Georgell saw an approaching officer and asked where Jackson was. The officer pointed to a group of men in some sort of huddle and Georgell hustled over. They were discussing logistics and cleanup of the crime scene when Georgell interrupted. "Excuse me. Sergeant Jackson, this is a long shot, but the kid from last night—is he still locked up?"

Jackson did not answer immediately. He thought for a moment as the other officers looked perplexed. The detective noticed the intrusion and walked over to the group with the unlit cigarette still clinging to his mouth. "What's going on," he asked.

Georgell looked at Jackson, as did the other officers and finally Jackson answered, "Mr. Butler might have another possible lead." He then went on to explain the altercation from the previous night and how Bug had basically saved Georgell's life.

Fitzhumme listened intently and then asked, "Well? Is he locked up?"

Instead of an answer Jackson promptly directed one of the junior officers to radio dispatch. When the officer returned he was shaking his head. "He's out, released on bail yesterday afternoon. His parents sent down a personal lawyer to expedite his processing."

Fitzhumme looked at Georgell and then at Jackson. "What was the name of the kid?"

"Louis Alder," Jackson replied.

The detective's face seemed to brighten and he elbowed Georgell. Then, as if sharing some insider news, said, "The owner of this club is a Mr. William Alder. Quite a coincidence, huh?" He then shot a serious look at Jackson, pulled the cigarette from his lips, and began barking orders, "I want an APB out on this kid and I want Mr. Alder down at the precinct in twenty minutes. Hop to it, boys, we have our primary."

Revenge, Georgell thought. *Could that be the only reason?* He watched the officers heading toward their specific assignments and pondered the situation further. Then in a moment of clarity, he was hit with a sudden realization that guardians may have been involved. Georgell headed back to the alley. He wanted to examine the body, no matter how gruesome; he had to check for guardian scars.

"Where you going," Jackson asked as he intercepted Georgell.

"I need to see the body again."

"That isn't a good idea. Come on let's get you home."

"No! I need to see the body," Georgell said sidestepping Jackson.

Jackson stepped in front of Georgell again and put his arm out to stop him. "You can't see it."

Georgell stood and eyed Jackson, he wanted to knock his arm down, pass him; he needed to see the body. A rage began to rise in Georgell's mind. He was angry about the whole situation and the weight was bearing down on him. His jaw tightened and his blood boiled.

"Not here, Doc," Jackson said in a calming voice. "Give me some time to get things under control. I'll get you a look at the morgue. Give me some time."

"Is there a problem?"

Georgell and Jackson turned to see Fitzhumme walking towards them and with a gruff look he repeated the query "Is there a problem?"

"I'm sorry," Georgell said to the detective. "I'm a bit shaken up by this whole scene and I wanted to see Chris one more time before I left." The detective was about to speak when Georgell cut him off with a raised hand and continued. "I know that I can't. Sergeant Jackson made that clear. I'm tired, can Jackson take me home?"

The detective pulled a pack of Marlboro's from his suit coat and slipped a fresh cigarette in his mouth. He looked at Jackson, who gave no indication as to his preference, and then spoke up, "Take him home Sergeant. I'll get Freddie to finish up here."

As they pulled away from the crime scene Jackson said, "The body will be sent to the city morgue where an autopsy will be performed. If it gets there before six I can get you in for a look but I can't promise anything. Why do you want to see it anyway?"

"I appreciate the help," Georgell said and then described the circular scarring he was looking for.

Jackson listened but didn't understand. "The wounds wouldn't be scarred over yet," he said confused.

"I know," Georgell said and tried to think of a way to curb Jackson's inquiry. "They would be from before, old wounds."

"Drug related," Jackson asked.

"No!"

"What then?"

Georgell didn't know how to answer and wished he hadn't brought it up. *I should've just waited to see the body*, he thought. "It's a gang thing," Georgell lied. "Can Bear come with me to the morgue?"

"I guess," Jackson answered but not allowing the subject change, added, "I've never heard of a gang brand like that. Are you sure?"

"No I'm not, that's why I want to see the body," Georgell said with an edge in his voice.

"Alright relax," Jackson spouted back. "Why you snapping at me? I'm trying to help!"

"I know, I know," Georgell pressed fingers into his closed eyes forcing flashes of white to dance in his mind. "I'm sorry."

"Listen, I didn't see any scarring but I didn't undress him either. There was nothing like that on his face or hands though."

When they pulled up to the house, Jackson scribbled Georgell's cell number onto a pad of paper and promised to call the minute he could get him in. Georgell asked for the address to the Morgue and said he would be waiting near the building. Jackson thanked him and drove off.

Emma opened the door as Georgell walked toward the house. They embraced on the porch for a moment and then went inside. Georgell explained the situation and Emma listened. He then told her that he had to get Bear and head to the morgue.

"Is that necessary?" she asked.

"I have to see if there's any guardian scarring."

"Okay, but why take Bear."

"Honestly, I would rather take you," he said. "But that isn't possible and I just need some support. Another set of eyes on this, I have one shot, and I don't want to miss anything."

Emma nodded with reluctant acceptance and grabbed Georgell's hands.

He pulled her in for another long embrace and said, "This sucks!"

Georgell changed into some jeans and laced up his boots. He grabbed his Lil' Devil skull cap from the shelf and pulled it over his head with the smiling little red devil facing the front. On his way to the kitchen he snatched a jacket from a hook on the wall, expecting rain. The smell of frying eggs brought on the only smile of the morning and Georgell swept into the kitchen as his stomach growled.

Two egg sandwiches with melted cheddar cheese and ham waited on a plate next to a large glass of orange juice. Emma was frying more eggs and explained that Bear would be hungry as well. Georgell nodded with his mouth full and Emma handed him a paper towel. Georgell wiped the dripping yolk from the corners of his mouth. Emma placed the hot sandwiches in a plastic container and sealed the lid over the top. The container steamed up immediately and Emma slid it across the table toward Georgell.

Georgell stood and guzzled the remainder of his juice. He grabbed the container of sandwiches, kissed Emma, and snatched the keys from a hook next to the door. The door groaned as Georgell pulled it open and stepped out into the gloomy darkness.

The Blazer started with no trouble and Georgell sighed. He then noticed Emma standing in the doorway holding the cell phone and a can of Coke. *I love this woman*, Georgell thought and rolled down the window.

Emma smiled and said, "What would you do without me?"

Georgell took the items with a wink. "That isn't possible. We're one, remember?"

Emma stood in the driveway with her arms folded as Georgell backed out and drove away. Her hair was a mess, her eyes were red and puffy from lack of sleep and the tears she had shed for Bug, a little smudge of yellow yolk rested on her cheek from Georgell's sloppy kiss, and her faded old red robe, the bottom in tatters, clung to her body.

What a vision, Georgell thought, seeing through her dishevelment. She disappeared from his rear view mirror and he moaned. It was 4:33 in the morning and the deep vibe of Tom Shear's voice and brooding Lullaby echoed from the speakers,

> *. . . And if fate should choose to smite you*
> *Stand your ground, never walk away*
> *Please don't ever let the world defeat you*
> *Don't get buried in its decay . . .*

☼～ **22** ～☼

Bear's car was gone and the rusted old Mazda pickup that belonged to Alys was missing as well. Georgell called Bear's apartment but no one answered and to his surprise he found the apartment door locked. He thought about checking the apartment where Alys lived but could not recall the number. *Where could they be?* he wondered, returning to the idling Blazer. Deciding there was no time to search he called Moose instead. The phone rang as Georgell pulled out of the apartment complex and accelerated onto the deserted street.

"Hello," Naomi answered in a groggy voice.

"Naomi, sorry to call so early, can I talk to Moose please. It's an emergency," Georgell apologetically said.

"Are you okay?"

"I'm as fine as can be expected. Bug is dead—he was murdered. I need Moose to go to the morgue with me." Georgell heard a disturbing gasp from Naomi and then a rustling noise as she tried to wake Moose. There was some muffled conversation as Moose stumbled out of bed, then a thump as Naomi handed him the phone.

"What? What's this about Bug?"

Georgell quickly explained the situation and heard Naomi gasp again as she listened on another line. Moose said nothing but Georgell could picture his face. He could almost feel the anger it was no doubt gathering.

"Listen I'll be pulling up in about five minutes and I need you waiting out front. We only have one shot at this so we have to be ready when Barney calls."

Moose said nothing and Naomi finally cut in and said, "He'll be ready, Georgell."

It was 5:17 when Georgell pulled onto Moose's quiet street. Moose stood in front of his house pacing with fists tightly rolled and pumping hard against a defenseless air. He wore a tattered brown jacket that billowed over a Summer Slam tee-shirt and slapped against his camouflage cargo pants. He also wore a pair of unlaced brown boots and a worn black baseball cap with Dewey's Bail Bonds stitched across the front in white. He was seething with anger as he jogged over to the Blazer and opened the door. Georgell hoped the sandwiches Emma made would calm him down a bit; *Either way*, he thought, *I'm glad he's coming.*

The night was wet and the drizzling rain tapped lightly against the windshield with the intermittent sound of wiper blades slashing at the moisture. The only light in the exterior darkness was the surreal vision of Naomi's concerned face in her brightly lit kitchen window, a phone snug against her ear. She was speaking slowly into the receiver as she watched Moose hunker into the blazer. Georgell figured Emma was on the other end and wondered what they were saying. Cold air bit his face and snapped him back to reality as the passenger door slammed shut.

Georgell handed Moose the still-warm container with egg sandwiches and pushed on the gas. Moose accepted the food with a nod and ate as Georgell described the situation with more detail. The drive was easy in the traffic-free morning and despite the humming heater a chill loomed heavy in the vehicle as they drove. The light drizzle gave way to a pelting rain that assaulted the car and surrounding streets. Steam filtered up from the asphalt and seemed to glow in the gloomy light.

The cell phone rang as they pulled into a nearby lot. Jackson spoke quickly, "Doc, you've got about fifteen minutes. I'll have the ambulance garage door open on the north side. Hurry up."

"Copy," Georgell hastily responded, as if heading to a brawl in a nightclub. It was 5:35. He placed the phone on the dashboard, not wanting to take it for fear of unwanted calls, then both Moose and he jumped from the Blazer, slammed the doors, and ran the two blocks to the morgue.

Moose was breathing hard and still chewing the last bit of egg sandwich as they entered the dark garage. The heavy door rolled shut behind them as Jackson's unmistakable voice and a light appeared from an opening near the back of the garage.

"This way guys," Jackson said.

As they approached, Georgell could see a look of concern on Jackson's face and said, "Bear wasn't home and I needed another set of eyes."

"What's wrong with my eyes?" Jackson asked.

Georgell stopped in the entrance and said, "We see things a little differently." Then to avoid further questioning stated, "Aren't we on a time crunch?"

"Right!" Jackson exclaimed. "You've got to make this quick!" He then rapidly led the dripping bouncers down the hall. "The Medical Examiner will be in at six sharp and I think the kid's parents are on the way down to identify the body as well. The on-duty examiner owes me a favor and she's waiting for us; please be brief, neither of us can afford any heat from you guys getting busted."

They hurried down a long white hall with bare walls and dim lighting then followed a rounded corner. At the end of the hall a small mousey looking lady wearing a white physician's coat held open a door and motioned quickly with her hands. "Hurry," she said, voice shrill.

An odd aroma of decay and disinfectant stung the senses as Moose and Georgell entered the spacious, gymnasium-sized room. It was glaringly well lit with two rows of florescent lighting humming overhead and to Georgell's surprise; a warm air flowed through the space, not the expected cold air of death. The wall on the left side of the room had a row of numbered stainless steel doors stacked two high. Behind each door was a sliding shelf that would hold a body until its autopsy or the inevitable delivery to a mortuary. The right wall held numerous shelves and closed cupboards holding various tools, machinery, and tomes of medical knowledge. Computers sat on cluttered desks throughout the room and eight numbered tables covered the remainder of the floor space with rolling trays and chairs next to them. Most of the stainless steel tabletops were empty but a few held the motionless forms of humanity under heavy plastic body covers.

Georgell wondered which of these tables carried the lifeless shell of Bug. The mousey lady, as if reading his mind, stepped to table number three and pulled back the cover with a crinkling whoosh. She then went into a clinical description of the wounds and bruises but Georgell wasn't listening. He ignored the multiple punctures on Bug's chest and neck and paid no regard to the bruising that decorated Bug's stomach, legs, and back. The point of captivation was the guardian scarring that disfigured the lifeless body like a horrific Halloween costume. Patches of circular scarring covered his chest amidst the gruesome punctures. There were marks on his right shoulder and arm, more on his neck and back; even his face displayed a mark near his mouth and two on his left temple. The woman said nothing of these scars. In her mind, the odd scars were not relevant to Bug's death and therefore warranted no discussion.

The warmth that had once blanketed the room gave way to a cold shudder as Georgell felt examining eyes staring at him from every corner. He darted his gaze quickly around the room but saw no one. Cold shivers vibrated through his body and mind as he continued to feel unseen eyes boring into him. *Where are they*, he thought.

Moose stepped closer and grimaced in disgust as the examiner lifted the body to show the bruising on Bug's back. Suddenly, Moose cursed aloud and slammed his closed fist hard to the table. The display of rage startled the doctor and she jerked back, eyes wide and looked at Jackson with concern as Bug's body fell back to the table with a sickening thud.

"You're telling me those marks are some sort of gang branding," Jackson asked pointing at Bug's chest and ignoring Moose's outburst. Georgell didn't respond but stood motionless with his eyes closed and head tilted towards the ceiling. The doctor turned her eyes back to the torso and looked with renewed interest at the scarring.

"What?" Moose growled.

Georgell lifted his hand to calm Moose and, with his eyes still closed, softly said, "In a manner of speaking." Frosty shivers of death raced up his spine and slid like a noose around his neck. Georgell felt a smidgeon of relief as Moose postured against him, back-to-back in a defensive stance. He quieted and Georgell figured he too was feeling the ominous presence of others.

It was silent for a moment then Georgell began to see them. Not with his physical eyes, but in his mind, he could see them staring. They looked out from the numbered shelving units, their features garish, protruding like trophies from the closed doors. Forms loomed over the corpses that lay on examining tables. Georgell felt his breathing stiffen. The light seemed to dim and his whole body went cold. He felt a slight shiver and wasn't sure if the feeling originated from Moose or himself.

With trepidation, Georgell opened his eyes hoping to focus on something concrete, real. He saw Jackson, obviously spooked by Georgell and Moose, looking around. His hand slipped to his gun, he unclipped the cover, and rested his palm on the exposed grip. Then, ever so slightly, he raised the gun and swiveled his back against a nearby cabinet. The examiner was oblivious and looking intently at the guardian scars on Bug's body.

Another shiver touched him and Georgell was certain it came from Moose, their backs still rigid against each other. With laborious effort he tried to slow his breathing then closed his eyes again to aid in the concentrated focus. It was darker than before and Georgell wondered if the lights had been physically turned off. He opened his eyes and saw nothing, then realized his eyes were still closed and confusion began to broaden his sense of doom. The darkness felt complete, his movement slow and rigid in the freezing room. He tried to take comfort in the physical presence of Moose, but could not. All seemed desperately lost; he was suffocating, could not think. *How is this happening? How can I fight?*

A gradual sensation slowly pressed on Georgell's shoulders and with a haunting realization he identified the cause as fingers and hands. The touch was warm and strong and Georgell grew increasingly stressed knowing it wasn't Jackson, who could still be heard shuffling near the bookshelf, or the examiner still mumbling to herself about the guardian scars, nor Moose, who maintained a back-to-back cover with Georgell. The hair-raising sensation moved over his shoulders and up his neck. The unseen hands removed the taut strain from his muscles. His stress began to dissolve, the hands massaging deeper than any physical touch could reach. Tender fingers tapped on his closed eyes and Georgell opened them—focused.

Looming spiritual forms massed before him. Georgell could not only feel their cold gazes but could see their lifeless eyes glaring. They were everywhere, hundreds, thousands, pressing in on him with suffocating force. The scene was overwhelming and beyond any horror Georgell could imagine or hope to survive. But inches from him, eye-level and smiling his sarcastic grin, hovered the spirit of Bug with a radiant glow of hope. Bug rested his hands again on Georgell's shoulders and nodded. He then deftly motioned with his head toward the exit and Georgell distinctly felt a voice penetrate his mind, "I'm okay Doc! Thank you . . . Now go!"

Georgell felt an incredible surge of power course through his body and evaporate the despair that arrested him. He gave an understanding nod to Bug and then with a deep war-like grunt hammered back his elbows and yelled, "MOOSE!"

Moose shuddered from the force of Georgell's blow and weakly turned to face him. Georgell spun as well and grabbed Moose by the collar with both hands. "Come on!" he roared. His eyes seemed to be glazed over and flitting about the room in unfocused awe, "Moose, Let's go!" Moose's eyes quit their frantic dance and his pupils focused strongly on one spot, not on Georgell, above him, then, with animated force his face hardened and color rushed back into his sallow cheeks.

Yes, Georgell thought and swiftly turned toward the exit. Still holding Moose by the collar with his right hand, Georgell focused through the mass of swirling bodies and faces at the doorknob, the goal, and barreled toward the door with his left hand probing for the knob. The men plowed through the curtain of death, through the entry door, rushed down the long hall, the garage, blasted through the exterior door and headlong into the thundering rain. Georgell felt an incredible sense of exuberance as he stopped in the street and looked at Moose.

Jackson was close behind, his gun held in a defensive posture at the closing door. With a thud, he smacked into Moose, did a deflective bounce, a half spin, and dropped to his knees on the wet road, still pointing his weapon at the exit.

Moose stumbled a bit from the collision but recovered as Georgell, still holding tight to the collar of his jacket, helped balance him. Moose looked at him wide-eyed, then at Jackson, then back at Georgell and with a heartfelt tribute to William Wallace, screamed, "FREEEEEDOM!"

Georgell let go of Moose's collar and realized he had bent a few fingernails back when a car honked. Jackson stood; whistled and waved the car passed with an official gesture as he holstered his gun. "Let's get out of the rain."

☼~ **23** ~☼

"Alright, what was going on in there? I felt something . . . I mean my skin was crawling," Jackson said as the three men settled into the cruiser, Jackson in the driver's seat, Moose and Georgell sitting in the back.

"Your skin would've come off if you saw what was in there," Moose said rubbing his face.

"It's hard to explain," Georgell injected. "I'm not sure it would be wise for you to hear it all."

Jackson gave him a stern look and Georgell backtracked, "Okay, do you think after a night's rest you could reason out the feelings you had in that room? I mean do you think you could logically explain what was going on?"

Jackson shook his head, slowly. "No! I can't explain what I felt. Maybe it was instinct or training, but that gut feeling doesn't come unwarranted; especially as sudden as it did. And sure, maybe I would eventually create an explanation in my head, but . . ." he said with emphasis, turning his body to get a better view of both Georgell and Moose, " . . . you turkeys know the cause of my feelings. I don't want to make up a solution, I don't want to forget what I felt, and I don't plan on letting you out of my car until I get some answers." The doors locked and a sinister grin rolled across Jackson's heavy face.

"Quid pro quo," Georgell smiled back.

"Fine," Jackson responded.

"Any progress on the Alder kid?"

"Not yet, but we did scare up some possible hangouts."

Georgell gave Moose a quick glance and then turning back to Jackson asked, "Can you get us some face time when he's caught?"

Jackson shook his head, surrendering. "You're trying to force me into retirement aren't you? Face time is very unlikely. Any of a hundred cops might pick that kid up and then he becomes pigeon food for Fitzy and the prosecutor." Jackson shook his head some more and continued talking, more to himself than to Georgell or Moose. "I know a lot of guys and I can put the word out to call me but the chances are slim at best. Slim at best," his voice trailed off.

"You can try, though, right?"

"I'll try, but you better come clean with me." There was a pause but Georgell knew there was more to come. Jackson was notorious for long pauses between sentences. A bus rolled by and sprayed the windows. Jackson eyed Moose. "What happened in there?"

Moose fidgeted under Jackson's hard stare then spurted, "Did you notice the medical examiner?"

"Yeah," Jackson answered. "Nothing concerned her but your freakish outburst."

"I know. Wasn't that crazy," Moose said almost giddily.

Georgell interrupted, trying to redirect the conversation, "Those scars are a sort of gang brand but the gang isn't one you would outwardly be familiar with."

"Don't be so sure," Jackson challenged.

"We're sure," Moose said, chuckling.

"Let's cut to the meat," Georgell said. "Give me some answers, and I want you to be straight, because this conversation is going to get real fuzzy real quick unless we have some common ground."

"Alright," Jackson said.

"Do you believe in God?"

Jackson nodded.

"Do you believe in Heaven and Hell?"

A call blurted over the radio and Jackson reached over and turned the volume down. "Sure," he said retraining his eyes on Georgell.

"Do you believe in angels and demons?"

Moose chuckled a bit and rubbed his knuckles as Jackson again nodded, "Okay, yeah, I believe in angels and demons."

"How about guardian angels?"

A pause lingered and Jackson's eyes narrowed but he nodded affirmatively.

"You can't see them but you believe they exist. You believe they can direct people and protect them."

"Yes, I do!" Jackson answered emphatically. "Where do you think that gut feeling of danger comes from? I've been protected. I don't think I could do this job if I didn't have some sort of faith in a higher power. I can't see it but I can feel it."

Moose began to seriously laugh to the dismay of both Georgell and Jackson. In the midst of his fit, he said, "I love this part," motioning for Georgell to continue.

Georgell shook his head at Moose then leaned forward in the seat and without flinching said, "Barney, I can see them. Moose can see them. Bear and Chopper can see them. We can see what you feel."

Jackson held Georgell in a silent gaze. Moose composed himself and sat up in the seat. Georgell felt confident that Jackson was hearing him; he hadn't jumped in with another question or found distraction in Moose's laughter. He was listening, mulling the words over in his mind. "There are guardian demons just as sure as guardian angels. That Alder kid has one; both he and his evil guardian tried to kill me because I could see." Georgell didn't stop. He could see the wheels turning in Jackson's mind and wanted to keep the information flowing. "Those brands are scars from the dark guardians. The wound heals instantly. Not one of those scars was on Bug's body before tonight. You know that! You spoke with him yesterday; dark or not, you would have noticed the marks on his face, you know I'm right."

Jackson didn't flinch but Georgell could see the belief coming to his eyes. Georgell turned to Moose, lifting his eyebrows, and both pulled off their soaked shirts.

"I'm always undressing in public for you," Moose grumbled, trying not to distract from the moment.

Jackson pulled a flashlight from his belt and aimed it at the scars each man displayed.

"We call them guardian scars," Georgell said.

"Okay," Jackson said. He pointed at the garage entrance to the morgue. "What about in there?"

"That was insane," Moose said, hitting the back of Jackson's seat. "They were everywhere! Hundreds of them pushing in and trying to squeeze the life out of us!"

"That's right," Georgell said. He shivered. "It was unbelievable. They were looking out at us from the shelves and then they just seemed to multiply by the second. That's what you felt. How could you not? It was the most oppressive feeling I have ever encountered and that was before I actually opened my eyes and saw the horde."

Jackson scratched the back of his neck, as if wiping away a chill, and listened, captivated by every word. He didn't seem to blink or even breathe as Georgell continued, "Bug saved us. His spirit was there and he snapped me out of my stupor and empowered me to get out of there. He smiled at me, and, and," the memory caused him to stutter as he recalled Bug's gratitude, "And he thanked me." *Why did he thank me,* Georgell wondered. The gratitude seemed so out of place and unwarranted yet sincere. "Anyway—he helped us escape!"

"It was intense," Moose added, hitting the back of the seat again. "Let's go back!"

Georgell and Jackson both shot Moose a look.

"It was a joke, relax! There's no way I'm setting foot back in that room, or the building. In fact I think I will just avoid the whole block to be safe."

Georgell smiled and was about to comment when Jackson broke in, "Francine must be desensitized. Doctor Shea, the examiner." Jackson half pointed at the morgue. "She's in the middle of that creep show so much she doesn't even feel it. She must be desensitized. She was pretty much hiding under the table when we bolted out of there though. I should give her a call."

"It was us," Moose blurted, his eyes flaring. "When you can see those buggers it must bring them out! She probably doesn't have that many hanging around in there usually. We opened a door; or more than a door, a guardian grenade went off in there."

Georgell laughed. Moose had a way of finding humor in the bleakest of situations and though an obvious defense mechanism, it was a talent and quite endearing as well.

"Why didn't they attack? If there were that many, and they could in fact see you, why then aren't you riddled with guardian scars and lying dead as well?" There was no immediate response and Jackson didn't appear to solicit one as he fumbled with the heater controls. "Maybe they weren't bad guardians. What if they were just lost souls or something? They weren't directing anyone. No, if they were dark guardians you'd be gone."

No questions, no probable explanations, Jackson seemed to have accepted what he heard as truth and engaged in the conversation as if he had always been a member of the seeing. His acceptance seemed too quick and too easily gained and Georgell wondered what else had occurred in Jackson's life to make acceptance so easy. Despite the ease of his conversion, Georgell knew it was genuine and was pleased to have gained another ally in the strange war.

"You're right," Georgell agreed. "Maybe they weren't trying to kill us. I suppose it's as probable as anything else that they were just drawn to our sight. I can't argue with that but I am certain that we would have died had we stayed; spiritual suffocation or something."

"Yeah, send Chopper and Bear if you want to test that theory," Moose said.

Hours later, the men sat in a Winchell's Donut on State Street, crumbs, Styrofoam cups and crumpled napkins strewn about the table. Moose snored, his head wedged between the table and window. Jackson stirred some creamer into his third cup of coffee while Georgell sipped hot cider.

"Right, so we get this Alder kid and strap him down to a chair for you to interrogate. What then? What do you hope to discover?" Jackson asked.

"Honestly, I don't know. Maybe it will be enough just to see how the guardian reacts. That's really all we have. We're at a complete loss for any other direction," Georgell answered.

"Right," Jackson said again after a long drag of his steaming brew. Georgell winced expecting a reaction but not even a flinch of pain crossed Jackson's brow. "And we are certain that Sanctuary is a haven for dark guardians. I mean that many scars didn't come from one guardian. Alder had accomplices."

"Accomplices with dark guardians," Georgell added.

"Exactly," Jackson continued, "accomplices with dark guardians. Maybe Alder can see as well? Maybe he knows what's going on more than he lets on? That's where the interrogation needs to go. That's where some answers can be gathered. I'll get him Georgell! If I have to call in every favor owed me, I'll get Alder! You'll have your face time."

☼~ 24 ~☼

A noise from the kitchen woke Georgell. He opened his eyes and tried to focus on the clock. It was close to five in the afternoon and he had been sleeping for over two hours. The evening sun seeped into the room through slits in the curtains and cast shafts of light like spears onto the bed and floor. He could smell chocolate chip cookies and drew in a deep breath, devouring the thought of the warm morsels in his aching stomach. Sounds of laughter could be heard out in the yard and Georgell thought maybe he could steal a few cookies before the kids knew of their existence. Muppet rustled beneath the blankets.

"Here Kitty-Kitty," Georgell called to the slumbering Chihuahua.

Muppet pressed her way through the blanket and emerged with a wide yawn. Georgell scratched behind her ears and laughed at the sight of her tiny little body. *How did you get into this family*, he thought. "I was obviously duped," he said in a baby voice as Muppet snuggled up against his scratching hand.

Georgell felt rejuvenated by his slumber and realized he had not dreamt of the shooting. *Maybe*, he thought but dared not hope. A voice echoed from the kitchen, and this time Georgell recognized the fast-speaking voice. It was Alys. He focused his thoughts and listened. Sure enough, Bear and Alys were in the kitchen talking with Emma and it sounded pretty heavy. *She told them about Bug*, Georgell figured. He slid out of bed. Muppet jumped off the bed after him and raced to the door with a yip. *Oh now you hear them*, Georgell thought with a chuckle.

"It just keeps getting deeper, doesn't it?" Bear asked as Georgell entered the kitchen.

Georgell nodded, taking the half-eaten cookie from Bear's hand as he noticed the empty plate on the table.

"There's more in the oven," Emma said with a motherly tone.

Georgell sat at the table and swallowed the cookie. "It sure does, deeper and deeper," he said to Bear. He turned to Emma, "How much have you covered?"

"All about last night," she replied.

"Did you slip in any of the good news?"

Emma gave him a quizzical look. "No then," Georgell presumed with a loving smile. "Well the good news is that Barney is going to help. He believes us and is going to try and get us that Alder kid. Not sure exactly what we will do with him but it's worth a shot."

"That's cool," Bear said with muted enthusiasm.

Georgell filled in the gaps of the previous night, emphasizing his interaction with Bug. Bear listened and ate cookies as Georgell talked and ate just as many. As the evening wore on, their discussion morphed into a strategic staffing plan for the club. They were talking about club coverage when Emma interrupted and informed Georgell he would have to leave for work soon. As Bear and Alys left, Georgell jumped into his pre-work routine, hopeful that Jackson would be successful.

It was a quiet evening and most of the crowd had dispersed after the Monday Night Football game. Moose hung around the sports bar where he kept an eye on a group of boisterous men while watching a documentary on the Road Warriors. Chopper was at the entrance with Red and Pineapple roamed the dance floor. Georgell and Terrance had spent the majority of the evening discussing the new security budget and calling perspective applicants.

Yes, Georgell thought as he hung up the phone. Thinking on his feet he said, "That was Sergeant Jackson." Terrance didn't seem to pay any attention. "Hey I've got a pretty big favor to ask."

Terrance looked up from his stack of applications and said, "Really?"

"Remember that kid from Saturday, the one with the knife?"

"Yeah, the one wanted for Bug's murder," Terrance replied. "Alder, right?"

Georgell was impressed. Terrance never ceased to amaze him; he was a lot more knowledgeable and intelligent then he appeared. *But then who am I to stereotype*, he thought. *I'm a bouncer with a degree in English and a collection of turn-of-the-century literature.* "Yeah, Louis Alder. Anyway, Jackson has him and is bringing him here."

Terrance leaned back in his chair, concern creeping over his face. "Might I inquire as to why?"

"I need to ask him a few questions."

"Again," Terrance said opening his hands. "Why?"

"I just need some answers about Bug and I'm not sure the police can get those answers."

Terrance hunched back over the desk. "Ahhhh, an interrogation no less. Tell me," he said with intense eye contact. "How violent is it going to get, and who's paying for the damages?"

"He'll be cuffed to a chair. Nothing is going to happen."

"Where?"

"I'd like to bring him in through the exit in the sports bar and question him down there. I'd have to clear it out though."

"Come on! We still have forty minutes before closing."

"I'll pay the difference," Georgell offered. "Check the sales for last week, one-thirty to two. I'll match the sales. I need this, T!"

"Alright-alright, do it. But I know nothing. I don't want this to bite me later. I'm staying right here in my office and I better not get called out." Terrance scooped up the pile of applications and again leaned back in his chair.

"Thanks Boss," Georgell said, heading toward the door.

"And I don't expect you to pay, just do your business and get it done before closing time. And please, no sirens!" Terrance added as Georgell left.

"Moose, Pineapple, clear the basement," Georgell barked into his microphone as he headed toward the dance floor. "Chopper, dance. Red, Sergeant Jackson will be pulling up front in his truck, direct him to the side exit." A barrage of acknowledgements echoed back and he knew his crew was on task. Pineapple was coming down from the donkey bar when Georgell exited the office hall. He pulled the door shut and catching Pineapple's gaze, motioned him over.

"Pineapple, I want everyone out! Employees too, I want it empty down there." They walked together toward the slope and Georgell added, "When it's clear I want you to post on the right slope. No one comes down!"

Pineapple looked confused and Georgell said, "No time, I'll explain later."

With a nod, Pineapple hustled down the slope. Chopper entered the dance hall and Georgell waved him over. After a brief rundown of the situation, Georgell told him to cover the left slope. Chopper gave a big grin of excitement and moved into position. Some of the patrons were looking at the bouncer frenzy and seemed a little uneasy but Georgell didn't have time to calm their growing concern. He ran across the dance floor, through the tunnel, and to the front desk where a slightly heavy, dark-haired girl with amazing eyes, sat playing solitaire on the front desk computer.

"Mercy, I need you to cover the front. I'm pulling Red inside," Georgell said, passing the desk and heading down the stairs.

"Lame!" Georgell heard as he hustled down the stairs. Pushing open the exit door, Georgell saw Red talking with Jackson and pointing to the corner. "Wait," he shouted. Red turned and Georgell ran up to address him, "Red, give Jackson your radio and grab another one from the front desk. Mercy will watch the door. Go to the dance floor and watch the left slope. Don't let anyone down. Oh, and send Chopper to the basement."

Red pulled the radio from his pants and handed it to Jackson then headed back into the club as Mercy exited. Georgell looked into the cab of Jackson's truck and saw Alder unconscious between Jackson and a heavily tattooed Hispanic man. Alder wore a cumbersome cast that extended from the pit of his right arm, to his wrist. The arm was bent in a right angle at the elbow and was propped shoulder-level height by a rod that ran from a thick belt around his waist to the underside of his forearm.

"Wow," Georgell said while handing Jackson the radio and staring at Alder's peculiar contraption. He then recalled the urgency of the situation, "Listen, I'll radio when we're ready for you to bring him in. Moose will help. Let me know when you're in position."

Jackson agreed, then acknowledging the other passenger, said, "Once we've got him in place where do you want my friend Santos to go?"

Georgell recognized the man but didn't really know him. He was big and had a reputation for being tough but never really hung out in the bars or circles Georgell was familiar with. He looked at Santos, who returned his gaze with a serious air. "Can you follow directions?" Georgell asked. Santos gave a slight nod. "Look there's no time for a crash course but if Jackson thinks you can help . . ."

"He can," Jackson assured, giving Santos a cold don't-screw-this-up glare.

"Fine, are you familiar with the club?"

Santos shook his head.

"Okay, when you're done helping Jackson in the basement go up the stairs and to your left. Red, the bouncer I just sent in," Georgell pointed at the entrance, "will be at the end of the corridor. Tell him you're covering and send him down. All you have to do is guard that entry. Don't let anyone get by you. If a fight or something happens on the dance floor follow the lead of Pineapple, he will be guarding the other entrance." As he spoke Georgell pulled off his security shirt and tossed it to Santos who nodded his understanding. He also stripped off his radio and while handing it to Jackson asked, "Can you give him the basics?"

Jackson nodded and Georgell turned to enter the club. Mercy blocked his entrance. She stared at Georgell's bare chest and the protruding stitches on his abdomen then gave him a devouring smile as she stepped aside. "Nice," she purred suggestively as he passed.

Rummaging through the front desk, Georgell tried to shake off the unhinging moment he had just shared with Mercy. Despite the urgency of the moment and the pending confrontation with a guardian, one word and a provocative look from a female, not even a particularly attractive one, had distracted him. With a shake of his head, Georgell pressed on and found another shirt and radio in a lower drawer. He quickly pulled on the shirt and attached the radio then headed through the tunnel and back across the dance floor. Red and Pineapple were in place which meant the sports bar had been cleared. Georgell told Red about Santos and explained that he should come downstairs when the new bouncer arrived. He also informed Pineapple of the situation and told him to keep a close eye on the new guy. Both understood and agreed to their tasks.

Moose and Chopper waited in the sports bar and both approached Georgell as he entered.

"Moose," Georgell directed. "Jackson is waiting out there with Alder. His guardian doesn't recognize you so I need you to help secure him. Chopper and I will be waiting up the stairs and we'll come in once you've got him locked down."

Moose nodded and slapped Chopper on the back. Chopper flashed a golden grin and followed Georgell out of sight.

"Radio check," Georgell spoke into his Microphone.

Chopper gave him the thumbs up and Moose loudly said, "Copy," without engaging his radio.

"Ya," returned Red.

"Copy," Pineapple answered.

"Copy, I'm on," said Jackson.

"Ready," Santos responded.

"Bring him in," Georgell said.

Alder was obviously awake as they hauled him in because Georgell could hear his irate screams. It took some time but finally Jackson radioed that they were ready and Moose added, "Eyes on." Alder's guardian was in the house.

Santos came up the stairs and Georgell directed him to the right. As he passed Georgell asked, "What's your name again?"

Santos responded as he continued up the stairs but Georgell wasn't clear on his answer. *Santa*, he thought, *that's a little strange*. He shrugged his shoulders and then tapping Chopper on the back headed down the stairs.

Alder was positioned on a stool on the right side of the bar with his left hand cuffed to a rail. Jackson stood behind him and had a tight grip on the rod that held his cast upright. Moose was pacing and tapping his fists together roughly. The music was off and the cleaning lights had been turned on so the space was well lit. Alder was yelling and struggling to stand but Jackson kept yanking him back to the stool.

The guardian did not lunge or show any sign of aggression as they entered and, to Georgell's surprise, he was not holding his wicked dagger. He seemed completely aware of the situation and simply hovered above Alder with his arms folded and stared with icy contempt.

"Nice to see you again," Chopper sarcastically said to the guardian.

Red came up behind them and asked, "What for me, Doc."

Georgell pointed at Alder and said, "I don't want him to move."

Red moved directly to Alder and motioned Jackson away. Jackson stepped back and looked above Alder curiously. Alder stood and swung a feeble kick at Red with his left foot. Red ignored the kick and pushed him back to his seat. Then with his left hand he reached for the supporting rod, where it connected to the cast, and bracing Alder's chest with his right hand, yanked the bar free of the plaster. Alder screamed as his arm dropped. Red caught the cast, raised it up, and gruffly warned Alder not to move.

Georgell was pleased with the maneuver and again congratulated himself on acquiring Red for his team while silently wondering if pain and interrogation were standard practices Red had learned while serving in the Soviet military.

Jackson nodded with a note of approval at the simple technique and looked again above Alder as Chopper said, "Where's your pretty knife. Big bad dude like you and all you have is a dagger, pitiful, man."

The guardian ignored his screaming speck and stared only at Chopper.

"Man, step on down here. Come on, you don't need that kid. I can see you—you can see me—let's do this!"

Georgell saw Red look at Chopper then at him for further direction and Georgell shook his head and motioned for him to let it go.

Chopper began to circle Alder. "Yeah, that's right, follow me. I see you plottin'—make a move! Bring it Mystic Pizza! Pull out that shavin' stick and bring on the dance!"

Georgell watched the guardian follow Chopper with his eyes. Alder still winced and whined about Red's brutality but didn't seem the least bit concerned about Chopper so Georgell stepped closer and barked, "Alder! Why did you try to kill me Saturday?"

No response.

"Why did you kill my friend last night?"

Still, Alder said nothing.

"Did you do it alone?"

Nothing.

"Or did Daddy help?"

Alder looked up and said, "You've got nothing! No proof, no witnesses, nothing! So what are you going to do, beat me up some more?"

Georgell lost his composure and, forgetting his place, took a few more steps, reaching for Alder's throat. The guardian swiftly pulled his dagger from an unseen sheath and lunged at Georgell but Moose had intervened and yanked Georgell back by his belt.

"You can't touch me," Alder mocked then began a heckling laugh. The laugh turned into a violent scream as Red dropped his injured arm.

"I can," Red said as he lifted Alder's arm back to a comfortable position. He then slapped him on the head.

"So can I!" Moose stepped closer and pressed a thumb hard on a lump above Alder's left temple. Nothing happened, the guardian returned his arms to their once folded state on his chest, looked again to Chopper, who resumed his taunting, and ignored Moose altogether.

Alder winced and spat at Moose. Red dropped the arm again and gave him another slap on the head. Alder screeched in pain.

Chopper piped up, "Sweet move girlfriend. Did you learn that spin from Buffy? Check yourself—I think I heard a rip in your Armani crotch."

Jackson watched the bouncers as their eyes kept darting from Alder to something above him and seemed intent on Chopper's banter as if documenting the specifics and committing them to memory.

Georgell pondered his next move as Chopper continued his verbal assault. He ignored the hovering guardian and tried to focus on Alder. "So you can see him," he said nodding up at the man. "You know he's there, don't you. You do what he wants willingly. You enjoy it, don't you? It's fun!"

"Whatever," Alder said looking away. "You don't know the first thing about my Dad. He's got your number though, all of you; he'll take care of things."

"What are you talking about?" Georgell said.

"What are you talking about?" Alder shot back and screamed as Red dropped his arm again.

"Your Dad? Who's talking about your Dad?" Georgell looked to the other guys and said, "Did I mention William Alder? Anyone hear me say Dad or William, Willy, Will, anything. I wasn't talking about your Dad, you little wenker; but obviously Mr. William Alder has a little more to do with this than we thought."

Alder flipped him off with the hand that protruded from the end of his cast and said, "Screw you! I'm not saying another word."

Red quickly grabbed the extended finger and brutally snapped it sideways with a crack. Alder let out a new and surprised yelp as he stared at the broken finger in shock. Jackson winced at the brutal tactic.

Chopper's taunting turned violent and louder as he raised his right arm and barked, "You gave me this beauty mark and I want another one! Come on, give me another one!" He lifted up his shirt and slapped his chest. "Right here, right here in my heart. Do it! DO IT!!" He stepped closer to Alder and the dagger appeared in the guardian's hand as he motioned for Chopper to keep coming. Chopper obliged, stepping closer with enflamed eyes, his face visibly shaking, and with spit spewing from his mouth, he again screamed, "DO IT!"

Red turned his eyes toward Chopper and with a confused glance back at Georgell, shook his head. Alder began to cower, no longer concerned with his arm or broken finger, he stared with wide-eyed horror at Chopper. Jackson stepped warily toward Chopper but Moose intercepted him first. Chopper tried to shove Moose aside still glaring psychotically at the guardian. Moose deflected Chopper's arm and gave him a hearty shove as Georgell swept his feet from behind. Chopper fell to the ground.

"Stop," Georgell said with a calm poignant glare at the fallen bouncer.

Chopper looked startled, the crazed look gone from his eyes, and leaned up on his arms.

"Get me out of here!" Alder said, face ashen with pain and fear. "He's crazy!"

Chopper shook his head as if shaking away cobwebs and then gave Georgell a nod of acknowledgement.

"Dance, Dance, Dance!" Pineapple's voice echoed in the radio.

Moose bolted toward the stairs. Chopper leapt to his feet and followed. Georgell turned to Jackson and pointing at Alder said, "You got this?"

Jackson nodded.

Red carelessly dropped Alder's arm at Jackson's response and followed Georgell to the stairs. Alder's scream accompanied them as they bounded up two and three steps at a time. When they reached the top Georgell ran right and Red headed left.

The dance floor was a frenzy of action, but to Georgell's relief no guardians were involved in the melee. Near the middle of the dance floor Pineapple had a drunken guy pinned to the ground with his foot and another in a choke. A third was lunging toward him but fell victim to a full on blindside body check from Moose. The guy sprawled limp across the floor. Georgell could see Santos in the middle of the crowd with fists flying and rushed in to help.

From the backside of the melee, Georgell saw Chopper wade in pulling fighters off each other and deflecting fists as he pressed on. An off balance body slammed Georgell from the left. He spun right, canted his left leg slightly up to catch the man's feet, then completing the spin, crushed the falling man with a right elbow to his chest. The man fell like a rock to the ground and Georgell squared off to face whoever had pushed the man towards him. Pineapple smiled and Georgell realized it was the man Pineapple had been choking earlier. Georgell turned back to the fallen man and slammed his boot hard against his chest and up to his neck then looked back to Santos and Chopper.

Chopper had tossed a smaller man out of the fight and was immediately assaulted by another with obvious boxing ability. Georgell was about to head over when Santos stepped in and pushed the boxer back. The boxer lunged with a quick jab that connected with Santos but his next swing flew wildly over his head as Santos ducked then followed with a forceful uppercut that snapped the boxer's head back. Santos then pushed the man hard into Red who was advancing from behind.

Red caught the boxer and locked his huge arms around his midsection. He then lifted the man high above the crowd and fell backwards. Both hit the dance floor hard but the boxer's head bounced off the surface and his body went limp. Red rolled out from under the dead weight and scrambled back to his feet.

Chopper, obviously not bothered by the recent assault, began ushering people out of the club. It was ten minutes early but for any incident of this magnitude closing time was adjusted.

Georgell, still with his foot to the throat of the man below him, surveyed the scene. Pineapple was standing over a guy who desperately tried to get back on his feet. Moose had two guys pinned face first against the back wall. Red was looking down at the unconscious guy he had suplexed to the floor. Chopper was still directing people to the exit and Santos stood in the middle of the dance floor looking right and left, uncertain of what to do next.

"Santa, help Chopper clear the floor," Georgell radioed. He didn't seem to respond so assuming his radio was damaged in the brawl, Georgell caught his eye and motioned for him to help Chopper. Santos understood and began barking orders for people to leave.

The music stopped and the overhead lights flickered on. Most of the patrons had gone and only the brawlers remained. Georgell let up on the man under his foot and the guy immediately began vomiting. Georgell cringed and walked over to Pineapple. "What started all this?"

"They were fighting over the football game. Someone owed someone else money. This guy . . ." he said nodding at the pitiful man barely standing next to him, then pointing at others said, " . . . and his buddy over there by Red, started swinging at the puker you slammed and some other guy. The rest just joined in."

"Raiders and Broncos?"

"Yeah," Pineapple responded with a shrug.

"Moose, let them go," Georgell shouted across the room. He then engaged his microphone and said, "Chopper stay out front. Keep it cool and send Santa back in to escort these other guys out. Jackson, Moose is coming down to help you with Alder. Get him out. I'm done with him!"

"Copy," Jackson responded.

Georgell motioned for Moose to come over, knowing he had lost his earpiece during the brawl. He always had a hard time keeping it in during fights. Georgell directed him to the basement and Moose nodded, heading toward the slope. Santos entered from the swerve and guided the staggering puker and the guys Moose had been holding out of the club. Georgell looked over to Red as a volley of profanities came from the rousing body he was dragging over by the boots.

"Shut up," Red growled and stopped near Georgell.

"We're going to keep you two here while everyone else clears out," Georgell said. "We don't want anymore trouble tonight and I'm sure you guys would rather not end up in a cell. Am I right?"

Both begrudgingly nodded.

"So how did Santa handle the fight?" Georgell asked, addressing Pineapple.

"He can definitely handle," Pineapple responded, then with his foot, pressed the boxer back down as he tried to stand. "He fronted this dude when he saw him knock the other dude out."

The man slapped Pineapple's foot away and stood, staring menacingly at his oppressor. Pineapple grinned and stared back invitingly but the man did nothing. He continued, "Took some pretty good shots but gave some too. It erupted pretty quickly so I didn't see much else after that but he's still standing and that's saying a lot. This dude here . . ." Pineapple smiled wickedly as he gave the boxer another provoking shove, " . . . can fight."

The boxer snarled at Pineapple and mumbled something but made no aggressive movement. Pineapple retained his wicked grin and mockingly said, "I see you've met Red." He slugged Red in the arm. "That was a sweet suplex brother!"

Santos entered the dance floor and Red smiled, pointed at him, and said, "Santa tossed to me. It was perfect setup."

Santos shook his head, raised his hands, and said, "Hey, why do you guys keep calling me Santa? It's Santos, San-Tos."

Georgell's brow furrowed, "Uh, sorry, I wasn't clear on the . . ."

A round of laughter interrupted the apology and Georgell grinned. "Get them out of here," Georgell said, directing Red and Pineapple to the exit. They complied and followed the boxer and his friend out of the club, still laughing.

Georgell stuck his hand out to Santos. "I'm Georgell or Doc," he said pointing to the nametag on Santos' shirt. "You're a little rough around the edges but you've got a job if you want it."

Santos looked down at the nametag and sheepishly accepted Georgell's hand.

After the shake, Georgell reached into his pocket, pulled out the night's tips, and handed the cash to Santos. It was only about sixty dollars but Georgell figured for thirty minutes of work Santos would be grateful. He was.

"Terrance, I'm sending in a new employee. Hook him up," Georgell said into his mike. He directed Santos to the office, and then headed to the basement.

"Any damage out there?" Terrance's voice came back.

"No damage and the club is clear. Relax and take care of my new guy. I'm out," Georgell said, removing his earpiece. He began to descend the stairs but Moose met him halfway.

"He's gone. Jackson said he would call later."

"Albertos?" Georgell winced staring at Moose's swollen and mangled eye.

"Albertos!" Moose emphatically agreed. Then seeing Georgell's stare, he shrugged. "Lost my eye patch in the brawl."

☼~ 25 ~☼

As they sat around their booth; nachos, drinks, burrito platters and rice strewn about the table, Georgell, Moose, and Chopper discussed their thoughts about the evening. It was clear that a guardian was helpless when its speck was immobilized, but it was also clear that getting anywhere near the speck would incite an attack from the guardian. All agreed that the problem still remained; they could not affect the guardian without hurting the speck. It seemed they were no closer to solving Bear's predicament than before.

However, they were pleased to discover, through Chopper's part in the interrogation, that guardians had some sort of influence through eye contact. Alder's guardian used Chopper by slowly turning his taunting into anger and eventually rage. Chopper came at him, where the guardian—were it not for Moose's interference—would have stabbed him, turned him, and had an immediate ally to free his speck.

As Georgell thought about the incident, he couldn't believe how obvious the guardian's ploy had been. Chopper couldn't touch him. Nobody could. While they believed Chopper was cleverly distracting him, the guardian was actually slowly hypnotizing Chopper and pulling him within range. The guardian knew the others were distracted by his speck and used their tactic as his own ace, flipping it around to defeat them.

"You know, when the guardian . . ."

"You mean Mystic Pizza?" Moose interrupted.

"What?"

Moose chuckled. "Mystic Pizza, Alder's guardian, you don't remember Chopper calling him Mystic Pizza?"

Chopper rolled his eyes and Georgell said, "That's right, Mystic Pizza—I like it. Where did that come from Chop?"

"Man, whatever, I was in the moment."

"Mystic Pizza it is then," Georgell snickered. "Anyway, when Mystic Pizza first recognized me at the concert, I couldn't move either. It's like I was frozen, just waiting for him to stick me with his dagger."

"Had some moments like that too," Moose added.

"I wasn't froze, but I know what you mean man. I was walking right into it and man; I can't even tell you why. He had me man. Crazy!"

"So, it's agreed that looking at a guardian, recognized or not, is dangerous."

"Yup!" Moose chugged some more Coke and, with eyebrows raised, Chopper nodded.

"Mystic Pizza." Moose said again.

Chopper whacked him hard with a plastic fork. "In the moment, man!"

Jackson entered the restaurant looking quite haggard. His red checkered flannel shirt was mostly untucked and barely restrained behind his suspenders, the lace from his left mountain boot was dragging behind him untied, and his a eyes were puffy and red with fatigue. He wandered over to the table shaking his head. "Moose, why are you always laughing?"

Moose pointed at Chopper and Jackson simply nodded with understanding. Another round of laughter pierced the small dining area and Jackson squeezed into the booth beside Georgell. "Alder is on his way back to jail. Police picked him up in Pioneer Park."

"Nice," Georgell said. "You know, despite my desire to say otherwise, I really don't think Alder is aware of his guardian. Do you agree?"

"Yes I do," Jackson mumbled, "the kid is too ignorant but I would wager my truck that his sweet old Dad has an inkling."

"Yup!" Moose agreed.

"Any luck bringing him in?" Georgell asked.

"Not yet but the net is spread wide and I'm sure I will be notified."

The men discussed their recent conclusions with Jackson and he agreed but had little else to say. Realizing the man hadn't slept in over thirty hours; Georgell thanked Jackson for all his help and told him to go home. Jackson agreed and promised to call as soon as he had sufficient rest or heard anything about Alder's father.

"And tell me about Santos," Georgell said as Jackson shuffled off.

"You mean Santa," Jackson said with a laugh, exiting the building.

☼~ 26 ~☼

Months passed and the Holidays came and went. Valentine's Day fast approached with a huge event planned at Club Euphoria; flyers and advertisements touted the night as an evening with angels and devils (much to the consternation of Georgell and the others). *Come as an Angel or a Devil*, the ads explained. *Enjoy fire and ice, pyrotechnics and Cupid's arrow. Don't miss your chance at love!*

Georgell studied the flyer in his hand. He had seen it a thousand times but now, sitting at the kitchen table and waiting for Emma to come home, he really got a good look. Two women, a blonde and a brunette, stood on a flaming stone precipice while swirls of ice and snow swarmed around them. The rosy cheeked blonde smiled sheepishly with her arms and hands disappearing behind her back in an innocent pose. She wore a sheer, low-cut, form-fitting white gown with wings that extended from her back to her shoulders and a halo glowing above her head. The brunette had a sinister grin. Her right hand rested provocatively on her hip while her left hand held a coiled bullwhip. She wore a tight red leather corset and skirt with webbed black stockings and arm sleeves that ended above her elbows. Small curved horns rose from her thick mane of hair and an evil little imp hovered nearby with a tiny trident.

Georgell was impressed with the design of the flyer and figured it would definitely bring in a crowd. He thought about the club, the guardians, and the new bouncers. He was pleased that his core group of guys had become such a tight knit group and pleased that the new bouncers were starting to come around as well. Some were a little raw but it allowed Georgell the opportunity to train them correctly. One new guy was too high strung and despite efforts to train him otherwise he still caused more fights then he prevented. Finally, after Nemesis had an altercation with the guy for hitting a friend of hers, Georgell accepted the fact that he had made an error in judgment and fired him.

Even guardian intrusions had become a somewhat expected and controlled routine. Chopper and Moose had honed there skills as a team and could aptly handle most encounters. There had been a few sightings that Georgell was excluded on, and although he had sternly voiced his concern about the matter, he eventually relented and agreed to let Moose and Chopper call when and if they felt it necessary. No other recognition had occurred since the Alder event and the majority of guardian removals had become a discreet endeavor. There had been some pointed questions from other bouncers about curious things they witnessed Moose and Chopper do but Georgell had always been able to cover up any concerns.

Georgell wondered what was taking Emma so long. He had skipped Alberto's and come home early hoping to catch Emma awake but found a babysitter at the house instead. The babysitter explained that Emma was helping a friend but had no other information. Georgell paid the sitter and let her go but was curious who Emma was out with and couldn't sleep until she returned. He wasn't concerned about infidelity but more about whomever it was Emma had to run out and help.

Seeing the cordless phone lying on the table, Georgell picked it up and began scrolling through the received call list. He noticed a few calls from Alys and immediately began to wonder if Bear was in trouble. He felt sick at the thought of Bear allowing his beastly guardian to gain control but figured he would have been informed if that were indeed the case. Still, Georgell was discouraged. Despite all they had learned over the last few months, Bear was no closer to freedom and growing worse by the day. He hoped the Alys calls were innocent but his gut said otherwise.

Lights flashed through the curtains as a vehicle pulled into the driveway. Georgell got up and hastily walked to the door and outside. A cream colored, 1971 Buick Skylark idled in the driveway and the distinct smell of burnt rubber hovered in the chilly air. Emma exited the passenger side of the car. *Why has she been with Flip* he immediately wondered?

Flip leaned out the window. "You missed out man, crazy night!"

Flip Hernandez was a bounty hunter that Jackson had introduced to Georgell a few days after the Alder interrogation. He was an ex-con with the majority of his stocky Hispanic frame covered in prison tattoos. His real name was Raúl but a decision to go straight after eight years of hard time coined him the nickname, "Flip."

Emma walked toward Georgell and he could smell cigarette smoke and alcohol on her clothing. Her blouse was torn and dark stains disrupted the smooth lines that patterned the garment. Emma raised a hand slightly and Georgell understood by her smile and gesture that everything was okay and she didn't want him to ask any questions while Flip was still around. He smiled at Flip, his mind racing with concern. "Looks like it," he said pointing at Emma's clothing. "You two cheating on me again?"

"You know it man," Flip said with a snort. "I'm out! Some of my boys got busted up pretty good. Gotta head back to the scene y'know? Catch up tomorrow?"

"Yeah," Georgell waved as if everything was perfectly normal and watched as Flip drove away. Turning to Emma he said, "What the . . ."

"Not out here," Emma said, shivering with cold, and led Georgell back into the house.

As they entered the kitchen, Emma pulled off her bloodstained blouse and threw it into the garbage. "Look," she said turning to face Georgell. "I don't want you to get all bent out of shape. Especially since everyone is okay."

Georgell lifted his hands in confusion and wanted to speak but Emma wouldn't let him. Standing there in tight jeans and a frayed pink bra that screamed for Georgell's attention, she just kept yapping away. He tried to focus.

" . . . anyway, Bear decided to go to Sanctuary."

"He what," Emma's alluring outfit ejected from his mind, Georgell shook his head and repeated, "What?"

"You heard right. He went to Sanctuary. Alys wouldn't let him go alone so she went and secretly called me as well. I agreed to get some help without calling you guys and the only person I could think of was Flip. He agreed to go and called a bunch of guys too; I wasn't aware of that until it was all over though. It was scary but everything turned out okay."

Georgell couldn't wrap his mind around her words, "What?" He said again. There was no way Bear would be foolish enough to go to Sanctuary—especially alone; but even more ridiculous was the idea that Emma and Alys went along without informing anyone.

"I know it was a bad decision but Alys wanted me to be discreet. Bear was adamant that they do it alone and so I did my best to keep her out of trouble. Besides, you know there is no way you would have let him go and

Alys didn't want a confrontation between you guys. I guess Bear is really struggling with his control and Alys is near her wits end as well."

Georgell slumped into the kitchen chair still dumbfounded by the news.

"I'm sorry Georgell. Listen—let me change and I'll tell you everything." She didn't wait for an answer, just left.

"He's losing it," Emma said as she walked down the hall from the bedroom. "Bear, I mean." She entered the kitchen while tying her battered robe, the stench of cigarette smoke from the club still clinging to her. "He can't stand sitting around while that thing weighs on him y'know. He just wanted to help and for some reason figured a trip to Sanctuary would do the trick. Crazy I know but lately, well, you've seen the apartment: all those candles and that new age music constantly playing to keep him calm. Did you know all his old CD's and movies are out of the apartment?"

Georgell shook his head. He recalled the fight Bear and Alys had a few weeks back; Bear wanted to go to work and Alys, his peaceful thoughts guru, said no. Bear was listening to some thrashing music and simply lost his cool and rushed her. Georgell could picture Alys blasting Bear with pepper spray as he charged. *What a brutal deterrent,* he thought. It was then that they decided to remove the anger provoking CD's and movies but Georgell was unaware that the purge had actually taken place.

"He's desperate Georgell. He wants that thing gone and hates that he can't help find a solution. Alys told me that there are times when he stays right by her and keeps a hand on her the whole day. She says he hardly sleeps and it scares her but she doesn't want to leave him alone."

Bear's desperation was understandable but Georgell still could not fathom his suicidal desire to walk into Sanctuary. Jackson had discovered that Sanctuary was only one of many clubs that William Alder owned. There were Sanctuary type clubs all over the country and internationally as well. All the clubs had a similar theme and seemed ripe for harboring dark guardians. Alder seemed to be a dark guardian Godfather and his clubs quite possibly a gateway of sorts but Georgell had not allowed anyone to test the theory. Bug's death, and the visible guardian scarring on his body, seemed proof enough.

"Georgell?"

"Huh," he said looking up at Emma who stood above him.

"What are you thinking? You've barely said two words."

"I don't understand," he grabbed the knot of her robe and pulled her closer. "I just don't understand why he went—why you went?"

"Try and see it from my perspective; Alys was frantic when she called. I guess they discussed it all morning and she knew it was not worth fighting him over. It took her awhile to convince him to let her go but he finally agreed and they spent the entire day at the spa getting pampered in preparation. At some point she snuck away and called me, told me about the plan, and wanted my advice. I told her I would get help and promised that I wouldn't involve you or the others."

Georgell listened. He wanted to be angry with her but somehow knew she had done the best she could under the circumstance. It was frustrating that she kept things from him but, in certain situations, he had been guilty of doing the same thing.

"I wasn't going to go," Emma said. "But I wanted to be sure Flip understood the situation without knowing the real situation y'know."

"So what happened?"

Emma grabbed a glass from the cupboard and filled it with water from the kitchen tap. She then pulled a chair near Georgell and sat down after taking a long drink from the glass and placing it on the table. "I gave a note to Snake at the back door and he promised to slip it to Alys without Bear noticing. It basically told her that Flip and I were in the club and not to worry y'know. Anyway, we sat on the upper level and I was beginning to think they weren't going to come but sure enough, a little after midnight, they wandered in from the back. Snake was behind them and gave me a thumbs-up so I knew Alys had my note."

"Bear was looking seriously angry and Alys was holding onto him but he didn't seem to notice or even care. All the tables were taken but he scared some guys and they left one pretty quick. It was perfect because they were almost directly below our balcony so Flip and I had a great view."

"I really didn't know what to expect or even look for y'know. I mean I knew Bear was trying his best to stay focused and that he was hoping to learn something about the club or guardians or whatever so I wanted to give him space. I told Flip that when I gave him the go ahead he just needed to get Bear out of the club. So we sat there just watching."

"It didn't take long because a bouncer saw him scare away the guys at the table and he immediately went over to confront him. I saw Alys and the bouncer talking but Bear wasn't saying anything. Then the bouncer put his hand on Bear's shoulder and that was my trigger to send Flip. Bear stood and it looked like Hell was about to erupt but Snake stepped between them and walked the bouncer away. Alys got Bear to sit back down and Flip started coming back up the stairs but I waved him back when Bear stood up again. Alys tried to get him to sit but he totally ignored her and headed toward the dance floor. That's when I went down stairs."

Emma took a long drink from her glass of water and Georgell took a swig as well. "Here's where it all kind of went bonkers. Bear was pushing into the crowd and just stopped and stared above everyone. It was a creepy scene and even the people on the dance floor gave him space. I knew he had to be looking at guardians but no one else did. I told Flip to be prepared and he told me if it got crazy to grab Alys and go to his car."

"I stopped Alys as she tried to go to Bear but almost let her go again when I realized he was just standing there not doing anything; then without warning—like something released him—he threw his jacket to the floor, ripped of his shirt and rushed the bouncer that had talked to him earlier. Flip chased after him and a bunch of guys from all over the bar seemed to get involved when the bouncers stepped in. There were fights everywhere!"

"I didn't see what happened because Alys and I ducked under the stairs and stayed there until we thought it was safe. We finally got out but not before I got knocked over and ripped my blouse on a chair. I'm not sure how I got the blood on me; the chair, floor, I'm not sure—we just got out as fast as we could. Anyway, when we got to the car Bear and Flip were already there."

"That's when I found out that all the guys fighting the bouncers were with Flip. I guess he hired them to distract the bouncers and cause a scene so that he could get Bear out. It worked; Bear was roughed up a bit but was laughing when we got to the car. Flip tazed him! He zapped him and then he and another guy cuffed him and dragged him out the back entrance. Some bouncers chased after them but I guess Snake got in the way and covered their exit."

"As we were getting in the car I heard someone in the parking lot yelling, Flip peeled out before the door was even closed. Guess the bouncers were coming after us!"

Georgell was caught up in the retelling of the event and shared Emma's excitement although he knew it could have been disastrously worse and wished he had been part of it all. Emma took another drink and Georgell asked, "So what did Bear say?"

"He couldn't really discuss it with Flip around. He just said that he lost control when he thought he saw a gun under the bouncer's shirt. Flip seemed to buy the story so we left it at that. He did whisper to me that he saw a lot of guardians though. I didn't here anything else. I figured he would talk to us tomorrow so I didn't press the issue."

"So if you left early, why are you home so late and what do we owe Flip?"

"Oh, yeah, we took Bear to get some stitches from a friend of Flips then went and got some food. Flip wouldn't let me pay him—said he still owes Jackson and not to worry about it. Y'know I haven't seen Bear that happy and animated since before the Momentum shooting. He was his old self and Alys seemed to enjoy every minute of it. I didn't want to end the moment, sorry I didn't call but I figured you and the guys would go out to Albertos and we would get home at the same time.

Georgell wished that he too could have witnessed the old Bear. He often thought of the days back at Momentum when he and Bear roamed the club at top form, before the shooting, before the sight, the guardians, and the stress that he now faced. The stresses of old seemed so insignificant now, pointless. The universe had opened up its secrets just a crack and the distractions of mortality seemed so petty now.

"So how much trouble am I in?"

Georgell smiled at Emma. He was still disappointed that she didn't let him know what was going on and the anxiety of what could have been still lingered in his mind; but ultimately she was safe, they were together, and he was extremely tired, "Let's just go to bed."

☼~ 27 ~☼

The sun hid behind looming clouds and the temperature dipped below thirty. The driveway at the Butler home was lined with cars and the Sunday afternoon gathering was underway with emphasis on the first birthday of Moose and Naomi's youngest. Food had been eagerly consumed, presents opened, and the kids had playfully dispersed around the house while the adults sat in the living room and kitchen recovering. Conversations hummed with intermittent fits of laughter and the occasional scream shot from the boys' room like an audible stab of lightning.

A heavy feeling of frustration pressed at Georgell and though he joked, talked and generally kept himself busy, he couldn't shake his disgust for Bear's reckless decision to act alone. He tried to remain casual during the dinner and birthday celebration but his annoyance was hard to mask. Avoiding Bear had been the only way to keep his frustration in check and yet the longer he waited the more his anger seemed to concentrate on the issue. If it wasn't confronted soon, Georgell knew his irritation would overcome his ability to think rationally.

Where is Jackson! Georgell thought, *we got to get this thing moving before I lose it.* He stood at the kitchen sink blankly staring at the pile of dirty dishes on the counter and realized a distraction had been found. Methodically he began stacking the plates, bowls, and cups in the sink and spun the hot water knob to the on position. The water made a hollow rumbling sound as it streamed from the tap and quickly filled the topmost bowl then spilled over and filled the next. The water cascaded down the remaining bowls and plates and began to pool at the bottom of the sink. Georgell squeezed a drop of yellow dish soap into the water and stared. The water immediately bubbled where the soap had been introduced and the bubbles followed the cascading water down to the rising pool. A soapy scent of lemon pierced Georgell's nostrils.

Despite the distraction, Georgell's thoughts returned to the growing concern. He had no doubt that it was a delicate situation and knew once the conversation started it would have to be handled swiftly. Bear's hair-trigger rage had to be avoided. Losing him over heated words wasn't worth the battle but Georgell had decided, despite the possible risk, Bear had to agree never to act alone again. Bubbles began sneaking over the edge of the sink and Georgell turned off the water.

Bear walked into the kitchen fiddling with a broken toy pistol. Georgell stayed focused on washing dishes as Bear sat on a chair against the far side of the wall. Alys helped Gina cover the remaining lasagna and cake while Flora cleared the table.

Chopper entered the kitchen and snickered at Georgell doing the dishes. He snatched up a piece of garlic bread before Gina could cover the bowl and then, intruding on Bear's tinkering, said, "Check it out man." Beaming with pride, Chopper twirled his arm in front of Bear's face. Bear looked up from his project and marveled at the tattooing that Chopper displayed. Within the circular diameter of each guardian scar sat a peace-through-power symbol etched in black ink on the skin.

"Peace-through-power man," Chopper said. "I finally did it."

Georgell could see the interaction between Bear and Chopper in the small mirror above the sink and, despite his desire not to watch, he couldn't help staring as he briskly scrubbed the plate in his hand far longer then was necessary.

Bear seemed impressed and actually turned Chopper's arm upward to scope the whole job. "You're the last one man. When you going to ink yours?" Chopper asked.

"What?" Bear said with obvious irritation. "Everyone has done this but me? Where? Who?" His tone was sharp, almost accusatory.

"You know man, Rembrandt—at Dragon Tattoo," Chopper answered and then with a little bark of his own added, "Why you getting angry?"

Bear responded with added sarcasm to his escalating voice, "I'm just a little upset that I wasn't told about this little rite of passage. I mean the symbol comes from my wall. The meaning comes from my girlfriend. Why am I the last to hear about it?"

Chopper stepped back.

"Moose had it done two months ago," Georgell said flatly from his place at the kitchen sink. "He showed you. Just after Christmas I had it done and I showed you. Now Chopper has joined in. You're the only one that hasn't shown any interest. You've been here every Sunday, seen our tats and heard us talk about it. This isn't something new."

Bear seemed genuinely surprised and, after a subtle nod from Alys, he dropped his eyes back to the toy in his hands. "Sorry Chop, I . . ." Bear shook his head but didn't look up.

"Man, don't sweat it. You've got a lot on your mind," Chopper said with a warm grin.

"Literally," Alys added dramatically with an exaggerated glance above Bear's head.

"Seriously though," Georgell said. Water and bubbles shot from the bowl in his hand as he spun around to face the others. "Why do you think this is the first time you've acknowledged the tattooing? Where have you been? Are we wasting your time? Do you hear anything that we discuss?"

Bear looked up, his eyebrows strained and lips pursed.

"I've been forcing him to come." Alys interjected red-cheeked.

"Why?" Georgell slid the bowl on the counter and snatched up a nearby hand towel. The bowl banged against the splashguard, came to a stop on the edge of the sink, teetered for a moment, then slid back into the soapy water. Georgell wiped his hands dry and stepped towards Alys.

"He's felt useless," Alys said resting a hand on Bear's shoulder.

Georgell wasn't sure if the gesture was for comfort or restraint but didn't really care either way. Bear looked as if he were going to leap from his chair but somehow remained seated and Georgell stepped closer, daring him to make a move.

Moose shuffled into the kitchen bouncing baby Marla on his arm. He leaned against the doorframe and curiously looked everyone over as Flora and Gina scooted by to escape the pending discussion.

"And last night . . ." Georgell said with obvious annoyance.

Alys leaned a little heavier on Bear.

"I'll talk about it when Jackson gets here. I don't want to repeat myself," Bear said icily.

Georgell nodded briskly and threw the towel on the counter, "Fine!" *Whatever*, he thought as he marched passed Moose towards the living room. He was disappointed in the lack of control he'd displayed and needed to sit down, calm down—breathe some control back into his thoughts.

"What did I miss?" Moose questioned wide-eyed.

As Georgell found a seat in the living room he heard the kitchen door close and Chopper, in his deep baritone, say, "Man, that's a trip."

"What?" came the response from Jackson.

"Timing man, that's all, freak show timing!"

Georgell looked up as Jackson came into view—his head bobbing from side-to-side as he smiled goofily at the baby in Moose's arms. "Marla, Marla, Marla, I've got a present for ya." Marla stared with her big brown eyes as Jackson placed a pink box with a white ribbon on her stomach.

"I don't have much time," Jackson said looking at Moose then Georgell. "Let's get to it so I can skedaddle."

Georgell was utterly relieved at Jackson's suggestion and nodded as Naomi got up from the couch and snatched Marla from Moose. She walked into the kitchen and down the stairs, then, with a motherly tone that easily carried upstairs and into the living room; she pronounced instructions to the children below.

Bear and Alys entered the living room and Georgell felt a shift in the air as if a shroud of anger had followed in behind them. Jackson and Moose snatched some food from the kitchen table then they too found seats in the living room. Chopper pinched some olives from Moose's plate as he flopped onto the living room floor.

Gina hustled into the living room and grabbed the diaper bag that Naomi had left next to the couch. Bear grabbed her as she passed, handed her the toy gun he had fixed, and said, "Give that to Wolfy please."

Gina agreed and took the gun as Wolfy walked into the room, saw the exchange, and screamed, "That's mine!" He then raced across the carpet and tackled her. Baby powder shot out in a poof of smoke from the diaper bag as Gina fell hard to the ground.

Chopper laughed heartily as Emma pulled Wolfy off Gina, scolded him, and sent him away with a whack on the butt. Gina, unfazed by her brother's brutish behavior, stood, gathered the diaper bag, and then, catching up to Wolfy, slyly hit him on the head as Emma turned away.

Chopper continued his hearty laugh and somehow managed to say "Maaaaan," at the same time.

"What?" Emma asked.

Moose began to echo the contagious laughter and, as if discovering the source, he pointed at Chopper and said, "Bronco."

"What!?" Jackson echoed with his mouth full of food.

Chopper nodded at Moose, agreeing that he was correct in his assumption and Moose began laughing a bit harder. Having a shared recollection, Chopper began laughing harder as well. Finally, holding back tears and fits of laughter, Moose tried to explain, "Wolfy—tackling Gina—it reminded us of last night." Gaining control he continued, "There's a new bouncer—Bronco . . ." Chopper erupted with a new fit of laughter. Moose held his composure but grinned widely as he finished the tale. "Anyway, last night there was a call about a girl swiping beer without paying. Chopper was about to intercept her when out of nowhere Bronco busted through the crowd and tackled her like a crazed linebacker. He knocked over a few other guests and demolished a table too."

Jackson started to choke on a roll as he tried to chew and laugh at the same time which instantly caused the ruckus to increase and even Georgell found it hard to suppress a smile, but like Bear, he found a way to distance himself as the rest of the group joined in the fun. As the laughter began to wane, Emma nudged Jackson and asked, "Why were you late?"

The group quieted when Jackson nonchalantly replied, "Oh, there was a huge brawl at Sanctuary last night and I was cleaning up some loose ends."

Georgell saw an immediate regret flash from Emma and he took the moment to jumpstart his inquisition, "Really?"

Jackson looked quizzically at Georgell, who looked at Bear, and then back at Jackson. The quick exchange was enough and Jackson said, "Wait a minute. There was a pretty good description of the instigator and I'm just now making the connection—Bear?"

Bear stood abruptly, addressing Georgell with a growl. "What is your problem?"

Georgell wanted to stand; he wanted to snap back at Bear to make him realize how stupid his decision had been and yet he knew he had to stay cool. Instead of reciprocating with anger he opened his arms to display the audience and slowly said, "Everyone's here."

It was clear that Bear did not appreciate the manipulation but Georgell said nothing more. The silence lingered as Bear fumed. Alys softly said, "Bear . . ."

The plea seemed to calm Bear a bit and with a deep breath and a shake of his head, he returned to his seat. Alys placed a calming hand on his back and slowly rubbed his taught muscles. Finally, with another slight shake of his head, he spoke, "Okay—but I'm not going to apologize for the choice I made. What's done is done."

Emma gently placed her hand on Georgell's arm and he knew she wanted him to leave it alone. He said nothing, just nodded. Bear nodded as well and after another deep breath said, "I went to Sanctuary last night . . ."

As Bear relayed his reasoning, Georgell noticed concern on most of the listening faces but as he turned to Jackson he was surprised to see a growing air of annoyance.

" . . . I wanted to do this alone. I wanted to see again. I wanted to help. Alys was coming no matter what I said to deter her and she somehow roped Emma into the mix as well; but without my knowledge." Bear paused for a moment than softly concluded, "Honestly though, I don't think I would have made it without their help. I'm seriously grateful . . ."

Georgell appreciated the glance of gratitude Bear shot Emma and as he listened his anger began to soften as Bear talked with excitement about seeing guardians again. Georgell remembered the first few times he had seen the guardians and the excitement he had felt. Bear was finally in on the discussion of guardians, he had finally really seen them, and the intensity in his voice was unmistakable.

" . . . It was so surreal—I could feel the influence of my guardian and his strength and power seemed to lift me up and make me feel almost invincible—like I could do anything. There were three other guardians in the club, all above bouncers and each looked at me and nodded then bowed at my guardian. It was absolutely exhilarating!" Bear looked around but only looks of concern were returned.

"Look," Bear said, lowering his voice. "I know that having this guardian is not a good thing but I'm telling you, it was a feeling of power I can't begin to explain and I think it's important that I express the feelings I had so that we can understand its power."

"You're right," Georgell said. "Go on."

Bear nodded, and continued. "So like I was saying, my guardian seemed to have some kind of leadership over the other ones and—it's crazy—but I felt superior too. Anyway, after a few moments another guardian entered the club only this one wasn't like mine or the others—he seemed scared and immediately crouched into a defensive pose above his speck."

"I remember the speck specifically because I had the most overwhelming desire to destroy the kid—more than just kill—I literally wanted to decimate him. He was with a group of other kids and seemed concerned as his friends jumped up and down with excitement. I fed off his concern and it excited me more, I wanted to see him dead, I wanted to kill him so bad . . ."

Naomi gasped and Moose glared at Bear.

"Sorry Naomi," Bear said. "I just want everyone to understand the emotions and how powerful they were—I don't mean to get caught up in it but it was hard not to feel energized and even now I can't shake the excitement I felt."

"So, why didn't you go after him?" Georgell asked.

"I couldn't," Bear flatly stated. "My guardian prevented me. I couldn't move, my desire to destroy the kid was intense but the need to comply with my guardian's commands seemed more powerful and I simply refused to disobey him. He didn't want me to engage, so I didn't. I'm glad I didn't though because I had a front row seat to the guardian battle—it was intense. I know now that the kid's guardian was good and all the others were no doubt bad, mine especially so. The good guardian took out two of the bad ones in the fight but was impaled on a spear and vanished just like the ones he had killed. Now—here's where the crazy notches up a bit—a new guardian appeared over the kid that had the good one only this time it wasn't good, in fact I think he was of a higher rank then the other dark guardian and, even more bizarre, two other guardians appeared over a couple of the boys that came in with the kid . . ."

The urgency that had waned a bit over the last few weeks lurched mightily in Georgell's stomach as Bear continued. He talked of being released by the guardian once the ethereal battle had concluded. He said an enormous need for violence rushed over him and though he no longer had the desire to hurt the kid, he instead keyed in on a bouncer that had annoyed him earlier in the evening, a bouncer without a guardian.

" . . . I ripped off my shirt, like some goofy Hulk Hogan wannabe and totally rushed the dude. The crowd went completely wild but I was so focused on damaging the bouncer, I didn't see much else. I know it was mayhem though, and then, out of nowhere, I was tazed!"

"Wait—what? Man you serious?" Chopper interrupted.

"Yeah, it was Flip," Bear said pointing at Jackson. "He's a crazy dude—funny now though."

"Flip was in on this too?" Jackson said, his eyes glowing with serious anger.

Georgell noticed Jackson's glare but Bear did not and continued on, still amped on the retelling of the night's events.

"He totally tazed me!" Bear said shaking his head in remembrance. "I remember being dragged out of the club by him and some other dude and seeing fights all over the place, but more than anything, I remember looking up at my guardian . . ." Bear's jovial speech halted and he continued in a somber tone. " . . . He glared at me and I can't shake the intensity of his eyes as he spoke to me, 'you're mine,' he said, and I felt a complete sense of loss and yet accepted his words, almost embraced them willingly—at that point I think I seriously gave in and decided to no longer fight the influence—I wanted to be his tool," Bear said, as if to himself, like he had just now realized what he had nearly done or agreed to, his head lowered but he shook it off and bringing his voice back up, said, "Anyway, the guardian vanished somewhere in the parking lot and I was eventually thrown into Flip's car."

Jackson began to visibly fidget in his chair and looked near an eruption when Emma abruptly stood and said, "Listen I know this looks bad . . ." She paused for a moment then continued, " . . . I'm sure there's a lot of harsh feelings and anger but let's remember why we're here and try to keep things in perspective." There was a pause without comment as Emma walked over and put her hand on Bear's shoulder. She then continued, "We're here to help—and number one is this guy. Please don't turn this into something we'll all regret."

Georgell agreed and nodded thankfully at his wife as others did the same.

Jackson was the first to break the acceptance of Emma's plea and with a stern look at Bear, said, "I thought we decided not to go there. Didn't we all agree that Sanctuary was off limits? And what happened to the team? Why weren't we involved in this insane plan?"

"Because none of you would let me go!" Bear said as Alys leaned in to keep him seated. "I had to see! Foolish or not, it was something I had to do."

An equalizing weight of thought blossomed in Georgell's mind as Bear's fiery reaction hit home. *He's right*, Georgell thought. *Would I do nothing if the roles were reversed?* With his new perspective, Georgell felt ashamed for the angry thoughts he had carried the majority of the day and yet still hoped to prevent Bear from stepping out again.

Jackson was about to bite back when Georgell cut him off, "Listen, I've been locked in anger mode all day but Emma's right, there's nothing we can do about what's done—It's over." Then with an earnest air he added, "Now was it a waste or did we learn something?"

The glare did not leave Jackson's eyes and Georgell knew there was more on his mind but he seemed willing to back off as Chopper jumped in, "Remember when Georgell and I saw the good guardians kill the bad one in church?" A few nods were enough and he continued, "Man, when the bad guardian disappeared the speck seemed to snap out of her darkness. Her eyes softened. She was different—better. Man, I really saw a change." He then looked at Bear and said, "Now you're saying that the bad guardians killed off a good one and a bad guardian took its place. Is that right?"

Bear ignored Jackson's glare. "Yeah, not only that but two more guardians appeared."

"Over the one speck?" Moose quickly spurted.

"No, like I was saying early—they appeared over two of the kid's friends."

A quiet thoughtfulness settled on the group.

"I haven't been able to think of anything else," Alys said. "And I think there's a basic pattern here that may apply in all cases . . ."

Everyone turned their attention to Alys. Even Jackson seemed interested in her idea and pulled his gaze from Bear. She continued, ". . . Think of it as sitting on the fence. Okay, we've all had friends that have been influences on us, some good some bad. Sometimes the influences contradict each other. So let's take this group at Sanctuary as an example. Here are some boys that sit on the fence, they aren't bad kids, just undecided in their allegiances; but one of them, for whatever reason, is protected by a good guardian. It's safe for us to assume that this kid is probably a good influence on the group. He most likely didn't want to go to the club but agreed when all the others pressured him into it—that could explain their giddiness when they first got there as opposed to the concern on the protected kid."

Silent nods spurred her on, "Okay, so inside Sanctuary, a place of dark music and darker emotions, the good guardian is attacked because he is obviously not welcome. He is destroyed and immediately a bad guardian replaces the good one. Why?"

Georgell thought of the question and felt confident that the answer had to be simple, a basic idea. Still, he wasn't sure and tentatively said, "Because he has influence—before he was good and now . . ."

"Exactly!" Alys agreed. "He becomes a recruiter of sorts. The new guardian is not just a defender against good but an outward influence of bad as well. He's different from most guardians because he isn't gained through evil acts or bad decisions; he comes from force and remains through force. He influences his speck and fights to keep him on the bad path and hopes that the kid will eventually do something that will cement his choice to remain in darkness."

"See what I mean?" She said shaking her hands at the others. "Seconds after last night's battle the friends who sat happily on the fence of noncommittal, were no longer held back by the protected speck and his positive influence. They fell from the fence, to the bad side, and gained dark guardians as well. The difference is that they had earned their guardians by previous actions, choices or whatever, the protector kept them at bay—am I making sense?"

Jackson, obviously fascinated by the theory as his pending anger seemed less on the verge of eruption, said, "Right, so there are different types of guardians: soldier guardians called up by specks doing evil, recruiters that are called on when a good guardian is defeated and which specialize in the emotional turning of a speck, and warriors or maybe we can call them generals, like the one on Bear. Generals are gained through mortal sight and become not only recruiters but tend to direct the other guardians like military commanders."

"All generals and recruiters are able fighters too," Georgell added. "Because like Chopper said, they are the ones that will most likely face good guardians, and more than likely two or three."

"Right," Jackson agreed.

Moose raised a hand, "Wait, I don't think Alder has a lowly old soldier guardian. That dude is smart and calculating. He may not be big like Bear's but I'd put him on the same skill level."

"I agree," said Georgell.

"Played me like a fool," added Chopper.

"So maybe based on speck action or power in this world—I mean it seems Alder has some great connections and influence—maybe those types of mortals receive powerful guardians as well, or gain stronger ones over time." Georgell surmised.

"It has to be organized," Jackson jumped in again. "There has to be some kind of authority structure. I'm sure there's a high command in that other realm planning and directing strategic maneuvers like in any other war. And don't kid yourselves; from what I've heard about these guardian battles, this is a war."

Everyone brooded over the magnitude of the new conclusion for a moment when amidst the quiet, Marla, napping in Naomi's arms, let out a sigh that seemed to come from a deeper sleep than she had time to gain. Naomi stroked the child's face then, in a near whisper, stated, "So there is no peace. There cannot be good and bad guardians in the same place. When they come across each other they have to fight. There is no discussion or possibility of living in harmony. They will, and must, fight; is that right?"

"Good and evil." Moose kissed Naomi and pulled her in closer.

"They can't exist together," Emma added. "The nature of opposition prohibits it. True opposites simply repel one another—like magnets—they can't coexist."

"Why don't the good guardians have recruiters?" Chopper asked.

Alys began to answer and Jackson broke in as well but Georgell wasn't listening. His mind was caught up in thoughts of Milton's Paradise Lost, the stories of creation from the Bible, and the test that mortality seemed to be. He thought about William Blake and his many colorful plates depicting good and evil. One plate in particular: a Godlike being squatting down from the sun amid dark parting clouds and reaching down toward an unseen Earth with a compass as if measuring us, our choices and actions, this picture had always affected Georgell, and now gave meaning to his thoughts and Chopper's query. "That isn't part of the deal," He said interrupting the conversation and looking at Chopper. "We, as mortals, have to choose the right and make an effort to stay good. We've been given that agency as part of our existence. Satan, on the other hand, is fighting to eliminate our conscience—our natural filter to know what is right and wrong so that we blindly do what seems easiest."

Georgell looked around the room. "We all believe in a higher power, and no matter what faith we choose to align ourselves with, there is a basic understanding that we are here to succeed in this mortal test and earn a place in Heaven—right?"

No one seemed to balk at the idea so Georgell continued, "So why would God try and sway us? He wants us to make the right choices on our own. We can ask for help but ultimately we need to choose the right and earn our place. Good guardians can protect us by physically eliminating the dark ones but they can't force us to be good. We have to make that choice on our own."

Chopper sat up straight and pointing fervently at Georgell said, "The dark side will cheat and do whatever it takes man! Satan could care less about the rules—he wants us to fail and be miserable—jacked up man, jacked up!"

"So we have protectors but not recruiters," Emma clarified.

"Yeah but that doesn't mean there aren't varying degrees of good guardians. Again, back to the war thing, there has to be some sort of structure and power dynamic that makes this all work." Georgell leaned back in his chair and stretched his back from side to side.

Alys nodded. "I like the idea that they're protecting us from those unseen influencers. I think we should use that as a distinction so we're not confusing good and bad guardians all the time."

"Protectors and guardians," Moose said and everyone agreed.

"Why don't any of us have a protector? Haven't we made good choices? Am I an on-the-fence person?" Naomi asked.

"This isn't a battle ground," Georgell answered scanning the room. "I don't think they can reside here. That doesn't mean their influence can't be felt but it isn't as strong. I think places of worship are the battle grounds; churches, clubs, any place that exists for the express purpose of dark indulgence or righteous praise. Those are the battlefields."

"A home can be a place of worship," Naomi said. "I would guess dark guardians dwell in homes with meth labs or people engaged in child pornography and the like. And I wouldn't be surprised if there were protectors around homes or families that are doing their best to be good. I believe my home is protected—I truly do."

"You're right, I'm sure there are battles in some homes but maybe it's a matter of concentration. Maybe it's the number of people involved that makes the veil between this world and that thinner. All assumptions of course but I just don't think homes are major battle fronts. The amount of mortal traffic in the majority of homes just doesn't breed that kind of conflict."

"So where else do protectors hang out?" Chopper asked.

"I don't know but I would bet schools, hospitals, maybe even police precincts," Georgell guessed with a nod at Jackson. "Not jails or prisons though, those places definitely harbor guardians."

"And Naomi, just because we don't have a protector doesn't mean we're on the fence or bad. It just means we don't currently need one or they're needed somewhere else. But let's not try to second guess things we can't begin to comprehend. There's a lot to learn. We know that a portion of the big picture has been given to us through our sight and we need to use that knowledge to help."

Bear stood up. He excitedly looked at the others and said, "That's it. I have to go to a battlefield, a good place, like a church, and have my guardian destroyed by good ones." He then looked earnestly at Chopper and asked, "Which church had those two protectors you talked about?"

Chopper jumped to his feet. "Yeah—yeah, in the avenues, we can still make the service . . ."

Jackson reached up and, with a brusque tug on Chopper's belt, pulled the big man back down to the floor. "No you don't"

Chopper snapped his head at Jackson but said nothing as Georgell quickly stated, "We can't let you do that Bear."

"Why?" he gruffly barked.

"Still too many questions."

"I don't care, I'll take the chance."

"No you won't," Jackson sternly said.

"Why?" Bear huffed, "Who's going to stop me?"

Jackson placed his hand on Chopper's shoulder and purposefully stood while holding Chopper at bay. Georgell and Moose stood as well.

"Whoa—whoa—whoa!" Emma jumped to her feet motioning for everyone to calm down.

Alys stood, gently stepped in front of Bear and placed her hands on his shoulders.

"Sit down!" Emma glared at Georgell. "This is a discussion. We want to help, not provoke."

Georgell did not sit back down, there was no way he could allow Bear to traipse into a church and hope for the best—he returned Emma's glare.

"He doesn't get it!" Jackson said, standing firm, his hand still pressing down on Chopper.

Bear pressed into Alys as he took a step closer to Jackson. "Get what?" he growled.

"People are in the hospital because of you. That little riot you caused last night landed four people in jail and three in the hospital. One is critical. Because of you a little girl is sitting in the hospital and hoping her dad doesn't die."

Bear stepped back as if slapped by an invisible hand. "What do you mean? Who?"

"I can arrest you! I can lock you up! I can stop you!" Jackson said. "You can't go to a church, or anywhere else, because you can't control yourself and you'll physically harm anyone with a good guardian or . . . p-p-protector!" He stammered. Realizing he had touched his anger threshold and also hit a nerve with Bear, Jackson backed off. "I won't let you hurt anyone else, including yourself," he said evenly.

Bear slumped back into his chair, face ashen, and Alys sat beside him grasping his hand and squeezing tightly.

Jackson steadied his voice. "It was Snake."

Emma gasped.

"He was badly beaten. That's why I was late. I had to pick up his daughter from the sitter's and take her to the hospital. No one can locate the girl's strung out mother."

Bear dropped his gaze from Jackson and stared sullenly at the floor.

Naomi looked at Moose quizzically and he quietly responded, "He's a friend, a bouncer." She then raised a hand to her mouth and shook her head in disbelief as Marla began to stir.

Georgell stepped in front of Emma and could see her shaking, her eyes welling up; he knew she was blaming herself. "Sit down," he softly said while guiding her back to a chair. She sat and placed her face in her hands.

"Bear, I'm not going to arrest you. This incident will blow over like any other club brawl; but it doesn't change the fact that we have to trust each other." Jackson looked down at Chopper and then the others.

"We have to bring the protectors to you," Georgell said. "And I don't think any less than three will do the trick. Your guardian is more than just a general."

Bear nodded his consent without looking up.

Georgell continued, "But please don't go on anymore solo missions. We're all trying to work this thing out and yes your excursion helped us learn some things; but it's just not safe. Not for you and certainly not for those that get in your way. Can you give me your word on that?"

Bear again nodded without taking his eyes from the carpet.

"Man, I should round up some protectors," Chopper volunteered.

"What are you going to do, kidnap church officials and old men?" Moose raised his eyebrows with a grin.

"Why not?" Chopper asked.

Moose shook his head and Georgell said, "No—we're not forcing good people into this situation. There has to be another option."

Bear stood then dropped his hand to Alys. As he helped her up he said, "My future lies with this group and I couldn't ask for a better team; but until there is a tangible way out for me I can't keep attending these meetings."

"I'm not angry, just realistic," he added as he and Alys crossed the room toward the front door. Alys squeezed Emma on the shoulder and Emma looked up with a broken smile, her eyes red and filled with concern and guilt.

"I'm getting worse and my rage is barely kept in check as it is. I just think I should stay home and wait this out." Bear pulled open the door, stepped out and holding the door open as Alys passed by, looked back at Jackson and said, "Barney, we okay?"

"We're okay," Jackson answered.

"Maybe you should lock me up." Bear said taking a half step back, "I'm on the edge as it is and if I get to the point where I don't feel controlled anymore—like I might hurt Alys or something—well then I want you to lock me up. Can you do that for me?"

Jackson nodded.

"You going to the hospital?" Georgell asked.

Bear looked at Alys and said, "Yeah, I've got to know that Snake is okay."

Alys nodded her approval.

Georgell stood and said, "Emma and I will come too."

Emma looked at Naomi and received a silent nod that she and Moose would hang out with the kids until they returned. Chopper mumbled something about going to church and excused himself to the restroom as Jackson headed to the kitchen for a second helping of lasagna and garlic bread to go.

"See you there," Bear said to Georgell, and shut the door.

☼～ **28** ～☼

Five days later, on a chilly Friday-the-thirteenth and just a few minutes after ten, Moose and Chopper tossed a speck from the club. There were no problems and the speck had no other friends to contend with. Everything went smoothly and afterward they found Georgell to relay the details.

"That had to be the ugliest guardian I've ever seen," Moose said as they found Georgell sitting at a table near the donkey bar.

"Man, it had a disease or something. I didn't want to touch the speck!" Chopper agreed.

"What?" Georgell looked at them, confused.

"I think it had leprosy," Moose said with a raised eyebrow.

"What?"

"The guardian had leprosy," Moose clarified. "Seriously! It had leprosy. Its face was bubbling up and peeling off—not a pretty sight."

"Maybe it was the Elephant Man," Chopper added, eyes wide.

"Nooo," Georgell said. "Not John Merrick. I'm sure he would be a protector."

"Who?" Chopper asked.

"The Elephant Man, John Merrick," Georgell said while slightly nodding his head and smiling.

"Right, Professor!" Moose said with a jovial snarl. He hit Chopper with the back of his arm and said, "Let's go talk to someone on our level."

"Yeah," Chopper agreed. "Where's Bronco?"

They all laughed and Georgell waved them off with a grin. The conversation was oddly comforting. The staff had really come together as a team over the last few weeks and there had been few incidents requiring more than two bouncers. The most positive change was the guardian intrusions; they didn't cause as much of an uproar as they had in the past.

Chopper, Moose, and Georgell had encountered quite a few, but they had successfully removed them all without incident or recognition. They had learned to be aware of both the crowd and the space above the crowd. They could fight and handle incidents without the need to look up. They knew when a guardian was there and watched without looking.

Listening to his friends, Georgell realized that guardian situations had become just like any other part of the job. The possibility of going to work and getting seriously injured was there, just as it always had been, and though the edge was more acute with the guardian factor, work was still work. The only exceptions were the recruiter guardians or, even worse, the generals. Georgell was learning to decipher the differences, and though he allowed Moose and Chopper to deal with most guardian situations alone, he always wanted to see the being in case he felt a need to impose stronger tactics. Tonight was an exception because there was an obvious opening right when the guardian revealed itself and Chopper was correct in taking immediate action. More of that would happen, Georgell supposed, and hoped they wouldn't get too lax in their judgment.

Moose and Chopper were an affective roaming team but Georgell looked forward to the day when Bear returned so that he could split them up again. It was good to have fun, but Georgell felt it would be better if they were teamed with a more subdued partner. In the meantime he had taken Santos on as his protégé and was teaching him the finer points of bouncing. Of all the staff he had hired, Santos had proven himself time and again as tough, patient, and surprisingly willing to set aside his ego and learn. He had even accepted "Santa" as an alias and seemed to enjoy the notoriety it gave him.

Georgell waved Santos over, "I want you to look out on the dance floor and tell me if you see a problem." He was becoming more adept at preemptive marking but Georgell kept him on his toes by constantly pointing out things he hadn't noticed or people he should watch.

Santos eagerly looked over the crowd and cursed when he spotted the situation. "That guy with the yellow hat," he answered.

"Right," Georgell agreed. "Why?"

"He keeps bumping that other dude and eyeballing his girlfriend."

"Good," Georgell praised. "Call it in."

"Pepper," Santos radioed.

"Go ahead."

"Pull the yellow hat, ten feet out on your left, prevent."

Prevent was the term used to note that a pointed target was irritating another and that a situation needed some attention. Pepper, so named because his afro had patches of white, would give the guy two options: go to the opposite side of the dance floor or go home. The guy would certainly protest but Pepper had to be firm and stand his ground.

Georgell was pleased that Santos gave the call to Pepper because he hadn't seen him in action yet. Pepper was a lanky kickboxer with fast reflexes, a smooth attitude, and no fear; but he wasn't as physically imposing as the other bouncers and therefore people didn't tend to listen to him without argument. Georgell was curious how he would handle the situation and stood to get a better line of sight.

Pineapple and Nemesis, whom Georgell had made the other roaming team, stopped to back up Pepper as they entered the dance floor from the tunnel. Bronco, Pepper's designated partner, closed in from the other side of the dance floor.

Pepper pushed through the crowd toward the guy in the yellow hat and Santos made another radio call, "Pineapple two guys from the wall, intercept."

Georgell was impressed. Two guys had moved from the perimeter when Pepper pushed into the crowd and Santos was sending in help just in case they were friends. *Good eye*, Georgell thought but decided to hold off on the audible praise until the situation was over.

"Copy," Nemesis responded for her partner as they pressed in.

Pepper reached his target and stepped in front of him. He then leaned in and gave the guy his options. With a menacing stare the guy angrily removed his hat and seemed to question Pepper's authority.

Georgell tapped Santos on the shoulder and said, "Go." Removing the hat was probably a signal for help which in turn meant definite trouble. Georgell stayed in position and watched. He was confident that the situation would be handled and wanted to observe the action. He keyed his mike, "Red, we are tossing three."

"Yellow hat?" Red asked having heard the previous chatter.

"Copy," Georgell responded. "And friends."

The guys from the wall pushed swiftly through the crowd but found their way deterred as Pineapple and Nemesis stepped into their path. They stopped and wavered as Pineapple pointed to the tunnel. After his target removed his hat, Pepper stepped closer and said something inches away from the man's face. The guy looked toward his friends, who were being escorted from the floor, and reluctantly nodded his head.

Santos followed them through the tunnel and out of the club. Red gave the all clear signal and Georgell proudly sat back in his chair. *A well oiled machine*, he thought.

"Chopper, front desk please," Mercy radioed.

"Copy," Chopper responded.

A few minutes later Chopper and Moose exited the left slope, pressed their way through the crowd, and disappeared into the tunnel. Georgell leaned back over the table and studied the budget sheet he had grabbed from Terence earlier. A slew of radios were broken and Georgell had to generate some extra funds to buy more. *If Moose doesn't wear one we'll be fine*, Georgell thought. *He ruins more equipment than any three bouncers.*

"Doc, meet us at the left slope, eyes on," Moose radioed.

Georgell stood immediately, snatched up the report, and shoved it into his pocket as he headed toward the left slope. As he walked his eyes scanned the dance floor and tunnel for Moose, Chopper, or any sign of a guardian. Finally he saw them clear the tunnel and begin skirting the dance floor toward the slope. A young guy and girl accompanied them and Georgell was surprised to see an exceptionally beautiful protector above the girl. The protector's full length brown skirt flowed above her speck like an umbrella of protection as they walked. She had long brown hair in a tight braid that draped over her left shoulder and rested on a yellow blouse. As they approached, Georgell could make out an obvious look of concern on the protector's face and knew she wasn't happy by the way she spun her glimmering white staff in a defensive grip.

Georgell caught the protector's wide-eyed gaze and gave a slight bow. She returned the gesture but with a pleading stare. Georgell felt her concern and nodded with understanding. *Why are they here?* He wondered. The girl seemed oblivious to her protector and cordially greeted Georgell as Chopper introduced her and her boyfriend.

As they headed to the basement Moose leaned in and said, "They're from one of the churches Chopper attends."

"I thought we decided not to involve innocent bystanders?" Georgell questioned.

"Me too," Moose answered with a shrug.

The group pressed through the dance floor and made it down to the sports bar where Chopper escorted them to a nearby table. When they had settled and ordered drinks from a passing server Chopper returned to Georgell and Moose. Both men stood dumbfounded near the stairs.

"Her brother didn't come. Man you should see his protector. Dude carries an awesome sword. I watched them take out a guardian in church a few weeks ago."

"Why are they here?" Georgell interrupted.

"I didn't force them," Chopper said defensively.

"But you did invite them, right."

"Yeah, but man if they can take out a guardian then we can help Bear."

"She is alone, Chop!" Moose pointed at the girl.

"I know, I'm sorry, I wasn't going to tell her she couldn't come in without her brother. Come on man," Chopper pleaded.

"No, Chopper, this is wrong," Georgell roughly said. "Have you seen her protector's face? She's scared! You've got to get them out of here!"

"How?"

"I don't care, lie to them, but get them out as soon as you can. Until then you are right here," Georgell pointed at the ground. "You don't leave until they are ready to go and then you escort them out personally. All the way to the car, understand?"

Chopper nodded without further excuse or protest.

"Doc, come to the Donkey please," Emma's voice called over the radio.

Georgell shot Chopper another look of extreme irritation and then headed up the stairs and radioed Pineapple.

"Go ahead."

"Moose and Chopper are hanging in the basement. Roam top only."

"Copy," Pineapple responded.

As Georgell entered the dance area, veered to the right and up towards the donkey bar, he immediately noticed the looming figure of a guardian and stopped for a moment to gather his thoughts. The guardian stood above a well dressed man amidst a group of Greeks. Like the protector in the basement, the guardian had his weapons drawn, a dagger in one hand and a short sword in the other. The guardian looked tough and had an expression of excitement on his hardened face as he looked toward the slope. His dark hair was short and his clothing ragged, almost in pieces and barely hanging from his muscular frame, but he still looked menacing.

Georgell wondered if he could feel the presence of the protector and exasperated by the situation, took a deep breath and continued toward the bar while radioing a warning to Moose and Chopper, "Moose, stay put! Eyes on, I repeat, eyes on—stay put."

Moose acknowledged and Georgell scrambled to formulate a plan. Emma pointed at Georgell as he approached and Cosmo turned with his arms outstretched and bellowed, "What's up Doc?"

Georgell embraced Cosmo and the others he knew then smiled at Emma and gave her a quick nod toward the new guy. She didn't understand at first but after Georgell directed a nod above the stranger a barely visible tell of concern crossed her brow and Georgell knew she was cued in.

"Ahh yes Doc, this is Devon my cousin from L.A.," Cosmo said as he put his arm around Devon. "He's visiting us, in a little trouble back home so he came out here to let the heat settle, know-what-I'm-saying?"

Georgell nodded and stretched out his hand toward Devon who shook it warmly. "Great club, Doc," Devon praised. "What's down there?"

"Sports bar," Georgell answered. "But the women are up here."

Cosmo laughed. Then, with mock seriousness he looked at Devon. "This man knows what's important." Then nodding at Emma said, "Cherub here—is his beautiful wife."

Emma shrugged with a girlish grin and Georgell reached over the bar and squeezed her hand knowing that Cosmo's compliment was also a sly way of letting his cousin know that she was off limits.

Devon looked toward the basement again and Georgell tried to distract him by pointing to a group of blondes standing like sheep near the tunnel. "Like I said," Georgell directed. "The action is up here."

Cosmo smacked his cousin on the shoulder and said, "Beautiful." He then motioned for his crew to escort Devon to the women and like ravenous wolves they eagerly obliged.

"Not playing tonight?" Georgell asked Cosmo as he watched the Greeks mingle with the playful girls. Devon kept looking toward the slope and Georgell knew he was fighting the urge to go down. The guardian pointed toward the slope but Devon resisted the influence as a girl latched on to his arm and pulled him toward the dance floor.

"Not tonight. My girl is coming and I told her to meet me here at Emma's bar."

"Your girl?" Georgell asked, astonished.

"Yeah, my girl, Linda. I guess I'm getting hooked."

"Really?" Georgell was dumbfounded.

"She's got a couple of kids but hey, the girl has my number—y'know? I'm hooked."

Georgell pointed to a vacant table just below the bar and they sat. Twenty minutes passed as they discussed Cosmo's budding romance. Georgell grew increasingly concerned about how to deal with the situation discreetly. He silently hoped for a break but nothing seemed obvious. After a few more minutes a beautiful dark haired woman arrived and Cosmo cordially introduced her to Georgell. He then led her to the donkey bar and introduced her to Emma. They bought some drinks and then returned to sit next to Georgell at the table.

"Doc, muscle heads in the club," Red's voice informed through the radio.

Georgell couldn't believe his rotten luck; the situation was getting worse by the minute. The Greeks and muscle heads hated each other and there were always problems when the two groups met. "Copy," Georgell responded, grasping desperately at his thoughts for a way out.

Then a solution hit him. It wasn't the best idea, but under the circumstances it would have to do. Devon was being directed to the tunnel and Georgell assumed he was heading to the bathroom. It was a perfect opportunity. Georgell stood, excused himself from the table and headed toward the tunnel. Santos was already in the foyer and Georgell quickly radioed for his assistance, "Santa, go to the men's room. I'm following a blue silk shirt. Cover me."

Santos responded affirmatively.

When Georgell strolled into the bathroom, Santos was washing his hands at the row of sinks and Devon was busy at a nearby urinal, his back to Georgell. Ammonia and a striking berry scent fought at Georgell's senses as Santos raised a finger and pointed at an occupied stall. Georgell nodded and motioned toward the door. Loudly pulling towels from the dispenser, Santos dried his hands and exited the bathroom. Georgell heard him tell some guys that the bathroom was closed as the door shut behind him.

Frustrated by the additional occupant, Georgell hesitated for a moment but knew he had no choice—he had to act fast. Devon whistled as he concentrated on his aim, clueless to the coming assault. Ignoring the looming guardian, Georgell grabbed Devon by the head and with pinpoint accuracy rammed it against the hard tile above the urinal.

Devon's body slumped as a sickening crack echoed from the walls. The guardian dissipated. Georgell caught the unconscious form, pulling him quickly to an empty stall as the sound of rolling toilet paper sounded from the occupied one. A stream of blood trickled down from the wound on Devon's forehead but Georgell thought it best not to doctor the gash. He placed him on the toilet and leaned him upright against the partition, locked the door and stealthily climbed out of the stall as he heard pants rustling and a belt being fastened. Georgell slipped from the bathroom.

Santos looked over and raised an eyebrow as Georgell exited. "Everything cool?"

"Yeah, listen," Georgell hastily spoke. "You remember what that guy looks like, right?"

Santos nodded.

"He's sleeping now but when he wakes up he's going to have a headache and a lot of justified anger. The Greeks are going to be hungry for revenge. You've got to play it real. Like you don't know what happened, got it?"

Santos seemed confused but nodded anyway.

"Contain the rage as long as possible and run it like you would normally; radio for backup, everything."

"Understood," Santos replied.

"Tonight is going to get crazy and you need to be on your toes. Remember, the Greeks are on our side and we need to back them up if possible."

"Isn't he a Greek?" Santos thumbed back toward the restroom.

"Yes, but—I can't explain . . . just stay on top of it." Georgell headed through the tunnel and barked into the radio, "Moose, now!"

Within a couple of minutes, Georgell saw Chopper exit the slope followed by the girl, her protector, the boyfriend, and finally Moose. He met them as they skirted the dance floor and said, "Take them all the way out."

"Got it," Chopper answered.

Georgell grabbed Moose and quickly relayed the situation. A glint shimmered in his eye and he readily agreed to the task of prepping Pineapple and Nemesis for a Greek and muscle head confrontation.

"Red," Georgell radioed.

"Go ahead."

"Keep an eye on Chopper. He's exiting now."

"Copy," Red responded.

Georgell looked around the dance floor to evaluate the situation and noticed the muscle heads had congregated by the donkey bar as well. Cosmo was talking to Linda and paid the group no mind. The other Greeks were engaged in flirtatious conversations with the girls they had met and didn't seem to notice the muscle heads either.

"All staff," Georgell radioed. "Greeks and muscle heads are in the house. Be alert!" Everyone knew of the rivalry between the two groups and he wanted them to be extra attentive. He then did a radio check and headed back up to speak with Cosmo as the bouncers responded in turn.

"Sorry to interrupt," Georgell said with a hand on Cosmo's shoulder. "Can I talk with you for a moment?"

Cosmo smiled and said, "What's up?" without the usual "Doc" attached to his query.

Georgell nodded at the group of muscle heads and Cosmo looked, as did Linda.

"Thank you for the warning," Cosmo said.

"What?" Linda asked concerned.

"These guys are a problem," Cosmo said flatly. "Don't worry though, it'll be okay tonight. No problems, I promise," he said with a smile. Linda didn't seem convinced but scooted her chair closer and kissed Cosmo anyway.

"Doc, entry, now!" Santos radioed.

Here we go, Georgell thought as he excused himself and headed to the foyer. Before he could enter the tunnel, Pineapple intercepted him and asked where he should position. Georgell whisked by and directed him and Nemesis to shadow the muscle heads.

In the foyer Santos listened to a couple of Greeks as they heatedly explained where and how they found the unconscious Devon. Georgell approached and they began spouting the information again while trying to support their bloodied cousin. Georgell marveled at Devon's grisly appearance and silently applauded his scheme. The guardian was still nowhere to be seen and the damage to Devon was minimal but appeared horrific.

"Someone is going to pay," a hotheaded young Greek screamed.

"Who did this?" Georgell asked, looking from the irate Greek to Santos.

Another Greek had wandered into the foyer and overheard Georgell's query as he noticed the bloodied visage of Devon. He became immediately outraged and pointed frantically back toward the dance floor. "Those muscle pricks are here. I bet they did this!"

Georgell saw that his ruse was working and—though unlikely—hoped he could resolve the situation without too much trouble. He took a deep breath. "Listen, you've got to get him to a hospital." He put his hand on the shoulder of the newly arrived Greek and said, "Go get Cosmo, tell him what has happened." Then pointing at another said, "You go get the car and pull it up to the exit door." Georgell then directed Santos and the last of the men to get Devon down the stairs and into the car.

The guys accepted and broke into action as a distress call came blaring over the radio from Emma, "Donkey, Donkey, Donkey!" Georgell saw Santos look back, questioning, but pointed sharply at the exit. He knew Santos wanted in on the action but Devon was a priority and had to take precedence. With the reassurance that Santos would follow through, Georgell bolted into the tunnel.

By the time Georgell reached the bar, the incident already appeared to be contained. Cosmo was taunting some muscle heads while Nemesis ushered him back to the table where Linda anxiously sat. Four other members of the group tried unsuccessfully to press through Moose, Chopper, Pepper and two other bouncers while Pineapple held a fifth in a tight full nelson. Georgell recognized the flailing muscle head in Pineapple's grip as Brisco, a heavy supplement user that bulged from every muscle and often had fits of steroid rage. Even his bright blonde curls seemed to bulge from his overly tanned head.

Georgell chuckled as he watched Brisco try to flex out of Pineapple's hold. He figured Pineapple was likely the strongest bouncer on staff and Brisco had no chance of out-muscling him. With a shake, a lift, and a hard drop Pineapple said, "Relax bra, you ain't going anywhere!" Georgell smiled and directed Pineapple to eject him then asked Emma what happened.

"He spit on me!" Emma exclaimed. "He cut in line, I refused to serve him, and he spit on me."

Georgell felt a sudden blast of wrath and looked sharply back toward Pineapple but realized he had already dragged Brisco out of sight. Unable to vent his sudden fury on its cause, Georgell silently fumed.

Emma continued, "I slapped him and he would've hit me but Cosmo hit him first."

Cosmo sat quietly at his table with a smirk on his face and Georgell directed Nemesis to go down and help Pineapple. "Tell him I'll be out shortly," he added in a barely controlled whisper. Nemesis nodded and headed toward the tunnel. Georgell engaged his radio and forcefully said, "Red, coming your way. Keep him out! Way out!" Then Georgell leaned over the table where Linda held Cosmo's hand and said, "Thank you Coz, but keep it cool now?"

"Depends on them."

"Let me take care of them."

"Can you?" Cosmo answered.

"Listen." Georgell leaned in closer to strengthen his response. "You know I can! And you know I will! Don't think for a moment that I won't do what it takes." He paused for a moment to let the words sink in. Then he added, "You've got other problems. Devon was jumped in the bathroom. Your boys have taken him out to the car and you need to get him to the hospital."

Cosmo stood up with a burst. "Take me to him," he said. He turned to Linda. "You should go. I'll see you later."

With a threatening glare, Linda stood and said, "You'd better!"

As Cosmo followed the Greek sent up from the foyer, Georgell turned toward Linda. Touching his arm with a smile and raised eyebrows, she said, "Nice to meet you?"

Georgell nodded but was unable to return her smile. He watched as she left the dance floor. He turned to face the angry muscle heads and eyes glaring said, "Brisco was the problem. Not you guys—he's lucky I wasn't here. He spit on my wife." Three of the guys showed varying degrees of surprise while the fourth just creased his forehead and looked over at Emma with contempt.

"That's right," Georgell added. "Then he tried to hit her." He let the statement linger for a moment. "Now if any of you feel like I was wrong to kick him out, please feel free to follow him—but know this; he is gone for good, and anyone that follows is done as well."

"Why did that grease ball jump in?" the contemptuous one asked.

Georgell stepped up to the questioner. Barely holding back his choking rage he growled, "Because my wife was about to get hit!" Lowering his voice to a whisper, he finished, "He has no problem with the rest of you staying and I suggest you back off. Do you agree or can I vent some of my anger?"

"Dude, whatever," the guy answered daring Georgell to make a move.

Chopper stepped between the two and shoved the muscle head back and laughed at him. "Man, you really that stupid?"

"Stay away from the Greeks." Georgell said, pleased that Chopper intervened. "My crew will be watching. If any of you get within fifty feet you're done. Do you understand?"

"Fine dude, but keep them out of our way as well," one of the bigger guys said, shoving Pepper out of the way as he passed.

"Leave it alone," Moose said to Pepper, grabbing his arm.

The muscle heads left the dance floor and headed down to the sports bar where Georgell was certain they would regroup and begin calling the rest of their pack. *This isn't over*, he thought, watching the group disappear below.

☼~ **29** ~☼

Over the next few hours Georgell gained control of his anger but still felt the itch of confrontation and knew that the night would not end pleasantly. Cosmo had returned, and though he promised Georgell that nothing would happen inside, there was no guarantee that the muscle heads wouldn't alter that oath. For the time being he sat quietly, seething, waiting for the club to close. Around Cosmo, his crew sat talking with each other and making discreet phone calls. No one disturbed Cosmo as he contemplated what was to come.

Overhearing a few conversations, Emma let Georgell know that the Greeks were calling others and telling them to wait outside. Minutes later Moose informed Georgell that Cosmo's cousin was still around as well because his guardian loomed distinctly over a black suburban parked on the street.

Meanwhile, the muscle heads were gathering strength in the sports bar. They too had called friends, preparing themselves for the coming rumble. To make matters worse Georgell noticed three new guardians in the basement hovering over members of the plotting group. Neither Moose nor Chopper had seen them enter, and Georgell wondered if they had appeared because of the pending violence. He chose not to dwell on the subject.

As position bouncers watched the two groups, Georgell decided to set up a game plan. He gathered the roamers at the left slope, giving each team assignments for closing. Moose and Chopper would start from the slopes and corral guests down and out through the emergency exit in the basement. He gave Moose a key to turn off the door alarm.

Pineapple and Nemesis were to start at the slope as well but direct people from the dance floor and bars through the tunnel and out the front exit. They were also instructed to position the other bouncers appropriately once they were all outside.

"If we can get all the muscle heads out through the basement, and if I can keep Cosmo and the Greeks inside and upstairs, then we can at least prevent anything from happening in the club." He also explained that he would call the police and hoped the entire situation could be diffused without a fist being thrown. After a huff from Chopper and a laugh from Moose he shrugged with fragile optimism. "It's worth a try."

"What about coats?" Nemesis asked.

Georgell turned to Chopper and Moose. "If they have a coat check ticket let them up. If not—out the exit door." The men nodded and Georgell thanked Nemesis for pointing out the concern. Georgell then instructed Santos to stay in and together they would escort Cosmo to his vehicle and more importantly, through the entry doors. He then told him to have Red clear a spot in front for Cosmo's ride. Santos agreed and headed to the front.

Pineapple and Nemesis split up to more efficiently deliver the tactics to each bouncer on the upper level and then met at the front desk to explain the plan to Mercy and the coat check personnel.

Before Moose and Chopper headed down to inform the basement security of the situation, Georgell grabbed each by the chest, and squeezing a fistful of shirt, said, "Do not engage the specks unless a brawl ensues. There are too many and we need crowd coverage. Do what you can, but keep a low profile. I don't expect any problems until we close so let's just play it cool until then."

"Yeah-yeah, you owe me some chest hair." Moose slapped Georgell's hand away.

Chopper looked at Moose pitifully, shook his head, and giddily trotted off toward the basement.

Georgell made his way to the office and, ignoring Terrance, grabbed the portable phone from his desk and called Jackson. "Jackson, its Georgell. Listen there might be a huge brawl outside the club tonight and I sure could use some help."

"Sorry, can't . . ."

"Are you sure?" Georgell said. "It's the muscle heads, Greeks, and at least four of our friends. Sure could use you."

"I can't Doc—I'm in the middle of a botched sting and have no idea when it will clear up."

"Do what you can," Georgell said.

"Yeah, I'll send a squaddie and try to get there myself but don't count on it—be careful!"

Georgell hung up the phone and placed it back in the cradle. Terrance sat in his chair with his arms crossed, shaking his head.

"I'm just taking precautions," Georgell said. He then explained the plan to Terrance with as much optimism as he could but Terrance saw through the sugarcoating and sneered.

"I've already told Mercy to do the close out. I plan on being right out front with you guys," he said, rolling his head from side to side.

"What are you doing?" Georgell asked.

"Stretching, I'm getting in on this one."

"Oh, no!" Georgell protested.

"What are you going to do," Terence asked. He stood up then, keeping his legs straight, bent forward at the waist and pressed his palms flat against the ground. "Are you going to waste a bouncer trying to keep me out of trouble?"

"Just—be careful and don't aggravate the situation. Help solve the problem; don't become one." Georgell marveled at how limber Terence was. "Hey, I know its thirty minutes early but can we close the club? I don't want these guys to have any more prep time. Let's just get this over with."

"Fine," Terence said, pulling a knee up to his chest.

"Santa, flash the DJ booth. We are closing early. I repeat we are closing early. Clear the club," Georgell radioed. "Everyone get to your positions." Then, keying the mike again, he cautioned, "Stay with your partner and watch your back."

On his way out, Georgell switched on the overhead lights and lit up the dance floor. As he exited the office hall, pulling the door closed behind him, he saw a massive bottleneck of confused clubbers making its way to the tunnel. Cosmo still sat at his table by the donkey bar and motioned his crew to get the car. Santos, a few steps away from Cosmo, talked with Emma while she wiped down the counter. Three men stayed with Cosmo as the others strolled to the exit. One spoke on his cell phone and Georgell overheard him say, "Yes now! Pull up front."

Cosmo stood as Georgell approached. "Like I said, no problems in here. In fact I am going to walk out the front door and get into my vehicle. I will do nothing, and none of my boys will lift a finger either; but," he said with a smirk. "If those impotent puffs make a move between here and my car then I will teach them a lesson of respect they won't soon forget."

"Fair enough," Georgell said. "Do you mind if Santa and I escort you?"

Cosmo agreed and motioned to the others that it was time to leave. Santos took the lead followed by the three Greeks, Cosmo, and Georgell in the rear. Georgell was confident that no trouble would come from behind with Moose and Chopper clearing the basement and he began thinking that the situation had been diffused when he abruptly discovered the flaw in his plan. He had closed early, which meant the police would not be arriving for another twenty minutes at least. He silently cursed his mistake and hoped Jackson had sent coverage already.

"We're clear in the basement and the door is locked," Chopper informed.

"Okay in front," Red followed.

"Cosmo's ride is in place," Pineapple said.

"Everyone is in position," Nemesis added.

Georgell flexed his jaw and wondered if the muscle heads had decided not to try anything. He pumped his fists and wanted to believe that it was over but couldn't relax until Cosmo was in his car and rolling away. "We're coming out the front," Georgell informed, "Thirty-seconds."

Santos pushed open the entry doors and held them as everyone descended the stairs and walked outside. Cosmo grinned as he left the building and scanned the crowd. The muscle heads were nowhere in sight. He stopped a few steps from his car and turned to Georgell. "I knew they were bunnies," he said.

Georgell ignored Cosmo as he scanned the crowd and saw multiple guardians. Some hovered over the crowd to the right, others stood over a group of guys that rounded the corner on the left, and a few stood over parked cars on the street. The closest guardian was feet away and perched above the bed of a truck, directly in front of Cosmo's rig.

"Bunnies!" Cosmo exclaimed with a mocking laugh and stepped toward the waiting vehicle.

The next few moments unfolded in slow motion as Georgell saw and reacted to the movement of the guardian from the truck bed. The guardian leaned forward and Georgell knew this meant its speck was making a move as well. Georgell sprang into action and took two giant steps toward the truck as Brisco emerged from beneath a blanket brandishing a heavy aluminum bat that glimmered and steamed in the winter cold. His eyes burned red and his teeth were clenched in a concentrated grimace. The blanket fell from his body as he leapt from the truck and sailed toward an unaware Cosmo.

With a guttural roar, Georgell advanced two more steps and jumped powerfully toward Brisco. Georgell redirected Brisco's momentum back and to the left as he blasted him hard in the midsection. They landed with a heavy thump on the hood of Cosmo's black Suburban. Brisco's bat slammed into the windshield and a spider web of cracks instantaneously appeared. They slid across the hood, Georgell using all the strength he could muster to keep Brisco below him as they plummeted off the edge and toward the asphalt street below. As their bodies collided with the hard road, Georgell felt the air drain from Brisco's lungs. He knew he had the upper hand as they rolled toward oncoming vehicles exiting the parking lot.

"It's on," Santos blared into his radio.

A car screeched and swerved as it avoided Brisco and Georgell. A surprised van driving from the opposite direction had no time to react and the two vehicles slammed into each other. Georgell heard other cars braking, followed by crunching and screams. Traffic stopped in both directions.

When they finally came to a rest, Brisco lay beneath Georgell, swinging a weak cross at his head. The punch hit Georgell on the left ear but was too soft to cause any pain or damage. Keeping his face buried in Brisco's chest, Georgell reached up with both hands, grabbed Brisco by his wavy blonde curls, pulled his head forward, and then slammed it back to the ground. There was a groan of pain but Brisco was still conscious. In a swift motion, Georgell lifted himself up while still holding tight to Brisco's hair and hammered his forehead to Brisco's nose. A heavy crack sounded, a warm spray peppering Georgell's cheeks as the bridge of Brisco's nose caved in.

Georgell hammered Brisco's head to the ground a couple more times, overcome with blood lust. He wanted to continue hurting the man, a frenzy of hatred dancing in his mind, but he had to stop. He forced himself to pull back and instead screamed into Brisco's ear, "That's for my wife!" Brisco swore and covered his face with both hands.

A fist hammered Georgell from behind, then another. On the third strike Georgell realized it was a foot pounding him in the kidney. He rolled off Brisco and away from the kicks in time to see Santos tackle the kicker. Freed from his assailant, Georgell stood and rapidly looked around. Fights were everywhere; on the sidewalk, in cars, on cars, and on both sides of the street. He also saw flashing sirens coming from multiple angles and felt a surge of relief as he realized that Jackson had indeed sent help early.

Near the front of the club Georgell was dumbfounded to see a protector in the midst of battle. The protector swung a heavy axe and covered his massive weight with a tremendous shield as three guardians attacked. Two more guardians made their way toward the melee above muscle heads that fought through crews of Greeks. The desire to help pierced Georgell's mind. Assisting the protector might bolster his own attempt to acquire one, he thought, and scurried toward the scene.

A plastic cup hit Georgell on the side of his head, a wet spray of beer sloshing his face and clothing. He turned to confront the assailant and saw an irate girl screaming at him from the passenger side of a car. Then, from an unseen source, a spiraling bottle of water hit the screaming girl in the face. She yelped and slumped in the seat and out of sight as the window slowly raised and closed.

Georgell heard a new string of profanity bellowing from Brisco and turned to see Cosmo kicking him hard in the ribs. He was irritated by the new distraction but could not ignore it; the police were coming and he did not want Cosmo detained or involved any more than needed. He stepped toward Cosmo and pushed him roughly against his suburban then pointedly yelled, "No!"

Cosmo looked stunned and then, glancing to his left, unwittingly tipped off Georgell to a coming assault. Georgell leaned back and a fist grazed his chin. He then tilted his head as another blow struck him on the right cheek. A surge of annoyance gripped Georgell; he desperately wanted to help the protector, but continuously found himself side-tracked by other battles. He felt a loss of control brimming in his mind as he grabbed his assailant by the shirt and pulled him forward. The man tripped off balance as he stumbled over Brisco and fell hard, face first, to the street.

Seeing that the fallen attacker was a Greek, Georgell looked at Cosmo and barked, "Control your people!" He then pointed at the coming sirens and said, "Get out of sight."

Cosmo responded by kicking the downed Greek and saying, "Security is with us!" He then nodded at Georgell, understanding the warning, and escaped into his Suburban.

Two cops jumped from their vehicle as it screeched to a halt. Georgell hollered for their attention. They heard his plea and ran over, pulling their batons. Georgell grabbed the arm of the closest cop and pointed at Brisco. "This is the guy that started it all. Don't let him go!" He didn't wait for a reply just turned and ran back to where the guardians had been fighting the lone protector.

The protector was still standing strong and swinging his axe with practiced precision at the diminished guardians. *He's winning*, Georgell realized as he slid over the hood of a white sedan. Then, to Georgell's utter astonishment, he made eye contact with Moose.

"Wassssup!" Moose bellowed, bashing a guy in the head.

Georgell felt a rush of excitement as he marveled at his friend. Moose had a protector, a strong one at that, and the possibilities had just turned in a positive, powerful, direction.

With an awakening jolt, Georgell heard Emma call his name. The frenzied melee returned to his focus and he redirected his attention to the beckoning call. Emma pointed toward a nearby streetlight where Pepper lay curled up on the ground as two muscle heads blasted away at him with feet and fists. Georgell motioned for Emma to stay back and hurdled to the bouncer's aid.

Nemesis arrived a second before him and with an awesome body check, hammered one of the brutes into a nearby rose bush. Georgell grabbed the other thug in a rear choke and squeezed. His body went limp and Georgell let him slump to the ground. "Pepper . . ."

"I'm fine." Pepper stood, wiping his face and spat out a mouthful of blood. He then spun hard with a raised foot and kicked the shredded muscle head back into the rose bush as he tried to escape.

Nemesis smacked Pepper on the shoulder and ran back to the street where Pineapple held off some Greeks from the bloodied form of a writhing muscle head. As Nemesis ran by, Georgell noticed her ear was badly torn and bleeding and wondered what had happened. Then, realizing that Pepper was alone, Georgell turned to Pepper and hollered, "Where's Bronco?"

Pepper shrugged, spit out another spray of blood, and answered, "Don't know."

Georgell was immediately upset that the two were out of contact and concerned that Bronco may be in trouble as well. He rapidly scanned the chaotic scene; not finding the missing bouncer he barked, "Help Pineapple and Nemesis." Then pointing towards the two added, "And stay with them!"

Pepper was still a bit shaky but followed Georgell's direction without debate.

Police sirens blared all around as blue and red lights illuminated the mayhem. Georgell spotted Jackson pulling fighters apart with help from Santos and Terrance. He then noticed another cop further to his left pointing at Red with a baton and yelling at him to back off. Georgell recognized the cop as the one he had told to watch Brisco and immediately looked back to where Brisco had been. He was gone. Inspecting the area, Georgell promptly caught sight of Brisco and his lurching guardian jetting across the street towards an unaware Greek target.

Knowing he was giving Red license to assault an officer, Georgell yelled for him to follow and darted across the street. With Georgell's order Red stepped toward the interfering cop and caught the baton as he swung it toward him. He yanked the weapon from the officer's hand and tossed it onto the club roof behind him. He then hammered the officer to the ground and rushed to assist Georgell.

Brisco scrambled on top of the screaming Greek he had bulldogged to the ground, pummeling him mercilessly.

As he rushed to help, Georgell noticed the arm of the Greek skewed at a sickening angle; a bone protruding from his elbow. Another wave of rage racked Georgell as he thought of the damage that could've been avoided if the ignorant officer had listened to him.

Georgell approached hurriedly from behind, reaching for Brisco's shirt collar with both hands. With an infusion of adrenaline, he yanked Brisco from the unconscious Greek and tossed him. Brisco slid a few feet backward and slammed headfirst into the street curb with a thud. He looked up, still conscious and Georgell hammered a boot into his exposed neck affectively pinning him against the curb. Brisco wailed but didn't move and Georgell thought the situation was controlled until he found himself staring eye to eye at Brisco's guardian.

The guardian smiled wickedly, as if finally given license to attack a mortal, and with deliberate focus, slashed his blade across Georgell's neck. Georgell felt an excruciating wave of pain and nausea and lost the ability to breathe. Darkness dizzied his mind. Georgell felt an urge to fall—to quit, and fight no more. He wanted the pain to stop and the nightmares to go. He wanted the cackling laughter banished from his mind and his memories of darkness stripped away. *This is the way*, he thought, *I can just stop living. I can die, here, now, and the pain will be gone.* Acceptance closed in then a flood of oxygen filled his lungs as his wife and children screamed from his subconscious. Georgell bellowed, "No!!" and pressed his boot hard into Brisco's throat.

The damning fog lifted and the searing pain dissipated from his neck. The guardian was gone and Brisco lay motionless on the ground. Red came up behind Georgell and caught him as he faltered.

"Okay?" he questioned.

Georgell recovered his balance, hoarsely answering, "Yes." He then leaned over, hands on his knees, and sucked in deep gulps of air. The battle still raged around him. He could hear yells of anger, screams of pain, police barking orders, the blue and red flash of lights from all around and yet none of it mattered—he was breathing, alive. Heavy footfalls approached and without looking Georgell knew it was Moose and Chopper. He felt their hands press comfortingly against his back, both spouting queries about his health.

"I'm good," Georgell wheezed. As he raised himself back up to full stature, Moose immediately saw the guardian scarring across Georgell's throat and winced. Chopper too cringed at the sight, his eyes big. Then both looked away.

"Freeze!" A cop shrieked from behind. They all turned and were surprised to see a disheveled cop with his gun pointed angrily at Red. "Freeze!" the cop repeated.

Georgell stepped in front of Red, as did Moose and Chopper, and the cop screamed for them to move. Georgell shook his head and took a step toward the cop. Fuming with rage the cop pointed the gun to the ground and fired a bullet inches away from Georgell's foot.

"Hey," someone bellowed from across the street. Georgell looked over and saw Jackson hoofing it toward them. "Drop the gun," he ordered.

The cop ignored the order and raised the gun to Georgell's head. "Take another step hero," he dared.

With his own gun now raised at the officer, Jackson calmly said, "Roper, drop your weapon." The officer ignored the order again and Jackson roared, "Drop your weapon, NOW!"

Roper broke eye contact with Georgell, leering at Jackson. "That man assaulted me, Sergeant," he said, wagging the gun at Red.

Jackson kept his weapon locked on the officer. "Put the weapon on the ground." Another officer crept up behind Roper.

"But he assaulted me!" Roper protested again.

Jackson nodded and the second officer snapped into action, disarming Roper in a trained rear attack. He had him immobile and cuffed on the street within seconds of initial contact.

"Red?" Jackson asked.

"No," Red succinctly lied.

"Alright," Jackson said addressing the officer and returning his weapon to its holster. "Put Roper in a car and we'll sort it out later." The officer acknowledged the order, lifted Roper to his feet, and escorted him to the nearest squad car.

"Sergeant," Georgell said, using Jackson's title to eliminate the question of favoritism, "Can I speak with you?"

Jackson nodded and motioned for Georgell to join him by a nearby squad car.

"I'm going to give you a quick version of events so you can clear up the mess and get your boys on track!" Georgell said rapidly stepping over to the car.

"I don't appreciate the tone." Jackson raised his hands to his hips.

Georgell sharply raised his chin to display the new row of guardian scars on his neck. "And I don't appreciate getting my head severed because of the negligence of green cops that think they know everything."

"Alright, spit it out," Jackson growled.

Georgell gave Jackson a quick rundown of the night's events and then added, "I had him down and subdued. I handed him to your brainless rookie and the next thing I know Brisco is running across the street and busting up another Greek. Meanwhile your negligent genius has Red backed up against the wall while serious fights are raging all around him. I told Red to go through him so he could help me. I don't know what he did to your supercop but if anyone is to blame, it's me. Anyway now I have these beauty marks and that dude has a severely fractured arm," he said, pointing to the writhing Greek on the ground. "I want to press charges against that piece of . . ."

"I got it! I got it!" Jackson interrupted. "The kid is a fool—I'll take care of it. Are you done yelling at me?"

Georgell nodded, feeling a little foolish for unloading his anger on Jackson.

"Good, let me sort out this riot you've caused and we can talk later."

Georgell nodded again.

☼~ **30** ~☼

It took a few hours to clear the traffic and release all those involved. Eight muscle heads and two Greeks were arrested, but only three people went to the hospital: Devon, who could not maintain consciousness due to his severe concussion, Brisco, who needed extra care for his shattered nose and ruptured windpipe, and the Greek with the fractured arm. A number of vehicles were banged up in the fender bender and another had a caved in hood from a particularly nasty body slam credited to Moose. And, aside from a thrashed rose bush, Terrance was astonished to find no damage to the club, inside or out.

While statements were written, Georgell rustled through the lost and found closet and pulled out an ugly beige turtle neck. With a shrug he pulled off his security shirt and slipped the musty garment over his head. He figured the ridicule and laughter over the shirt would be easier to handle then the questions about his prominent new scars. As he tried to tuck the shirt in, Red came around the corner. "Doc what should I say in report?"

Georgell looked up. "Yeah don't say anything about the cop. Actually," Georgell said reaching into his pocket and pulling out some keys. He tossed the keys to Red. "The green key will open the roof door. Get the baton and discreetly take it to Jackson. When he asks—tell him the truth, he already knows I gave you the go ahead. Anyway, ask him about the report and he will tell you what to say."

Forty minutes flew by as everyone lounged on couches in the tunnel and traded moments of glory. Injuries were flaunted; most of the bouncers had minor scrapes and bruises while a few had lumps welling up on their heads and black eyes starting to form. Moose had a nasty scratch down the length of his arm and his shirt was ripped to tatters. There were also two pitchers of ice on his lap with his throbbing fists soaking inside. Chopper and Nemesis compared ears, as both had earrings ripped out during the brawl.

Bronco tossed Chopper his golden hoop and said, "I saw the dude take off with this and I grabbed it from him."

"Sweet, thanks man!" Chopper said snatching the hoop from the air and looking it over for damage.

Emma sat on the armrest of a couch and pressed a damp bar towel to a gash on Georgell's forehead. "How's that lip of yours Terrance?" she said.

Leaning against the wall across from Emma, Terrance smiled and said, "It's nothing, my knee hurts more than my lip." With a grimace, he then mimicked the motion of grabbing someone by the head and kneeing them multiple times in the face. A dark blood stain adorned his pant leg to prove his action and everyone seemed pleased by his willingness to help out.

Georgell gently moved Emma's hand and towel from his head and touched the injury. He was certain the deep cut was a result of head-butting Brisco and was pleased that the bleeding had finally stopped. He thanked Emma for her nursing then with excitement told the group about Nemesis body checking the guy into the rose bush and Pepper's stellar roundhouse kick that kept the guy tangled within. Everyone applauded, and then laughed as Terrance jokingly threatened to deduct the bush from their wages.

"Okay, I've heard all the highlights but no one has mentioned the best," Santos said, standing up and quieting the chatter.

"Whatever," Pineapple said.

A few other disagreements began to flare among the group but Santos raised his arms. "Just listen—I'm sure you will all agree." The din quieted as Santos continued, "The best moment, and I'll never forget it, was the start of it all. I mean Doc blasted that dude right out of the air. He was on him before anyone even knew the dude was there. It was unbelievable!"

"Awesome!" Pepper agreed.

"How did you even know?" Nemesis said.

All those that saw the action began to share their view of the event but Santos quieted the comments by loudly repeating the Nemesis question. Everyone looked to Georgell.

"I could smell him," he said, shrugging his shoulders. Most of the group laughed at the response but he could see that Nemesis and Santos were not satisfied.

A whistle blasted from Emma's lips and in the subsequent silence she said, "Wait—wait—wait, I disagree. If any of you could have seen my expertly thrown water bottle sail across the street and smack the screaming banshee I was aiming for, square on the nose, well then . . ." She smiled at Georgell proudly.

"That was you?" he asked, pleased by her diversion.

She nodded and Georgell pulled her to his lap and kissed her to a rousing applause. "That was sweet!" he said, releasing her.

Emma beamed with pride. Flexing her bicep, she boasted, "I do have a pretty good arm."

Georgell grinned, "Yeah, that too."

After a few more minutes Terrance finally rattled his set of keys and pointed to the exit. "Enough," he said. "Tomorrow is the big night, remember—angels and demons. I know some of you are scheduled to be here at ten to help with the decorations so let's call it a night; oh, and Happy Valentine's Day!"

☼~ **31** ~☼

"You should've seen it man! He cut through those guardians like butter. I don't know which ones he took out versus the ones Moose and I KO'd but it was awesome. He has a huge shield and a battleaxe and fought like, well, like Moose, only with weapons." Chopper slapped Moose hard on the back.

Moose choked a bit on the burrito he was chewing and gave Chopper a glare as Emma returned with another round of nachos. The smell of steaming meat, onions, and salsa enticed Georgell and he looked forward to eating more despite his already full belly. Emma placed the platter in front of the newly arrived Jackson and squeezed into the booth beside Georgell.

"Do you have any idea how he got there or what you may have done differently?" Georgell asked.

"No?"

"Do you think you can get him back?"

"I don't know," Moose answered, shaking his head and taking a long pull from his Coke.

"Why wasn't he there later, or even before the brawl?" Jackson asked, shoving a scoop of beef, chips, guacamole, and melted cheese into his mouth.

Moose shrugged again. "Don't know that either."

"Well, the fact is—he was there! That is a positive, and from the description it sounds like he could give Bear's guardian a good fight," Jackson said, chewing loudly.

"Maybe but we still don't want to attempt that without another protector, and definitely not until we can positively assure the protectors will be present. Besides I'm not certain they are always visible," Georgell added and then explained the appearance of the guardians in the sports bar and the one over Brisco. "Maybe they aren't constant, even on battle grounds; maybe they come and go as needed."

Chopper weighed in, "Man, that's gotta be true. My friend from tonight—you know from church, the one with the hot protector—well I don't always see her. I mean I see Sara but not always her protector. There's others like that too, people that usually have protectors. Most of the time I can see them but some days I don't. I thought it was me but maybe not, huh?"

"Something to think about," Jackson said.

"Here's another one," Georgell added. "They aren't as ignorant as we thought. I moved on Brisco because I saw a guardian not because I knew it was Brisco or that he was hiding in the back of the truck. The guardian made a move and I knew something was about to happen so I reacted. Without that added step and counter-surprise, Cosmo would be sipping through a straw right now. Anyway, I think the guardian knew I could see him and purposefully waited for me to inadvertently look at him. He positioned himself and got a look into my eyes. I nearly lost me head." Georgell inadvertently rubbed his neck. "Just be careful when you react to guardian movement. I'm guessing they have a pretty good idea what's going on around them."

"Speaking of injuries," Jackson said after a sip of water. "Tell me again about the Greek kid. What did you do to him?"

Emma and Chopper looked surprised at Georgell and he realized that no one except Santos knew what really happened. "I rammed his head into the ceramic tile above the urinal."

"While he was . . ."

"Yes dear, while he was . . ."

"Sweet," Chopper said. "Gotta remember that one, man."

"Santos already told me," Moose said, snatching a nacho from Jackson.

"No one but this table and Santos know what happened and I want to keep it that way. We want to keep Cosmo and his crew on our side."

They all agreed and Jackson added, "You'd better inform Santos to keep his mouth shut but I don't think it'll be a problem, he's had some run-ins with the Greeks in the past—besides, he thinks you walk on water." Looking at his watch, Jackson stood. "I need to report back and call it a night. Thanks for the nachos."

"Hey, can you give me a ride home? I've got to wake up Naomi and tell her about tonight, and especially about my protector. She's going to flip!" Moose said, sliding from the booth. "Sorry but I just can't wait any longer."

"Ice that hand," Georgell called after Moose as he and Jackson left.

At the door, Jackson stopped as Moose exited. "Roper is on administrative leave pending a psych evaluation," he said in his signature megaphone voice. "Thought you should know." He then waved and pushed Moose back through the exit.

"What did Moose do to his hands?" Emma asked.

"It's all about accuracy," Georgell answered. "If I could teach him how to aim he wouldn't be so apt to hit walls and floors and poles and what was it tonight?"

"A car," Chopper answered.

"That's right, and cars. He tends to swing without much accuracy and connects with a lot of solid objects. Doesn't stop him though, he probably has more fractured bones and calcium deposits in his hands than most people do in their whole body."

Emma shook her head. She leaned in, pulled down Georgell's turtle neck, and lightly touched the new scars. "You can't hide those. I suggest you make a trip to Rembrandt early tomorrow; otherwise you'll be flooded with questions. As much as I hate the idea of my husband having a permanent necklace of tattoos I'm afraid there isn't much else to do."

"You're definitely going to look more sinister," Chopper said.

"Well that's a plus," Georgell agreed with a smile.

"At least they don't go all the way around like Chopper's forearm. That would look horrible." Emma added as she touched the five smooth scars.

"Yeah, lucky," Georgell said sarcastically. "And lucky my head is still attached at all. That was not a pleasurable moment in my life. I honestly thought I was through."

"Man, so did we," Chopper agreed. "I don't know where you found the strength. That guardian was dropping his blade on your heart when he vanished. We thought it connected. How many times is that for you, man? Close calls . . ."

"Too many," Georgell answered. He looked at Emma and rhetorically asked Chopper, "Do you want to know where I found the strength?" Not waiting for a reply he continued, "Well, my friend, you need to find yourself one of these." He leaned over, kissed Emma softly, and whispered, "You're the reason, you and the kids."

Chopper huffed at the display of affection and picking at the remaining nachos, grumbled, "I'm working on it . . ."

☼~ **32** ~☼

Georgell sneered at his reflection in the bathroom mirror. He flexed his neck and rolled his head, admiring the five tattoos across the base of his throat. Rembrandt had done a good job and Chopper was right, the tattooed scarring did give him a more sinister appearance.

Earlier in the day Georgell and Bear visited Dragon Tattoo and had Rembrandt ink their scarring with the peace-through-power symbol. Rembrandt made quick work of the job and they spent the remainder of the afternoon talking and wandering around town. Bear seemed like he was enjoying himself but on the way back to the car he snapped at a truck full of taunting teenagers and chased the vehicle down as one of the boys flipped him off. He caught the truck at a stop sign and managed to punch a dent in the fender as it screeched away. He probably would have pursued them further but stopped when he saw Georgell laughing from a distance. Other than the one melt down, Bear controlled his temper exceptionally well and seemed surprisingly optimistic. Georgell was pleased with the day.

Back in the club, it was closing in on eleven, and the staff buzzed with chatter about the previous night. Grisly bruises and black eyes became trophies and everyone seemed in high spirits. Terrance was delighted with the turnout and giddily commended the staff on their hard work and preparation. Various costumed angels and demons wandered the club. There were big wings, white suits, capes, and halos mixed with devil-red miniskirts, horns, tails and tridents alongside the commonly dressed clubbers; everyone seemed to be having fun. The ornate decorations ranged from fiery torches to heavenly designed ice sculptures. Amidst the décor and costumes the sight of the battered bouncers and Georgell's new tattoos went totally unnoticed.

Georgell continued modeling his tattoo in the mirror and then pondered the odds of an unusually quiet evening. Serious issues seldom occurred during special events. Everyone came to celebrate the holiday and have a good time; and above that, the people seemed more forgiving than usual on big party nights. Besides, brawls never happened two nights in a row, and the bigger a brawl the greater the odds nothing would happen on the following night. It was a fact proven time and again. Georgell was certain the night would be quiet, and he looked forward to the break.

The light flickered out as Georgell left the employee restroom and poked his head into Terrance's office. "How's that leg?" he asked.

Terrance looked up from his numbers. "Bruised but fine." He gestured to Georgell's neck, "What's the deal with your neck, some kind of trophy?"

Georgell raised his eyebrows; the trophy idea was definitely something he could use. "Yeah—well, you've seen that Four Feathers movie with Heath Ledger, haven't you?" Terrance nodded and Georgell continued, "It's like that. Remember how the guy got a bigger trophy for every man he killed and finally a necklace after he killed ten?"

Terrance nodded, a smirk creeping across his face. "Yeah . . ."

"Well for bouncers, its hospitalization, and Brisco was the twenty-fifth person I sent to the hospital. I had no choice. This tattoo is a requirement under bouncer code two-three-two section B."

"Get out of here!" Terrance barked as he tossed a pencil at Georgell's head.

Georgell deftly avoided the missile. "I'll get you a copy of the manual; besides, after last night I may have to make you an honorary bouncer." He paused for a moment and then raised an eyebrow and added with a crooked grin, "You'll have to be hazed though."

Terrance searched for another projectile but Georgell ducked behind the door and escaped into the outer hallway. Under the dim lighting of an exit sign, Georgell stopped, and recalling the wad of cash in his pocket, pulled it out. He counted the bills and was surprised to total over three hundred dollars already. Greeks had been giving him handshakes of cash and appreciative embraces all night. It was a little embarrassing, but Georgell was glad to see that his act hadn't gone unnoticed. Every greeting he received, cash or not, was accompanied with a comment regarding his protection of Cosmo. *It'll be interesting to see how Cosmo thanks me,* Georgell thought.

Georgell relocated the money to his front pocket and then entered the dance floor. A hot wave of fire blasted over his head and he flinched with surprise. He then smiled as he realized the flames came from a fire-breather dancing in the cage above him. The half naked entertainer was costumed in red body art, horns, and a leather loin cloth but little else.

"Sorry," the fire breather said with a hand over his mouth as if holding back more flames.

Georgell waved him off, knowing it wasn't his fault. The other cages had fire breathers belching fire as well and the DJ booth shot rockets of snow into the undulating crowd. The scene was definitely one for the books. Georgell shook his head and grinned.

Santos stood near a group of guys on the elephant side of the dance floor and Georgell headed over to speak with him. He didn't wait for a lull in the conversation but curtly interrupted. "I'm going to check the front. Hang out here."

Santos agreed with a nod, resuming his conversation. Georgell stood back and watched after strolling to the tunnel entrance. He was impressed with the way Santos held eye contact with his listener but managed to watch the crowd as well. It was a skill that normally took years to perfect but Santos had acquired the ability in short order. A beam of pride arrested Georgell's mind as he gloated over his student, and more so, his own ability to teach. *If I had me as a teacher I would have been great in a month too*, he silently boasted.

A searching Greek noticed Georgell standing near the tunnel and briskly walked over, extending his hand. "I heard about last night. Come in and get some food. I'll take care of you," the man said. He slipped Georgell some cash and a business card as their hands clasped.

Georgell thanked him and quietly thought; *now that is a good tip*. He then headed purposefully through the tunnel and toward the entrance. At the front of the club, Chopper and Moose talked with Red while eyeing the throng of patrons waiting to enter. " . . . I just pushed him," Red finished as Georgell exited the club.

"Whatever, you ruthless brute," Georgell said, a hand on Red's shoulder. "A push from you could probably part the Red Sea. Maybe we should change your alias to Moses."

Red turned with a perplexed look but smiled as everyone laughed.

225

"You know, the Red Sea, the Bible man—when Moses was helping all the slaves and . . ." Red continued to stare blankly and Chopper gave up, replacing the tutorial with a fit of laughter.

Georgell gently elbowed Chopper and said, "Get it together, Giggles. Go help Santos on the dance floor. I'll hang out here for awhile. I need the air."

Chopper didn't respond, just turned and entered the club as he burst into another wave of comedic huffing.

"Doc, you copy?" Jackson asked over the radio.

The voice took Georgell by surprise and he answered, "Barney, is that you?"

"That's a big ten-four. I'll be coming around in fifteen. Meet me in front."

"Copy that," Georgell answered and looked at Moose.

Moose shrugged and said, "Got me."

Georgell thought it over for a second, confused as to how Jackson had acquired a radio; but, under the circumstances, figured it was a good idea. In tough situations he could radio Jackson for backup. Yes, it was good to have him monitoring the chatter.

"How do you think he got it?" Moose asked.

"I don't know but I don't care either. I think it's a good idea, don't you?"

"Yeah, sure," Moose tentatively agreed.

The line spread in a sporadic jumble down the stanchioned sidewalk and passed the haggard rose bushes, ending near the far corner of the club. Although coats covered most of the patrons a few braved the cold without them due to ornate costumes and accessories. Georgell walked over and shook his head at two such patrons that shivered pitifully in the line; the girls were scantily clad and sparkled with glittered makeup and wings that protruded from their backs. They smiled pleadingly and Georgell escorted them from the line and pointed to the entrance. They hugged him thankfully and scampered passed Red and into the club. Georgell sheepishly grinned at Moose who shook his head in mock disgust.

Further down the line Georgell found a couple of guys immaculately dressed in white tuxedos with halos attached ingeniously above their heads. He motioned them to the entrance as well but informed them that hugs were not necessary as some onlookers snickered. Others begged entry as well but Georgell shook his head and politely explained that only uniquely dressed individuals were afforded the pass. A particularly buxom girl touched Georgell's arm and motioning to her friends said, "I'll uniquely undress if . . ."

"Sorry," Georgell interrupted to a whimper of disappointment. He extended his gaze down the line as he continued to walk its length. Near the end of the waiting crowd a guy stood with his date holding tightly to his arm. They weren't particularly dressed up or unique but Georgell recognized the woman from gay night at Club Momentum and knew she was actually a cross dresser. She wore a long dark wig and heavy makeup along with black lipstick and Georgell figured she was going for a Morticia Addams look. Her sallow companion wore a dark suit with a blood red rose clipped to the lapel. He had ghastly pale makeup over his face and hands, dark red eye shadow covered the rims of his eyes, and he too wore charcoal black lipstick.

Apart from the obvious gender switch of Morticia the couple didn't seem too extraordinary except for the two guardians that hovered above them. The suited guy had a diminutive guardian with dark eyes, dark hair, and a brown eighteenth-century tuxedo with ruffles in the front and shirt sleeves that flared out and extended over his boney fingers. The figure reminded Georgell of Montgomery Burns from the Simpson's and he found the relation humorous except for the fact that size or appearance never equated fighting ability.

Hmmm, Georgell thought as he discreetly looked at the transvestite's guardian. A large woman loomed above her with severed shackles around her wrists and ankles. She was not muscular but stood a good six feet tall, was large in stature and girth, and towered over her companion's guardian. Her hair was shoulder length but unkempt and visibly dirty as was her tattered clothing. A scowl covered the guardian's face and Georgell figured it was a permanent mask of anger. He also found it exceptionally interesting that a woman guardian influenced a man that wanted to be a woman and wondered what that might implicate.

Hmmm, Georgell thought again as he turned and wandered slowly back to the front. "Have you seen the love birds at the end of the line?" He asked Moose who gave him a knowing nod with a raised eyebrow.

"I was going to radio Chopper."

"Morticia is really a guy."

"The guardian?" Moose asked confused.

"No the mortal," Georgell said. "I recognized him from gay night at Club Momentum—weird, huh?"

"Weird those two gay guys have guardians or weird that you recognized them?" Moose asked, even more confused.

"No Stimpy," Georgell said, raising his hand as if to backslap him. "Gays come in all the time without guardians. I mean weird that a guy dressed as a woman is influenced by a female guardian."

Moose looked at Georgell for a moment as if replaying the words in his mind, "Yeah, that is weird." Shaking off the confusion, he then said, "Should I radio Chopper?"

"No let's wait till they're inside. Trying to deal with them out here would draw too much attention."

"Right."

Minutes passed as they watched the slow procession of the line and Georgell contemplated the advantage of letting the specks in early. Red tapped him on the shoulder and pointed to the left of the building. Georgell looked and saw Emma approaching with Naomi. Both women had wide grins on their faces and Georgell's stomach lurched as he immediately noted the protector heavily armed above Naomi. She was an impressively built black woman with multiple piercings and intricate tribal tattoos covering her scantily clad figure. She wore only a bikini top that looked like it was made from the mane of a lion and her legs were covered in a similar material that extended from her sculpted abdomen, over her shapely thighs, and down to her knees. *An Amazon!* Georgell mentally cheered.

The Amazon began raising her lengthy spear and stood in a throwing stance while gripping a short sword tightly in her other hand. Georgell spun back, looked over the line, and was horrified to see the guardians approaching from the outside edge. Each carried a now-visible weapon; the diminutive man held a curved Arabian scimitar that did not compliment his appearance, and above her head, the woman swung two heavy chains in wide arcs, solid balls flailing from the spinning ends.

A barreling mass brushed Georgell off-balance as Moose rocketed passed, rushing furiously toward the guardians that targeted his wife and Emma. Georgell lurched into action and yelled, "Emma, stop!"

Emma halted immediately, eyes fixed on Georgell as he and Moose rumbled toward them. Naomi grabbed her arm, nodding at the two individuals walking swiftly toward them from the line. Neither woman understood the situation but both knew they couldn't see the real problem. The look in their husbands' eyes was information enough and both froze.

Ten feet away, Georgell marveled as the Amazon tossed her spear with unreal force at the coming attackers. The spear pierced the shoulder of the female guardian and carried through her body until it stopped midway and protruded three feet from either side of her frame. The guardian's face contorted and the chain held by her left arm vanished, but she did not.

Moose swung at the unaware speck beneath the diminutive guardian, blasting him hard on the side of the face. The waiting patrons squealed in disbelief at the attack and then followed their awe with gasps as Moose followed his left hook with a crushing right roundhouse that buckled the man. His momentum carried him over the falling body and he brutally collided with the startled transvestite. They slammed into a parked Explorer and Moose's crushing weight pinned her against the vehicle. Without concern for appearance, Moose brought his knee hard into the midsection of the speck and then stepped back as she buckled forward.

A few gasps broke from the crowd as they became unnaturally silent. Moose finished the assault by dropping his anvil fists roughly to the back of the falling speck's head. She dropped cold to the sidewalk.

"Chopper to entry," Red radioed.

Naomi screamed as the unconscious body of the seemingly petite woman drop to the ground. Georgell hopped over the unconscious couple and slammed into Moose. "It's over," he harshly whispered as he forced Moose back against the Explorer. "Now follow my lead or this is going to look real bad." Moose did not seem to hear, his vision still clouded with blood lust. "Push me!" Georgell growled.

Moose responded with a shove more powerful than Georgell had anticipated and he nearly fell over the prone figures on the walk. A commanding order came from the crowd before Georgell could recover his footing and set his plan into motion.

"Freeze, psycho!" A plain-clothed man said, stepping from the line and pointing a 9mm Glock at Moose. In his other hand he arrogantly displayed a vice shield as license for his action. The entry doors opened and Chopper exited followed by Santos. They immediately halted as Georgell held a hand up to keep them at bay.

"What the hell are you doing? Get down on the ground!" the vice officer bellowed at Moose.

Ignoring the weapon, Naomi ran to Moose and threw her arms around him. Moose gently pulled her to one side, away from the line of fire, and glared at the cop. He then looked to Georgell for guidance.

Georgell knew he had three bouncers that would assault the officer without question and saw Santos deftly moving into position behind the man. As he contemplated the situation, he reflected on the oddity of the circumstance: mere hours earlier, on essentially the same day, a similar situation had occurred. An irrational officer in an extraordinary moment pointed a gun at one of his bouncers. Here, at least, the guardians were gone and the specks were assuredly incapacitated—but to the naked mortal eye it was clearly assault. Georgell nodded at Moose to obey the officer and looked to Emma for assistance with Naomi.

Naomi screeched as Moose pressed her into Emma's arms. He shook his head and kept eye contact with Naomi as he dropped to his knees and lay prone on the ground.

The officer looked to Georgell and sarcastically bellowed, "Are you going to help or stand there gawking?"

Georgell felt a flash of steam boil in his mind but ignored the scathing sarcasm and motioned for Chopper and Santos to come over. He told them to get the unconscious couple into the club and out of the cold. He then discreetly eyed Chopper with the added instruction to keep them unconscious.

Chopper nodded as he and Santos gently lifted the limp forms and carried them into the club. As they passed the line a group of girls noticed the heavy makeup and slipping wig on Morticia and one exclaimed, "That's a guy!"

"It is a guy," another voice said from further up in the line.

"Eww, he deserved it," another voice said with echoes of approval from his friends.

Others in the crowd began harassing those that spoke out and a heated debate ensued. In seconds the extraordinary assault became a sexually motivated hate crime. Georgell shook his head disgustedly at the crowd as he watched Chopper and Santos disappear into the club.

"Hey, Dilbert, call the police," the officer derogatorily ordered Georgell as he pressed his knee into Moose's back. Georgell ignored the demand as he saw flashing lights appear at the corner and slowly roll to the scene.

Moose was roughly cuffed, to the disapproving sobs of Naomi. She wrestled out of Emma's hold and rushed to help her husband. Georgell intercepted her and lifted her off the ground as Moose called back, "I'm alright Nomi. Let Georgell handle this. I'll call you later."

Naomi began to cry but Georgell held her tight until she quit fighting. Then he gently handed her back to Emma as Jackson hurried over, questioning the vice officer as to the trouble.

"This bouncer assaulted two homosexual males without provocation. Both males have been taken into the club but are badly beaten." Georgell felt a pang of anger as the officer relayed the incorrect and derogatory motive.

"Are you sure there was no cause for the assault?" Jackson questioned.

The officer flashed an angry glare at Jackson and said, "Of course I'm sure and there are a hundred witnesses here who will agree. Now take the guy downtown and book him or . . ."

"Or what?" Jackson barked back at the seething man. "I'll do my job but don't think for a minute that you have any kind of jurisdiction here. You belong to the Department of Alcohol and Beverage which means you can back off and answer any question I decide to ask."

"Are you going to book him?" the man asked with a little more cordiality.

"Yes," Jackson responded as he motioned for him to get off Moose.

"Can I go with him?" Georgell asked Jackson.

"No!" The vice officer said, looking at Georgell like he were some kind of idiot. Jackson unhappily agreed with the vice officer, leering back at him with a bolt of disapproval.

Without a second thought, Georgell threw a hard right cross at the officer's chin and watched as the officer bounced off the Explorer then collapsed unconscious on the sidewalk.

Jackson looked down at the officer then shook his head as he rolled his gaze back to Georgell, eye-wide in shock. A smattering of applause and whistles erupted from the onlookers.

"Now can I go?" Georgell asked as the officer slumped to the ground.

Jackson shook his head in disbelief, motioning for Georgell to assume the position. Georgell leaned against the Explorer and Jackson cuffed him as a moan came from the fallen officer.

"What are you thinking?" Jackson asked.

"I can't let him go in a cell alone," Georgell answered.

"I understand that, but . . ." Jackson shook his head with a wide grin.

"He deserved it."

"Yeah but . . ."

His words were interrupted as a car alarm began to wail from the battered Explorer. *After all that*, Georgell thought. *Now it goes off?*

"Alright, come on," Jackson said. He pushed Georgell toward his car and then pulled Moose around and directed him to the car as well.

After both sat comfortably in the back of his cruiser, Jackson rolled down the windows, shut the doors, and said, "I'm going to gather some statements. I'll let your wives come over and talk with you while I'm away. Don't worry, everything will be fine."

"Thank you," Moose said, careening his neck desperately for a glance of Naomi.

"Can you have Red radio Pineapple please?" Georgell asked.

Jackson nodded then wandered back to the front of the club. He spoke with Emma and Naomi, then helped up the stunned vice officer and walked him toward the entrance. As he passed Red he said something and Georgell saw Red nod with understanding. Seconds later Red's voice broke over the radio and said, "Pineapple to entry please."

Naomi leaned in through the open window and with tears streaming down her face she draped herself over Moose. "I'm sorry Glen. I'm sorry I came to see you, I just wanted you to know . . ." She leaned in and kissed him with salty tears. " . . . I'm pregnant," she said. She kissed him again. "We only came to tell you the good news."

Moose stammered at the announcement, "Really?" he said, eyes-wide.

Naomi grinned through her tears and Moose beamed, "You should have seen your protector." He described the action with enthusiasm and relayed the information without concern for what the consequences might bring.

Leaning in the other window, Emma kissed Georgell and he apologetically told her that he couldn't let Moose go to jail alone. Emma begrudgingly understood. She pressed a hand against his face and admiringly mouthed the words, "I love you." She then stepped away as Pineapple approached.

"What's going on?" Pineapple asked Georgell.

"Sorry Pineapple, I'm leaving you in charge. Moose and I have to make an unexpected visit downtown. Can you manage?"

Pineapple nodded but was visibly concerned and confused by the situation.

"Can you engage my radio for me?" Georgell asked.

Pineapple leaned in, cued the mike, and Georgell matter-of-factly stated, "Moose and I are leaving. Pineapple is taking the lead. Santos and Chopper stay roaming. Sorry guys."

"What?" Terrance belted over the radio in response.

Georgell winced and mentally chastised himself for forgetting Terrance. He then motioned for Pineapple to cue the mike again and said, "Uh, sorry T. Moose and I got into a little trouble. Talk to Red he can give you the details."

No response came but Georgell knew Terrance was running to the front for an explanation. He then directed Pineapple and Naomi to remove the radios from him and Moose as he saw Jackson approaching with the vice officer.

The officer was holding an ice pack to his jaw and mumbling something about the assaulted party not wanting to press charges but assured Jackson that he would personally make a report. He then noticed the group around the squad car and the opened windows. Lowering the ice pack, he said, "Why are the windows down? What kind of operation are you running here?"

Jackson nodded at Pineapple, opened the front door, and apologized to Naomi as he said, "We need to roll." Naomi stepped away from the car and smiled at Moose, holding his radio in her quivering hands.

Jackson said nothing as he rolled up the power windows and fastened his seat belt. The vice officer continued to degrade his policing skills and question his methods as he strapped into the passenger seat and closed the door. Georgell could feel Jackson's desire to hit the whiner and marveled at his control.

Moose repositioned himself, sitting with a contemplative but happy smile. Georgell leaned over and ignoring the continuous jabber from the vice officer said to Moose, "So is Nomi some kind of bedroom name?"

Moose looked at him and then with a whisper, and ignoring the question, said, "I wish I could've seen you drop that dude."

"Yours was much more impressive," Georgell responded. "Did you see that spear sticking out?"

Moose nodded and they quietly relived the moment as Jackson patiently drove—the irate vice officer jabbering on incessantly.

☼~ **33** ~☼

A strong smell of coffee wafted through the processing area and Georgell couldn't put his finger on the source. The walls, benches, floors and desks, behind glass partitions, were a dull concrete gray and except for the bright fluorescent lighting, behind caged covers, and the likewise caged green exit signs that hummed a green glow, the space was not inviting at all. Still, Georgell was annoyed by the coffee smell. There were three other individuals waiting to be processed and Georgell looked at them, wondering what landed them here. There was a filthy unhygienic transient in a huge faded University of Utah blanket, sleeping on a bench with his arms skewed awkwardly. The other two men wore skin tight clothing and sat smiling, and giggling at each other. *Prostitution*, Georgell surmised.

Georgell and Moose sat side by side on a cold bench in the middle of a room and waited as Jackson discussed something with the processing clerk. "Where is that smell coming from?" Georgell said.

"I think it's the bum," Moose said.

"Wow, seriously?"

Moose sniffed in a long drag of air. "Positive, there's a touch of whiskey too."

"Huh," Georgell said still surprised by the smell and unable to catch any sign of whiskey in the air.

"His home is the dumpster by Beans and Brews," Jackson said as he approached carrying a cordless phone and some clipboards.

"I believe it," Georgell said.

"Listen guys, I'm going to do what I can to get you out of here, but with that idiot causing problems, my best may still leave you in a cell overnight." Jackson sat facing them on a nearby bench, "I'm going to make some calls and try to get this handled but I can't promise anything."

Nodding, Georgell said, "What about processing? How long before we actually get in a cell?"

"Is that decaf or whole brew?" Moose gestured to the sleeping transient.

Moose was nervous and Georgell knew he was turning to his ever-present humor channel to compensate. He laughed and shouldered him despite his own looming fear.

"You'll get your phone calls but I wouldn't count on bail this late. Like I said, unless I can pull some strings I'm afraid you're stuck here until morning." He then added in a softer whisper, "The good news is I'm holding all the eye witness statements and I can lose the negative ones; also Chopper and Santos somehow convinced the two assaultees not to press charges so that problem is gone. Our only concern is Mr. Bucking-for-a-Promotion. If I can get him to drop his charges and revise his statement then we're home free."

"Is that a possibility?" Georgell asked, astounded by the idea.

"Let's just say it's not impossible, okay. There is one shot—but don't get your hopes up."

Moose kicked Jackson to signify the return of the vice officer and the conversation abruptly changed, " . . . okay so who wants to make the first call."

"I bet they're still at the club," Georgell suggested. "Let's call Emma's cell phone."

Moose agreed.

"How can they . . . they aren't even processed yet," the officer objected.

Jackson turned to address him and said, "These two are not hardened criminals and they aren't a flight risk. I know them well and I know where they live, so go find someone else to pester and let me handle this."

The officer didn't say another word, just held his stance, folded his arms and glared with disapproving eyes as Jackson uncuffed Georgell from the bench and handed him the cordless phone.

"Do you know the number?" Jackson said, ignoring the hovering officer and releasing Moose from the bench as well.

Georgell nodded and keyed in Emma's number. Both phone calls were brief as the vice officer loomed and taunted the men with his stance, he wanted another tussle but Georgell refused to oblige and kept Moose from engaging the man either.

The fingerprinting, mug shots, and processing dragged on for two hours. Jackson clued Georgell and Moose in on his ploy to keep them from the cell while he waited for the call but incarceration was beginning to look inevitable as the night wore on. Georgell pressed to know what it was they were waiting on but Jackson refused to divulge the ray of hope, explaining it was a long shot. Even with a positive result Jackson couldn't promise that the officer would yield; the man was too fired up and wanted Georgell prosecuted to the full extent.

After a while Jackson pulled some strings and had the vice officer called out on a gig, to the gratitude of everyone in the now bustling center. Minutes later, with nothing remaining to do, and other precinct officers haranguing him about the extended length of his processing, Jackson begrudgingly accepted defeat and escorted Moose and Georgell to the holding cell. On their way he discreetly said, "Tell me how many are in each cell and I'll put you in the one least occupied."

Georgell knew Jackson referred to guardians, and a nervous quiver lurched at his stomach. Although the lengthy processing was appreciated, the extended time afforded a slowly mounting anxiety that Georgell could not shake. He had no idea what to expect and knew Moose was also apprehensive by his controlled breathing and purposeful gaze.

As the heavy door locked behind them and they rounded the corner towards the cells the incarcerated men and hovering guardians came bleakly into view. *I apologize for my lack of communication Lord*, Georgell prayed in his mind. *But I know you are there and I believe that you granted me this gift of sight. Please, help me now; let me continue to learn and do whatever it is you desire of me. If nothing else—for Emma, Gina, Gideon, and Wolfy—please, don't let it end here.* He repeated the names in his head, as if by doing so he would gain further strength and resolve to face the menace he knew was waiting.

Moose muttered something incoherent and Georgell looked over to see him walking with his eyes closed and mouthing a prayer as well.

Jackson broke the silence with a whisper, "How many?"

"Four left, three right."

Jackson swore under his breath and escorted them to the cell on the right. It was more crowded than its sister cell but the guardian threat was less, and that made the decision obvious.

As Jackson searched for the key Georgell felt the urge to look up and as he did so a wave of fire coursed through him. He felt energized and relieved as he stared at the Scottish warrior bouncing above Moose with his shield and battleaxe ready for action. The protector seemed excited and hungry to fight. His eyes stared straight into the cell where he appeared to be mocking one of the guardians. Georgell grabbed Moose's arm and as he turned said, "He's here."

☼~ **34** ~☼

Moose didn't understand at first but Georgell gestured above with a smile and Moose caught on. "Really," he said as a grin flashed across his cheeks. He lifted his gaze upward and then, eyes popping, returned his gaze to Georgell and said, "You too!"

Georgell then understood that his urge to look up was probably a prompting from his own protector. *Wow*, he thought, heart pounding, *this is insane.*

Glancing up again, Georgell noticed the Scot smiling down at him. He pointed above Georgell then flipped his shield around and the mirror-like surface on the inside reflected his own protector. The man was tall and bulged under a well tailored suit. In his left hand the protector held an ornate body shield like that of the Scot; it seemed from a different era yet he held the armament with knowing power. In his right hand a lengthy broad sword was held mightily above the protector's head and Georgell was certain it would take both hands of a normal man to wield the weapon. His face was etched with lines of experience and two jagged scars traversed his features from the left of his bald head, across a white blinded eye, his nose, cheek, and down to his jaw line. A heavy brown beard extended from the protector's chin and over his broad chest. The protector smiled a sinister grin directed at Moose and Georgell felt infused with a new found determination.

The Scot flipped his shield back around and slapped his sword against it, returning his gaze to the now lunging guardians within the cell.

"He really wants to get in there," Georgell said, mesmerized by the protector.

"Yours too," Moose said, bouncing on his toes and shaking his hands.

Jackson turned the key in the lock but before opening the entry said, "Wait until I'm out or I'll have to get involved."

"We'll try," Georgell said, pumping his fists and allowing the surge of adrenaline to course through his body.

"You guys going to be alright?" Jackson asked still concerned despite the knowledge that both carried protectors.

"Georgell definitely has a general," Moose said encouragingly.

"So does Moose," Georgell added.

"What about in there?" Jackson asked motioning to the cell.

"Only soldiers in our cell. We'll be fine," Georgell said.

"Yeah, let us in!"

Jackson slid open the entry gate and both men stepped in; halting as Jackson slid the door shut and reset the lock. Jackson then walked briskly away and exited the holding area without looking back. The heavy entry door closed and the bolt audibly locked into place.

Georgell looked at Moose and motioned to the far right to avoid any interference from the adjacent cell to their left. Moose nodded and they slowly made their way to the right as two specks followed their progression from the backside of the cell.

Moose began to laugh with a sinister chuckle as he eyed the biggest patron of the cell, sitting alone at the far right. The man wore obvious biker gear and his arms were covered in tattoos of violent scenes. He stood and appeared to be of larger stature than Moose. A mass of dried blood was visible in the man's matted hair and a lump protruded from his head but he seemed no less eager to fight. Above him a guardian held a coiled whip and danced with frenzied anticipation beneath the ceremonial white robes of the Ku Klux Klan.

"Check this out," a man said to his friend as Moose and Georgell approached.

"Oh yeah," the friend said with excitement.

The men then flinched as Moose jumped onto their bench and propelled himself at the approaching biker. Cheers began to buzz in both cells as the fight erupted.

The biker staggered backward behind the force of Moose's attack but stayed on his feet as they slammed against the brick wall at the far end of the cell. Moose thrust two heavy blows to the biker's stomach and the behemoth wrapped his meaty arms around him and squeezed. He then lifted Moose from the ground and tossed him hard to his left. The power of the throw wobbled Moose but he stayed on his feet and maneuvered so his back was against the cell bars. He then braced himself for the charge of the bullish man. A split second before contact, Moose dropped to his knees, planted his feet against the cell bars, and lunged at the biker's legs. The man barreled forward and stumbled as Moose hammered his knees and lifted him off the ground. The cell shook as his quarter-ton body thundered against the bars.

Moose jumped to his feet and spun toward the man who was slowly pressing up from the ground. The man's guardian was still visible and slashing the whip violently at the Scot who pressed forward behind his shield swinging at the elusive guardian with his battleaxe. Moose jumped on the biker's back. Sitting on his massive shoulders, he reached down and gripped the man's chin with both hands and pulled back, his biceps bulging from the strain. Seconds later the man went limp from a loss of blood to the brain and the guardian, unscathed, vanished.

Georgell stepped quickly to the back of the cell where he turned to face the other two specks. Moose had the biker under control and Georgell had to focus on the others. The men were not friends but came at him as if choreographed by one mind; one was a middle-aged black man with a large sumo-looking guardian tapping two clubs together, the other man was a thin weasel of a guy that Georgell immediately recognized as Manny, a two-bit dealer that Santos used to provide muscle for.

Manny allowed his coat to slip off as he advanced, flexing his wiry frame. Georgell wasn't impressed but wavered at the sight of the giant guardian above him. The guardian was also thin but immensely tall and his head seemed to scrape the high ceiling. His eyes bulged out of his reddening face like massive ping pong balls. A long staff with spikes thrust from the giants grip and Georgell felt a tinge of concern for his protector.

The black man shoved Manny back and lunged at Georgell with a right cross, easily dodged. Manny cursed at the man for shoving him as Georgell countered with a hard right uppercut to the man's groin. With a squeal the man dropped to his knees and Georgell followed with a crushing left jab that he swung with all his weight to the man's head. The man dropped, but to Georgell's surprise, had not been knocked unconscious.

A surprise tackle hammered Georgell from the left and he fell hard to the ground. The attack did not come from Manny, who Georgell could plainly see, but from an unseen attacker and Georgell immediately thought

Moose had failed and the biker was his new assailant. Manny took a giant step toward the fallen duo and with his right foot extended back, swung it hard at Georgell's face. With a twist Georgell shoved the man on top of him just enough to block the rushing kick and realized the man was too small to be the biker. The man grunted as Manny's foot thumped him solidly on the shoulder.

A painful jolt rocked Georgell's jaw as the man caught him with an uppercut and then pulled back to whack him with another. Georgell slashed his open palm across his body, deflecting the second uppercut harmlessly to the side. He then spun his body right, with the momentum of his block, and was able to roll the guy off. Another kick came from Manny but this time successfully connected to the back of Georgell's head as he continued to roll. The painful rock of the blow gave Georgell a rush of gratitude that Manny wore padded basketball sneakers.

Georgell completed his roll and dropped an elbow toward the prone man but he too had rolled and escaped the elbow. A shiver of pain shot up his arm as his elbow hammered the barren cement but Georgell did not falter. Above him he saw his protector blocking thundering blows from the sumo guardian's clubs and parrying the staff that slashed at him from Manny's guardian. He marveled at the powerful shield and the defensive skill of his protector.

From his periphery, Georgell saw another kick barreling in from Manny as the intended victim of his elbow scrambled to his feet. He canted his right arm and caught Manny's foot just above the ankle is it slammed into his jaw. With raging force Georgell rolled his body again to the right, while holding Manny's foot immobile, and rammed the solid base of his left palm with pinpoint accuracy to Manny's knee. The effect was sickening as Georgell felt the knee pop. Manny wailed in pain.

To the left of Manny, Georgell saw the eyes of his accomplice widen as a roundhouse blasted him in the face and propelled him toward the cheering crowd. A few men caught him as he fell and mercilessly tossed him headlong back toward Moose. Stepping in and raising his arm, Moose effectively caught the man in a clothes-line that lifted him of his feet and flipped him toward the ground.

No longer bothered with three fighters, and pleased that Moose had in fact defeated the hefty biker, Georgell pressed hard against Manny's knee and forced him to the ground. He then released his leg and rolled to the right over Manny's prone body, and this time, accurately connected with an elbow that crushed him in the mouth. Manny's screams of pain gurgled as busted teeth and blood rushed down his throat.

Looking up for another glimpse of the guardian battle, Georgell inadvertently made eye contact with Manny's guardian and felt a lurching regret pound his stomach. The guardian released his staff as Georgell's protector deflected it with his shield, then a serrated dagger appeared where the staff was held and with both hands the guardian gripped the dagger and lunged at Georgell. In a surreal visual display the guardian's head suddenly separated from his shoulder as the battleaxe from Moose's protector sliced it cleanly free. The guardian vanished not a second later and the Scot motioned Georgell to his feet, bowed, and then returned to Moose who stood more than ten feet away.

Manny spit out a tooth with a spray of blood and cursed with screaming pain. Without looking, Georgell cocked his elbow back, leaned a little further to the right, and drove it again to Manny's face. With an audible crack, Manny's screams halted and he lay unconscious on the grimy floor.

Georgell then realized that the sumo guardian was no longer above the whimpering speck against the wall; but that his own protector was smiling and motioning as Moose's had, for Georgell to stand. This prompted Georgell to wonder if it were unmanly to battle from the ground. He stood and felt dizzy from his multiple rolls but managed to look to the far right of the cell where the biker lay unconscious. He then walked over to Moose who stood gloating over the pleading victim of his clothesline.

"Are you Manny's new muscle?" Georgell asked the man writhing below Moose. The man nodded and in a moment of weakness Georgell said, "Find a new job," and kicked the guy in the head. He too went limp and slumped unconscious to the ground.

"Three for me and one for you," Georgell said to Moose as he rubbed his aching jaw. The men around them cheered and thanked the bouncers for the rousing entertainment then returned to their seats, chatting excitedly.

"No way, King Kong Bundy over there counts as three," Moose protested as he pointed to the downed biker. "Besides, that one was mine," he argued nodding at the man knocked out below him.

Georgell smiled and said, "Fine, two each." He and Moose then locked hands and congratulated each other as a commotion sounded outside the cell. A group of officers, including a smiling Jackson, stormed in ordering everyone against the back wall. The inmates moved sluggishly but did as they were commanded, including the black man who could barely stand from the pain in his gut.

"Who did this?" a perturbed desk sergeant questioned.

No one responded and a few laughs echoed in the silence. The sergeant asked again but received the same snickering response. Georgell enjoyed the sudden camaraderie that he felt with these men and tried not to look at Jackson who was holding back a fit of laughter. Then the coffee smelling transient, still draped in the U of U blanket and standing near the end of the line, pointed to the unconscious men and, with a gravelly voice, said, "Uh, sir, those guys were fighting each other. It was quite a stirring finish."

Everyone laughed at the remark, including a few of the officers, but finally the sergeant cut through the hilarity. Pointing at subordinates, he directed, "Put them in the other cell." Then pointing at the inmates in the adjacent cell, he barked, "You lot get against the back wall as well." He then unlocked the door as the inmates did as instructed.

The officers dragged Manny's unconscious bodyguard to the cell and lay him near the back. Georgell winced as they then grabbed Manny by the legs and dragged him over to the cell as well. Three other guards hefted the massive biker. Two grabbed his legs while the other held up his hefty arms, trying unsuccessfully to ease the strain on the other officers. The biker began to stir as they cleared the entry of the new cell but the officer in the rear lost his grip and the biker's head bounced off the cement. "Oops," the officer said as the man fell silent again.

After locking both cells the officers began to exit the holding area. Jackson shook his head with an amazed glance at Moose and Georgell. When the bolt locked on the heavy door a group of black men walked over to the rousing biker and kicked him till he quit stirring. Georgell guessed they were the reason he was in the cell to begin with and chuckled at the oversight of the sergeant.

Georgell beckoned Moose to the far right corner of their cell and Moose begrudgingly followed. The specks, watching from the other cell, cursed as Moose and Georgell walked away, their guardians pointing and lurching at the protectors with menacing hate.

"Come over here boys," an older man beckoned while pressing against the bars. "Let me give you a lesson in respect."

"I'll kill ya—I'll kill ya—I'll kill ya!" another spat, shaking the bars in a growing frenzy.

Georgell was aware that the protectors sought the battle just as eagerly. He felt an urge to fight like he'd never felt before and could see the Scot swinging his axe above Moose, though he was well out of range.

"What do you think?" Georgell asked.

"I think we should go over and get it on."

"No," Georgell hesitantly responded. "We can't maneuver through those bars. If it were an open area we'd have the advantage and I would agree, but not with those bars separating us. It's too dangerous." Then, with a sudden thought, said, "Your guardian left you."

"So," Moose queried. "Chopper said they leave their specks all the time to battle. He's seen it a lot."

"Yeah but don't the specks make physical contact first?" Georgell responded. He thought for a moment and then added, "Maybe only one has to touch; I mean if there are two guardians and one protector, one of the guardian specks has to touch the protector speck in order for the three to battle unattached, and vice versa."

Georgell continued to think out loud, "The only thing I've seen or heard contrary to that theory is the spear from Naomi's protector. In fact, that is the first time I've ever seen a projectile weapon in the hands of a guardian or protector. Maybe because she's pregnant she is extra vulnerable and therefore gets better protection? I don't know."

Pausing for a moment, frustrated, he then abruptly made eye contact with Moose. "I think your protector was able to leave you and help me because Manny's guardian recognized me. I mean he was nowhere near you and yet he beheaded the guardian as it lunged toward me." He looked at Moose for a response but received nothing.

Moose stared blankly at Georgell.

"So let's make eye contact. I know it means more guardians that recognize us but what if I'm right? If our boys can attack without us being near—I think it's worth the risk."

Moose nodded vehemently. "Absolutely, and if they do attack then let's make eye contact with the other two," Moose added.

"Right," Georgell said with a grin. "Start with the ones on the bench, then look to the ones at the bars. I'll go left, you go right."

Moose agreed and motioned to a bench in the middle of the cell. They walked to the bench, sat, and then in unison turned and glared toward the guardians in the other cell. Georgell made eye contact with a lithe guardian that thrashed and appeared to foam at the mouth with growing rage. The guardian had pronounced cheekbones, heavy eye brows, and a lengthy mustache. He wore a heavy black bear skin over his torso and legs and had a similarly bordered hat with a metal spike protruding from the top. In his gloved hands the guardian twirled two swords with trained precision. Georgell figured the harried warrior was Mongolian from his appearance, and felt certain that he was also a recruiter by his steady gaze and fluid movement. Rank had no bearing, though; Georgell knew they would have to engage every guardian and was oddly unafraid.

The protectors moved, just as Georgell had guessed, triggered by recognition. The Scot swung his axe and bolted headlong toward a guardian dressed in a United States military uniform while Georgell's protector lumbered slowly, purposefully, toward the frothing Mongolian.

"The others!" Georgell said, focusing his eyes on a hillbilly that loomed over the taunting old man at the cell bars.

The hillbilly danced a little jig as his eyes locked with Georgell's. A chilling excitement pressed at Georgell as the protectors and guardians engaged in their battle. Georgell stood and felt Moose stand as well; a cold shudder pricked his neck. The bystanders cheered, excited that Moose and Georgell were so willing to brawl again. Georgell put out his arm and held Moose back from a headlong rush. They moved deliberately toward the cell separation, causing the guardians to flinch at their approach. Georgell wanted to distract them from battle and his plan was working.

The hillbilly looked as they neared, and Georgell's protector thrust his sword into the distracted guardian's heart. The man vanished and his speck faltered, confused as to why he was pressed so firmly against the bars. The thrust exposed the right side of Georgell's warrior and the Mongolian slashed him with both swords. The protector spun his shield sideways and halted the swords from gaining a deeper purchase. The guardian followed the downward swing of his swords with a perfectly timed somersault that he landed without the slightest hint of imbalance, and then parried an attack with one sword while slashing high with the other.

He won't be distracted, Georgell surmised but also hesitantly figured the guardian was watching and waiting for him to get closer. He stopped, not willing to chance another near miss.

The Scottish warrior pressed his shield facedown toward the farmer and although he exposed his torso by doing so, the move lured an errant lunge of the farmer's pitchfork. Instinctively, the warrior snapped the shield up and pulled hard and high, disarming the farmer as the pitchfork sailed upwards, disappearing in the ceiling.

The soldier, instead of taking advantage of the protector's move, stepped toward the unarmed guardian and thrust his rapier into the farmer's neck. The farmer vanished and the soldier swiftly swung his rapier back at the protector. The point pierced deep into the protector's upper thigh but forced only a smile from the calculating Scot as he hammered his shield down, snapping the rapier to the ground, and thrust his axe forward. The solid head of the axe pummeled the soldier in the face and pressed him back. The warrior stepped forward; dropping the axe downward and in a high swinging arc over his head. At the apex of the swing, the axe fell with tremendous force and sunk deep into the soldier's chest. The soldier vanished and his speck crumbled to the ground in exhaustion.

Only the Mongolian remained, pressing on like a buzzing fly despite the odds. The guardian slashed and jabbed at the protectors as spurts of blood seeped from shallow wounds on the men. The protectors lunged at the agile man, fighting with frustrated rage as he continued to inflict aggravating wounds that whittled away at their strength.

In gaping astonishment, Georgell surmised that his original assessment was wrong. The vicious guardian was definitely some sort of general. Feeling the need to help, Georgell stepped toward the speck. A blade slashed inches from his face as the guardian rolled toward him and away from a plummeting axe. Georgell's protector shot him a warning glare and Georgell backed away.

Moose, unrecognized by the swift guardian, lurched passed, reached through the bars and, grasping the long hair of the Mongolian's speck, yanked the man's head hard against the cell bars. The fight still raged overhead and Moose repeated the action with better results the second time. The man slumped to the ground and his guardian vanished. A pitiful laughter rumbled over the audience as the man fell.

The Scottish warrior looked down at Moose and nodded solemnly as he resumed his position. Georgell's protector slammed his sword against his shield and grinned wildly as he too resumed his position.

"Three for me," Moose said softly as he lumbered passed Georgell and toward a bench that leaned against the back wall. The men who sat on the bench swiftly scrambled to other places as Moose sat down.

Georgell followed, mustering a laugh as his head began to pound from all the kicking it had endured. He too felt completely spent and collapsed on the bench, but before closing his eyes looked cautiously at the various participants.

Manny was waking, whimpering from the pain but without the guardian hovering over head. His hired hand leaned on a bench in the back, rolling his aching head; Georgell wasn't concerned with him though and felt oddly guilty for kicking the guy. The biker was vigilantly covered by the group of black men who punished him for every waking peep. The speck who remained in Georgell's cell, sat quietly in the corner, leaning forward to lessen his pain, but he too had no sign of the guardian that once stood above him. The three other specks were not in physical pain but seemed disoriented and lacked the exuberance they once showed under their guardian control. Georgell figured they were finished as well.

The only concern was the unconscious carrier of the Mongolian general. He would wake soon and the battle would no doubt commence. With this in mind, Georgell pulled a fifty dollar bill from his pocket and while pointing at the prone figure, said, "I've got fifty bucks for whoever keeps that man quiet."

A few men verbally responded but a strong odor of coffee blasted over Georgell as the Beans and Brews dumpster diver snatched the money and sauntered over to the cell bars. To prove his worth, the man sat down next to the bars, repositioned his faded blanket around his shoulders, then reached through and pulled the unconscious man toward him. With the first groan the bum slammed the man's face against the bars and let him slump back to the ground. Moose grumbled his appreciation and Georgell, satisfied with the solution as well, lay down on the bench and closed his eyes.

☼~ 35 ~☼

It was impossible to sleep; every clank of the door made Georgell jump with anticipation of a new guardian. His head pounded mercilessly and he couldn't open his mouth without feeling a shock of pain. In his repose, Georgell also realized his elbow was throbbing. He found it interesting that during conflict there was no pain but when silence came, and the calm of rest, the shield of endurance waned, and every scratch made itself known through various aches and throbs of remembrance. Moose grumbled some inarticulate complaint and Georgell guessed his body was voicing its displeasure as well.

The heavy door clanked again and Georgell snapped open his eyes to see an officer enter the holding area alone. The door closed behind him and he stood in front of the cells and looked down at his clipboard. He cleared his throat and in a raspy drawl said, "Georgell Butler and Glen Wallace." Georgell and Moose raised their beleaguered arms and the officer said, "Let's go."

Georgell was surprised at the news but didn't contest it. Moose stood with uncharacteristic speed and leaned over to help Georgell off the bench. As they made their way to the front, one of their cellmates raised his hand and said, "What club do you boys work at?"

Moose slapped his hand. "Euphoria, in the avenues."

"Awesome, I'll see you there. You definitely have a new fan."

Georgell nodded and slapped his hand as well.

From the back of the cell another couple of guys spoke up, "Great show!"

"Come back anytime."

Georgell looked back to acknowledge the kudos and saw the still aching black man holding his crotch and glaring at him with a raised middle finger.

"Don't worry about that fool." A man said from the adjacent cell.

Georgell looked over and a well dressed man stuck his hand through the bars. His face was familiar and his smile infectious. *Where do I know this guy*, Georgell thought and took his hand.

The man glared at Georgell respectfully. "My name is Lang and you guys did me a favor." He nodded back at the prone biker still sleeping soundly beneath the watchful eye of his men. "Listen, ever need anything come see me at the boxing center." He shook Georgell's hand and then, grinning broadly, grabbed Moose's outstretched hand and pulled him a step closer. "Three golden gloves boxers couldn't handle that meathead and you—you—my brother, please come and see me!"

Moose nodded, turning a little red with embarrassment.

"Come on," the impatient officer said.

Slapping Moose on the back and giving him a little shove toward the exit, Georgell looked at the familiar man and said, "Lang, right."

"That's right," Lang said, returning to a bench near the fallen biker.

As the cell door slid closed, Georgell glanced over at the Beans and Brews transient who looked him in the eye, nodded, and slammed the speck into the bars again. He then pulled the faded red blanket tighter around his shoulders and repositioned himself against the bars.

Moose chuckled as he caught the display; then groaned uncomfortably.

"What's your problem?" Georgell said.

"I'm starving. I haven't eaten since six."

"What time is it?"

"Almost four." The officer opened the holding area door and directed them to the front desk.

Before walking through the door Georgell noticed a new guardian appear over one of the specks. The new guardian was well-armored and looked like a Roman Legionnaire. He wore the familiar red and bronze trappings and gripped a short sword in one hand, a shield in the other. Georgell was perplexed by the appearance of the man but had no time to share the discovery with Moose.

The out-processing was swift and within minutes the two men were given back their personals and directed to the exit. *How?* Georgell thought, as he and Moose exited the building. All the charges had been dropped and they had been released without further explanation. Confused, but no less thankful, Georgell twisted the cap from his returned vial of Excedrin and tossed a couple into his mouth. As they lumbered down the front steps a squad car pulled up to the curb.

"Get in," Jackson barked as the passenger window lowered.

"Albertos, please," Moose begged from the front seat as they drove away.

"I'll buy," Georgell said. "But what happened? How were the charges dropped?"

"My ace came through," Jackson said. "I had a suspicion that Cosmo could help out and I was right. Believe it or not, that overzealous vice officer has his greedy little hand in Cosmo's pocket."

"He's on the take?"

"Not my jurisdiction," Jackson said. "But I had a hunch."

"For what?" Moose said.

"Again, not my jurisdiction—and don't act all surprised Moose, you know Cosmo is dirty."

"Yeah but . . ."

"Anyway," Jackson dismissed. "Cosmo wouldn't answer his phone so I cased the clubs and finally found him partying at The Lounge. After I told him what was going on he got real agitated and immediately dismissed the party, it was pretty hilarious. Anyway, he called the numbchuck and put the screws to him real hard. As a cop I should have arrested him for such threats to a fellow officer but I kind of urged him on. Needless to say the dirty punk retracted his statement and dropped the charges and, being the irresponsible cop that I am, I unfortunately misplaced the other statements. So, to make a long story short, you are both in the clear."

"Wow," Georgell said, he couldn't believe their luck and was thankful for the little acts of karma that seemed to continuously bail him out.

"Are we there yet?" Moose asked, eyes shut, and totally disinterested in the details.

Georgell shook his head in disbelief, both at Moose and the outcome of their evening, he too shut his eyes. Jackson let the two relax as he drove the remaining distance, chuckling as they pulled into the parking lot. Georgell opened his eyes and saw Chopper wandering toward his car with his back to them.

"Stay where you are," Jackson said in a heavy accent after turning on his flashing lights.

Chopper froze and raised his arms.

"That's cold," Georgell said with a smile while he watched Chopper's reaction.

Moose opened his eyes and laughed as well then reached for the microphone and said, "Now drop your pants and do the running man."

Chopper turned and without a word or even a glance at the vehicle walked back toward the restaurant.

"Hey we're not through with you," Moose barked.

"I'm calling the real police," Chopper yelled back as he pushed through the entrance.

The trio had a good laugh and then exited the cruiser after Jackson parked. They each ordered and took their drinks to where a scowling Chopper waited at the corner booth. Seconds after sitting down, Jackson was called out on a hit and run and begrudgingly had to excuse himself.

"I'll take care of your food," Moose said with a grin then cowered as Jackson unclipped his revolver. "Please?" Moose added.

"That's better." Jackson left.

After Georgell and Moose used Chopper's phone to contact their wives, they quietly ate their food. Moose didn't seem to breathe as he devoured his order and started in on Jackson's. Georgell chewed slowly to avoid the shocks of pain from his battered jaw. After his last bite he asked about the two specks at Club Euphoria. Chopper explained that Santos had found drugs on them and bought their silence by threatening arrest. He then said that the pair hastily left once the commotion settled.

"So my attack could have been justified," Moose said through a mouthful of beans.

"Still excessive," Georgell disagreed.

Moose shrugged and shoveled in another spoonful.

"What happened in there?" Chopper asked as Georgell pushed his plate aside.

"I'm not sure," Georgell responded. "I've been trying to work it out. Butler and Wallace took on seven guardians and . . ."

"Whoa," Chopper interrupted. "Who?"

"Oh, sorry," Georgell apologized. "Moose and I both had protectors in there." Chopper shuffled in his seat and seemed to lurch with anticipation. Georgell, seeing the excitement in Chopper's eyes, realized the magnitude of it all and exclaimed, "Yeah, man! We had protectors!" He then slugged Moose who dropped a fork full of beans.

After a few minutes of jubilee, Georgell settled down. "Anyway, we decided to call them by our last names. They're most likely blood-related anyway."

"Man, how do you know that?" Chopper said, shaking his head.

Pulling the straw from his mouth, Coke spraying a bit from the jolt, Moose said, "Butler's eyes are identical to Georgell's and they have the same intensity in their glare. And my ancestors were Scottish so it seems obvious."

"Right," Georgell said, eager to continue his narration. "And they're definitely powerful. They fought seven guardians!"

Chopper's eyes bulged at the news. Georgell leaned his throbbing head back on the padded booth thoughtfully. "Well, not completely. We did it as a team. We eliminated five of the guardians and left two, maybe three. One was a general that recognizes me and the other belonged to a biker that . . ."

"Hold it man," Chopper interrupted. "From the beginning."

Georgell quieted, rubbing his eyes, and after a moment decided he could spare the time. He started from the beginning, from first seeing the guardians outside Euphoria, and relayed the entire account. Reaching the end of the narration, he recalled the appearance of the roman guardian. "Moose did you see the guardian as we left the cell?"

"Yeah, barely," Moose said. "Did you see what happened to his speck in the battle?"

"The farmer?"

"Yeah," Moose said. "That soldier guardian killed the dude after Wallace disarmed him."

"That's right." Georgell recalled.

"A guardian killed another guardian?" Chopper asked.

Moose slurped down the rest of his drink and stood to go refill it. "Sure did, crazy huh?"

Georgell described the scene to Chopper as Moose wandered up to the soda fountain at the front. When he returned he placed two more drinks on the table, and grinning like a child who won a prize, said, "They made a new batch of horchata—we get free samples."

Chopper grabbed one of the drinks, closed his eyes and drank deeply as if the refreshment deserved all his attention.

"Why did he do it," Moose said.

"Who?" Georgell said, reaching for the other horchata.

"The soldier. Why did he kill the dude—they were on the same team."

Georgell thought it over as he too drank deeply from the refreshing rice drink. "Don't know, but he definitely had a new guardian, and the others didn't."

"Looked tough too."

Georgell nodded as he took another drag from his drink.

"So the first guardian was weak?" Chopper asked.

"Yeah," Moose answered. "Maybe that's it. Soldier dude killed him to get a stronger guardian in his place."

"Why not," Georgell said. It was as good an explanation as any. "And maybe if a protector kills a guardian the speck is changed somehow and a new guardian can't replace the dead one."

"Yeah," Moose said, snatching the drink from Georgell and handing him the Coke.

Eyebrows furrowed, Chopper said, "Man, let me get this straight—so the weak guardian is killed by another guardian so that the protector can't kill him. Then a new guardian appears, a stronger guardian, over the same speck right? And you guys think it's tactical; a way to keep a speck under a dark influence but better protected. Man, this is serious—I need a notebook to keep track of all this stuff."

Moose raised his eyebrows and shrugged his shoulders.

"Best we got," Georgell said.

Moose abruptly sat down his horchata. Pointing at Georgell, he said, "Hey, why was that soldier in a United States uniform? I mean a Nazi is one thing but why ours?"

"What do you mean?"

"You saw the uniform. It was definitely ours, right?"

Georgell knew that it was and had figured the uniform was either from WWII or the Korean War. He thought it over for a second, his eye caught by the flickering neon sign outside. "Just because our nation was involved in a war of good intentions doesn't mean the men that carried it out were." He said, looking back at Moose. "It doesn't matter how righteous a war is, or a group may profess to be, men still make decisions, good and bad. Do you think all the German soldiers were evil?" Georgell did not wait for a response but answered his rhetorical question without pause, "Of course not. It's individual action that dictates allegiance to right or wrong. Don't let a uniform or religious robes stereotype the person within it; everyone is capable of evil."

"Civil War," Moose said.

"Absolutely," Georgell agreed. "Despite the general belief that slaves were the issue; most of the soldiers in the south were fighting for their homes, families, and neighbors. The politics of the war didn't drive them to fight. It was a need to protect what was being threatened. The majority were good people just doing what they perceived was right."

The conversation piqued Georgell's mind. He thought of the many accounts he had read from both sides of the conflict. *Gods and Generals—The Killer Angels*, he thought, recalling some of his favorite books. "War is for the participants a test of character; it makes bad men worse and good men better."

"What's that?" Chopper leaned in, pushing an empty platter away from him.

"General Chamberlain said that; he's the one Lee surrendered to near the end of the war."

"That's good man, say it again."

Georgell repeated the quote and the three men sat, saying nothing for some time as the idea rested upon them.

"Can I take those?" A man in a white apron asked, pointing at the empty platters.

Moose snapped out of his contemplation first and gathered the dishes. "Thanks," he said, handing the stack of dishes to the waiting man.

"You guys want anything else?"

"Nah, we're good—thanks." Moose said again as the man returned to the kitchen.

Georgell jumped topics. "Hey the recognition idea seemed to work."

"It sure did," Moose said with a smile. "It's like they were given a green light to attack."

"I think it's more a defensive action than anything else. They're protectors, and given the weight of recognition, I think they attack to keep the guardians away from us so we can't be turned and forced into the dark ranks. Our protectors are taking the initiative to reduce that possibility."

"Exactly," Moose heartily agreed.

"Man, how did you get them?" Chopper erupted. "I've got to get one too."

Moose shrugged.

"I'm not sure," Georgell said. "We were going in and I said a quiet prayer for help and then noticed Moose's warrior. He noticed mine seconds after; but it can't be as simple as a prayer."

"Man, I know that's true. I pray all the time. I even ask for protectors. Has to be something else 'cause I ain't never had one," Chopper pouted, grabbing his horchata and leaning back against the seat.

"I prayed too," Moose added. "Just like I did yesterday before the brawl; so why isn't it that simple?"

The group thought over the enigma for a moment and then Georgell looked at Moose and asked, "How often do you pray?"

"I don't. Naomi does it enough for both of us but last night I was nervous and figured it wouldn't hurt; same with the jail."

Georgell let the answer roll over in his thoughts for a moment. "I don't pray much either. For myself anyway, I pray with the kids at night and before family meals; but when I saw those cells full of guardians I felt sick and I prayed to survive. I wanted to see my family again."

"Me too," Moose admitted.

"So what's the difference?" Georgell looked at Chopper. "When do you pray?"

"I'm always speaking to the Lord lately," Chopper responded. "I ask for his protection all the time. I don't see the difference other than you two have families."

"Could it be fear?" Georgell thought aloud. "I mean real fear. Fear for life? I'm not saying your prayers aren't sincere but maybe because Moose and I have families our fear of loss is a little more direct. When I was a single bouncer I admittedly did some crazy things and never cared about the consequences. The only person I was hurting was me; but with a wife and kids my mindset has changed. My instincts and automatic responses are the same, like what I did at Club Momentum, but overall I can't act without thinking of how it will affect my family. Am I making sense?"

"Yeah," Moose agreed. "A few days ago I saw my son get angry and punch the wall. He really hurt himself. Naomi gave me that look of hers, but she didn't need to; I was ashamed. He learned it from me—my stupid example."

"Wait man," Chopper sat up straight. "Are you saying my sincerity isn't as real as yours? I'm just as scared."

"No, not at all," Georgell said, he understood Chopper's frustration and did not want him angered or riled up when all they were trying to do was hypothesize solutions. "These things don't just go away. Some of those guardians are downright terrifying. I can't picture Bear's guardian, or even Bear, without butterflies lurching in my stomach. I know you have fear as real as any of us; but there has to be an added factor."

Chopper hit the table, not out of anger but with the face of discovery. "Them that fear Him! Man that's it!"

"What?" Moose said as Chopper shoved Georgell from the booth and wiggled out, leaping to his feet.

"Psalms, man," Chopper said as he ran toward the door. "I'll be back."

Moose and Georgell watched Chopper burst into the parking lot and trot over to his car. After a moment he briskly walked back toward the restaurant, thumbing through a book. He paused in front of the entrance and then, finding the page he searched for, pulled the door open, and ran back to the booth waving the book. "Here," he said, slamming a Bible to the table. "It's right here. Samuel Walker told me months ago."

"Who? What?" Georgell asked. "Slow down and explain."

Chopper took some deep breaths. "Remember that old speck from the church I told you guys about, the one with twin daughters as protectors?"

Moose and Georgell nodded.

"He told me a verse to look up, here in Psalms. I read it over and over again but never totally understood until now,"

Moose looked at the verse and Georgell shook his head in confusion.

Chopper took another long gulp of air then slowly recited the verse from heart while locking eyes with Georgell, "Psalms 34:7 . . .

> *. . .The angel of the Lord encampeth round about them that fear Him, and delivereth them."*

Moose read the verse over and over to himself as Chopper shook a finger at Georgell and added, "You were right Doc. Don't you see? It's fear; fear is the key; not fear of death or pain but fear of God. You both prayed for help . . ."

Moose interrupted Chopper and read the verse aloud again, "The angel of the Lord encampeth round about them that fear Him, and delivereth them." He looked up from the passage with a beam of light ablaze in his eyes. "Encampeth round about them and delivereth them—what do you think?"

"Fear like faith," Georgell said as the pieces connected. "I didn't ask for a protector when I prayed. I asked for strength and why would I do that if I didn't have some inner fear or respect for the power of God; a power greater than any guardian or demon."

Chopper jumped in and said, "I want to try. Where can we go?"

"Let's go to the club. I've got a key," Georgell said as he stood and fumbled through his pockets.

☼~ 36 ~☼

The bouncers settled into the club without turning on the lights, focusing on one another through the dim glow of the exit signs. Each man sat on a couch in the tunnel and tried to imagine fearful moments; each also concentrated on their faith in an all powerful being. Nothing seemed to happen.

"This isn't going to work," Georgell finally said, exasperated.

"Why?" Moose asked.

"There's no looming force to fear. We can't just sit in the dark and try to be scared. I'm not saying our idea is wrong; it's just there's no evil force to contend with right now. The club is closed. There isn't the influence of music or alcohol or hundreds of patrons with dark thoughts of sex, drugs, drinking, and violence. It's too sedate. I don't know what's going on in the spirit world but maybe they're busy. Maybe they're at war as well? Maybe they're fighting their own battles and can't just pop in anytime we try to call. What I'm trying to say is, we need something tangible. Something real that we can truly fear, understand?"

Chopper agreed but Moose said nothing.

"Moose?" Georgell questioned.

After a few moments, Moose raised his head and with visible concern, whispered, "The morgue, let's go to the morgue."

Georgell was caught off guard by the suggestion and felt pangs of anxiety. He knew Moose legitimately feared the place, and he too felt a shivering dance of fear on his neck.

"I'll go," Chopper said.

A hesitant nod came from Moose and then Georgell. The group reluctantly rose and headed solemnly back to Chopper's car. Georgell wasn't sure about the choice, but—like Moose—was willing to take the necessary risks for the sake of Bear. As they drove, he called Jackson, who had just finished his shift, and filled him in on the details. With little persuasion, Georgell agreed to pick him up at the precinct and take him along.

Jackson opened the front passenger door and eyed Moose, who grumbled but removed himself from the front and sat in the back with Georgell. "Only because your old and I was taught to respect my elders," Moose said.

"Whatever eases your mind, dear boy," Jackson retorted. He then leaned back and addressing all said, "I've got some bad news and some good news. First the bad news; I can't get you into the morgue. The county coroner is there today for some special inspection and he's a real by-the-book pain. But . . ." he said, pointing out the window. The rumble of a Harley could be heard in a nearby lot. With a roar, the impressive bike exited the garage and rolled out onto the street. A red flag flapped from a rod that poked up from the back of the bike, a black swastika printed on the center. Riding the hog, and oblivious to Chopper's Cadillac as it pulled in behind, sat the massive biker from the holding cell. " . . . I think there is another option."

"It's my buddy," Moose grumbled with mock cheer.

They followed the biker for a few miles, anxious to see where he might lead, when a tune began to play from Chopper's cell phone. Georgell immediately recognized ACDC and the unmistakable opening of Thunderstruck. "That's your ring, Doc," Chopper said, handing the phone back to Georgell. "Gotta be Emma"

"Do I have a special ringtone," Moose said as Georgell answered the phone.

"Iron Man." Georgell heard Chopper reply as Emma said, "Georgell?"

"Sweet," Moose said.

"Yeah what's up?" Georgell said to Emma, half listening.

Jackson said, "I'm afraid to know what mine is."

"Shaft," Chopper replied, with his signature huff.

Georgell laughed with the others.

"Are you listening to me?" Emma said.

"Sorry, what?" Georgell said

"Bear is gone!"

"What?" Georgell loudly repeated. The others quieted.

"Alys just called, she's very upset—you have to get over there."

Georgell hit Chopper on the shoulder. "Forget the biker. Get to Bear's apartment as fast as possible."

☼~ 37 ~☼

The mood in the vehicle was glum as they pulled into the apartment complex and saw the flashing lights of a police cruiser. A man sat cuffed in the back of the cruiser, his face a reservoir of drying blood, a nasty bump protruded from his forehead. The officer was a young, surprisingly tall, Asian that talked with a group of witnesses. The bystanders all stood around in bathrobes and coats that loosely covered their nightgowns and pajamas. The clock on Chopper's dashboard read, 6:30.

Breaking the silence, Georgell said, "We all know he's treading water with that guardian of his. Stupid things set him off. We may have to take a chance and deal with that beast a little earlier than planned." He looked the scene over and barely audible, said, "If he hasn't gone too far already."

Alys sat on the exterior steps of the apartment building, looking absolutely furious. Her red hair was in shambles, sticking out like dancing flames around her head. She held a blanket snug to her shoulders and her teeth were clenched tight. Her anger was vivid in the strained lines of her jaw and her searing eyes.

"I know the officer," Jackson said from the front of the car as Chopper parked. "Let me go talk with him. You guys get the real story from Alys."

Jackson exited the car and headed toward the officer as Georgell and Moose trotted over to speak with Alys.

"Chopper get away from the car," Jackson yelled and Georgell turned to see Chopper taunting the injured man in the car. The man spit a wad of blood at Chopper but he avoided the projectile and laughed at the guy then, seeing Jackson step toward him, Chopper raised his hands and walked over to where Moose and Georgell waited.

Alys stood as they approached.

"What's going on?" Georgell said.

Chopper stepped passed Georgell and wrapped his arms around Alys. She pressed her head against his chest. Georgell was surprised by the tender action and wished he had thought to comfort her first. Her anger seemed to diminish and after a moment she whimpered, "I don't know where he went."

"Georgell," Jackson beckoned.

Georgell looked to Moose and gestured for him to go over. Moose touched Alys on the shoulder and stepped away.

"But what happened," Georgell said, nodding at Chopper in appreciation of his gentle compassion.

Alys retreated from Chopper and sat back down on the steps. "When I came out after calling Emma I heard a shotgun blast and ducked. When I looked up again I saw Bear holding a shotgun and hitting the guy with it. I watched him throw the gun in the dumpster, get in his car, and drive off. I didn't even know he had his keys. I've been sitting here ever since."

Seeing Jackson and Moose approach, Georgell asked, "Are the police looking for him?"

"Yes they are. He shouldn't have left the scene but it was clearly self defense, at least I didn't hear anything contrary to that. He'll need to make a statement but they won't hold him. My concern is that he'll put up a fight and get himself into real trouble. We need to find him."

"Can Alys leave?" Georgell asked.

"Yeah, he's finished with her," Jackson answered.

Georgell turned to the group and jumped into commander mode, "Chopper, you and Moose head north. Check out the gym and cruise by Sanctuary. Alys, can you take me home?" Alys nodded, stood and scrambled up the stairs as Chopper and Moose set out toward the Cadillac. Georgell turned to Jackson and said, "What's the story?"

"Bear left the apartment and got into an argument with Mr. Petrov," Jackson said, nodding at the injured man in the cruiser. "Apparently Petrov retrieved a shotgun from his car and went after Bear. They had a scuffle and the weapon was fired without injury to either man. Bear wrestled the weapon away from Petrov and hit him with it—knocked him unconscious. He then tossed the shotgun in the dumpster, kicked Petrov a few times, and fled the scene in his Range Rover.

Georgell was pleased that no serious harm came to either man but could not shake his concern for Bear. If the rage overcame his ability to withstand the guardian then he could very well be on his way to commit an act that no one could cover up. He prayed they would find him. "Can you get a ride back to the station?"

Jackson nodded and Georgell said, "Call me on Emma's phone when you're ready to roll and I'll update you on our progress." Georgell then stepped in front of Chopper's car as it approached. "Moose, your house is on the way. Swing in and change out of that security shirt. You too Chopper." Both agreed, and the Cadillac rolled on.

After a few minutes Alys jogged down from her apartment in sweats and an oversized yellow hoody that Georgell knew belonged to Bear. They jumped in her car and headed out of the parking lot as another cruiser pulled in.

"How did this all start?" Georgell asked as the distinctive smell of Bear's cologne filled the car. He wondered if it were residual scent from the sweatshirt or if Alys sprayed the garment before throwing it on.

"It's so stupid," Alys sighed. "He cut himself shaving his head and then hit the mirror and carved his hand up pretty good. I went in the bathroom and tried to calm him down but he was fuming and wouldn't let me help. He just started screaming at me. Well, not me particularly, but everything, he was just ranting. The neighbor got upset at our noise and after pounding on the wall he came over and hammered on the door. Bear answered and you can imagine the exchange. Anyway, the guy left screaming about how tired he was and how he was going to finish the business outside."

"I thought the guy was about to back off but Bear provoked him. He agreed to meet him in the lot. I tried to stop him but he pushed me aside. I honestly don't even think he knew I was there, he was so angry. He got dressed and rushed out. That's when I called Emma."

"Over a razor cut?" Georgell asked, dumbfounded.

"Yeah," Alys said, rubbing her eyes as they came to a stoplight.

Emma and Alys had dropped the kids off with Naomi and checked out a few antique stores that Bear liked to visit. They then headed to Hogle Zoo. Bear kept his season pass in the glove box, and not having his wallet; Alys figured it would be a good place to search. Georgell wasn't sure but after Alys explained that she and Bear liked hanging out there and that he would often go alone while she was in class, he agreed it was worth a look.

Moose and Chopper hung out downtown and cased various locations including Sanctuary, the tattoo parlor, and a few places Bear liked to eat. Jackson enlisted the help of Flip, who picked up Santos, and they kept an eye on the apartment complex while Jackson stayed close to the precinct and monitored the scanner.

Around 3:00 in the afternoon Jackson overheard that the Range Rover had been located in a downtown parking garage and relayed the information to Georgell. *He won't go back to the car*, Georgell thought, assuming Bear knew he was wanted and dumped the vehicle. Still, he sent Moose and Chopper to sit on the vehicle and wait.

Georgell drove to the parking garage and parked on the street. He wanted to get a feel for Bear's thoughts and options. He wanted to get inside his head. *Where did he go? No wallet, little if any money, alone—come on think! You're Bear—where do you go.* Looking around, he found a bus stop and instantly knew Bear could use the change in his vehicle to ride the bus anywhere he wanted to go. *But where*, he thought, jogging over to the three-walled stop.

There were two benches in the open structure with destination maps on either side and advertising on the back wall. The map was largely daunting but Georgell could not shake the large patch of green that represented Liberty Park. He yawned and resolved to search the area.

"Where you going, boy?" A gruff voice said from the street.

What now, Georgell thought and turned to confront his questioner.

Moose laughed at him from the passenger side of Chopper's Cadillac and Georgell shook his head. He was happy to see his friends and as he approached the vehicle couldn't help but notice their haggard appearance and sagging red eyes. "Do I look as tired as you idiots?"

"Worse," Chopper said from the opposite side of the car.

"Find anything?" Moose said.

"He got on the bus. I'm going to drive down to Liberty Park and see what I can see. It's a shot in the dark but all I can come up with."

"Want to take one of us along?"

"Nah, stick together. You two need supervision when you're this tired."

"That's true!" Moose said, tossing Georgell an Amp as they drove off toward the entrance of the parking garage.

"Call Alys and Jackson," Georgell said, catching the cold beverage. Chopper waved and Georgell knew his whereabouts would be relayed.

The sun glared off the windshield, piercing Georgell's mind. His throbbing headache had returned and drowsiness, along with the stabbing sunlight, intensified the pounding. He washed his last Excedrin down with the remaining Amp and prayed it would lessen the pain and afford him a burst of energy. When he reached the park, Georgell drove slowly around the perimeter hoping to catch a glimpse of Bear but saw nothing.

Relenting, Georgell finally parked the car on the east end of the park and trudged up a paved walkway on a rising hill. He was confident that the elevation would give him a birds-eye view but the hope of finding Bear was quickly fading. A cool breeze stung his lungs as his heavy legs carried him to the top of the hill. He sat on a cold bench beneath a leafless walnut tree, his hands warming in his pockets, and surveyed the surroundings.

There was no sign of his friend and Georgell felt a wave of frustration. Emma's phone rang and startled him. He fumbled quickly for the phone and anxiously answered.

"Georgell, we've searched the entire zoo. I don't think he's here," Emma said, her voice discouraged.

"No luck here either," Georgell responded. "This really sucks!"

"I know, honey."

A dog barked in the distance. A leaf, finally freed from its frozen winter perch, lifted from beneath the bench and billowed up on a cold breeze. Georgell kept the phone to his ear, saying nothing.

"We'll find him. Where are you?"

Georgell watched as the leaf swam in the breeze. "Liberty Park, I thought he might have ridden the bus here but I haven't seen him."

"Listen, Alys and I are going to take some burgers to Naomi and the kids. Why don't you go to the car and get some sleep. We'll come find you. We shouldn't be more than an hour. Can you do that for me?"

"Yeah," Georgell said, still watching the leaf. "I don't know where else to look."

"Just get some rest and we'll see you soon."

"Okay," Georgell said, disconnecting. He looked around and sighed, taking a deep gulp of chilly air. The lone leaf flipped through the air again, landing in a patch of scraggly grass. The breeze picked up but the leaf was trapped, it struggled, fought to get free again but, as the breeze died down, the struggle stopped, and the leaf lay still.

Georgell wanted to stand, he wanted to go back to his warm car and rest but he couldn't. He sat mesmerized by the leaf and reflecting on his friendship with Bear. He recalled the first time they met; Bear laughing at two drunks who had fallen down stairs at Club Manhattan while Georgell tried to help them up. The infectious laughter caused Georgell to laugh as well and the hefty drunks weren't happy. It was their first night bouncing together, their first laugh together and the first time they got to fight together. He had so much control, his movements so calculated and swift; nothing deterred him or scared him. *Why*, he thought.

His eyes beginning to burn with fatigue and the stinging cold, Georgell blinked and turned away from the captivating leaf. "Okay," Georgell said again, repeating his last word to Emma. He stood, marveling at the glare of the sun on the patches of snow that still littered the park. A few joggers were running on a cobbled trail and a group of college kids were bundled up and tossing a football on the far end of the open field. *Life just keeps pressing on*, he thought. *Pain is constant, regret ever-present, friends have lost their lives and here I am on the verge of losing another, yet life goes on oblivious; insanity.*

Georgell pulled the beanie further over his ears and then stuffed his hands back in the warm pockets of his coat. He took a few steps and kicked the leaf free from its grassy tangle and smiled as it lifted on another chilly breeze. "Press on," he said to the leaf as it traveled. "Press on," he said again, to himself, and wandered down the opposite side of the hill. He decided to take the path around the small lake and then circle back to the car. He wanted to breathe in the cold refreshing air, feel the grass crunch beneath his feet as he strayed from the path, he wanted to ground himself in the reality around him and simply press on. *One more look*, he thought, as another gaping yawn pressed his mouth wide and sent a shock of pain through his tender jaw. His eyes began to water from the stinging breeze and he shuddered.

Some ravens scattered from beneath a tree where they had gathered as joggers ran by oblivious. The birds returned, slowly gathering, and Georgell saw the brief flash of a hand tossing crumbs from behind the massive trunk of a tree. His heart leapt. It was Bear; it had to be.

The birds scattered again as Georgell walked over to the tree. Verifying his hope, he slumped down with his back to the base of the tree and slightly rocked Bear as their shoulders bumped. "Nice day," Georgell said.

"Yeah," Bear muttered back.

They sat for awhile, saying nothing as Bear tossed more crumbs, beckoning the birds near. They pecked closer and closer as Bear lured them with handfuls of crumbs. Georgell watched for a moment, relieved. Bear was safe and feeding birds in the park. He smiled and shut his eyes. Of all the scenarios that crossed his mind, this quaint scene was nowhere near the realm of possibilities, and yet—slumber tickled his conscious. His thoughts fell away in the moment; the cold breeze, the rustling of the trees, the scent of stale wheat bread and the flap and shuffle of the hungry ravens.

"How serious is it?" Bear finally asked.

Georgell heard the question but wasn't sure if it were directed to him, it seemed so faint and far off. His mind wrestled with the quandary for a moment; then finally he snapped back to the park, the birds, the cold, and Bear. He pried open his eyes and answered, "He's not dead. He'll be alright and so will you. Jackson said it was clearly self defense; but you need to go in and make a report."

"I thought I killed the guy. I was completely enraged. I wanted to kill him. This isn't working anymore. I can't control myself. I . . ."

"I know," Georgell said, shoving Bear with his shoulder while keeping his hands warm in his pockets. "I know, and it's time we take care of it."

"How?" Bear whispered as if worried that anything above a whisper might wake his sleeping guardian. He tossed the remaining crumbs.

"We can summon the protectors. Moose and I have figured it out and I've seen them in action. I think we can make it work. Chopper is working it out too—I'm certain he'll be ready. With three protectors even your monster can't win. It's time, Bear. We can do this."

"When?" Bear asked, not yet ready to hope.

"The club is closed tonight so we'll have to do it tomorrow."

"Why do we have to wait?" Bear growled.

"It doesn't work like that," Georgell responded softly, trying to keep the conversation peaceful. "We've tried and it doesn't work. It has to be when the club is open. All the influences have to be in place. The alcohol, the music, the tension has to be there; that edge of evil feeling has to be prevalent.

"Somewhere else then," Bear pleaded.

"No, we have to be in control. The environment can't be one that is uncertain. It has to be Euphoria. It's only a day. We can make it," Georgell reassured.

"We," Bear snidely repeated.

Georgell ignored the sarcasm. "Yes we—all of us; Jackson, Chopper, Moose—we will all take turns watching your back, but don't even think about shaving." Bear said nothing but Georgell believed his old friend was grinning.

Bear finally nodded his reluctant approval and after a time, quietly said, "I can't feel my butt."

Georgell laughed and realized that his, too, was growing numb from the cold hard ground. He retrieved the cell phone from his pocket. They called Alys and Emma, then Jackson while they walked to Georgell's Blazer. Jackson quickly volunteered to escort Bear to the downtown precinct and Georgell agreed but made it clear that he too would accompany them.

Jackson volunteered to call off Flip and Santos and also agreed to stay at Bear's apartment through the night. Georgell was pleased and made the last call to Chopper.

"Yeah," Moose answered, Chopper growling in the background.

"I found him and we are heading to the station. Jackson is going to meet us."

"Hello," Chopper said wrestling the phone from Moose.

"Just put it on speakerphone!" Georgell barked, amazed at their playfulness.

"Oh yeah," Chopper said.

Georgell heard the phone drop then Chopper say "speakerphone" and the fight seemed to end as a high pitched yelp sounded from Moose. "Okay man, we're listening."

Unbelievable, Georgell thought. "We're meeting Jackson at the precinct."

"What should we do?" Moose said.

"I'm going to stay at Bear's tonight and I want you guys to be there as well. We can take shifts. We can't let him out of our sight."

"How long?"

"Until tomorrow night—it's time to end this, one way or the other." Georgell said, looking at Bear who sternly nodded.

"I'm in, man," Chopper said.

"No doubt," Moose agreed. "It's time."

Georgell knew they were serious by their silence as the line went dead. It was on—all in.

☼⁓ 38 ⁓☼

The dark windows lit up with a flash. No crack of thunder or burst of rain followed, just darkness and the apprehension of more lightning, closer. Bear's apartment was eerily still despite the soothing Celtic music, the deep snoring of Moose, Emma's heavy breathing, and the flickering glow of candles. Georgell couldn't sleep. He sat on the sofa gently caressing Emma's arm as she slept—her head resting comfortably in his lap. After moments without thought, he felt his eyes begin to water and realized he had been staring at Bear's bedroom door. He knew Bear and Alys were most likely sleeping, as he had left them an hour earlier when he and Moose were relieved by Chopper and Jackson; still, he couldn't sleep—he just stared, waiting for something to happen.

Moose lay with his back on the floor and his legs propped up on a chair but he too constantly stirred, waking every few minutes ready for a fight. Georgell watched his labored breathing and found himself in awe at their friendship. He marveled at their closeness, the deep respect that had grown between them. It had only been a few months but Georgell felt they had known each other forever. He wondered if a guiding hand pushed Moose to this place. *Was it more than mere coincidence? Was it fate or divine providence of some sort?*

With all they now knew, Georgell could not deny the grandiose scheme of creation. He could not accept coincidence and luck as floating powers that randomly attached themselves to unaware beings or situations. There was more. There had to be. He regretted his lack of theological knowledge but somehow felt comforted by the fact that his faith could no longer be denied or questioned. He knew a higher power was at work and with that knowledge he could not deny the existence of a higher evil as well. A battle was raging in the heavens that extended down to Earth, and Georgell had physically seen the proof.

The idea of a spiritual war settled on Georgell and he tried to mentally piece together its mechanics. It was more than just a war; the stakes were on a different level, a level outside of Georgell's grasp. He could not fathom a war without quarter. A war where opponents held no compassion for their enemy, where prisoners were not taken, surrender was never offered, and death was the only option. Every battle was life or death. *Or was it?* Georgell wondered. *Do they die? Where do they go when they vanish?*

Moose bolted up again and looked swiftly around the room. Georgell waved at him with a smile but Moose was blind to the gesture. He only saw the lack of contention, and—sufficiently appeased—returned to his restless nap. Georgell chuckled. He believed they had known each other before—maybe before this life. Not in a previous life, as Georgell had never bought into reincarnation, but in a pre-Earth existence. Their friendship began there and carried over into this world. Georgell had always believed this to be true with Emma, and now this short-fused barbarian of a man had garnered that same closeness. Life without Emma wasn't living at all and a battle without Moose seemed a looming defeat.

Emma stirred as Georgell slid out from under her. He quickly grabbed a throw pillow from the floor and gently slid it under her head then pulled her small blanket up and over her shoulders. He strolled over to Bear's door and cracked it open. An irritated huff came from Chopper as Georgell leaned in and saw him toss his cards on the small table they had set up in the corner. Jackson smiled and recorded the score on a small yellow tablet as Bear and Alys slept soundly on the nearby bed. Georgell pulled back and shut the door. Earlier in the evening Jackson had mixed a few sleeping pills into Bear's water and the concoction had swiftly put the brooding man to rest. There was no concern of his waking but his vigilant friends refused to leave, despite their delirium.

I'm so tired, Georgell thought. He leaned his back against the wall to the right of the door and slid to the linoleum floor. He began to ponder the power of fatigue and how sufficiently it drained his ability to think with any sort of clarity. The physical aches from two nights of battery had begun to voice their throbbing displeasure, a burning need to rest; but the unknown, the unseen, the possibility of action at any given moment, kept his brain functioning and his eyes open.

Rolling to his left, Georgell propped himself up on his knees, then using the wall as a brace, he rose back to his feet and stood. He snatched up a few burning candles from a coffee table near the couch, walked over to the small dining table adjacent to the kitchen, and strategically set the candles to best illuminate the area. He then rummaged through some drawers in the kitchen and found a pen and some paper.

"What are you doing?"

Georgell jumped, startled by the intrusion of his thoughts. He looked up and saw Jackson staring down at him quizzically. A quick glance to his right and Georgell could see 3:53 in green lettering staring back at him from the microwave in the kitchen. It had been almost two hours since he began writing but seemed like only twenty minutes. He smiled, pleased at the discovery. "I couldn't sleep."

"So do I need to slip you a pill too?"

"Please don't," Georgell said, returning his eyes and thoughts to the mess of crumpled papers on the table.

"What are you writing?"

"A poem," Georgell admitted. "I'm writing about the affects of fatigue."

"Really," Jackson said, walking into the kitchen. After refilling his giant mug with water, he took a long sip and said, "I may be able to help. Not with the writing, of course, but maybe with some insight."

"Actually, that's why I decided to scribble this down. No better time then the moment, right?"

"How much have you finished?"

"I think I'm done," Georgell said. He slipped the document across the table toward Jackson.

"Oh no, I can't read that scratch. You wrote it, you read it."

Emma wandered in and yawned as Georgell began to read;

> Fatigue anchors madness to thought and deed
> Burns the ice of moral creed
> Standards fall
> Logic mauled
> Chaos crowns the mental halls

Fatigue breeds visions of clouded kind
Clamoring forth with primitive design
Sleep ignored
Senses gored
Strings attached to puppetted whores

Fatigue slips numbness to the brain
Slaughters reason and hope defames
Blurs sight
Wrongs the right
Upends day with bitter-clad night

Fatigue destroys all crowning intellect
Cares not for worries or moments of retrospect
Buries life
Glorifies strife
Slices judgment with a wicked knife

Fatigue is the eighth of the deadly sins
No one can say where or when it begins
Welcome sleep
Sanity reap
Or fight for your life in the Hell of fatigue!

"Whoa, you'll have to read that again," Jackson insisted, and then scooted into Bear's bedroom and hauled out Chopper.

As Chopper walked by Moose he kicked him gently in the side. Moose yawned and inquired about the time, stretched, and finally joined the others around the small table. "Is Bear still asleep?" he asked.

"He'll be sleeping for a while yet," Jackson replied.

"So what's up?"

"Georgell wrote a poem," Chopper said, bobbing his head playfully.

"Let's hear it," Moose said, to Georgell's surprise. Then noticing the stares, added, "What? I happen to like poetry—read it!"

Georgell read the poem again and Moose reached across the table and snatched the paper. He studied the scribble and finally, with a smirk, said, "Wait, you just wrote this?"

Georgell nodded and Moose said, "It's good, and true. Clean it up and make me a copy. I'd like to keep it in my wallet with some other poems I've saved."

"Man, why?" Chopper asked. "I mean—it's good but why carry it in your wallet. Seriously, man, what's wrong with you?"

Again, to the shock of Jackson and Georgell, Moose stood upright and replied, "John Adams once said, 'A man is never alone with a poet in his pocket.' I guess I just took that literally."

Chopper began to snicker then, realizing Moose was serious, shook his head and slapped him on the back.

Georgell immediately wondered where Moose had found the quote. *What other gems of intelligence are hiding behind that brutish mask*, he thought. *And what are the other poems in his wallet?* He decided to leave it alone and after blinking a few times to help focus his sight and thoughts, said, "Look, my poem aside, isn't anyone else concerned about their fatigue? I mean seriously, we've still got at least seventeen hours to go, and by the time we make our move we'll each have fifty hours straight of little or no rest. Now obviously we'll have an adrenaline kick but Bear will be well rested and ready to rock. I'm concerned with our ability to perform. Will we be willing or better yet, capable of doing the job?"

"We're all more than willing," Moose said as he looked around at the others who nodded. "And like all the other situations we've somehow survived, I believe this too will end in our favor. That doesn't mean I ain't concerned, but what else can we do?"

"Man, Moose is right," Chopper chimed in. "Plus, being so tired maybe God will see fit to assist me with a protector, right?"

"You got it," Moose whole-heartedly agreed.

"Let's cuff him like we did Alder," Jackson suggested.

"Good," Georgell said.

"What about involving Red or Pineapple?" Emma said, pulling a chair next to Georgell and taking a seat.

"Not for this," Georgell answered. "I'll have Santos, Pineapple, and Nemesis come in early and post at the entries; but I don't want to involve them with this guardian mess. We'll play it just like we did with Alder only this time we won't be learning. We know what we need to do and we know what's at stake. This time we need to make a difference. Bear has to be freed. It's all or nothing, guys."

"Fight for our lives in the Hell of fatigue," Jackson said quoting the end of the poem.

"Yeah," Georgell smiled. "Something like that."

Though minutes pressed on like hours, night passed. The daylight eventually dawned and Jackson stole away to the market. He returned with fixings for a spectacular breakfast and to the delight of all, he and Emma made piles of pancakes, sausage, bacon, eggs, and hash browns. The preparation and consumption of the meal was a welcome distraction and the group seemed rejuvenated by its sustenance.

While they ate, ideas were batted around as to what they would do for the remainder of the day but nothing seemed to stick. The only real solution was to continue the vigil at the apartment though no one favored the idea. Cleanup wound down and the group quieted, accepting the fact that they would spend the next twelve hours together in the little apartment, bacon still heavy in the air.

"Let's go to the zoo," Alys said to Bear as they loaded up the dishwasher.

Overhearing the suggestion from his seat at the table, Georgell said, "It would definitely kill time."

"Who we gonna kill?" Moose shouted from the sofa.

"Bear?" Georgell looked at Bear for a response.

"We're gonna kill Bear?" Moose asked.

Bear nodded, "I'd enjoy that."

"You'd enjoy getting killed?" Moose stood as Jackson shook his head and Chopper began to laugh.

"We're going to the zoo," Georgell said, smiling at Moose who approached palms up and eyebrows furrowed in confusion.

"Can we bring the kids?" Moose said, cleanly yanked from his bewilderment.

Georgell looked at Emma and she nodded. "Sure."

Moose called Naomi and informed her of the trip and she excitedly relayed the news to the mass of children in her house. Georgell and Emma heard the zealous cheer of kids and laughed when Moose pulled the phone away from his ear in mock pain.

The logistics of preparing a lunch and transporting the group of eight adults and eight children was time consuming and proved a perfect way to burn a few hours. Eventually three vehicles were packed and loaded;

Naomi excitedly drove Chopper's Cadillac with Chopper and a mixture of the younger kids, Emma drove the Blazer with Jackson and the older children, and Alys drove the Range Rover with Moose in front and Georgell riding in the back with Bear.

The day passed without incident as everyone rallied around Bear and kept him sufficiently busy with pictures, churros and the distracting sights of birds and wildlife. Lunch came and went, Moose crashing hard and sleeping for an hour while everyone ate. A bird show, a snake show, and thirty minutes watching the monkeys, pressed the day and the sun slipped into the high treetops.

"The kids are cold," Emma said to Georgell as they exited the reptile exhibit.

He ignored her.

"Georgell," Emma grabbed his arm. "The kids are cold. It's time to go."

"This is working Emma," Georgell said, brushing her off. He immediately regretted the action as Emma glared at him. "Come on, seriously—it's working, just a couple more hours."

"No," she said not dropping her gaze. "We need to get the kids home."

Georgell felt his fatigue bubble forward as a slew of angry thoughts pressed hard at his mind. *Why is she doing this?* He looked around and saw two of the Wallace children whimpering, Wolfy already asleep in the stroller and Gina complaining about her feet. Bear was arm-and-arm with Alys, but he too seemed less jubilant as he had been. She was right, it was time.

☼~ 39 ~☼

A pothole rocked the Range Rover as it dipped down then hopped back to the smooth surface of the road. Georgell's head bounced on the back seat and then returned to rest against the cold window. *Whatever*, he thought. *Not like I could sleep anyway.*

The hum of the heater returned to sooth his restlessness and Georgell allowed his mind to wander. The many scenarios of the coming evening had already played out like a never-ending song and he tried to focus on something different. The protectors came to mind, the similar shields that Butler and Wallace carried. *Is the shield an identifier of rank?* He was curious about their origins as well and wondered if indeed they were ancestors of those they protected. He focused on Butler, relived the prison scene and tried to recall every detail of the man. He wore no rings and, other than the period look of his suit, there were no real identifying items.

Wait, he thought. *There was a pocket watch*! He pictured the battle Butler had with the Mongolian guardian and recalled one particular thrust of the guardian's sword where Butler twisted hard right and Georgell could see his full torso. Between the two front pockets of Butler's vest, a gold chain dangled. It was a small chain, actually two twisted strands of gold that separated slightly as Butler parried the thrust. A round pocket watch, with a strange engraving on the covering face, was also exposed as it was yanked partly out of Butler's left pocket during the same action.

Georgell thought about the watch for a moment and wasn't sure he could identify the engraving but was certain he would recognize the chain, if it were still attached. He would have to ask his father about the item, no, about Butler, then maybe the watch would come in handy as an identifier.

"Are they asleep?" Alys said from the front.

"Moose is," Bear said after a particularly loud snore from Moose. "And I think Georgell is too, why?"

Georgell listened. He had fretted over his decision to let Bear ride in front but decided not to argue the point. He didn't want Bear to have any need for anger until it was absolutely necessary and so he climbed in the back with Moose, who was sleeping before they even left the parking lot.

"Doc you awake?" Bear said from the front.

Keeping his breathing constant, Georgell remained still, curious.

The car rolled on for a few more minutes, stopping at a light and then picking up speed as they cruised onto the interstate. The sweet smell of orange nectar hovered in the vehicle and Georgell reminded himself to ask where the smell came from. It was nice and he hadn't noticed an air freshener on the rearview mirror.

"Everything changes tonight," Alys said, barely above a whisper.

Georgell wanted to see Bear's reaction but kept his eyes closed.

"There's no need for me to express my feelings for you," she continued. "I think my actions and friendship have been expressive enough. You know that I love you."

"But . . ." Bear added.

"But, I can't live with that presence anymore—it's too much!"

Bear said nothing as Alys seemed to pause for a reaction but finally, in a flood of words, she opened up, "This has to end tonight. I want to get to know the real Bear. I need to see if he loves me. You say you do, but you're in a crazy situation that requires a different kind of woman. I've been that woman and don't regret it, but I want to be pampered for awhile. No—that sounds bad—what I mean is, I'd like to go on a date without worrying. I want you to take me places, dote on me, treat me like a princess—I want to feel more than just needed."

Bear said nothing and Georgell couldn't resist the urge to look. He opened his eyes slightly and was pleased to have a perfect view. Bear stared blankly out the front window.

Alys continued, "This isn't the choice I want—but what I've accepted . . ."

Bear shuffled in his seat but maintained his forward gaze.

"If they can't make a difference tonight—I have to leave you. I know this is bad timing but there it is, I just—do you understand?"

Bear nodded and for a time nothing was heard but the passing cars and the steady beat of drums and bagpipes playing from the rear speakers. Then finally, in an emotionless tone, he said, "Like I needed more pressure."

Georgell heard Alys begin to speak but Bear cut her off. His voice was slow and steady. "I honestly can't believe you stuck it out this long? But you're not getting rid of me that easy; and don't for a second believe that I don't want to treat you like a princess."

Georgell was relieved at Bear's response. A weight lifted from his chest knowing the conversation could have erupted into something much worse. He wanted to sigh deeply and rejoice but remained calm. Bear turned his gaze away from the front and looked at Alys, and there, in his eyes, Georgell could see his friend. Bear was in those intense eyes, fighting the demon within and refusing to lash out. Georgell smiled, buoyed by the subtle display of defiance.

"But know this," Bear continued. "I'm coming out tonight, whole and free. Those guys won't let us down. They don't know how. We're going to survive this, and after a few months of serious courtship, I'm going to put a ring on your finger."

Bear raised a hand to her face. "Now don't ruin your tough exterior by crying, aren't you trying to break up with me? Be strong woman," he urged with a smile.

☼~ **40** ~☼

When the music began to play on the dance floor, Georgell and Chopper closed the sports bar and shuffled out the few patrons that were playing pool or watching games on the TV screens. Some argued but Georgell was in no mood to debate and gruffly rejected their legitimate pleas to stay.

Emma had arranged to work as the bartender in the basement and as the patrons were escorted out, she and Alys, who had been snuck in as a training bar back, closed down the bar and quickly handled the required cleaning. After posting Santos and Pineapple at the slope entrances, Georgell returned to the sports bar where he and Chopper shoved most of the tables and chairs away from the central area. Only one chair remained, placed near the rail as they had done during the Alder interrogation. Georgell looked around and was satisfied that the area was as prepared as it could be.

Earlier in the evening Georgell had attempted to explain the situation to his crew but couldn't dodge the prodding questions from Nemesis. After some debate, he finally explained that he didn't want to lie, assured them that he was not engaged in anything illegal, and again asked for their trust. Red quickly agreed and walked out of the meeting shaking his head and laughing at the others for their pointless inquisition. Santos consented as well but Pineapple and Nemesis took a little more assurance before they gave in. Georgell appreciated their trust and was confident that all would perform their appointed tasks.

Georgell had convinced Terrance to take the night off and was pleased that the present crowd was minimal. He didn't expect too many more; still, he wanted to get the job done as quickly as possible. Red was informed that the emergency exit would be propped open and the alarm disabled if they needed his assistance. If his name was called he would drop everything and enter through the emergency exit while Nemesis covered the door.

Chopper nudged Georgell and said, "It's time, man."

"Why do you say that?" Georgell asked.

Chopper bowed slightly then gesturing upward said, "Because, man, your boy just showed up and you're right, his shield does look like the one I saw Wallace use."

So they do come only when they are needed, Georgell thought, feeling more at ease. He then realized Moose could not escort Bear because he too would have a protector and he didn't want the battle to commence without all players in position. "Wait here," he said to Chopper and quickly stepped through the emergency exit.

"Red, can you go to the parking lot and escort Bear downstairs?" Georgell said as he rounded the exterior corner, motioning Red over. There were no customers in line and no one approaching so Georgell figured Red's quick escort would not cause undue stress on the front desk.

Red agreed, placing his clipboard on the high barstool and joining Georgell.

"Listen, I don't think Bear will put up a fight but if he does can you handle him alone?"

Red nodded as they walked to the rear parking lot.

"I need to get him in the bar and cuffed to the rail but he needs to be conscious. I need to talk with him. If he hesitates in any way just wrap him up and carry him in; but watch your nuts and nose, he'll do whatever it takes."

"I know this," Red assured. "I will handle."

When they approached the vehicle Jackson, Moose, and Bear stepped out and greeted them solemnly.

"I know you don't agree, Georgell, but I really think I should go in unconscious," Bear stated.

"No," Georgell flatly rejected. "You're still tough and I expect you to resist that thing long enough to get set. Jackson and Red will escort you in and if you struggle Red will assist the rest of the way."

"Watch your nose and . . ." Bear began but was interrupted by Red.

"Ya-ya, I know," Red smiled.

"Are the cuffs secured?" Georgell asked.

Bear nodded. To assure his friends he pulled and flexed at the restraints.

Red shook his head and looked at Georgell.

"Trust me, he needs them," Georgell said to Red then turned to Jackson. "What about the key?"

Jackson smiled and said, "Someone has it, yes." They had agreed not to divulge the whereabouts of the key just in case things didn't work according to plan.

"I saw your protection in place," Moose said letting Georgell and the others know that Butler was visible but currently gone.

"How far?" Georgell asked referring to the point at which his protector vanished from sight.

"About a hundred yards; that red car is a good spot." Moose pointed down the lot at a burgundy VW Jetta with a ski rack and then added, "A little further but it's a good mark."

Georgell nodded and said, "Okay, here's how we play this. Moose and I will go in and join Chopper on the stairs. You guys bring him in and secure him to the rail. If I hear a struggle we'll come out early but I want to have as much control as possible so try to be quick." Tapping Moose on the arm, Georgell then added, "Give us five minutes."

Jackson nodded and Red flexed his chest, rolling his head from side to side in preparation.

"Alright," Georgell said. He was secure with the plan but still reluctant to set it in motion. He stepped close to Bear. "This is going to work," he said in a low voice. "Tonight you will be freed and after a few months of serious courtship I will put a ring on your finger."

Bear gave Georgell a slight grin. "You were awake?"

"We don't know how to fail—believe it." Then, tapping Bear on the shoulder with a closed fist, Georgell said, "Let's do this!"

Moose and Georgell jogged to the club in silence. Georgell sucked in deep gulps of air, loosening his muscles as they ran. The butterflies faded, fatigue slipped away, and determination began to empower him. When they entered through the emergency exit of the sports bar they found Chopper pacing in anticipation. He faced them with a golden smile and a big nod, and Georgell was immediately relieved to know that both Butler and Wallace were visible.

Hiding behind the counter in the darkened service bar, Georgell saw Emma and Alys staring, wide-eyed. They had promised to stay clear of danger and leave if told to do so; but Georgell wondered how serious that promise was. He gave them the thumbs up signal and seeing a shadow of relief on Emma's face, he led Moose and Chopper up the stairs. The trio stopped at the top, the glow of red from the exiting slopes covered them and for half a second, Georgell wanted to keep walking.

"Don't worry about it," Moose said.

Georgell looked at his friend and found he was talking to Chopper who seemed to be hanging his head unnaturally. *He has no protector,* Georgell immediately realized with alarm.

"I'm good," Chopper lied.

Moose slapped Chopper hard in the chest with both hands.

Chopper flinched at the assault. "Man, I said I'm good."

"No, you're not!" Moose shoved Chopper hard against the wall.

Georgell understood. He too needed to snap out of his doubts and focus. It was the final hour, and they all needed to forget about their deficiencies and get pumped up for the task at hand. A surge of determination sparked through his veins and he too shoved Chopper against the wall.

"Man!" Chopper growled, giving Moose a thumping head butt. "I'm here! I'm with you!" Then he spun on Georgell and vigorously slapped him on the face.

Georgell accepted the sting of pain, smiling as his cheek reddened. He peered into Chopper's eyes and then at Moose, allowing his smile to broaden wickedly.

Moose nodded at Georgell, then Chopper, and then banged his head against the brick wall, grunting ferociously. Chopper bounced in place and began to shadowbox. Georgell simply rolled his shoulders and sucked in deep breaths of air.

The emergency door swung open. Georgell halted his breathing and motioned for the others to quiet. After a few moments passed with no sounds of struggle, Georgell relaxed a bit and thought over the plan again. Chopper would enter the bar and stand opposite Jackson with Bear between them. Moose and Georgell would flank Bear on the remaining two sides. They would effectively box him in but remain a safe distance apart. Once in position, they would each stare at the guardian, gain his recognition, and free their protectors to battle unhindered. Georgell had hoped Chopper would have a protector but felt confident that Butler and Wallace could handle the beast. With the demise of Bear's guardian they would release him from the restraints, congratulate him, and live happily ever after.

But . . . Georgell knew that was the perfect ending—and perfection never lingered in night clubs.

The lights flickered and Georgell released Moose and Chopper like dogs on a hunt. Bear's head twisted back as the trio entered, and he glared with sinister eyes as they swiftly surrounded him. The guardian hovered with monstrous bulk, every vein in his body visibly taut. A short spiked shield appeared on his left arm and a sword, the length of a normal man, materialized in the grip of his right hand. The beast seemed pleased at his predicament and he flashed a recognizing stare and menacing nod to each bouncer.

Silence lingered for a moment, then broke as Bear began to chuckle. The sound pierced Georgell's heart as if directly from his troubled dreams, intensifying as Bear burst into a fit of laughter, deep and foul.

Butler and Wallace did not charge as they had the guardians in jail. They stayed back, cautiously circling the beast while tapping their swords rhythmically against their shields. Georgell wondered why they stalled—and then understood as another protector joined their circling procession. *Chopper did it*, Georgell thought excitedly, then shouted, "You did it Chopper, Cross is hear! Look!"

Moose grunted a behemoth, "Yeah!"

The new protector was a solid man in heavily soiled overalls and no shirt. His chest and arms were chiseled with the muscular mass of a younger man, but the gray mutton chops beneath his darkened railroad cap, betrayed his age. He too carried a protector's shield like Wallace and Butler, but in his right hand he gripped a heavy sledge hammer with a colossal iron head and a leather strap that secured the weapon to his wrist.

The three protectors stopped circling and prepared for battle—but to Georgell's dismay the beastly guardian seemed to welcome the odds. He darted his sight equally among the three, waiting for the attack. Georgell didn't like it. He was planning something. It was obvious in his scheming eyes.

As chaos threatened to erupt, Georgell surveyed the surreal scene before him. Jackson stood to his left staring at Bear while tightly holding his police baton for security. He couldn't see the guardians or protectors but seemed in awe of the situation anyway. Across the room, Georgell could see Moose gravely watching the protectors with a smirk of mortal encouragement. To his right, Chopper stared with giddy wonder at his protector. He seemed completely enamored by the man and oblivious to anything else.

Jackson swore and Georgell swung his eyes to see Bear raise his arms, and with inhuman strength and a demonic groan, pull apart both pairs of restraining cuffs. Then with catlike speed he leapt over the rail and sped toward the unaware Chopper. Georgell watched in horror and tried to alert Chopper with a shout but his warning was too late.

Bear slammed into Chopper and the two men barreled violently into the back wall. A neon sign shattered and sparked beneath their weight. Chopper snapped out of his motionless awe, trying to react, but the damage was done.

The beastly guardian jabbed at Butler with his long sword, stepped free of Wallace who lunged with his shield, deflected Cross's swinging sledge with his own shield and limberly stepped out of the protector's circle with a clever spin. He then followed Bear with giant strides toward Chopper. Bear obediently stepped aside as the guardian arrived and plunged his sword deep into Chopper's heart.

The tide of battle quickly changed as Cross vanished and a dark guardian appeared in his place. A shadow seemed to pass over Chopper as his eyes darkened and his demeanor violently changed. He scowled deeply and turned a bitter glare toward Georgell.

Georgell's legs weakened. *This can't be happening*, he thought, trying to overcome a severe wave of nausea. It was now quite obvious how Bear had been turned, and with a frightful understanding, Georgell knew that Butler and Wallace were now greatly outmatched.

The new guardian was tiny compared to Bear's sizeable beast but seemed to gather shadows around him like a magnet of evil. His features were indistinguishable as he shimmered beneath a blood red haze and he carried nothing but a gnarled staff. Bear's guardian dropped to a knee and bowed in recognition of the powerful being.

Georgell shook his head in disbelief and keyed his radio, "Red, get back here!" Then from across the way, he saw Moose looking at the new guardian and shouted, "Don't get recognized!"

Moose dropped his eyes from the guardian and Georgell said, "It's on us." His words hit home and Moose rushed toward Bear with a deafening roar. Georgell turned to face Chopper and saw the shimmering demon pointing a withered finger at Moose. Bear and his guardian followed the directive, heading toward their assailant with ferocious determination.

Believing a headlong rush like Moose's approach would do more harm than good; Georgell approached Chopper methodically, trying to lure the big man into an attack.

A crack sounded from across the way as a stool, flung by Moose, shattered at Bear's feet. Bear stumbled on the obstruction and Moose hammered him with a right hook that dropped him to the ground. Moose reached down to snatch Bear out of the rubble but missed as Bear rolled out of his reach, grabbing a leg of the broken stool. Bear swung the club at Moose's face and connected. Moose dropped to a knee.

No, Georgell thought, seeing Moose falter and Bear scramble to his feet.

Chopper faked a jab and moved into a defensive stance.

The action frustrated Georgell and he immediately knew Chopper was too smart to make the first move. There was no time and despite not wanting to break any bones or damage Chopper in any unnecessary way, Georgell had to take the initiative knowing Moose was in a vulnerable state.

Bear hurled the club at Moose's face but it veered right as Moose deflected it with his forearm. Moose spit a mouthful of blood at Bear who followed his projectile by leaping from a nearby chair. Bear was blinded by the red mist but still managed to secure a front choke on Moose by lodging his shoulder under Moose's chin and gripping his elbows behind Moose's neck.

Sliding to the right of Chopper, Georgell flashed his arms apart while stepping into the big man's reach. Chopper took the bait, throwing a hard right jab. Georgell dropped his forehead to catch the jab but Chopper had expected the tactic and adjusted the blow enough to blast Georgell just below his right eye. Despite the miscalculation, Georgell's distraction worked as Jackson blindsided Chopper's exposed flank with a heavy swing of his baton. Chopper stumbled with the blow and smashed into another neon sign. Green and yellow sparks lit up the scene.

Jackson pulled the baton free and swung it hard at the back of Chopper's knees. The blow successfully connected but Chopper blasted Jackson with an elbow as he fell. The officer's shoulder popped. Chopper snatched Jackson's shirt, yanking the man forward and off his feet while his own knees compacted onto a bed of broken glass. Furious, Chopper twisted Jackson's limp arm and reached for the baton but Georgell had already wrenched it free.

Jackson grunted with pain as his arm stretched further out of its socket.

As Georgell stepped back with the baton, he heard a howl from Bear and realized Moose had somehow pried Bear's legs apart and flung him down on his knee. Despite the crushing blow to his groin, Bear did not release the choke and Georgell knew the situation was getting more desperate.

Lunging forward, Georgell punched the baton into Chopper's right kidney. Chopper arched his back and flung his head to the rear in a reflexive motion that Georgell anticipated. Stretching his hands to the ends of the baton, palms up, Georgell reached over Chopper's head and hooked the exposed shaft under his chin. Chopper tensed and Georgell swiftly released the baton, letting it roll down his forearms and settle into the crook of his elbows as he reached behind Chopper's head and clasped his hands tight.

Chopper released Jackson as Georgell squeezed. Jackson shuffled to his knees, ignoring the shattered glass, and pressed Chopper into the wall with his good shoulder. The big man swung at Jackson with his left, successfully hitting him several times, but finally lost consciousness and fell limp.

"Stop!"

Georgell held his choke but turned back toward the scream and found Alys swinging a stool at Bear's back. Moose had dropped to his knees again; seemingly unable to release Bear's grip. The head of the stool caught Bear at the base of his neck and the impact forced him to release the choke. Bear fell backward as Moose fell forward. Wiping the blood and spit from his eyes, Bear stood and lunged toward Alys. Moose grabbed Bear's foot, causing him to fumble forward off-balance.

A glance above showed Wallace and Butler trying to frustrate Bear's general but their efforts seemed useless as the monster kept forcing them back. They tried to lure him into overextending an attack but the savvy guardian never fell for their ploys. The battle raged and Georgell could only imagine the deafening sound as the swords clashed and the shields blocked merciless hammering. No one seemed to falter or back down but lunged and parried with inexhaustible calculation and determined vigor.

To his relief, Georgell realized Chopper's shimmering guardian was gone and he gratefully released the choke. Red pushed through the emergency door and ran toward them as Chopper slumped to the ground. Georgell jumped to his feet. "Stay on him," he said, gesturing to Chopper.

Red looked confused at the order but stepped toward Chopper anyway.

"He's with them," Georgell hastily explained, pulling Jackson to his feet. *That was dumb*, he thought as Red looked around, more perplexed. "Just keep him down!"

Georgell turned his attention back to Bear. He was on his feet and advancing toward Alys as Moose groggily stood. Jackson yelped and Georgell wondered why but kept his attention forward. Alys pulled a canister of pepper spray from her belt and reached toward Bear but he cut the distance and knocked the canister out of her hand before she could use it. In a brutally quick motion, Bear then grabbed Alys by the throat, lifting her off the ground. Her eyes bulged and she screamed with what air she could muster. He then slid behind her and applied a threatening lock around her head and roughly tugged on her hair. "I'll snap her neck!" He screamed as Georgell and Moose hunkered near.

"Let her go," Georgell barked as the blood drained from Alys' face.

"Your call," Moose grumbled to Georgell and spit out some more blood.

"Don't do it," Jackson said, approaching from Georgell's right with a Glock pointed at Bear.

"What are you doing?" Georgell said to Jackson.

"I won't let him kill her."

Bear laughed and in a voice deeper than his own, said, "This life is meaningless. I don't care about mortality. Her death will only cement my place in the kingdom. I will kill. If not her, someone else, my mortality is only a stepping stone to eternity." He began to laugh again, slowly backing up, dragging Alys helplessly with him. Alys did not fight but tears rolled over her pale cheeks and regardless of her situation, her eyes begged Jackson not to pull the trigger.

Georgell felt completely defeated. This was not going well and his options were slipping away. Two friends were lost, another near death, and he had no idea what to do. He knew it wasn't Bear who spoke of fateful acceptance or laughed with demonic contempt but still, he was puppetted far beyond anyone's control and Jackson was about to shoot him.

Another step back and the heckling laugh stopped as Bear's eyes bulged from his face. He gasped for air, buckled to the left, and to everyone's relief, dropped Alys. Pineapple delivered another deadening punch to Bear's left kidney as Alys scooted toward her canister of pepper spray, weeping. A crack echoed and Bear gulped for air, his ribs fracturing beneath the second crushing blow. Pineapple followed the kidney shots with a full nelson, hoisting Bear off the ground.

"What's happening?" Pineapple screamed.

"Just hold him," Georgell ordered as Emma ran over, helping Alys to her feet.

An immediate sensation screamed for Georgell to duck and he did so as the sword of Bear's guardian flashed overhead.

"Watch out!" Moose screamed, a hundredth of a second late.

Georgell scooted forward, still crouching, and saw Butler and Wallace step over him, pressing the guardian back. *Aaaaargh*, he silently screamed. *This is insane!*

A demonic growl shot from Bear and he windmilled both arms to Pineapple's head. The broken cuffs and dangling chains still attached to Bear's wrists, smashed into Pineapple's exposed temples. The hold was released and Bear dropped to the ground and rushed Moose who sprang forward.

Bear and Moose collided again, swinging viciously at each other. Bear bit Moose's shoulder and yanked out a chunk of skin as Moose lifted him from the ground and battered his cracked ribs.

"Drop!" Georgell ordered.

Moose wrapped his arms around Bear and lunged forward, landing hard on the ground—smothering Bear beneath him. Georgell jumped on Moose's back and felt the weight of Pineapple as he joined the pile as well. Jackson stepped on Bear's clawing hand.

"Get her out of here!" Jackson said.

Georgell twisted beneath the weight of Pineapple and saw Emma pushing Alys up the stairs. Forcing his head back toward the sports bar, he saw Butler and Wallace still battling the resilient guardian. They were haggard and thoroughly beaten as their thrusts became less and less frequent. The beast was tiring as well but became the aggressor and pushed Wallace and Butler back, ever closer to their mortal wards.

The protectors stepped together and locked shields. Georgell watched in growing horror as the beast pounded at the men, forcing them closer still. The hulking monster tossed his shield, sensing victory, and grabbed his sword with both hands. With feeble effort, Butler and Wallace lifted their shields as the massive sword rose above the monster's head. The beast shrieked a soundless howl and brought it crashing down. Simultaneously, Butler and Wallace released their shields, spinning out on either side of the monster as he battered their armaments to the ground.

Georgell gawked in amazement as the beast realized his mistake and froze with a hardened look of disgust. Butler's sword pierced deep into his side. The beast dropped his massive weapon—it fell and disappeared. Gripping the hilt with both hands, Wallace swung his battleaxe in a high sweeping arc and plunged the weapon into the muscular bulk of the guardian's back. The hulking figure fell to his knees and looked at Georgell with careless disdain as Butler's sword severed his colossal head. The menacing figure's body faltered, toppled forward and vanished.

"Get off," Georgell hollered at Pineapple while trying to muscle out of the pile. Pineapple rolled off and Georgell saw the welcome sight of a tall Viking protector standing over him. *Bear*, he immediately thought, *Bear's protector!* The imposing figure had a long blonde beard with braided strands, and lengthy blonde hair covered by a helmet with two horns protruding from the front. The man grinned with a toothy smile and beckoned him to rise. Georgell moved from the pile, wondering why protectors were always asking him to stand up.

Moose rolled off Bear and grudgingly stood as well. Jackson refused to move from his spot on Bear's arm. "Alright Barney, I'm good!" Bear spat and coughed up blood. With the earnest plea, Jackson released his weight and gently helped Bear to his feet. More blood dribbled from his lips but Bear forced a smile. "I'm in a lot of pain," he said.

"Yeah!" Moose covered the bloody gash on his shoulder. "We all are, but this ain't over yet." He then pointed to Red, who sat poised above Chopper with a look of sheer bewilderment on his face. Above Red and Chopper, the hooded guardian hovered with his arms folded.

"What's going on?" Pineapple said again, gently massaging his bruised temples.

"Later," Georgell said. "Right now I need you to help Red."

"Red don't need help," Pineapple protested.

"Just do it! Please," Georgell growled. Then he looked at Bear with a serious gaze and said. "Can you hold on for a few more minutes?"

Bear nodded and Georgell said, "If you need incentive—look at your protector."

Bear darted his eyes upward, and after a short, wide-eyed gaze, stood upright and shook off Jackson's assistance with gruff appreciation. Moose looked at the Viking as well, and then he too, seemed to straighten a bit as Wallace rejoined him. Jackson repositioned his useless arm and asked, "What's the plan?"

"We've all got to recognize at the same time. Our protectors have to be free to battle. I don't know how powerful that thing is but Bear's beast seemed to take orders from it. We have to stay away—far away. We can't let him take any of us!"

"I agree," Moose said.

"I'll help with Chopper," Jackson said. "He can't see me." After a nod from Georgell, Jackson grabbed a chair and dragged it over to where Chopper lay on his back with Red straddling his chest and pinning his arms. Jackson placed the chair over Chopper's legs and sat down, the baton gripped tightly in his left hand.

"What do you need me for?" Pineapple asked.

"It's no problem," Red said, shaking his head.

"Yes, it is," Jackson said. "Bear ripped through two pairs of handcuffs. I guarantee it's a problem!"

Pineapple kneeled down near Chopper's head and pressed down on his forearms. Red grunted and situated himself better on Chopper's slow breathing torso.

"If I yell 'out,' put him out," Georgell directed the restraining trio.

"Copy," Pineapple answered.

"Toss the sword," Moose urged. "Let's finish Longshanks!"

"Right," Georgell said with a final nod to Moose and Bear. "Now!"

The three men peered at the guardian simultaneously. The guardian smiled and pulled his staff from oblivion. The protectors did not move and Georgell wondered why. They stayed glued to their respective bouncer but readied themselves as the guardian steadily approached.

"This isn't good," Moose said, unable to take his eyes off the approaching demon.

"Back up," Georgell whispered and the group did so.

With their backs against the wall, Moose said, "Now what?"

Darkness began to swamp the room and a suppressive feeling crept up from the floor like a rising tide. Georgell felt evil grip his mind, fear began to envelop him, but in his haze he saw Emma and Alys descending the stairs. "Emma go!"

To his sinking relief, Georgell heard the women scramble back up the stairs. The dark menace moved closer and with each step the hope of life faltered. *Out!* Georgell screamed in his thoughts. Red and Pineapple did nothing, they heard nothing, the words were constricted in Georgell's throat and despite all his effort—he could not vocalize the saving plea.

The demon pointed his boney finger at Georgell then Bear and finally Moose. The gesture was immediately recognized as the same directive

Franklin received prior to killing all those people at Club Momentum. Death had been ordered. The pointing finger wavered then darkened as Georgell lost all vision. With every ounce of strength he could gather, Georgell reached to either side, grabbed Moose and Bear, and pulled them close. He could not speak but begged them to hear his mental plea. *We have to break this trance, we have to move now or it's over.*

Nothing seemed to happen but Georgell felt a warm sensation began to tickle his back and work its strengthening vibe up his spine. *Bug*, he thought, then repeated his mental plea, *Now, now, now* . . .With each repeated effort the word strengthened and his resolve heightened. *Now, now, now* . . .he silently continued to rage. The veil of darkness faltered. The mantra continued until the strangle-hold on his throat weakened, "NOW!" he shrieked.

A white flash burst into Georgell's mind and he suddenly felt free of the crippling grasp that held him. He wrenched forward, pulling Bear and Moose with him, they crashed headlong into tables and chairs.

No longer hindered by blindness, Georgell looked up to see Butler and the other protectors viciously defending against the flailing blur of the demon's attack. A crash sounded from the other side of the room and Georgell was astonished to see Red, Pineapple and Jackson sprawled out on the floor. Chopper had freed himself from the trio and scrambled to his feet. Moose let out a stunned gasp of excitement and Georgell realized three new protectors quickened from the dust above Red, Pineapple, and Jackson.

Why now? Georgell wondered, marveling at the new protectors.

"They encampeth round about and delivereth," Moose whispered as if answering Georgell's silent query.

Pineapple's protector was a meaty islander with no shirt, no fear, a massive afro, and a body full of tribal tattoos similar to those on Pineapple. He wore bracelets and anklets of bone, a necklace of shells bounced on his heaving chest and he rushed forth with a spear in one hand and a fish net spinning over his head from the other.

Surprisingly, Georgell saw the slender figure of an Indian warrior advance from Jackson. The warrior gripped a feathered tomahawk in each of his white-knuckled hands, and his long black hair danced on the ethereal breeze behind him as he darted forward. His mouth was agape and Georgell guessed he was shrieking an invigorating war cry. The warrior had a disturbing stare of intense wrath that chilled Georgell but bolstered his hope in the outcome of the battle.

A thick coat of brown fur covered the short stumpy man that harried forth from Red. He wore a thick fur hat and with his long brown hair and bulky beard it was hard to see any semblance of a face, but his eyes were dark, pointed, and focused on the flailing demon. In one hand he held a long dagger and in the other a heavy axe, and though he trailed behind the other protectors, he looked no less ferocious.

Steps behind the rushing wall of protectors, Georgell saw the unholy gaze of Chopper pressing forward as well. His heart sinking for his friend, Georgell released a grunt of exhaustion and stood. With admiration he saw his team rise beside him. Both spat blood from their mouths and prepared themselves for another fight. Despite injuries, fatigue, and mental exhaustion, every man was willing to continue at any cost.

Jackson's Indian sprang forward, sinking his tomahawk into the demon's robes before having his neck splayed by the guardian's unseen dagger. The Islander tossed his net and jabbed his spear at the demon with futile effort as the Indian vanished. The demon deflected the net with his wicked staff, spun around with lightning speed and rammed his blade into the nape of the Islanders neck. The Russian ran through the Polynesian's dissipating form and forcefully bowled into the demon. The menacing figure plunged his dagger multiple times into the Russians back but not before being carried several yards and thrown at the feet of the remaining protectors.

Butler slammed his shield on the demon's wrist and kicked the dagger out of his grip. Wallace destroyed the dark guardian's staff with a swing of his axe and simultaneously dropped his shield, pinning the demon's free arm. The Russian remained visible, his body still weighing heavily on the demon's torso and legs. Tossing his shield to the side, the Viking gripped his sword with both hands, and stepped in.

Caught up in the battle above, Georgell didn't notice Chopper pick up a table and hurl it with tremendous power; Chopper's accompanying growl was the only warning. With no time to react, Georgell tried to move but the table caught him square in the chest, propelling him several feet backwards. Air blasted from his lungs and stomach as he hammered the ground. The table continued forward and raked his lips and nose as it tore across his face and finally came to a rest against the wall behind him.

Chopper's eyes bulged with intensity as he continued forward, intent on Georgell. Bear stepped up on a rail, leapt and clothes-lined him with a high flying arm bar. Moose lunged from the opposite side and clipped Chopper low on his already battered knees. Chopper roared as his mass blasted mercilessly to the ground—feet from where Georgell lay stunned.

As Georgell labored to get back to his feet, fighting desperately for oxygen, he viewed the final moments of the guardian execution. Butler and Wallace stood stoically, eyes closed, on either side of the demon, pinning his arms with all their weight. The Viking lifted his sword high and as the Russian protector finally dissipated from his multiple wounds, the Viking plunged his sword with great accuracy into the uncovered chest of the shimmering menace. There was no scream or lightning rift, just silence and the devil was gone.

Wallace and Butler fell exhausted to their knees and the Viking knelt between them. Each bowed their heads in a united prayer of thankfulness as Georgell fell back to the ground, gathered his voice, and yelled, "It's over!"

Georgell lay completely spent. He heard the rustling of the others but didn't care to look. A curious prick of thought then urged Georgell to open his eyes and he did so. The protectors stood with faces of stone and haggard bodies, welcoming the reappearance of Cross with outstretched arms. Each nodded at the others, eyes full of mutual respect and gratitude, then parted company and returned to their respective bouncer.

Georgell and Butler locked eyes for what seemed an eternity, speaking volumes of esteem for one another in their gaze. Butler nodded and Georgell experienced a communication he couldn't have fathomed months earlier. A vision of possibilities, of the future, both grim and blissful, along with an inkling of the war in heaven, opened in his mind. Butler pleaded with Georgell, his eyes ablaze with intent. He wanted Georgell to accept his mortal purpose. The plea was unclear but Georgell nonetheless accepted. Butler stroked his heavy beard in contemplation and reached for his gold watch. He held the item in his ghostly hand, smiling, then slowly faded from Georgell's sight.

Seconds seemed like an eternity as Georgell tried to internalize the meaning of it all. He now understood that the white flash had come from his own mind. Butler, Wallace, and the Viking did not immediately attack the demon because they were compelled to defend their mortal hosts. The demon attacked with an unseen weapon. He had the uncanny ability to attract darkness, altering the mental will of mortals that recognized him—he had essentially hypnotized them and made them helpless to his will. The protectors stayed with their hosts in an attempt to bolster their mental resistance. The added will of Butler, along with the empowering memory of Bug, helped Georgell break the demon's hold and freed the others as well. The white flash was his mental refusal to give in and it somehow severed the demon's hypnotic spell. It also freed the protectors as they no longer had to mentally defend their mortal hosts.

As for the new protectors, Georgell could only assume they had been somehow summoned. Ultimately, angels had indeed been sent to encampeth round about them and above all, had come to destroy a demon of evil that seemed only subordinate to the ruler of darkness.

Red and Pineapple staggered over, reaching for Chopper in the mess of furniture and battered men. They too seemed physically exhausted, and slumped to the floor when Jackson whistled at them. "Leave him alone boys. The war is over."

"What's going on?" Pineapple asked again, rubbing his head. "And what was that flash of white light?"

"Peace through power brother," Jackson mumbled, then started to laugh, slouching onto the only chair in the area still upright.

Georgell was taken aback by Pineapple's question and wondered if everyone had seen the light. *Was it that powerful?* He thought. *No wonder the door opened for the other protectors.*

"I really need to get some medical treatment," Bear mumbled, face down on the disheveled floor.

"Ow!" Chopper moaned.

Moose opened his eyes, looked at Georgell who lay motionless on the ground next to him, and slowly reached out an arm to pat Chopper on the leg. "Yeah, I think we all need treatment."

"Can someone please pull the barstool out of my butt cheek?" Bear pleaded.

Georgell began to laugh, then, ignoring the request, pointed at Jackson and said, "You have Indian blood."

Jackson quit laughing and stared wide-eyed at Georgell as Moose and Bear joined in the moment with their own painful giggles.

"Dance, Dance, Dance," Santos radioed.

Red smirked at the sprawling mess of men and furniture and headed toward the stairs. Still rubbing his head, Pineapple playfully kicked

Georgell, beckoning him to get up, and then followed Red to the dance floor. Moose, Bear, Jackson and Georgell didn't budge.

Chopper stood, looked at the others, and said, "Man I haven't done anything good all night—I'll go." He limped toward the stairs but then paused, addressing Bear. "Ain't no way I'm calling that Viking, Robinson. Come on, man, definitely not Robinson!" He then huffed at the idea all the way out of sight.

Hurrying steps could be heard coming down the stairs and Georgell knew the women had been notified. Moose morphed his chuckling into snores and the laughter of his friends intensified.

"Bear!" Alys wailed as she gingerly entered the room, holding her sore neck.

The laughter waned and Bear bellowed, "Here, but please be gentle."

Steps behind Alys, Emma held a phone to her ear and with tears in her eyes cried, "Yes, they're alright. It's over. Everyone's okay." She handed the phone to Moose and said, "It's Naomi."

Georgell's heart was full as he heard Moose speak to his wife, his voice choked up. As Emma knelt over him, Georgell felt his own words falter as he looked into her eyes. He said nothing, just smiled as she leaned over him and gently kissed the bloody bruise beneath his eye and then his torn lips.

A scream shot from Bear as Alys yanked the protruding shard of wood from his butt. She pressed her hand on the draining blood and said, "That's for my neck—I love you."

☼~ **41** ~☼

On a bright Easter Sunday afternoon, the group sat under trees in Castle Park enjoying the crisp spring air as the kids chased each other around the playground. The fried chicken had been demolished and the salads put away. Drinks still littered the area along with brownies, crispy treats, and colored egg shells; but the feeling was one of peaceful contentment.

"Let me see that ring again," Emma said to Alys.

Alys displayed her engagement ring with beaming pride while Bear rolled his eyes behind her. Moose snickered and Alys rammed an elbow back at her sarcastic fiancé. Bear buckled as the elbow smashed his still tender ribs and he choked out an apology.

"It's amazing," Emma said. "Are those emeralds in the base?"

"Yeah," Alys said. "Bear actually designed it."

Bear nodded with pride and Alys elbowed him again.

Jackson slept quietly under a nearby tree with little Marla napping happily on his lap. Moose lay on his back with Naomi leaning against him. She pulled her feet underneath her and rubbed her barely-showing stomach. Emma saw the tender act and smiled. "Are you done after this one?"

"No," Naomi responded. "Two more waiting to join us. Twins I think."

"Eight?" Georgell said surprised.

"How do you know?" Alys asked.

"I just feel it," Naomi said with a motherly grin. Moose banged his head in the grass and Naomi shot back a look of disdain but said nothing.

"Let's see those teeth," Bear said in an attempt to change the subject.

Moose raised his head, smiled, and pulled his cheek aside with a finger. Two gold teeth gleamed in the back of his mouth where Bear had knocked one loose and fractured the other with the barstool leg.

"Gold?" Emma questioned.

Naomi smiled and said, "That was my idea."

Georgell wondered how they could afford the pricey job but thought the crowns added some class to the jovial brute.

"And the bite mark?" Bear asked proud of the scars he had imposed on his friend.

"It's fine," Moose sneered. "How's your butt?"

"Touché," Bear responded.

"That's right," Moose said mockingly. "Call it what you want; toosh, butt, glutious maximus, or my favorite . . ."

Naomi ribbed Moose and he defensively said, "What? I was gonna say donkey."

"What are we talking about?" Chopper asked, approaching from behind the group.

A beautiful tall woman accompanied him and waved her son off to play with the other kids at the castle. "Please don't get grass stains on your church pants, David." The woman said as the boy tripped and nearly fell.

"Battle scars again," Emma said to Chopper. She stood and gave him a hug.

Pointing to some picnic tables off in the distance, Georgell said, "Yeah, notice we are eating far away from any tables so don't even think about table tossing."

Chopper huffed at Georgell's remark and then with a knowing smile, he grandly gestured at his date and said, "Everybody remember Chandra?"

Georgell loved that Chandra and Chopper were together. He remembered her from their first meeting at the church and knew that Chopper still had the note she had given him. She was good for him, strong willed and attractive too. Everyone had already met her but Chopper always introduced her, as if proud to show her off.

Emma ignored Chopper's question and hugged Chandra, "Glad you could make it."

"Me too," Chandra said.

"Check this out," Alys said, beckoning Chandra over while displaying her engagement ring.

"Oh, Alys that's beautiful—who gave it to you, not Bear surely?"

Alys smiled and Bear growled.

"Who did you say?" Chandra asked Alys, wide-eyed with anticipation.

"Chopper," Bear said. "She's doing it again . . ."

"Sorry, man—I love her but you know I can't control her."

"Congratulations, you two," Chandra said, winking at Bear.

Jackson woke from his nap. "Hey Chop, I hear Cross had quite a game last night."

Georgell wasn't sure Chandra knew about the guardians yet and it was apparent that Jackson didn't know either as he used the word 'game' in reference to a guardian battle.

"Man you know it," Chopper answered. "He took care of business before Wallace even showed up; dropped the hammer like a champ."

"Wish I could've seen it," Jackson said, repositioning Marla on his lap as he sat up. "Oh Doc, you'll be interested to know that there is in fact Indian blood in my family. Cherokee, three generations back on my mother's side. I've really gotten hooked on genealogy. I'm discovering all kinds of cool family history."

"Sweet," Georgell responded. "I've discovered that Butler was a well paid bodyguard in the mid eighteen-hundreds. Lance Butler—I even have that pocket watch that he wears. You know the gold chain?" The bouncers all nodded their recognition. "My uncle gave it to me; I'm sure my dad paid him something for it but whatever."

"Man what's the decision on Red and Pineapple? They keep nagging me," Chopper asked.

"I don't blame them," Jackson informed. "The exhaustion I felt after the battle was different than anything I have ever experienced. The death of my protector took a toll on my physical being and I honestly felt completely wasted, like part of me was gone. The feeling didn't last long but I know those two felt the same draining exhaustion. They just don't know the cause. Tell me again how my protector died?"

The various conversations waned and everyone looked to Georgell. He mulled over Jackson's comments for a moment. When he finally spoke, his voice was quiet. "They were sent for a purpose. That demon was no ordinary guardian. He was a higher rank and more powerful than any we've ever seen. He was beyond our ability to fight and even that of our protectors. Remember how the protectors refused to leave us? They knew the demon had power over us beyond physical sight and remained by our sides to strengthen our mental resolve against that influence."

"I've only seen one other like him." Georgell said. Everyone looked at him in surprise. Georgell hadn't discussed this with the group yet, but after much contemplation and the nightmare that still intruded on his dreams, he was certain that he had seen a similar demon before. "He wore the same robes and had the same destructive power. He was above Franklin, at Club Momentum. I have no doubt something similar and just as horrific was in the works for us. We were his pawns to direct, and who knows what mayhem he would have forced us to do. But those three protectors appeared. They didn't hesitate for a moment. It was like they were debriefed before they arrived. Their single objective was to distract the demon and set him up for the warriors. Each of those men knew they would die but performed their duty without question. They sacrificed themselves for the benefit of every one of us."

"Besides," Bear slipped in. "What is death to the protectors? Who's to say they really die? Maybe they're removed from this realm but continue on in another place. Maybe by performing such a selfless act they earned status or promotion. I don't think we can assume they ultimately died. Maybe they return someday and this time carry the shield of a warrior protector. Who knows."

"Absolutely!" Moose agreed.

"So," Chopper said, eyebrows raised.

Georgell looked at him, confused, and then remembered the original question? "Right, bringing Red and Pineapple in on the truth depends on what we plan to do. I mean there are four of us with sight and four more with knowledge."

"Five," Chandra chimed in.

"Really?" Emma asked surprised.

Naomi nodded and audibly whispered, "I told you" to Moose.

Chopper smiled and reddened as Bear shook his head.

"Okay, so five," Georgell continued with a nod to Chandra. "The thing is, we are complacent with the current status. Dark guardians have no chance in our club. We have honed our abilities and can call on our protectors at will. We seldom even raise a finger of violence anymore. Our protectors do all the work. So I find myself wondering, what now? Are we happy to stay at Euphoria and affect change when it comes to us, or is it time to branch out?"

Alys and Emma looked at each other with concern but Naomi assertively said, "As much as I hate the idea, Georgell is right. It is time to do more. The sight is a gift and yes, you're using the power to eliminate evil when the moments arise, but maybe that isn't enough."

"I've been thinking the same thing," Bear added.

"Naomi and I have discussed it a few times," Moose said, squeezing his wife's hand.

"Okay, so what we need to do is vote on the matter," Georgell said.

"Wait," Alys interrupted. "Let's first get your definition of branching out. What do you plan on doing?"

"I don't know? Maybe once a week we can go to another club or something; Sanctuary, for instance. Look, I know this is another step into the unknown but look at our strength. We're a small army of power both mortally and above. We took down a guardian master. I don't know how common that is but I think we've accomplished something pretty fantastic, don't you?"

Heads nodded and voices mumbled agreement.

"Besides, there's something else I can't shake," Georgell added. Looks of bewilderment met his quiet tone. "I'll never forget what Bear said while he was threatening to kill Alys. Remember? Something about the things he did here would cement his place in another kingdom. And the words that really got me I can recite verbatim, 'My mortality is only a stepping stone to eternity.' Those words have really been haunting me."

The group said nothing. Georgell let the thought linger, hoping everyone would agree to the decision. Finally he said, "I don't want to complacently sit back anymore. I want to cement my place in the coming Kingdom. I have no doubt that there is a war in heaven and when my day comes to cross over I want an immediate commission in that army. Eternity is a long time but why waste this mortal stepping stone. Let's use it to our advantage. I know the future may be uncertain and our lives will be put on the line but I'm willing to take that risk. I know that sounds pretentious but how else can I put it?"

"Nail on the head man," Chopper commended.

"Thanks Chop," Georgell said. He then looked at Alys and asked, "Did I answer your question at all?"

Alys sullenly nodded, wrapping her arms tightly around Bear.

"So we vote and if everyone agrees we let Red and Pineapple in on this circus. Is that about right?" Jackson asked.

"Yes," Georgell answered. "Nemesis and Santos too if the need arises."

Jackson nodded and said, "I'm about due for retirement and no offense ladies but I'm having a hard time swallowing the fact that I'm the only man in this party that can't see. I intend on changing that no matter what I need to do, whatever it takes, I'm in."

"Thank you Barney," Georgell said with a nodding smile as a warm feeling began to flame within him. He looked to the others.

"We're in one hundred and ten percent," Moose answered for both Naomi and himself.

Emma reached for Georgell's hand and squeezed. She smiled and said, "Yes."

The blanket of warmth thickened over Georgell and began to tickle his neck with its overpowering force. Bear looked to Alys, his face hopeful. She sighed deeply and nodded without a word. With utter excitement and joy, Bear forwarded the nod to Georgell and pulled Alys close.

Chandra felt the gravity of the moment and whispered, "I'm too new to vote but I like what I've heard and I want to be a part of it."

Chopper grinned at Chandra, and then gave the group a smirk. With his trademark huff and a positive thumbs up, he said, "Man, you know I'm in."

Moose and Jackson chuckled at Chopper's response. Respect and admiration lingered in the small group and a wave of pride welled up in Georgell. He could not speak. The group had made their decision and all had agreed to step toward an unknown future in search of a better understanding. He was overcome with emotion and could only manage a smile.

Moose noticed Georgell's lack of speech and broke the heavy moment with a quote, "Its okay Doc, strong men also cry—strong men also cry."

CPSIA information can be obtained at www.ICGtesting.com
Printed in the USA
LVOW092221031211

257698LV00002B/101/P